SCIENCE, MYSTICISM
AND
EAST-WEST DIALOGUE

SCIENCE, MYSTICISM
AND
EAST-WEST DIALOGUE

Edited by
Job Kozhamthadam

Indian Institute of Science and Religion (IISR)
2016

SCIENCE, MYSTICISM AND EAST-WEST DIALOGUE—jointly published by the Rev. Dr. Ashish Amos of the Indian Society for Promoting Christian Knowledge (ISPCK), Post Box 1585, 1654, Madarsa Road, Kashmere Gate, Delhi-110006 and Indian Institute of Science and Religion (IISR), Delhi.

ISBN: 978-81-8465-547-6

Laser typeset by

ISPCK, Post Box 1585, 1654, Madarsa Road, Kashmere Gate, Delhi-110006
• *Tel:* 23866323/22

e-mail: ashish@ispck.org.in • ella@ispck.org.in
website: www.ispck.org.in

To

Theodore Bowling, SJ

Jesuit Priest, Scientist and Teacher

Contents

Dedication ... *v*

Acknowledgements ... *ix*

Preface ... *xi*

Introduction ... *xiii*

Science-Mysticism Dialogue: A Surer Path to Fullness
Job Kozhamthadam ... 1

Symbiosis and the Transpersonal Quest For Oneness
Lancy Pereira ... 19

Inner Net of the Heart: The Fractal Nature of Consciousness
Will Keepin ... 63

Pathway To Reality
N.V. Kulkarni ... 84

Mysticism and East-West Dialogue on Darwinism
T.D. Singh ... 125

Science and the Sacred, Silence and Service:
Towards a Dialogical Enrichment between
Eastern and Western Mysticism
Kuruvilla Pandikattu ... 149

Self-Organizing Systems and Final Causality
    Joseph Bracken   ...   163

The Theory of Evolution:
Input for a Teilhardian Mysticism
    Kathleen Duffy   ...   177

Mysticism as Re-Enchanting the World:
Teilhard de Chardin and Albert Einstein
    Sarojini Henry   ...   196

Islamic Perspective on Mysticism and Modern Science
    Yusuf Amin   ...   211

Modern Science, Mysticism and East-West Dialogue:
Tribal Perspective
    Nirmal Minz   ...   222

Concept of Reality in Aad Guru Granth Sahib
and its Physical, Metaphysical and Mystical Aspects
    Hardev Singh Virk   ...   232

The Puzzle of Experiential Primacy and Consciousness
    Sangeetha Menon   ...   242

Engaged Contemplation for a Troubled World
    William Grassie   ...   251

Contributors   ...   268

Index   ...   270

Acknowledgements

This volume owes a great deal to the generous support and active collaboration of many organizations and persons. To mention a few, Fr. Theodore Bowling and Mr. Denis Rodrigues went over the manuscript and gave valuable comments and suggestions. Ms. Sheeja Mathew and Mr. Printo Augustine helped me with the typing and other secretarial tasks. I remain grateful to these generous persons for their valuable assistance.

As mentioned in the introduction, this volume has arisen from the international symposium organized by IISR which was supported by a grant from the John Templeton Foundation – exploring the creative interface between science and religion. Without this generous help this project in its present form would not have been possible. I remain deeply indebted to the Templeton Foundation. However, the opinions expressed in this volume are those of the authors, and do not necessarily reflect the views of the John Templeton Foundation.

ISPCK has graciously agreed to co-publish this volume with IISR. I sincerely appreciate this valuable collaboration and express my gratitude to ISPCK.

Job Kozhamthadam

Preface

One of the greatest insights of modern developments, particularly in the light of the phenomenal growth of science, is that ours is a dynamic universe, a constantly changing and evolving universe. An evolutionary universe is an interacting one, where progress is achieved by mutually collaborating and contributing to each other. The 14 papers of this collection focus on one area of this ongoing interaction: modern science and mysticism. In the past very often it seemed that any such creative interaction was foreclosed, mostly under the influence of the Mechanical Philosophy of Nature and its 20th century reincarnation of Logical Positivism. The authors of this volume point out that such a view need not be, and even cannot be, the case, rationally and historically, in principle and in practice. In fact, a constructive engagement between science and mysticism is to be expected, given the complex, essential composition of the human person – rational and emotional, discursive and intuitive. Indeed, it is becoming more and more clear that a more comprehensive and genuine knowledge and experience of reality can be had only when all these different dimensions are allowed to intermingle and interpenetrate. The papers also bring out another aspect of this interaction between modern science and mysticism: it can be an effective catalyst for promoting a healthy dialogue between the East and the West. Traditionally it has been found that science, especially empirical science, is closely associated with the West, whereas mysticism is closely associated with the East, although both of these are not the monopoly of either the West or the East. These points take on special significance in our contemporary scenario of the ongoing process of globalization. It is hoped that this volume will add its mite towards enriching the different ferments operative in our world today.

Introduction

Rudyard Kipling in 1889 opened his well known poem "The Ballad of East and West," with the declaration: "East is East and West is West and never the twain shall meet." Today over one century and a quarter of opportunities for the twain to mix and mingle, the scenario has changed considerably. No doubt, both the East and the West continue to keep their unique identity. But the two have come closer to learn and know each other better, to understand and appreciate each other better, to share and enrich each other more in an attempt to grow together. A similar situation can be seen in the case of science and mysticism. Over a century ago it was generally believed that these two had hardly anything in common, particularly in the heydays of Mechanical Philosophy of Nature and Logical Positivism, its 20th century reincarnation. Today in the aftermath of the relativistic-quantum mechanical revolution and subsequent developments in science, many have begun finding welcome and wholesome possibilities for modern science and mysticism to come together and creatively interact with each other. The present work is an exploration into the various dimensions of science-mysticism interfacing and the contribution it can make in providing an effective platform for further East-West dialogue.

The 14 papers of this collection are the fruit of a symposium organized by Indian Institute of Science and Religion some years ago as part of its mission to bring together the latest findings of modern science and the deepest insights of religions in order to build up a better world and a better humanity. The first paper by Job Kozhamthadam, "Science-Mysticism Dialogue: A Surer Path to Fullness," introduces the whole book by posing two simple but probing questions: 1. What is the relationship between modern science and mysticism? 2. Can such a relationship lead to a constructive dialogue between the East and the West? Concerning the first question three different views are presented. The first is the "Strong-Interaction View," subscribed to by scholars like Fritjof Capra, Gary Zukav, Murli Manohar Joshi, former Indian Minister of Human Resources, etc., which sees both science and mysticism mutually supporting and enriching each other. On the other hand, the second view, the "No-Interaction View," advocated by scholars like Ken Wilber, Jeremy Bernstein, etc., sees no such interlinking between science and mysticism. Kozhamthadam finds both these views one-sided, each going to the extreme, and hence presents his own perspective which takes a middle position. He sees a healthy complementarity between modern science and mysticism, but points out that the locus of interaction is not so much any individual scientific theory or religious dogma, but the life-experience of the human person. The primary role of this interaction is to enrich and enlighten human life by giving it a richer and deeper grasp and appreciation of reality. He sums up the nature and need for interaction between science and mysticism as follows: "Science without mysticism is stagnant, mysticism without science is sterile." With regard to the second issue of the possibility of science-mysticism dialogue leading to an enriching East-West dialogue, the paper remains optimistic. Since traditionally the East is closely associated with mysticism and the West with empirical science – although neither mysticism nor science has been the monopoly of any particular nation or geographical region – any rapprochement between mysticism and modern science will inevitably have its ripple effect on East-West relationship. Because science is noted for its universal spirit and mysticism for its unifying spirit, the paper concludes on a positive note with the hope that a constructive and creative interaction between modern science and mysticism can pave the way for the breakdown of all barriers of geographical boundary, caste, creed and colour, and assist in the creation of a united universe of fraternity and mutual enrichment.

In the second paper "Symbiosis and the Transpersonal Quest for Oneness" Lancy Pereira invites the reader to look at both science and mysticism afresh, emphasizes the need for a healthy and creative interfacing of true science and genuine mysticism and suggests new ways in which this can be carried out. His focus is on science as seen through the integrated consciousness of the mystics. In the first three sections of his paper he attempts to explain the nature and characteristics of mysticism. He takes special pains to bring out the human dimension of both scientists and mystics. In his view mystics are persons of flesh and blood, vibrant, competent, deeply compassionate and fully involved in the here and now. Coming to scientists, he points out that the greatest scientists are first, foremost and always human beings. He sees the spirit of adventure written deep both in science and religion/mysticism: science is a human adventure moving to the realm of ever new and ever ingenious ideas, whereas religion is an adventure in God-experience leading humans to elevating mystical experience. Commenting on the integrative spirit of mysticism, he says that the great masters are persons who spontaneously integrate conflicts, polarities and diversities into a symbiosis. With regard to the close relationship between mysticism and science, he agrees with Fritjof Capra to say that mystics tend to understand the roots of the tree of Reality, while scientists understand better the branches. This means that humans with genuine interest in all of Reality need both science and mysticism. In the final part of the paper, focusing on his own specialized field of microbiology, he argues at great length that the "chance-alone" hypothesis of certain scientists, especially Darwinian evolutionists, to explain the origin and development of the universe and living beings simply fails to satisfy an inquiring mind. On the basis of his long study and research in the field of microbiology he concludes that microbiology points to the hidden face of God. In his view it is this God whom the mystics seek to be united with.

Will Keepin in his contribution, "Inner Net of the Heart: The Fractal Nature of Consciousness," attempts to link science and mysticism through a Bohmean holistic perspective of reality. The scientific world defines reality in terms of the dual forms of matter and energy, as given by Einstein's equation $E = mc^2$. David Bohm points out that this model of reality remains incomplete and inadequate. The holistic perspective of reality recognizes the existence of a realm beyond and behind this dual model. Only in recent times science is discovering this world, but the mystics had discovered it eons ago. David Bohm calls this invisible but real realm the implicate order. It is the world of consciousness, the world of meaning, the world of spirituality. This is also the world of the mystics. In the light of all these developments, Bohm presents a tripartite structure of reality consisting of matter, energy and consciousness or meaning. According to him, our universe is a holomovement − a dynamic, continually changing system with a kind of holographic structure − in which each part contains the whole, which is illustrated by fractal geometry characterized by "nested sets of self-similar structures." In the Bohmean perspective of reality the dual world of science and the mystical world of consciousness together constitute reality in its fullness. Keepin discusses these and related points in his paper and emphasizes the need for reclaiming genuine mystical practice in the western tradition.

N.V. Kulkarni in his paper, "Pathway to Reality," gives the reader a taste of the Indian perspective of science-mysticism interfacing, although he brings in also the western dimension, particularly from the perspective of a comparative study. Like several other scholars in this book, he too highlights the need for bringing in the mystical perspective for getting a fuller grasp of reality from a consideration of the inadequacy of science. More specifically he points out that modern science, despite its breathtaking achievements, still leaves many everyday phenomena unexplained or inadequately explained. For instance, we can take the puzzle regarding the arrow of time: we see eggs breaking, not un-breaking. Why doesn't this phenomenon happen symmetrically? Also it has been found that relativity and quantum theory, despite being two of the most creative and successful scientific achievements of humans, remain inconsistent. Since relativity focuses on the megaworld of large bodies and quantum theory on the microworld of minute bodies, bringing these two in a consistent way is necessary for further progress of science. In recent times superstring theories and M-Theory have been proposed to tackle this challenging problem, and thus get a clearer and fuller understanding of reality. Kulkarni points out that mysticism is the pathway to reality. It aims at apprehending reality directly and fully. The paper also introduces the reader to the different aspects of mysticism. It points out that mysticism is not confined to India and the East only; it is a universal phenomenon. The paper takes special pains to present the striking parallels between the East and West with regard to the understanding and practice of mysticism. Being a loyal disciple of Guru R.D. Ranade, he shares the perspective of this spiritual master on mysticism, particularly the five successive steps the unitive life of mysticism passes through.

The paper by T.D. Singh, "Mysticism and East-West Dialogue on Darwinism," also touches many aspects of mysticism from the Indian perspective, particularly the Vedantic. It attempts at a synthesis of the eastern and western evolutionary views of life to arrive at a holistic perspective. According to Singh, the western tradition focuses primarily on the structural aspect of life, whereas the eastern tradition is more concerned about the evolution of consciousness. In his view the need to have recourse to mysticism comes about because of the almost inexhaustible richness of reality, which cannot be fathomed by science alone, however developed and sophisticated. In fact, every victory won by science opens up a new challenge to explore further. The more we know, the more challenging the yet unknown territory. Humans are as it were forced into the realm of mysticism when confronted by the many unexplored mysteries of nature. Before this mysterious nature scientists are also drawn to become mystics. He gives also a well-informed critique of the Darwinian perspective of evolution. He believes that the nature of life still remains an enigma and all available data indicates that a purely mechanistic explanation of life falls seriously short. Following the scientific tradition, Singh coins the word "spiriton" to describe the spiritual dimension in humans such as consciousness, free will, humility, love, etc.

The next paper by Kuruvilla Pandikattu, "Science and the Sacred – Silence and Service: Towards a Dialogical Enrichment between Eastern and Western Mysticism," attempts to go beyond the popular stereotypes of the spirituality of the eastern and western traditions. The mysticism of the West he broadly categorizes as a "mysticism of service," whereas that of the East as a "mysticism of silence." From the perspective of the mysticism of service, serving one's neighbour is serving God, as is clearly given in the statements of Jesus in the Gospels. A corollary of this perspective is a positive attitude towards matter and the human body. This also implies a positive attitude towards science since it involves study of matter and the material universe. In the western tradition this outlook makes technological advancement something valuable and desirable, and becomes a means for better and greater service. Thus the material becomes related to spiritual wellbeing. The mysticism of silence is not to be taken in the narrow negative sense of mere absence of words and activities. Rather it is to be taken positively in the sense of nirvana, a silence of fullness where the ephemeral, external sounds are transcended to reach the depth of the absolute. *Maunavrata* is meant to lead one from absence of words to absence of the ego or self. This can endow one with special powers and lead to *nishkama karma*. In fact, the focus of the mysticism of silence is to realize one's total union with the whole, to forget oneself to attain the Ultimate. Pandikattu illustrates his point by presenting the cases of two eminent men who have personalized these two strands of mysticism: Raimundo Panikkar and Bede Griffiths. The author then proceeds to trace out a mysticism that responds to the needs and aspirations of contemporary men and women.

He believes that developing this form of mysticism requires a true dialogue between the service tradition and the silence tradition. According to him, such a dialogue can deepen the spiritual unity of our religious communities and at the same time further the wellbeing of all creatures.

Taking inspiration from the ideas of Michael Polanyi in his *The Tacit Dimension* and Rupert Sheldrake in his *A New Science of Life*, and using Whiteheadian process philosophy, Joseph Bracken in his paper "Self-Organizing Systems and Final Causality" develops a process-theological perspective of the universe, particularly with regard to its directionality. From the 17th century onwards, with the development of the mechanics of Galileo and Newton and the rise of the Mechanical Philosophy of Nature, teleology and explanation of natural phenomena in terms of it became a medieval pariah in the world of scientific explanation. Not only in the physical sciences, but also in the biological sciences this spirit began to prevail. Charles Darwin's theory of evolution through natural selection was a clear illustration of this spirit and practice. Although the vast majority of the scientific world went along with this trend, serious dissenting voices could be heard in scientific circles. Polanyi and Sheldrake were two such scholars who appealed to immanent teleology within cosmic evolution by means of their concept of morphogenetic fields. Bracken discusses these ideas and goes further to point out that, if these morphogenetic fields are interpreted as Whiteheadian societies in the sense of structured fields of activity for their constituent actual occasions, it can give rise to an explanatory mechanism for "bottom-up" and "top-down" causation at different levels of existence and activity within nature. According to Bracken, this involves a dialectical process in which in one step "the constituent actual occasions by their dynamic interrelation are giving shape to the 'common element of form," in the next step "the same 'common element of form' heavily conditions the next set of self-constituting actual occasions." He believes also that this Whiteheadian approach to reality has some affinity to classical eastern conceptions of the Ultimate Reality. The author presents this view as a counter-suggestion to the claim that cosmic evolution is "a direction-less process going nowhere slowly."

The next two papers focus on Teilhard de Chardin, well-known French Jesuit, scientist, philosopher and mystic. In the first one, "The Theory of Evolution: Input for a Teilhardian Mysticism," Kathleen Duffy traces the roots, the development and the blossoming of Teilhard's mysticism, pointing out the impact it had on his own thoughts and writings and through them on his readers. Teilhard was a born mystic, one with a natural mystical bent in every aspect of his life. Union and communion – with God, with fellow-humans and with nature – is the essence of mysticism, and Teilhard had it as an inborn trait. Since he was also a scientist by temperament and training, he was able to blend these two harmoniously in his person, life and writings. Duffy discusses his essay "The Mystical Milieu" in which he narrates the roots of his mystical growth in terms of different expanding circles. The first one is the Circle of Presence, followed by the Circle of Consistence. Then come the circle of Energy and the Circle of the Spirit. Finally he arrives at the Circle of Person. According to Duffy, Teilhard was familiar with the three principal mystical currents of his times: eastern religions, humanist neopantheism and Christianity. Teilhard's was a curious blend of these three currents, in the form of Hindu 'totality,' western 'technology,' and Christian 'personalism.' According to her, his mystical bent integrates what he considers the best of the three worlds: the nature of a personal God, a cosmic sense and a drive for progress. Teilhard manifested his mysticism in different ways. For instance, for him evolution and Incarnation became interlocked and provided a single view of reality. The cosmic Christ who resides ahead of creation and in the future, drawing all things forward becomes the force behind evolution. Again, it is pointed out that in the Tilhardian perspective of evolution the three Christian mysteries of creation, Incarnation and Redemption, which are generally considered logically independent, become one. The Teilhardian system was a grand synthesis of mysticism, science and Christian theology.

The universe is indeed the masterpiece of the Creator, most beautiful and most enchanting. But developments in science, particularly mechanical science with its mechanistic worldview, have taken the charm and beauty out of it; it has been reduced to a set of numbers, equations and formulas. In this world of science in order to know the world one has to distance oneself from it. No doubt, science has done a lot of good to humanity; it has banished many a superstition, has unpacked many a riddle, has furnished very valuable information and insights about the universe. But it has also reduced the universe to a dry and disenchanted one. As the poet John Keats laments, Newton has destroyed the poetry of the rainbow. Sarojini Henry in her paper "Mysticism as Re-Enchanting the World: Teilhard de Chardin and Albert Einstein" makes a plea for moving from the disenchanted world to a re-enchanted one. This re-enchanted universe is suffused with aesthetic and spiritual sensibilities and will foster intimate links between humans and nature. It is hoped that such a disenchanted view will penetrate into the different dimensions of life, inviting us to rediscover our world in its original state of simplicity, beauty and wonder. She thinks that mysticism can make this process of re-enchantment happen. In this connection she presents Teilhard de Chardin and Albert Einstein as two eminent persons who could remain great men of science without losing the enchantment of nature. They could achieve this feat because they could blend science and mysticism harmoniously. According to her, their mysticism was one of involvement in, not withdrawal from, the world. The universe with its "deep mystery formed the basic foundation for their mystical sensibilities." Both were "constantly moving freely around the two poles of thought and feeling, truth and beauty." For both the physical world was a setting for a profound mystic vision of the Ultimate Reality. The major difference between them and ordinary scientists was that for the latter the world was just a storehouse of raw materials, whereas for the former it was a source of mystical illumination and aesthetic beauty. The fundamental message is that in our world driven by science and technology it is necessary to have the balancing spirit of authentic mysticism.

Mysticism has always been closely associated with religion, each one having its own form of mysticism. The paper "Islamic Perspective on Mysticism and Modern Science" by Yusuf Amin discusses mysticism in Islam, particularly its nature and place in the Islamic religious world. He points out that Islam subscribes to a knowledge-oriented mysticism. The Islamic form of mysticism is known as Sufism. According to Amin, Sufism is an Islamic entity, both phenomenologically and historically. Coming to the place of science in Islam, he states that it has a clear locus in the hierarchy and vista of knowledge, albeit with certain limits and limitations. Not only is Islam opposed to all forms of scientism, it also accords to science a rather limited place. Science is considered a part of philosophy, coming below metaphysics, mathematics, etc. The place of science is specified in terms of a "descending arc of knowledge." At the top of this arc is the knowledge of God (or the Absolute). This arc provides justification, locus and character to science and other cognitive systems. Furthermore, "the progressively descending knowledge systems, including science, are not of course ends in themselves, but a preparation for embarking on the ascending arc of knowledge, i.e., attainment of Gnosis by seeing everything with God." Amin points out that Islam has a positive attitude towards nature. For instance, the Koran holds observation as a valid means of knowledge. Islam and Sufism are critical of certain aspects of modern science. According to Islam, science has caused the undermining of spirituality since it leaves out higher realities and the human spirit. Also scientific theories like evolution can mislead people by concocting and imposing philosophies in the garb of facts. It also criticizes modern science for replacing the Universal Substance by matter alone, either by denying the universal principle or reducing it to matter or some kind of pseudo-absolute from which all transcendence has been eliminated. Amin believes that "mysticism had a crucial role in nurturing and guiding science in Islamic Civilization."

The tribals/adivasis/indigenous population forms a significant segment of India's population, making up almost 9%. No serious study of science-mysticism interfacing can overlook this important group of India. However, there are people who think that the tribal people have neither religion nor science. Nirmal Minz in his paper "Modern Science, Mysticism and East-West Dialogue: A Tribal Perspective" wants to dispel this myth and point out that the tribals do have their own form of religion and science. According to him, it is true that the tribals usually do not engage in scientific experiment and study in the modern sense and practice. But they have tested the workings of nature in their own way and have found effective solutions to some of their problems. This is particularly true of their medicine and medical practices. Also in their everyday life one can see them following customs based on careful experience. For instance, the practice of sleeping under peepal tree is strongly supported by science since this ensures good supply of oxygen – something very much needed for healthy life. In the field of religion they have developed their own form of belief and worship. God, spirits, ancestors, etc., find due place in their religious beliefs and practices. Creation myth is central to tribal cultures. Interconnectedness and interdependence are part of the essence of mysticism. In the tribal life and tradition also these aspects are very pronounced. Tribals see nature, human and spirit in a continuum. Also they have an organismic view of reality. Minz points out that in actual practice the impact of modern science and technology on the tribals has not been a blessing; in some ways it has done much harm to them. Projects like indiscriminate mining and other industrial developments often lead to the destruction of tribal cultural life and large scale displacement of tribal population.

Sikhism is one of the major religions in India. The next paper "Concept of Reality in Aad Guru Granth Sahib and Its Physical, Metaphysical and Mystical Aspects" by Hardev Singh Virk is a contribution to the theme of this book from the perspective of Sikhism. It is an attempt at understanding Reality in its various aspects, particularly as given by Aad Guru Granth Sahib (AGGS). It points out that humans have been engaged in fathoming Reality from time immemorial. The first part of the paper explores science's ongoing odyssey to comprehend fully the physical aspect of Reality. Although science has made much progress in this adventure, science cannot claim total success as relativity and quantum theory have shown, particularly in the context of the Uncertainty Principle, Complementarity Principle, etc. Coming to human endeavour to apprehend the Ultimate Reality, he says that this concept is trans-empirical and trans-scientific and so we need to go to the realm of mysticism, and in this regard AGGS has a unique contribution to make. According to him, the concept of the Ultimate Reality in AGGS is most scientific, precise and dynamic in nature. It presents an integrated view of the fundamental Reality that is monistic, but whose manifestation is pluralistic. It explains the nature of the Ultimate Reality and presents means to attain it. It emphasizes the reality of the created universe and encourages serious study of the same. Thus Virk brings out the wealth and depth of AGGS.

It is a puzzling paradox of human life and experience that often what is most commonplace and most intimately associated with it happens to be the most intractable and least known. Consciousness is one such intriguing phenomenon. It still remains an enigma even now, despite millennia of serious effort to unpack it, despite the explosive growth of scientific knowledge and technological breakthroughs. "The Puzzle of Experiential Primacy and Consciousness" by Sangeetha Menon is a contribution to uncover the mystery still surrounding the concept of consciousness. Starting with the distinction of David Chalmers between "easy problems and hard problem" in the study of consciousness, she explores the possibility of arriving at an explanation for the mutual influence of neural events and subjective experiences. It is an attempt to identify the defining characteristic of consciousness – neural events which belong to the third person discourse or subjective experience which belongs to the first person discourse. The paper apprises the reader of the complexity and challenge posed by this puzzling problem of the nature of consciousness, although it continues to remain resistant to any satisfactory solution. The paper concludes with a short discussion of the Indian perspective on the theme.

The final contribution by William Grassie, "Engaged Contemplation for a Troubled World," is an extended meditation on our confused and confusing world scenario. It dwells at length on the many and varied challenges of social transformation in our troubled and wounded world. The author presents a panoramic view of the paradoxical predicament our world is in – of burgeoning technological growth and mounting insecurities, glamour and gloom, prosperity and poverty, promises and perils, hopefulness and hopelessness. It is an exposition of our world trapped in the maze of manifold problems and endless challenges. It attempts to charter the complex trail one has to tread to rescue today's society from the malaise it is in, with no guarantee of success. It compares our society to an addict and the attempt to extricate itself from the enslavement to that of an alcoholic trying to liberate him/ herself from the clutches of the addiction. But the world is not lost; it is not without hope. There is a way out. The nursery rhyme of the children: "People are dying, Children are crying, Concentrate! Concentrate!" rings time and again as a chorus. The author interprets the rhyme to convey the message that "the way to create a safer and healthier world is through a profound awareness of the present condition and not a predictive managerial control of the future's unfolding." The paper points out that in this context world religious traditions can make a substantial contribution since they can go a long way in integrating the past and living fully in the present moment, thereby giving rise to a better tomorrow. The right attitude to take is: on the one hand, like children live fully in the present and, on the other hand, like adults keep alive the hopes for a bright future. In short, this paper is an attempt to weave science, religion and mysticism together in an appeal for a novel mode of spiritually-based activism.

The papers above make it abundantly clear that a creative and constructive interaction between genuine mysticism and true science is not only possible but also necessary for a fuller and fruitful understanding and appreciation of reality. Three powerful and well-supported considerations seem to lead to this conclusion: the almost inexhaustible richness of reality, the limitedness of science and the relentlessness of the human quest for knowledge. Towards the end of the nineteenth century many scholars, particularly scientists, had thought that the resources of reality were well within human reach, and it was only a matter of a few more years before science had exhausted all the secrets of nature. In fact, some scholars, including the teacher of Max Planck, had predicted the advent of the day when science would have accomplished this feat. But they were all badly mistaken. The Relativistic-Quantum Mechanical Revolution that unfolded in the beginning of the 20th century revealed that reality was far more complex and rich than what Classical Science had anticipated. Subsequent developments in science were even more surprising, even shocking. It became known that there were certain limits to science's capability to fathom reality beyond which it could not go. Not only were the resources of reality overwhelming, there were certain limits put on science, which prevented it from exhausting the full richness of reality. But the human spirit refused to honour these limits and restlessly ventured beyond them. Particularly the human mind, never bound by these limits of science, dared deeper into the secret depths of reality. This is where mysticism found its natural entry-point. This became clear from the fact that many scientists in their creative moments became mystics. In the light of these developments it becomes clear that genuine mysticism when applied appropriately, far from being a stranger, needs to be recognized as a natural partner in the ongoing task of understanding and appreciating the fullness of reality.

Science-Mysticism Dialogue

A Surer Path to Fullness

Job Kozhamthadam

What Is Mysticism

Controversy has been the constant companion of mysticism. Although this phenomenon is as old as the human race, being found in all cultures and ages, there is no consensus about what its actual nature is. Plagued by unclarity and vagueness, no definitive definition can be given for this phenomenon that can capture the many aspects attributed to it. Already in 1899 Dean W.R.Inge listed 25 different definitions for mysticism. Today that figure must number many times more.

Usually mysticism is spoken of in two different but related senses - a broad sense and a narrow sense. In the broad sense it refers to the direct, experiential knowledge of the spiritual realm. This arises from the firsthand experience of direct intercourse with the Divine. In the narrow sense it refers to the theologico-philosophical doctrine of the union of the soul with the Absolute Reality, i.e., God. Understandably, this flight of the alone to the Alone is no easy path, being steep and hard, lonely and arduous, involving "ladders," "steps" and "ascents." Traditionally three grades are given, in progressive order: The purgative, the illuminative and the unitive stages.

It must be noted that these two senses are closely related since this union with the Absolute can be considered the cause of the special spiritual knowledge attained. The direct access comes because of the person's total absorption in the Divine. Since mysticism involves invoking powers which are usually unused, it requires special techniques to unleash such powers. Unlike intellection which requires only a part of the person, mysticism is a holistic process involving the whole person.

Mystical experiences are context-sensitive, expressing the unique and special characteristics of the person involved. According to Gershom Scholem, "There is no mysticism-in-general. Only particular mystical systems and individuals: Hindu, Christian, Jewish, Muslim, etc." However, they all show family-resemblance and their general characteristics can be identified.

Some Special Characteristics of Mysticism

William James in his classic, *The Varieties of Religious Experience,* points out a number of features that distinguish mystical experience from other phenomena.

1.   Ineffability

Mystical experience is deeply personal and private, and hence is characterized by a form of incommunicability. The mystics may write page after page about their experience, but they all fail to communicate exactly their experiences. The experience seems to be beyond words. As Lancy Pereira puts it, "When one can fully come to terms with the enthusiastic babble of mystics from all times and climes, one may appreciate what it means for infinities to converge at a point of indescribable beauty and love. The 'music' one then hears is beyond hearing, the 'science' beyond understanding. The enchantment takes a quantum leap, and the darkness spills over into new abysses of wonder."[1]

2.   Noetic Quality

Experts point out that mystical experience usually does not lead to new theoretical or technical knowledge, although this is contestable. But the deep insights and unique illuminations on complex and incomprehensible themes that often accompany mystical experiences certainly belong to the noetic order. Speaking on this noetic aspect, Rufus Jones writes: "It is not necessary to conclude that 'oracular communications,' or mysterious information, or ideas with novelty of content come into the world through the secret door of mystical openings." At the same time he adds, "The mystical experience has undoubtedly a noetic nature. But it consists of leaps of insight through heightened life, in an intensifying of vision through the fusing of all the deep-lying powers of the intellect, emotion, and will, and in a corresponding surge of conviction through the dynamic integration of personality, rather than as a ready-made 'gift.'"

3.   Passivity

Mystical insights are "given" gratuitously, not "acquired." Although proper preparation and a certain mastery over specific methods are prerequisites for reaching the mystical stage, once the higher powers take over, all voluntary preparations seem to lose their efficacy. One cannot predict with any measure of exactness what results one is going to get, unlike as in the case of science.

4.   Transiency

Mystical experience is short-lived, lasting only small spells of time. Although this view has been contested, there is no guarantee that mysticism will remain a permanent feature of the person.

5.   Integration

The mystical consciousness is capable of crossing the boundaries and bringing about an integration of different elements, including what is usually deemed as opposites, when it is in touch with a higher reality.

Scholars point out that this list is not exhaustive; nor is it strictly followed in all cases.

A Phenomenological Description of Mystical Experience

As mentioned already, mystical experience defies any definite description. Yet a detailed study of the experiences of mystics from various cultures and ages reveals certain outstanding common features. For instance, in this experience the subject-object distinction gets obliterated since it is marked by the emergence of a type of consciousness which is neither sharply focalized nor clearly differentiated into a subject-object state. The person is flooded with an onrush of deep feelings from the depths of his/her inner life. Deep-lying, powerful, dormant powers are unleashed and the person feels a sudden liberation deep within, and gets charged with unanticipated vigour and activity. The walls of all kinds of compartmentalization, categorization and distinction seem to collapse. And one experiences a sense of unity and wholeness with nature. The person feels gripped by transcendent energies. These are accompanied by a lofty appreciation of beauty or sublimity, serene companionship with nature and the surroundings, absorbed relishing of music, sudden flashes of insight into deeper mysteries, sudden apprehension of the meaning of truth, strong awakening of love, moral exaltation of life in the pursuit of duty, etc. In some cases, the person sees visions, hears voices and is taken up in ecstasy. The element of going "beyond," and being "above" are characteristic marks of mystical experience.

Mysticism and Renunciation

Mysticism is a demonstration of the power of the spiritual. According to many masters, this power is obtained not by amassing wealth, particularly material wealth, but by renouncing all forms of things. As the old Sufi master has said, the mystic renounces "first, what is not lawful; then what is lawful; and finally, whatever is not God."[2] Growth in the mystical life involves a progressive shattering of the ego so that the energy normally expended in maintaining the ego may be placed at the service of humanity in a life of compassion and service.

Mysticism and Religion

Although mysticism is religion-related, it need not be religion-rooted. It is not necessary for someone to belong to any religion to embrace the path of mysticism. Some of the mystically-inclined modern scientists whom we will discuss in this paper did not belong to any religion, and could not fit into any of the official religions. It may be noted that Albert Einstein and Werner Heisenberg did not believe in a personal God. It may also be mentioned that although some of the mystics were endowed with special powers like performing miracles, this ability is not a requisite for being a mystic.

Mysticism and Reality

Mysticism and mystics are often relegated to the realm of the impractical, being lost-in-the clouds. But this seems to be a hasty conclusion based on inadequate information and insufficient reflection. Many mystics in the

Christian religion, like St. Ignatius of Loyola, were founders of highly successful religious congregations whose members have been rendering outstanding service in various parts of the world. Many scholars argue that mysticism, far from taking people away from reality, makes them more sensitive and alive to reality. According to Pereira, "the mystic is one who really knows, one who is really at home in the universe, one who reminds us of who we are and what we can be."[3] According to Hocking, "it is the mystic alone who is fully at home in the universe; the rest of us merely use the earth as a business address."[4] The communion they experience with the Divine provides them with added impetus to reach out to others and perceive the spark of the divine in them. "In bonding themselves absolutely to the divinity they experience, personal or otherwise, the mystics proclaim in a manner most powerful, that there has to exist in each of us that which, primarily, makes the bond feasible."[5] This bonding is not confined to fellow-humans only, but extends to the cosmos at large: "Unlike the scientist or musician, the genuine mystic cannot live without uniting the personal consciousness to everything else that exists."[6] Mysticism enables the mystics to make the whole universe their home: "The mystic's 'God' is identical with 'the Mystery' and, as a result, the true mystic knows exactly who she/he is and becomes perfectly at home everywhere in the universe. The 'other' world is right here. Death is welcome as a transition into new regions of blissful wonder."[7]

MYSTICISM AND MODERN SCIENCE

The Possibility of a Dialogue

In the past even the mention of a dialogue between science and mysticism would have been considered odd and suspect. Science is science, mysticism is mysticism and they have nothing to dialogue about. In fact, some would have considered such a proposal an insult to science. Even today some of the major bookstores put books on mysticism under the category of the "occult," books that promote obscurantism and superstition. Today, strangely, with the development of science this attitude has changed. Books are available on the theme of science-mysticism dialogue. Two of Fritjof Capra's works, *The Tao of Physics* and *The Turning Point* became international bestsellers, and have been translated into many languages. National and international conferences are being organized quite frequently in various parts of the globe on this theme. This shift in perspective has not come about accidentally. As we will discuss later, this came as part of positive developments in the field of both science and mysticism.

Some Reasons for the Downgrading of Mysticism

1.   Cartesian Dualism

Descartes in the 17th century made a strong and sharp demarcation between matter and spirit, body and soul. Although in the religious world the spirit dimension occupied superior status, in scientific circles the material dimension dominated. With the development and phenomenal success of science, the material dimension, with its characteristic clarity, exactness and reliability, began gaining greater acceptance. Simultaneously the spiritual dimension with its intrinsic sensory and experimental inaccessibility began to be downgraded. The dimension of emotions and feelings became even more suspect. Since mysticism was closely linked to the spiritual world and had many emotional overtones, it became highly suspect.

2.   Mechanical Philosophy of Nature(MPN)

This philosophy arose as a spin off from the tremendous success of science, especially of Newtonian Mechanics. Intoxicated by this success, it claimed that science could explain every phenomenon worth worrying about, using the laws, principles and methods of science with mathematical clarity, exactness and accuracy. If something could not be so explained, there was something wrong with it. Since mysticism was not amenable to such mathematical analysis, it was concluded that it belonged to the world of obscurantism.

3.   The Enlightenment

This was a philosophical movement that swept the intellectual world of 18th century Europe with extreme emphasis on reason and rationality, an excessive reliance on empiricism and a strong spirit of skepticism in social and political thought. This excessive reliance on the rational and the sense-observable led it to a downgrading of all that is related to emotions and feelings. Naturally mysticism became a sure victim of this movement.

4.   The Influence of Thinkers like Hume, Marx, Comte, Russell, etc

These thinkers were highly gifted, articulate and influential. They all emphasized the empirical, material aspect of reality. All of them were staunch opponents of matters of God and religion, and debunked all forms of mysticism and spirituality. Their writings were clear in their ideas and persuasive in their arguments. Under their combined onslaught mysticism suffered greatly.

5.   Logical Positivism (LP)

This philosophy of science, which dominated the philosophical world in the first half of the 20th century, subscribed to an extreme form of empiricism, and claimed that all true knowledge must be based on sense data; otherwise it was meaningless. Since mysticism and related phenomena could not be anchored on strict empirical data, they debunked mysticism.

6.   Attitude of Religious Persons

The otherworldly and complacent attitudes of many religious persons, particularly religious leaders, led to an insensitivity to developments in science and other fields, and consequent alienation. The gulf between the traditional supporters of mysticism and its opponents began to widen.

The Emergence of a New Positive Outlook towards Mysticism

However, this process of denigration of mysticism did not continue for long. Nor did it lead to a wholesale disappearance or abandonment of mysticism. Ironically, several recent developments in science - like the rise of the theory of evolution, relativity, quantum theory, and chaos theory - far from strengthening the hold of the Mechanical Philosophy of Nature and Logical Positivism, dealt a deathblow to many of their claims. Many of these claims and expectations were shown to be unreal, unrealizable, and unnecessary. For instance, in the past it was thought that stability demanded immutability; a changing world was an unstable and hence unreliable world. But evolution showed that reality could change without ceasing to be stable. Space, length, time, mass, etc., were considered to be absolute in the world of MPN. Relativity showed that this absolutism was an illusion. According to MPN and LP, reality must be determinate and definite. But the wave-particle duality of the quantum theory showed that fundamentally nature is indeterminate and indefinite, and yet is law-governed and reliable. According to MPN and LP, scientific knowledge must be exact and certain. But Heisenberg's uncertainty principle revealed that the search for fully exact and certain knowledge in science was an impossible dream. It was claimed that science could give a complete, unambiguous explanation of natural phenomena. But Bohr's complementarity principle argued that a complete explanation could be obtained only through a complementary, piecemeal approach. MPN and LP had perfect faith in reductionism, and never ceased advocating its use in science. But today reductionism seems to be an endless road. The reductionist search for the ultimate fundamental particle seems to defy detection; any chance of seeing clear light at the end of the tunnel seems to be slipping away. Chance and chaos were relegated to the realm of the meaningless and worthless. But now they have taken center stage in scientific investigations. In 1980 when Stephen Hawking was appointed to the Lucasian Chair, in his acceptance speech he spoke of the imminent completion of the search for GUT (Grand Unified Theory) and thereupon the triumphant finale of physics. But today, after over 75 years of relentless efforts by some of the best of brains in the world, persevering in the pursuit of the GUT theory seems to require all the guts in the world! In fine, practically every claim made and every criterion imposed by MPN seems to have been shaken up and shown to be in need of radical reconsideration.

Certain Findings from the Research in the History of Science

A close look at the history of science reveals that science and mysticism were no strange bedfellows. All through history we see outstanding geniuses and other scholars who combined science with genuine mysticism, without experiencing any serious tension. In fact, in many ways, the two supported and reinforced each other. Some well-known examples are Pythagoras and his followers, Plato, Aristotle, Plotinus, etc., in ancient times; Copernicus, Kepler, etc., in modern times.

As has been mentioned already, in the heyday of the Enlightenment there was serious tension and conflict between the two. But further developments in science, particularly from the 20th century onwards has changed this scenario.

Scientist-Mystics of Recent Times

From the twentieth century onwards, we are witnessing a whole long line of outstanding scientists who have combined science with a certain form of mysticism. They all experienced the need to embrace some form of mysticism and there is no good reason to believe that this rendered their science any less effective or successful. In some ways it enriched and ennobled their scientific life. We discuss a few of these eminent scientists.

1.   Einstein

He talks of the need for attaining "a humble attitude of mind toward the grandeur of reason incarnate in existence, and which in its profoundest depths, is inaccessible to man." "This attitude," he continues, "however, appears to me religious in the highest sense of the word. And so it seems to me that science not only purifies religious impulse of the dross of its anthropomorphism, but also contributed to a religious spiritualization of our understanding of life."

2.   Eddington

According to him, mysticism is necessary since science alone fails to map the world of our experience. "The 'something to which truth matters' must surely have a place in reality whatever the definition of reality we adopt. In our own nature, or through the contact of our consciousness with a nature transcending ours, there are other things that claim the same kind of recognition – a sense of beauty, of morality, and finally, at the root of all spiritual religion, an experience which we describe as the presence of God."[8]

3.   Pauli

Pauli believed that "natural science of the modern era involves a Christian elaboration of the 'lucid mysticism' of Plato, in which the unitary ground of spirit and matter is sought in the primeval images, and in which understanding has found its place in its various degrees and kinds, even to knowledge of the word of God." But Pauli warns that "this mysticism is so lucid that it sees out beyond many obscurities, which we moderns dare not and cannot do."[9] According to Heisenberg, Pauli allied himself, rather, with those who "emphasize the role of intuition and the direction of attention in freeing the concepts and ideas necessary for the establishing of a system of natural laws (i.e., a scientific theory) – ideas which in general go beyond experience."[10]

4.   Louis de Broglie

Taking inspiration from Bergson, he says that our human body is expanding, thanks to developments in technology. "Our enlarged body clamours for an addition to the spirit."[11] "Now, in this extremely enlarged body, the spirit remains what it was, too small now to fill it, too feeble to direct it." "Let us add that this increased body awaits a supplement of the soul and that the mechanism demands a mysticism."[12] "Humanity groans half-crushed under the weight of the advances that it has made. It does not know sufficiently that its future depends on itself. It is for it, above all, to make up its mind if it wishes to continue to live...."[13]

5.   James Jeans

He talks of some "Eternal Spirit" in whose mind everything subsists, after the view of Berkeley. His is a mathematical mysticism: "The Great Architect of the Universe now begins to appear as a pure mathematician."[14]

6.   Werner Heisenberg

According to him, science can make statements "about strictly limited relations that are only valid within the framework of limitations."[15] Science is limited in its domain and method. His central theme is of the "Central Order" "whose existence seems beyond doubt," which can be reached "as directly as you can reach the soul of another human being,"[16] "whose outer manifestations may be highly diverse and pass our understanding."[17] It belongs not to the immediately visible world, but to the "region of the structures lying behind it, which Plato spoke of as the world of Ideas, and concerning which we are told in the Bible, 'God is spirit.'[18]

Different Views on the Science-Mysticism Relationship

A wide spectrum of views exists among scholars concerning the relationship between science and mysticism. First we will discuss below the two extreme views of strong-interaction and no-interaction. Then I will present my own views.

Strong-Interaction View

Mainly proposed by Fritjof Capra, Gary Zukav, Lawrence Beynam and others. Modern science reveals a number of characteristics for the universe: interconnection, unity, intrinsic dynamism, space-time transcendence of reality, indeterminism, fading of the subject-object and observer-observed distinction, etc. The proponents of this view point out that many of these cosmic features were already discovered by the ancient sages thousands of years ago. This close parallel between the empirically-based findings of modern science and the intuitive insights of the sages is too striking to be ignored or relegated as merely accidental. In fact, they see the discoveries of modern science, in a way, confirming what the sages had discovered ages ago. Thus this Strong-Interaction view argues for modern science supporting or even "proving" mysticism. Capra wrote about it in his *The Tao of Physics* in 1977 and Gary Zukav in *The Dancing Wu Li Masters* in 1979. Lawrence Beynam said in 1978: "We are currently undergoing a paradigm shift in science – perhaps the greatest shift in its kind to date. It is for the first time that we have stumbled upon a comprehensive model for mystical experiences, which has the additional advantage of deriving from the forefront of contemporary physics."[19] In 2000 Murli Manohar pointed out that "scientists today are discussing questions like 'reality,' 'being,' 'non-being,' etc. in almost the same language which the Upanishads and other schools of Indian Philosophy have done."[20] Capra in his most recent writings has reaffirmed this view: "When I first discovered parallels between the worldviews of physicists and mystics, more than 30 years ago, ... I had the strong feeling that I was merely uncovering something that was quite obvious and would be common knowledge in the future; and sometimes, while writing the book, I even felt that it was being written through me, rather than by me. The subsequent events have confirmed these feelings."[21] He continues: "The reluctance of modern scientists to accept the profound similarities between their concepts and those of mystics is not surprising, since mysticism – at least in the West – has traditionally been associated, quite erroneously, with things vague, nebulous, mysterious, and highly unscientific."[22]

No-Interaction View

On the other end of the spectrum is the No-Interaction View, strongly propounded by Ken Wilber, Jeremy Bernstein, Richard Jones, etc. For them, the case of modern science supporting and proving mysticism not only has never happened, but also it is just impossible. In fact, such a claim commits "a violent fallacy known as category error."[23] In his view the Strong-Interaction theory is based on "wild generalizations" and "on the use of accidental similarities of language as if they were somehow evidence of deeply rooted connections."[24] Wilber does not rule out the claim altogether since he concedes some limited similarity. While Capra sees modern science uncovering a remarkable interconnectivity at the cosmic level, Wilber finds mutual interconnectivity of the elements in the world of non-living matter only. In his own words, "I suggest that the new physics has simply discovered the one-dimensional interpenetration of its own level (non-sentient mass/energy). While this is an important discovery, it cannot be equated with the extraordinary phenomenon of multi-dimensional interpenetration described by the mystics.... To put it crudely, the study of physics is on the first floor, describing the interactions of its elements; the mystics are on the sixth floor describing the interaction of all six floors."[25]

Here Wilber is referring to the so-called perennial philosophy which in his view underlies all Eastern philosophical tradition. The perennial philosophy looks at the cosmos in terms of a hierarchy of six levels, arranged in an order of superiority. The higher one contains the lower, but not vice versa. The different levels are physical, biological, psychological, subtle, causal, and ultimate. Mysticism belongs to the sixth and last level and hence is superior to all others and pervades all levels, whereas science belongs to the first level only, and hence is at the lowest level and least pervasive. Clearly, Wilber's point is that any claim to equality or close similarity between the new science and mysticism goes against the perennial philosophy, and hence is wrongheaded. In fact, such a claim commits the fallacy known as category error.

The conclusion follows that the interconnectedness of the universe discovered by the new science is, at best, applicable only to the first level. Being the first level, it can never hope to reach out to any higher level, much less to the all-superior and all-pervasive sixth level of mysticism. The physicist "tells us, and can tell us, nothing whatsoever about the interaction of non-living matter with the biological level, and of that level's interaction with the mental field ...."[26] Of course, since the sixth level of the mystic comprises the first level, a very limited level of agreement is possible. However, further considerations show that "even the agreement between mystic and physicist on level-one must be looked upon either as somewhat tenuous or as a fortunate coincidence."[27] This comes about because the new science is very much limited to the micro-world only. It doesn't seem to be applicable to the macro world of every day experience.

According to Bernstein, any attempt to equate the findings of modern science with the intuitions of the East, will be a disservice to the latter. In his own words, "If I were an Eastern mystic the last thing in the world that I would want would be a reconciliation with modern science."[28] His main argument is that science and scientific knowledge are built on the shifting sands of change, and hence subject to revision, whereas the truths given by the sages of the East are religious truths which are immune to revision and change. It also cannot claim any consensus among its practitioners. Naturally, "to hitch a religious [transpersonal] philosophy to a contemporary science is a sure route to its obsolescence."[29]

Many may be inclined to see a relationship of complementarity between modern science and eastern mysticism. Wilber is of the opinion that this betrays an incorrect understanding of what such a relationship is. As Niels Bohr has articulated it, two items A and B are complementary if they are mutually exclusive and jointly necessary. Wilber thinks that science and mysticism are not mutually exclusive since one and the same person can be a scientist and a mystic.

Wilber concludes his well-thought out and clearly-written critical remarks with a few words of warning: "Take Bernstein's warning with you: thank the new physics for agreeing with you, but resist the temptation to build your transpersonal models upon the shifting sands of changing level-one theories."[30] His final parting message is even more indicative of his dissatisfaction: "Unwarranted and premature marriages usually end in divorce, and all too often a divorce that terribly damages both parties."[31]

Some Critical Comments and Reflections

1. The parallels identified by Capra and others are too striking and pervasive to be deemed mere accidents or mere linguistic coincidences. True, some of the insights may be questionable with regard to details, some of them may lack the sophistication of the findings of contemporary science. But

these inadequacies cannot offset the value and significance of these findings. They are to be looked upon as the first, crude findings that need to be developed through further research and reflection. This has happened time and again in the history of science. For instance, it is well recognized that the ancient Greek atomists were the forerunners of modern atomism. Although the idea of atomism has evolved and developed considerably since then, the basic idea has not changed from what it was in the time of Democritus, Leucippus and Epicurus.

2. It is important to note that the parallelism is perceived in the case of wider and deeper truths, not in the case of particular, specific features. The truths the mystics have discovered are limited and few. The claims that the ancient sages knew of specific modern theories will have to be subjected to strict and critical scrutiny. This also explains why these parallels were discovered only in the post relativity-quantum mechanical revolution era. Thanks to this revolution, science is in a position to address larger and deeper truths about the universe. The genetic revolution has gone even further.

3. It is true that some of the concepts involved are vague and on occasions the proponents of the Strong-Interaction have cashed in on this vagueness. Also at times some of their interpretations of eastern concepts are questionable and smack of inaccuracy and superficiality. This can weaken their thesis, not invalidate it.

4. The claim that modern science supports mysticism needs a closer and critical reflection. If by support is meant proving, as some of the critics interpret, then the claim is unsustainable, particularly proving understood in the strict sense. On the other hand, a claim of a weaker form of support can be defended.

5. The contention that mystical insights are unchanging, whereas scientific findings are transient, also needs careful scrutiny. Today many philosophers and other thinkers show strong reservation towards the claim about unchanging truths. They point out that such claims are based on presuppositions that cannot be defended in a non-question-begging manner. Capra points out that science does not change in a totally discontinuous and abrupt fashion. Even in the most radical scientific revolution one can discern an underlying thread that is immune to mutation.

According to him, it is these sacred threads that the sages have succeeded in identifying.

6. The claims of the Perennial Philosophy upon which Wilber's criticism is anchored are questionable. With its multi-tier, sharp distinction of hierarchical levels, it is a version of the Great Chain of Being. According to its hierarchy, mysticism is the highest level and science the lowest. Since any higher level contains the lower ones, the mystical level contains the scientific level and not vice versa. This means that the mystical can influence the scientific, but the scientific cannot influence the mystical. Since the biological level is higher than the physical level, this means that the biological can influence the physical, not the other way around. In the light of recent findings on psychosomatic effects, this theory is highly questionable. Today many admit that mysticism is context-sensitive, and, since the physical is an integral part of the context, the physical can have an impact on the mystical. More importantly, it should be noted that the Perennial Philosophy is not a universally accepted philosophy.

7. Furthermore, we have seen that most of the creative scientists were mystics of one kind or other. There is no reason to believe that their mysticism impeded their science or vice versa. On the other hand, we can give good evidence from the history of science to show that, at least in some cases, the mystical streak proved beneficial for their scientific work, particularly in their most creative and innovative moments (Kepler, Newton, Kekule, etc). Also, there have been cases of their scientific work triggering mystical sense in them (Francis Collins, Einstein, etc.). All these go to show that science and mysticism are not strange companions. They can and do interact with each other.

My View: Complementarity

It seems to me that both the Strong-Interaction and the No-Interaction views have gone to two extremes. The truth seems to be in the middle. Science and mysticism do interact, but not as one proving the other, rather one complementing the other. I propose a complementarity view which respects the importance, value and validity of the other; one brings in something important which the other cannot, without leading to any conflict or tension; one completes and enriches the other in a holistic and harmonious way.

I see this complementary relationship at work at least in three aspects: at the level of the different abilities involved in the process of knowing, at the level of the mode or method of knowing, and at the level of the person knowing or the knower. Talking of the different abilities of the human mind, we can identify the rational and the intuitive. Western science refers mainly to the rational, and mysticism or eastern wisdom mainly to the intuitive. Of course, the intuitive does not fully exclude the rational, and vice versa.[32] Rational knowledge is discursive, moving step by step through a chain of reasoning process. Intuitive knowledge is direct, without any noticeable mediation, taking place suddenly as it were in one swoop. Rational knowledge usually proceeds by a definite plan, while intuitive knowledge usually comes unexpectedly, in a flash as it were. Rational knowledge is very much analytical and logical, while intuitive knowledge is very much synthetic and follows no identifiable logic. Rational knowledge compares, classifies, divides and distinguishes, whereas intuitive knowledge interlinks and unifies. Rational knowledge is highly selective, while intuitive knowledge tends to be holistic. Rational knowledge is characteristically deliberate, definite, accurate, clear, and objective. Intuitive knowledge is characteristically non-deliberate or subconscious, indefinite, inaccurate, vague, and subjective. Rational knowledge is for the most part articulate and communicable, whereas intuitive knowledge is often inarticulate and incommunicable. Obviously, here I am not claiming a complementarity relationship in a very strict sense. However, it is clear that these two are highlighting two distinct polarities of human knowledge.

Coming to the mode of learning, we can consider the free, daring mystical spirit and the critical, cautious scientific spirit. The mystical spirit is free, unbridled by space-time limitations. It can soar high and lose contact with the ground-reality. Science, on the other hand, keeps it in touch with reality. But empirical science limits itself to the observable world of space and time. That can leave it dry and uncreative. The mystical spirit urges science to dare to detach itself from the narrow confines of the observable world to venture into the richer and wider world. We may summarize the situation as Einstein did on a related theme: "Science without mysticism is stagnant, mysticism without science is sterile."

At the level of the knower also we can see a complementarity relationship between science and mysticism. The meeting point of science and mysticism is the person of the scientist, the life of the scientist. A life that is guided solely by dry, rigid, heartless scientific principles can often lead to a machine-like existence, lacking direction and meaning. On the other hand, a life that is given totally to mystical, ecstatic exuberance can lead to unrealism and unproductivity. A person in whom both science and mysticism meet in a complementary way avoids both these pitfalls and attains harmony and holism. Capra has depicted this scenario beautifully: "Science does not need mysticism, mysticism does not need science, but humans need both."

Science-Mysticism Dialogue and Genuine Globalization

I am optimistic that a serious, creative science-mysticism dialogue can lead to an enriching East-West dialogue. Traditionally, mysticism has been closely associated with the East, whereas empirical science has been linked with the West, although neither mysticism nor science has been the monopoly of any particular nation or geographical region. The different virtues of science and mysticism admirably equip them to be apostles of a global spirit. Science is characterized by a universal spirit, as is evident from the fact that scientific laws are universal in their application. Similarly, science's concern for objectivity allows its findings to be independent of any particular person, place or time. Mysticism by its very nature aims at transcending all narrow boundaries to embrace unity and oneness of all. A constructive and creative interaction between modern science and mysticism can pave the way for the breakdown of all barriers of caste, colour and creed, and help in the creation of a united universe of fraternity and mutual enrichment. Science-Mysticism dialogue can really be a surer path to a genuine global spirit.

Endnotes

[1] Lancy Pereira, *Our Enchanted Universe* (Anand: Gujarat Sahithya Prakashan, 1997), p. 82.

[2] Pereira, *Enchanted Universe*, p. 86.

[3] *Ibid.*, pp. 81-82.

[4] *Ibid.*, p.89.

[5] *Ibid.*, p.85.

[6] Lancy Pereira, *The Enchanted Darkness* (Anand: Gujarat Sahithya Prakashan, 1995), p. ix.

[7] *Ibid.*, p.ix.

[8] Ken Wilber, *Quantum Questions* (London: Shambhala, 1984)p. 175.

[9] W. Heisenberg, *Across the Frontiers* (New York: Harper Tochbooks, 1975), p.33.

[10] *Ibid.*, p.31.

[11] Ken Wilber, *Quantum Questions*, p.121.

[12] *Ibid.*, p.122.

[13] Idem.

[14] *Ibid.*, p.136.

[15] *Ibid.*, p.73.

[16] Werner Heisenberg, *Physics and Beyond* (New York: Harper Torchbooks, 1972), p.215.

[17] *Ibid.*, p.216.

[18] Werner Heisenberg, *Across the Frontiers* , pp. 219-220.

[19] Quoted by Ken Wilber, in "Physics, Mysticism, and the New Holographic Paradigm," in *Re-Vision* (Summer/Fall 1979), p.43.

[20] Murli Manohar Joshi, "Science and Religion, " in Stephen F. von Welck (ed.), *Crossing Borders, Stretching Boundaries* (New Delhi: Manohar Publishers, 2000), p.62.

[21] F.Capra, "The Tao of Physics Revisited," in Job Kozhamthadam (ed.), *Religious Phenomena in a world of Science* (Pune: ASSR Publications, 2004), p. 97.

[22] *Ibid.*, p.100.

[23] Job Kozhamthadam, "Modern Science and Eastern Intuition: Coexistence or Complementarity?" in *Disputatio Philosophica* 3 (2001), p.124.

[24] *Ibid.*, p.123.

[25] Ken Wilber, "Physics, Mysticism, and the New Holograpahic Paradigm," p. 47.

[26] *Ibid.*, p.47.

[27] Idem.

[28] *Ibid.*, p.48.

[29] *Ibid.*, p.48.

[30] *Ibid.*, p.53.

[31] *Ibid.*, p.55.

[32] As I have said earlier, strictly speaking complementarity requires that one aspect excludes the other and vice versa. We take a less strict view here.

Symbiosis and
the Transpersonal Quest For Oneness
Lancy Pereira

Introduction

In spite of heavy involvement over many years with research activities in modern microbiological science and the training of many research students in that and related fields, I have decided in this paper to focus on science as seen through the integrated consciousness of the mystics - including those scientists who have shown mystical tendencies. Among those who have deeply influenced me are good scientists and gifted mystics, but I do not claim to be a member of either category.

The first three sections of the paper are devoted to explaining what mysticism is about, fostering thereby my cherished mania that thoughtful human beings would do themselves a service by taking the claims of the mystics seriously.

A longish section four then proceeds to offer some ideas on how to enjoy a dialogue that grows into a symbiosis with scientists who are "unbelievers." The approach I suggest - centred on a calm, respectful, non-egoistic, intelligent but not purely intellectual interaction, where both sides win - is very much in the traditions of "the East."

That permits me in section five to talk directly about the grey areas in science which one hardly hears about, at least from the learned university professors I have known, in both the East and the West.

Finally section six explains why the insights of molecular biology when applied to the brain and the human embryo's growth in the womb render the statements found in several of today's best-selling books insufferably naive.

The Inner World of Consciousness

Seen from outer space by advanced cameras in satellites and spaceships, our earth is one single beautiful sphere twisting in serene majesty through the cosmos. This paper is however mainly devoted to our earth as seen from inner space by enlightened human spirits - and here too it is one, as many great scientists and all true mystics, East and West, have realized. For those advanced minds, not only our earth but also the entire universe and everything that exists are pervaded by a single consciousness.

The mind which functions in inner space is our link to that one all-embracing consciousness. The discoveries of scientists and the intuitions of mystics do little more than reveal in bits and pieces the unfathomable depths of wisdom locked into that one consciousness. Nobel Prize winning scientists, among other geniuses, have made clear to us that the most surprising disclosures of the 20th century were the uncertainty of our knowledge and the extent of our ignorance.

One wishes one heard more of such basic, truthful, scientific realism from the mass media, the scientists who write bestsellers for the general public and the learned professors of science in the better universities. But to do that one needs to venture without fear to the edges of the darkness. It is far more comfortable to be bathed in light and public admiration - including that of our adoring students, especially if they are good-looking. "The small head of our Professor contains so much knowledge. Where does he keep it all?" Which teacher is willing to say: Is "what I know" really mine – and, by the way, who is this "I"?

Scientists make exquisite use of their conscious minds to work, but science itself cannot explain consciousness and provides no proofs to validate mystical awareness. However, as human beings, several scientists reach a basic intuition close to that of the great mystics - that Someone or Something permeates all the realities of our existence (Immanent) without being part of them (Transcendent). The great difference is that the genuine mystics also experience *union* with that All-pervading Reality and some then will proceed to talk endlessly about that mind-blowing experience while insisting that their words are useless. Other mystics are more logical and shut up - which may be good for them but leaves the rest of us panting.

Where indeed are the boundaries of the universe, whether cosmic or personal? Was Nelson Mandela right when he said that we need to fear not our weaknesses but our strengths?

Perspectives, stretched endlessly towards the ever-receding horizons of outer and inner space, are in practice more easily available to those willing to function in the Transpersonal mode. Each human being has the hardware and software built in for the Transpersonal mode, but we need to press the proper buttons.

Transpersonal mode? What's that? One must move beyond the overwhelming compulsions of the ego and the personal, individualized self. Crushing the ego can release energies more powerful than splitting the atom. Mystics have made major contributions to bettering the world. Among such mystics we find - in both the East and the West - scientists, poets, artists, musicians, philosophers and the founders of the major religions as well as several smaller religious orders/groups.

But certainly we have also to function as practical citizens of this bent world. It is not my point that we must give up the need to develop talent and ego. In fact it is healthy and useful to become somebody before reaching for the sublime joys of being nobody. That *is* a joy which makes no logical sense, but it is very real. The individual self may be nothing, but more accurately it is "no-thing" because it is also capable of oneness with everything - nothing excluded, including *that* which cannot be named.

Hence the paradox. The hallmark of truly extraordinary human beings is a profound, truth-based humility. They achieve so much for being acutely aware of the enormous potential of emptiness in themselves and their world.

Note these intellectually brilliant and profoundly beautiful words of Jalaluddin Rumi, the Sufi mystic, whose poetry skirts tantalisingly the dangerous edges where human merges with the divine. The Great Lover speaks: "When you are with everyone but me, you're with no one ... When you are with no one but me, you're with everyone...Instead of being so bound up *with* everyone, *be* everyone ...When you become that many, you're nothing. Empty."[1] Science insists that iron is really empty to the percentage of 99.9999999999999 (yes! 13 decimal places after the first 99). So too, perhaps emptier, is my soft-brained head. But I will not now try to test this hard-to-believe fact by banging a bar of iron on my poor skull. The scientific experiments can wait. I want to finish this paper!

The Transpersonal Quest of Mystics

Our Symposium is devoted to Modern Science, Mysticism and East-West Dialogue. It surely took some courage to bring together such vast areas of human striving under one umbrella. But then, good human beings are ever bent on trying to reach beyond what is neat and predictable.

Science, with its immense modern ramifications, would by itself have been difficult enough to manage within a few days. The interactions between Science and Religion would naturally be a little worse. But to have Science plus Mysticism together with East-West Dialogue thrown in, as either pickle or an overall "masala," would seem to be a spiced meal dangerously tilted towards a stomachache.

However, what we have said in Section I about consciousness could provide a way out. One could work towards an integrating consciousness - admittedly difficult! - that brings all that we care about into fruitful contact.

The print media, TV and the Internet provide a widely available nervous system geared to blend us all into a single, vibrant, interacting community on all matters of common human interest. We know that the tsunami of late December 2004 instantly produced a massive psychological wave which touched millions all over the world. It is just possible that as a race we are being prepared for a quantum leap into the kind of shared warmth of unified awareness experienced by the mystics.

That possibility would hardly appear strange to anybody who has tried to come to terms with her/his own personal depths. There are mountain peaks inside there and forests with wild animals and swift rivers rushing to the ocean from which everything comes, and to which all things eventually return. Each one's consciousness is in fact flexibly structured to expand into lengths and breadths and depths beyond measure. One can absorb and integrate into a single human consciousness quite diverse fields of knowledge. What one needs to do is to experience them from the inside, binding them into that joy which erupts spontaneously from touching the deepest springs of all that exists.

Enlightened human beings speak from a wisdom that bubbles out effortlessly from within and imparts an added lustre to all the other forms of genuine knowledge provided by art, poetry, literature, university courses, Ph.D. dissertations and music - I would say especially music, which has the power to move the free spirit beyond what all words, images and concepts can do. This is why Einstein loved to play the violin.

The transpersonal quest for oneness is a royal road to the wisdom of the enlightened, provided it is sought with great longing joined to freedom from fears over the effort and tears involved. It does not matter what your head studies. What matters is where your heart is centred and where that heart is headed.

Mystics as Persons of Flesh and Blood

In this new section I would first like to draw attention briefly to Cusanus and Al-Ghazali, two mystics from the past who integrated with ease and style the secular and the sacred. They predated Copernicus, Kepler and Galileo and therefore were not directly involved in all the great developments of science from the 16th century onwards. But it is the mentality of these two that is of interest to bolster the points stressed in the first two sections. In their mystical awareness, we find that they both manifest a certain pattern for breadth and depth of intellectual work - embracing many forms of human activity - which is common right from the seers of the Upanishads to some of the great quantum physicists of the 20th century.

We first look at Nicholas of Cusa (1401-1464), noted German mathematician and Cardinal of the Catholic Church. Adept at both ecclesiastical and secular politics, he was also a first-rate mystic. "The fabric of the world has its centre everywhere and its circumference nowhere" is the mantra he created, even if today that has been hijacked as a slogan, among others, by the so-called "New Age" people of the West.

The intellectual brilliance of Cusanus allowed him to get away with his paradoxical (tongue-in-cheek?) ideas about "learned ignorance" and "the coincidence of contradictories." Five centuries later his words were echoed in a different form by the 20th century voices of our top quantum physicists. In his own times what saved Nicholas was that he could interact on the same level with leading figures from the world of mathematics and politics. One is reminded of Picasso, who always retained the capacity to draw a cow that actually looked like one.

Al-Ghazali (1058-1111) was an equally versatile genius who about three and a half centuries earlier lit up the skies more to the East. He became a Sufi master with acknowledged expertise in matters both sacred and secular (among other things, he is credited with important scientific discoveries). In the remarkable document "Maps for the Seeker" widely attributed to him, one finds a clear description of the stages by which the human spirit is purified for divine union. What much later came to be called "the dark night of the soul" and "the role of the unconscious" were already known to the Sufis in words appropriate to the culture of their times.

The integrating mystic consciousness has been present amongst us human beings for over 25 centuries now, despite many variations of type and intensity in that consciousness. Our own Upanishads in India tried to go as deeply as possible into the common human experiences of people, and they were composed by mystic seers, perhaps more than five centuries before the Christian Era. Approximately around the same time, Pythagoras appeared in Greece and he was interested in mysticism, music, mathematics and politics. The intriguing Tao Te Ching of China is considered a mystical work and some scholars date it to the late 4th century B.C. It too teaches a whole philosophy touching numerous aspects of life.

It is a modern conceit - both false and damaging - to regard mystics as unpractical, "airy-fairy" dreamers divorced from the real world. In fact the exact opposite is true. As someone put it so well: The mystic is unique in being fully at home in the universe - the rest of us use this world as a business address. And this world is a world where many people suffer. So, to be brutally clear, let me stick my own neck out and say: If anybody is uselessly incompetent at work or unable to actually influence the practical lives of others or show deep compassion to those in pain, then s/he cannot possibly be a true mystic. Genuine mystics accept the world of flesh and blood human beings and take care to make it a better world.

A simpler and more positive criterion would be: How joyously peaceful within is this person, despite all the horrors of external circumstances? The logic behind mentioning the peace and joy comes from those amazing intuitions about humans and God so dear to us Indians: "Tat tvam asi" and "Saccidananda."

Another positive criterion: Does this person give importance to the *whole of reality* without losing sight of the *parts*, to the courage as much as to the pain, to the sensual and visible as much as to the spiritual and invisible? Here the logic would be that integration implies a thrust towards wholeness as well as wholesomeness. The genuine mystic is a two-legged holistic masterpiece from the creativity of the Formless One. The spiritual and the material interpenetrate each other - "There is another world, but it is this one."

Wilber's *Quantum Questions* (mostly about brilliant physicists) and, even more, Weber's *Dialogues with Scientists and Sages* (many types of each kind) provide plenty of evidence that today's mystics are quite attractive people, vibrantly alive, professionally competent, deeply compassionate, and much valued for their contributions to our flesh and blood world.

By now, readers will have guessed what my hidden agenda from square one has been! So let me now come clean and admit that the rest of this paper will pursue the same agenda from a different angle. In the process I hope to focus more on science and, within science, to point up a few of the more biological aspects which tend to be neglected.

The Symbiosis between Science and Mysticism

Section IV is devoted to an approach where the mystical ideas of the first three sections are applied to dialogue. It is addressed to "believers" (of any religion) interested in sharing life and ideas with scientists who are "unbelievers." When about halfway down the line in this section I use the word "you," I mean "believers" interested in the give and take of that true dialogue which in its fulness flowers into a symbiosis. Our green earth exists in reality as a symbiotic world in which the various life-forms assist each other to benefit and grow, even if in the process there is some sacrifice. On the average, the total number of cells of other small living things in and on a single human body is estimated to exceed the total number of human cells which constitute that same body.

We have arrived at the point where the reader could fairly say: It is fine for the present writer to have insisted thus far that there *need not be* any problems between science and mysticism - at least in the East with its strong mystical tendencies. In India there has been hardly any sign of the kind of direct conflicts between science and religion which have played a rather significant role in the historical development of society in the West.

But in practice the Indian Universities, with English as the chief language of instruction, have - for better or worse - inherited the problems of the West, especially of the English-speaking West. (In Germany and France, for instance, the Darwinian approach to evolution has never been too popular). So, in practice, even in India *we do have* problems - or, if not problems, at least serious misunderstandings. Hence I would now like to share a few ideas about handling these problems and misunderstandings on a more personal level.

In the first place, the most basic problem of "non-believer scientists" is whether we need God at all. Science is enough. Religion is "kind of O.K" for those who think it useful, but then if we look at Bush or Bin Laden religion itself turns out to be an awful problem. As for mysticism, what kind of animal is that?

Secondly, mathematicians, for instance, see the pros and cons about God and religion differently from, say, evolutionists - and both in turn differently from molecular biologists. In fact each science - from its own specific professional ground - has also its own kind of religious difficulty. In any dialogue conducted through books and articles, it may be entirely safe and indeed even necessary to deal with science and religion in general, but on the personal level one must take into account the specific sciences and also include the human faces and the individual human histories involved. The written literature can however help much to prepare us intellectually for the personal encounter.

Thirdly, if the scientist with problems about God or religion is an Indian and Hindu, I breathe more easy. I find many such Indian scientists often highly critical of authoritarian organized religion and the antics of "holy men," but at the same time willing to make a pilgrimage to Tirupati and consult horoscopes for their daughter's marriage - while functioning at a deeply spiritual level as good Vedantins. In other words, there are "gods" and there is a *God* beyond all names and concepts and religions. Fair enough!

My own first reaction therefore when faced with a "non-believer scientist's" critical remarks is to laugh it off and say: "How interesting! Tell me about it." At times they may even like me as a person and want playfully to find out how "shockable" I am. It is necessary then for all of us in these situations to check further in order to discover what is really going on.

My own history compels me to make such distinctions. Both in India and abroad my life has been extremely varied. In the many different things I do, I have been forced at times to sit up, rub my eyes and try to decide whether I am functioning as a Jesuit priest, a trained scientist, an idealistic administrator, a dubious educator or - let me admit it — a happy clown enjoying life's circus. And often these roles can run into each other.

There is worse. By the undeserved grace of a mischievous God - joined to the wisdom of kind religious superiors unusually gifted for making unpleasant decisions - I have found myself involved in taking or conducting all sorts of peculiar courses. For example, to take science alone, I have studied more branches (physical, chemical, mathematical and biological) than has been safe for either my sanity or my digestion. But the net result - for surrender brings its own rewards - is that I have had the good fortune of sitting dazzled at the feet of great Masters in each of the four areas of our Symposium : Science, Mysticism, East, West (in India and abroad).

Consequently I have made an interesting discovery. Masters of real quality teach us to be ever open to wonder and to being surprised by life. In interactions with ordinary folk like us they go beyond what we commonly call "dialogue." The enlightened ones quite spontaneously tend to integrate conflicts, polarities and diversities into a "symbiosis." Penetrated by the wisdom of their lived experience, the dialogue can then move into a vast space where the participants become mutually nourished by the hidden wisdom within themselves - and that is a rich source of influence most individuals are hardly aware of.

Every human individual, however uneducated or unwashed, is truly a centre of the whole universe and - as the mystic Masters say - carries an uncreated spark *within*, a spark which can be nursed into radiance. My problem is that even those who do have doctoral degrees and take a regular shower with foreign soap actually behave as if their claims to fundamental respect are merely based on living in the vertical slums of south Mumbai - or having an upper-caste background which may include a cousin who is a senior bottle-washer in some multinational company in New Zealand.

In what follows for the rest of this section, I assume that the reader who is intent on dialogue has first also become intellectually competent to engage in it. The three volumes published by ASSR - please see the "Hints For Further Reading" at the end of this article - would be very helpful for that purpose.

Once the intellectual element has been looked after, the next best thing for interaction with a scientist, however famous, who has problems with religion or mysticism is to listen respectfully without feeling in any way threatened or overawed. One must learn to relativise everybody, including oneself. After all, like everybody else, the great man is also a centre of the universe but went to the toilet in the morning. He was once, like all the rest of us, not much bigger than a full stop in his mother's womb. He had to start life greedily sucking in milk, and later had to be toilet-trained. Today, he might even be subject to pains in the pancreas and will certainly one day sicken and die - so that somebody else will have to wash up his body with soap that is not too costly.

If he has problems with science and religion, what about you? Do you realize for yourself what science can and cannot do? (If your honest answer is NO, then Section V to follow may provide some hints). And how does your dialogue-partner respond to your ideas - can you get under and beyond her/his words, to learn from what s/he is trying to say?

Perhaps in the end both sides may come to understand that life is not only interesting because of the material and organizational problems which can be solved, but also entirely fascinating because of all the beautiful mysteries of life and love which can only be experienced. For this kind of dialogue, which, because holistic, might verge on the symbiotic, a little beer will be found more helpful than orange juice.

All participants in a dialogue are first, foremost and always human beings. To the biological factors mentioned earlier, one could add several other possible social and psychological determinants. I do not say that intellectual problems have not to be handled on their own grounds, but merely that nothing is purely intellectual.

To crown it all, as said earlier, each human being carries within a spark of the divine. For some Indians each human being is also essentially divine. Well, the rest of you may be divine, but I personally am too full of juicy little sins to feel comfortable with that idea.

It is my conviction that the decisions we take and the opinions we spout emerge in practice from head and heart and gut - in varying proportions of course, depending on the circumstances. I say this not only from my own experience but also from closely interacting with others in several courses conducted in India, Germany and the USA. Moreover I think that for most of us the divine seems to work at the gut level and that of the unconscious.

When years ago I wrote *The Enchanted Darkness,*[2] I had hoped to offer to fellow-professionals - clowns included - some intellectual reasons for a holistic approach to life through science, music and mysticism. Not *only* intellectual reasons. The non-rational factors were given much importance in that work, and for me that emphasis deserves to stand. But if I had to rewrite that book today, I would add some newer insights from biology, because molecular biology when applied to embryology and to neurobiology have made even more clear in the last ten years how utterly enchanting our darkness is.

Some Reflections on Science and the Possibility of Science-Religion Interfacing

The Grey Areas in Physics

There are a few who have the opportunity and the urge to do science through lab and field experiments, and there are the many who teach and practise science through fixed syllabi in classrooms and student labs.

As an aside, let me point to an interesting parallel. There are a few mystics who do research into their own consciousness of Reality, and there are the many who teach and practise religion, based on discoveries made originally by mystics. And the richness of Reality - as in all research - remains endlessly to be discovered by others still to come.

Back to science again. The scientific researchers are far more likely than the teachers to realize from practical experience that science is basically an *adventure* where the drive to constantly improve received findings is absolutely central. Nothing is fixed; discoveries serve as steppingstones to further progress. That at least is the ideal nobody will attempt to deny.

But science is also a *human* adventure and, human nature being what it is, Max Planck's mischievous comment remains valid : "A new scientific truth does not triumph by convincing its opponents and making them see the light, but rather because its opponents eventually die." He should know. It was Planck who came up with the idea of "quanta" which radically upset and altered physics.

Those who teach science based on fixed syllabi are rarely in touch with the research which made that syllabus possible. The question is: Must that always be so?

The most outstanding classroom lectures I ever had in my life were from the geneticist, Prof. Adrian Srb, at Cornell University. He possessed the confident learning and the critical insight to trace historically up to the late 1960s the path by which the major, extraordinary discoveries in genetics were made. There was a syllabus but he went inside and around that official syllabus with the help of the research findings.

What rendered Dr. Srb's lectures unique was his showing us how the route to great achievements often involved blind alleys, unexpected detours, wrong turns and at times simply getting lost. Big names were involved. This was science in the making - we loved it and wanted to be part of it.

Another aside. When religion is presented as an adventure in God-experience, believers more easily become enthusiasts - and will perhaps even develop a further interest in genuine mystical experience.

Anyone with a feel for science who reads the "Special Einstein Issue" of *Discover* magazine[3] might experience something of what Dr. Srb's students felt. Many of the articles in that issue are by highly rated scientists but written in a popular, humanly interesting way. For instance, one is brought to realize how dissatisfied Einstein himself was with his own relativity theories, and how he spent fruitless decades trying to bring Quantum Mechanics under the umbrella of General Relativity. After his celebrated feud with Niels Bohr in 1927, Einstein went off on his own and trod a lonely path without support from any of his eminent colleagues. At one point Schrödinger, admittedly not in good health at the time, in exasperation called him a fool!

Around 1953, two years before his death, Einstein wrote with serene wisdom: "Every individual...has to retain his way of thinking if he does not want to get lost in a maze of possibilities. However, nobody is sure of having taken the right road, me the least." The greatest of scientists are first, foremost and always human beings.

And today it appears that it is Einstein who has the last laugh. String theory - or, in its developed form, "M-theory" - is the modern reincarnation of Einstein's quest for a unified field theory. There is even a powerful string theory group working at our own Tata Institute of Fundamental Research in Mumbai.

Many today consider General Relativity to be the greatest theory of the 20th century. However, Prof. Michael Turner, writing in the *Discover* issue just cited, offers the view that Einstein's theory fails to answer not only the question of how gravity is reconciled to Quantum Mechanics but also some other profound questions such as: What is space and time and where do they come from? What lies at the heart of a black hole? What happened before the Big Bang? Why is the expansion of the universe speeding up and not slowing down? What is the ultimate fate of the universe? Perhaps the greatness of a theory should be judged not only by the problems it solves but by the value of the magnificent new questions it generates. Why shouldn't great theories remind us of God?

To move next to "Particle Physics," which deals with particles such as electrons, quarks, gluons, photons and the rather mysterious Higgs bosons, the so-called "Standard Model" covers these particles along with three of the four known forces[4] - gravity being the odd man out. In an article for *Scientific American*[5] Prof. Gordon Kane tells us that the Standard Model explains most phenomena but remains inadequate, and he gives ten reasons for the current dissatisfaction. In other words, the Standard Model is not up to standard in its present form. Like every other theory we know, this model will, it appears, be always subject to further improvement. Otherwise, it will not be science but something else.

Let me wrap up this section by talking about Roger Penrose of Oxford, a mathematical physicist and theoretician who, in my opinion, is in a class by himself. He has published most recently *The Road to Reality - A Complete Guide to the Laws of the Universe.*[6] This is a massive tome of 1094 pages, to be recommended for humbling anyone who has delusions of being a genius.

We have here a truly amazing masterpiece. It carries every relevant nuance of the views of more than a hundred experts in mathematical physics, each minutely analyzed with a minimum of words. Here and there I do manage to understand something, and that is enough to both drain and excite me.

After presenting each view with accuracy and fairness - I extrapolate from the topics I know something about - Penrose is never afraid to tell the reader what he thinks about that view. In other words, he talks about all his agreements, disagreements, doubts and prejudices (which incidentally he admits are his prejudices!). This then is also the kind of book to seduce teachers of physics in our universities into admitting that "education is the process of moving from brash ignorance to thoughtful uncertainty."

Underlying this whole subsection has been a submerged purpose I want now to bring clearly to the surface. If scientists are always trying to improve what they are saying, we may be fighting with what they have stopped saying. Why not give them a chance to do things their way and to change when they want to? People with genuine preoccupations about religion or mysticism have enough to bother about anyway in their own areas of interest and competence.

But if scientists insist on sticking stubbornly to some theory as the immutable, unassailable truth, we can point gently to top-notch scientists like Einstein and Penrose, smile and wonder why these outstanding figures remained so uncertain of many things even in the best theories.

One of Roger Penrose's greatest achievements was to work out with Stephen Hawking the singularity theorems which guaranteed the existence - under certain conditions - of a boundary for space and time, thus making black holes and the Big Bang understandable. The enormous scientific reputation of Penrose has hardly been complicated by the influence of the mass media. On that point he is quite different from Hawking to whose case we now turn.

The Transforming Power of Love

I had stressed above that dialogue needs to consider both intellectual and non-intellectual factors, more especially since the latter can exert a powerful influence. By way of illustration it will help to look carefully into the absorbing history of Stephen Hawking applying the viewpoint of an integrating, holistic consciousness to go beyond purely intellectual considerations. Commonly regarded as "the new Einstein," Hawking has today become the best-known mathematical physicist in the world. His public image has certainly not suffered by his sharing the same birth date as Galileo and occupying in Cambridge the position of Lucasian Professor of Mathematics, the same Chair which Newton held.

The three major theoretical contributions of Hawking to cosmology are: "the singularity theorem," "the Hawking radiation" and "the universe as a wave function." Explaining each of these further at this point would be counterproductive. The interested reader may kindly consult the Schaefer(1994) lecture cited in the "Hints for Further Reading" at the end of this paper.

Hawking's *A Brief History of Time*[7] has sold in excess of 25 million copies. From the same publishers a more recent book - dealing with quite complex developments such as string theory and far more lavishly illustrated - is entitled *The Universe in a Nutshell*, but does not seem to have achieved similar success. The earlier book was dedicated to "Jane" and in it Hawking wrote about his deep involvement with a "Theory of Everything" which would allow humankind to "see into the mind of God."

Hawking, however, has been afflicted for many years with ALS (amyotrophic lateral sclerosis)which affects the motor tracts of the spinal cord and causes progressive muscular atrophy. At the present time he is extensively paralyzed except for some slight movements of his fingers which allow him to operate a specially designed computer. As a result he can convey his thoughts and answer questions through a disembodied electronic voice which seems to emerge fom outer space.

He travels to other parts of the world and was in India a few years ago. His "lectures," which inevitably leave the large audiences spellbound, are of course the toast of the mass media. Who can respond without emotion to this extraordinary, amazing genius whose brain can play with more than 40 pages of memorized equations and whose mind, locked into a helpless body, still ranges freely over space and time grappling with the most abstruse problems of cosmology and philosophy? What a man! What courage! What brilliance!

Still, it remains true that, in 2004, Hawking has had to publicly retract two of his most cherished views. He now admits that thanks to Goedel's theorem there can never be a "Theory of Everything" and that black holes do not forever annihilate all traces of what falls into them. However, this does not take away, in my opinion, from the greatness of his achievement. Neither does it reduce my admiration for the unemotional dedication to scientific truth, shown both by him and by a few other leading scientists, who have been disagreeing for years with him - precisely about those two points trumpeted earlier by him to the whole world through TV and the press.

ALS or no ALS Hawking and his critics realized that scientific truth could not be compromised. Is this not a manifestation of their willingness to struggle for the truth even if it involved the crushing of the ego? Of course, in the process, the critical colleagues who stuck their necks out against the great Hawking were finally proved right.

The ALS diagnosis was made when Hawking was about 20/21 years old, and at that time a rather average student at Cambridge. He was given two years to live and told he would slowly get worse. That makes him a medical miracle also, since he has today already reached an age of about 65!

At a New Year's Party on December 31, 1962, there occurred for Stephen that central event which - in the opinion of his biographers White and Gribbin - gave him courage to live and something to live for. At that party he met his future wife Jane Wilde and everything changed for him. Though the ALS diagnosis was made about a month after the party, Jane and he had remained close and they finally married in July 1965. Stephen began to blossom into a consummate genius while defying the two-year death prediction.

So, shall we admit that love, perhaps the least rational of our emotions, can actually improve the functioning of the rational mind? What would have happened if Stephen had never met Jane Wilde? What will it take to release the genius hidden in so many of the rest of us who muddle along unaware of who we really are?

To make matters even more complicated, Hawking several years later thought fit to divorce Jane and to remarry. That is a strange story that I do not wish to involve the reader in now, especially since Jane Hawking has preferred to be very silent about it. Many geniuses seem to carry some striking flaw and some of Hawking's statements about other personalities raise suspicions of his being somewhat adolescent psychologically. Why, for instance, in a short essay on Newton at the end of *A Brief History of Time* should Hawking have to bring in prominently - for no compelling reason - how unpleasant and devious Newton could be?

Hawking is adamant that he is not an atheist. Perhaps the designation of "agnostic" or (like Darwin, I think) "deist" would be more appropriate. Jane Hawking however is a Christian with a doctorate in Medieval Portugese Literature. In 1986 she made clear that it was her faith in God which gave her the strength to marry Stephen in the first place, while already fully aware of his deteriorating health.

So, are we willing to say of her: What an utterly amazing woman? What faith! What courage! From the holistic point of view, would it be wrong to think of Jane as a human being at least as great as Stephen?

The Limitedness of the World of Science

There is a sound basis for that last question about Jane Hawking. Let us imagine that Stephen Hawking or some other brilliant mind indeed discovered a "Theory of Everything" (T.O.E.) in the form of one master equation or a set of master equations. What then would "everything" mean? Surely "everything" would have to include love, loyalty, compassion, courage, joy, support, relationship, admiration, enthusiasm and the many other human values which make life - and especially the life of Stephen Hawking - worthwhile. How do equations cover the many things really important to all of us? Science does not and cannot deal directly with qualities and ultimate questions.

Hence there is no need to make idols of Hawking, Einstein or anyone else. They deserve their fame, but they are merely, as Newton said, picking up seashells on a vast shore. That insight has been given a different, less personal expression in our own times by the great physicist John Wheeler, and it goes something like this: The larger the island of our knowledge grows, the more we are made aware that the coastline separating us from the ocean of our ignorance has only become longer.

For mystics, the more reliable form of a T.O.E. would be that there exists an intelligence too immense for our grasp underlying all phenomena. That statement has been verified "CONTENTWISE" by thousands of mystics using methods as reliable for the self inside as the methods of the scientists are for matter outside. But "EXPRESSIONWISE" that same content may vary in the words used, according to the culture and personal history of each mystic. That is necessarily so because mystic statements are *first-person* accounts to be confirmed by others within the laboratory inside. Till that is done, mystic statements may well appear unbelievable to others.

Scientific statements, on the other hand, are *third-person* accounts which can be confirmed by anybody anywhere. The quality of the individual consciousness does not come in, but only the appropriate scientific training. It is not surprising then that scientific statements appear to be more reliable to most human beings because they lack the training for first-personal mystic awareness and no university degrees are available for acquiring such skills in a personal way.

A practical example may help. Two poetic individuals expressing in first-person terms the experience of being loved or rejected or of feeling ecstatic after watching a beautiful sunset will not use identical words and their experiences do not become verified by recording changes in blood pressure, neuropeptides or brainwaves. The words of these individuals may be imprecise scientifically, but the expressions remain humanly precious. Scientific statements have their limitations but so do the statements of the mystics. As human beings we need both!

The Important Contributions of Science

The value of scientific discoveries becomes clearer when we reflect on how their applications have transformed human living all over the world.

Here is a concise list of improvements based on science in a few key areas: lighting, telephones, sanitation, food and water supplies, weather forecasting, crop yields, transportation, hydroelectricity, computers, mobiles, human fertility, survival rates after birth, modern materials and devices for protection against the elements, medical drugs and diagnostic tools such as X-rays, ultrasound, tomography, catscan, MRI... The list is easily extendable. The technology involved was built on what began in a research scientist's brain or laboratory. In fact there exists today in India the real danger of fostering a dependence on external aids to ensure healthy, relaxed living, but at the expense of effective measures which will ensure the inner peace and joy not dependent on any external factors. Here too one needs to fashion a symbiosis of science and mysticism, of the comfortable lifestyles of the West and the traditional simplicities of the East. There *are* individuals who care about that kind of symbiosis and succeed in style!

When two rivers flow into each other, there is a temporary turbulence followed by a peaceful merger with stronger flow. For the symbiosis of the East and the West, of science and mysticism, one can *consciously* adjust the direction, pattern and force of the two flows. But if the end result is a decrease in overall peace and joy, then something has gone wrong somewhere.

A French thinker who greatly admires the culture of India but wonders what the future will bring recently asked: "Will India resist the Indians?"[8] Good question. Difficult answer.

Science for Rationality, Religion for Values

The most important contribution of science to our lives is, however, that it has encouraged human beings to think rationally and creatively, without dependence on authority as interpreted or exercised by others whether in secular or religious fields. Today we have developed the confidence that humankind can indeed understand nature and wrestle with our problems, however difficult. This mentality is an enormous gain. It is difficult for modern people to realize that only a few hundred years ago the human race did not think in this way at all.

Faced with new diseases such as AIDS or natural calamities such as tsunamis, science encourages us not to throw up our hands and rush to placate the gods. It is routine now to work at solving problems rationally, or at least reducing their impact.

Still, the further step to the notion that it is only a matter of time before science will solve all problems and explain all mysteries is truly naive and can be positively dangerous. For instance, how helpful is it to claim that science will one day abolish death or at least old age? Does it not make much more sense to spend time and energy on ensuring that the existing millions who live sub-human lives will have effective access to food, water, shelter, hygiene and medical facilities?

There is a common view that value systems which inculcate the non-negotiable dignity of each individual emerge more strongly from religion than from science. Personally I cannot subscribe to that view unreservedly. After all, what often emerges on supposedly religious grounds - which other believers seem far too silent to oppose - is that men continue to get killed and women downgraded. Technology based on scientific discoveries is also used to destroy people and cripple alien civilizations for political gain.

But all religions teach the dignity of human beings and I find it easy to be filled with awe and wonder over what science reveals about the marvel and mystery of the human body - without any help from religion. Here then is one more area in which Einstein's insight remains valuable: "Science without religion is lame, religion without science is blind."

And what about the mystics? Well, they tend to embrace gladly everything that exists: human, animal, plant or mineral. The experiences of the true mystic are never purely individualistic and self-centred. They take place within a broad, universalizing, spiritual context. For instance, the old Sufi saying goes: "God sleeps in the rock, dreams in the plant, stirs in the animal and awakes in man." The mystic relies on no external authority, religious or secular - the contextualized, inner experience cannot be doubted. The people around will, however, notice the elevated and selfless quality of the mystic's life. No drug-induced highs produce that effect.

The Approach of Religion and Science to Suffering

This is a world in which millions everywhere are in constant pain. To totally forget that in a Symposium on Science, Mysticism and East-West

Dialogue would be to run away from the bitter sea of suffering in which many human beings today are immersed. Any realistic dialogue with so broad a panorama as that offered by this Symposium becomes tasteless if we show ourselves to be blind and deaf, plus dumb, remaining out of touch with human suffering. In any case, mystics take suffering very seriously.

Science seeks no explanations for suffering, but instead renders great practical service to all in the East and the West through constantly improved medical interventions. Young doctors attached to organizations such as "Medicine without Frontiers" have done yeoman service in troubled areas of the world precisely because their work is so easily accepted - they are skilled human beings caring for other human beings in need. No religion or ideology is involved beyond the ideal that our shared human nature demands that we reach out.

The different religions do offer explanations, too varied to go into just now. On the practical level they teach their followers to "surrender to the will of God," to pray and meditate and make offerings in holy places, and to reach out to those who suffer. When religious approaches are linked to medical treatment, admitting the spectrum offered in that treatment by Ayurveda, Unani, Homeopathy, etc., the combined effect can be really powerful. Religious acceptance of the pain does much to bolster the medical initiative.

Whatever the explanation religion offers, it remains true that suffering is not a problem to be solved, but a mystery to be experienced - just like selfless love and unrewarded caring. We understand mountaineers who say they climb Everest "because it is there." Is it so different for those who dive into the fathomless depths of suffering?

One influential form of the theory of "karma" common to religions of "the East" does provide a deep rational satisfaction for inexplicable present suffering by linking it to misdeeds in a past life. To me that would be fine as long as such views do not in practice prevent individuals from seeking medical treatment or from responding with sensitivity to the pain of others. Suffering *is* suffering, whatever brought it on. An individual may imagine he/she has a headache, but alas the imagination is real!

Buddhism, at least a section of it, stands apart as a religion or philosophy of life in that it does not depend on belief in God. What matters is the strategy to extinguish desire in order to escape the cycle of rebirth through which suffering is made possible. Buddhism lays great stress on compassion for all living beings in pain. Let it be noted in passing that the "agape" of Christians and what the Buddhists call "compassion" resonate beautifully together when it comes to selfless caring. Buddhists do not talk about God, and yet their universal compassion must surely inspire the rest of us who take pride in being God-believers.

Buddhism is for me a way of reaching out to what is truly beyond us without calling it "God." In their own unique way they vibrate with the divine and in practice continue to produce excellent mystics. The Zen Masters, for instance, are superbly mystical.

Within the garden of the various religions, mystics both in the East and the West emerge as the sweetest-smelling flowers. They seem most at home with suffering simply because they regard pain as integral to our *experience of reality as it is.* Pain is central to human experience and mystics make it their business to relate to all facets of reality - central or peripheral, sacred or secular, divine or human. It exists...It hurts... Here we are... Inter-related...Cheers!

A few mystics such as Aurobindo teach that one can be brought to a point where pain comes to be regarded as "a fiercer form of delight." Good for them! Personally, I do not think they are saying that pain is not real, but that the individual can become spiritually evolved to the point where pain is absorbed into a broader and deeper context - and there pain loses the awful power it usually has, becoming transformed instead into a quite different kind of integrated experience. In such cases the assistance of doctors may be less important. I have sometimes gone to comfort patients severely ill with a painful cancer, and ended up going down on my knees, before leaving, to ask for their blessing. They became priests to me.

Some mystics stress the intuition that if this world is indeed God's chosen world, then God has also chosen to suffer with us, in us and through us - an intuition irrelevant to science, strange perhaps to several types of religious believers, but obvious to these mystics. They may even say that

God's self-awareness becomes complete only with the deliberately chosen divine plan to personally experience the joys and sorrows of creatures. Good for God!

Whatever one's religious beliefs or mystical inclinations, it remains true that a major proportion of suffering and pain in human beings is caused by other human beings. Hence it is neither helpful nor realistic to look for answers to all kinds of interesting theoretical questions from God alone. In any case, on the practical level - through those they influence - science or technology, religion or mysticism, the East or the West have each a specific and non-transferable role to play in alleviating suffering.

The points discussed aboove provide, among other things, some points of view helpful for a symbiotic dialogue with scientists. In this last subsection I am concerned with ideas I want to stress specially or with authors to whom I feel particularly indebted. For instance, Ken Wilber is an extraordinary thinker and a marvellous integrator of mystical currents in the East and the West. He argues for an "all-level, all-quadrant" transformative practice. And as for the specifics of transpersonal development, he distinguishes four major stages which are sequential: the Psychic, the Subtle, the Causal and the Nondual. He even boldly goes into what he considers the pathology of these stages before the crowning Nondual stage is reached.

Why then have I referred to him by name so little? Well, I feel rather uncomfortable about squeezing the unique richness of his thinking into a few pages here or there. Wilber is too complex an author for a short paper as crowded with topics as this one.

Further there are also - in my never humble opinion - some significant deficiencies in Wilber. But here again, I find it quite unfair for me to point out what I think these are, without the reader having first been exposed to the magnificence and brilliance of his overall presentation. That exposure is out of the question for us here and now.

On a beautiful face, a mole may even increase the sense of beauty. But the mole by itself...? Which means that those who desire to contemplate the beauty of that face are welcome to ponder Wilber's massive *Sex, Ecology and Spirituality - The Spirit of Evolution*. A truly "sexy" book, to borrow a term dear to our young people. However, the curious may need to be warned that the book is excellent on mysticism but has little to do with sex.

Overtly or covertly, in what ways has Wilber's thinking contributed to this paper? Principally on two points. First, he has me convinced that the evolution of human consciousness progresses beyond those states described by recognized Western experts on human development such as Abraham Maslow, Lawrence Kohlberg and Jane Loevinger. For Wilber, an adequate understanding of his four transpersonal states mentioned earlier requires a study of the mystics of the East and the West - for instance, Ralph Waldo Emerson, Teresa of Avila, Meister Eckhart and Ramana Maharishi.

Scholars who scorn or otherwise neglect mystical consciousness deprive themselves of what must properly be considered "super consciousness" in comparison with the states described by the western transpersonal psychologists. The transpersonal developments for which Wilber keeps providing detailed descriptions is about the self-transcendence beyond self-actualization. Teachers in our universities may want to look into this point further for themselves.

Secondly, conflicts between the spheres of science and mysticism are for Wilber less likely if each is valued as distinct. Mysticism is concerned with spirit (transcendent) or Spirit (Immanent) and is at the top level of the "Chain of Being." Science is at the bottom of this Chain and is concerned with matter. So each sphere has no need of support or confirmation from the other. Each has its own methods, its own forms of evidence, its own proofs and its own peer-group competent to validate knowledge claims made in its own specific sphere.

Put by Wilber in more scholarly fashion: Whether one is referring to scientific or contemplative (mystical) traditions, any kind of "valid knowledge quest" involves three strands — *injunction, illumination, and confirmation*. The first strand means "Do this" if you want to get to the next strand of "illumination," which, of course, must then be necessarily subject, in turn, to "confirmation" by a community of peers.

Personally, I consider these views of Wilber fine and helpful, as long as the three strands of the "knowledge quest" (a Gnana Marga?) do not exclude, for mysticism, the desire for union with the transcendent spirit or the Immanent Spirit. Having expressed my gratitude to Wilber, I can pass to two others.

Extensively consulted too has been Prof. Huston Smith, whose book, *Beyond the Post-Modern Mind*, offers much that is relevant to the topics of science, mysticism and East-West dialogue. Huston Smith's thinking is very direct. He writes with real flair and is easy to take in. One of the major strengths of his book is in the devastating attacks he mounts on what he calls the "Modern Western Mind-set" (MWM). Smith considers science to be centrally important to this MWM. Hence he is at pains to cut down to size all overblown scientific claims and to focus on the deficiencies which science prefers to overlook.

Like Ken Wilber, Huston Smith insists that there is a perennial philosophy shared and abidingly valued by human beings in the East and the West - long before science came along. It is likely that several readers will prefer Smith's account of the planes of Reality (terrestrial, intermediate, celestial and infinite) as being more sensitively geared to common human experience than Wilber's more intellectual account of the "Great Chain of Being."

Smith is also brilliant on the distinction between "God" - which priests and prophets tend to focus on - and "Godhead" whose wondrous, hidden depths are so attractive to most mystics. In a creative insight precious for East-West dialogue, he describes a "jivanmukta" as an enlightened being in touch with the "sacred unconscious.".

An aside. My own mischievous impression is that the MWM is insidiously present in numerous science departments of our universities. For those who may wonder whether they have been infected, reading Huston Smith could be an eye-opener.

This brings us finally to Renee Weber and her *Dialogues with Saints and Sages - The Search for Unity*. This book edited by Weber is packed with a series of absorbing interviews she personally conducted. The scientists chosen were David Bohm, Stephen Hawking, Ilya Prigogine and Rupert Sheldrake. The sages were Lama Anagarika Govinda, Father Bede Griffiths, the Dalai Lama and Krishnamurti.

Here again the topics of the Lonavla Symposium come into consideration implicitly or explicitly and there is so much to learn from both the scientists and the sages. Still, for me, the best thing in this stimulating book is the Introduction by Renee Weber herself entitled "The Search for Unity" - brilliant and down to earth.

If Ken Wilber is most helpful when striving to induce an interest in East-West mysticism and Huston Smith to reducing an overdependence on science, Renee Weber places before the reader a rich and varied feast with uncommon charm and great persuasiveness. She has a keen, incisive mind, and knows how to prod her galaxy of stars into providing perspectives that open up vast spaces for awe and wonder. I hope other readers will enjoy and profit as much from her book as I did.

In concluding at long last this section, I may be permitted a few remarks about my very Indian preference for mystics whose principal focus is personal love or "bhakti." Such mystics through their songs and poems bring joy and warmth each day into the hearts and homes of millions of Indians, good scientists included. Among them are Meerabai, Kabir and Tagore.

Mystics come in many varieties and all have a deep desire for union with God/Godhead. In every mystic there seems to be some influence from each of the four traditional Indian paths: knowledge, love, selfless action and meditation. But not every mystic gives to loving devotion a principal focus.

For all mystics the "Many" (multiple forms) of this world's diversity owe their origin to the "One" (single, unnameable, all-pervading Reality beyond all forms). It is an insight which in the West is prominent already with Plato and Plotinus.

But what then becomes obvious to the "bhakti-type" mystics in the East and the West is precisely that everything must be loved - *everything*, including all that exists and every person however uneducated and unwashed. Why? Simply because everything from the Many has a face which is a single, tiny facet of the Infinite, Inexpressible Beauty of the Faceless One. Hence everything that exists has to be cherished, nourished, loved and selflessly served. How's that for a "Theory of Everything"?

Mystics of the bhakti type reveal a craziness that is enormously charming. They want union with the One with a far, far greater intensity than that shown by two human lovers longing for each other. As Rabia said to her Lord: "All that You have kept for me from the goods of this world, please give to my enemies...And all that You have kept for me from the goods of the next world, please give to my friends...You alone are enough for me."

Conclusion: Microbiology and the Hidden Face of God

To begin with, a few comments will be offered in favour of a dialogue along the lines of science-mysticism. Those comments will provide some needed perspective before tackling "molecular biology," which in any case is to be presented as a new field with the capacity to bring one close to a mystical outlook.

Mysticism is for religious mystics a subset of their religion. Put differently, every science-mysticism dialogue is implicitly also a science-religion dialogue. However, the reverse may not be true especially if the representatives of the religion concerned do not value their own mystics - and that alas is all too common among devotees of every major religion I know!

There are a few "nature mystics," but the majority of mystics work from within a specific religious system. However varied those religious systems, it seems clear that mystics of one religion relate easily to the expressions and experiences of mystics from other religions. Hence the chances increase for better mutual interaction when in Symposia mystics are compared and contrasted rather than religions. It is common to hear of mystics being killed for their beliefs, but far more difficult to point to mystics who defend the killing of other people on such grounds.

Mystics accept the creed, code and cult which characterize the ground from which they spring. But then they also testify to the experience of an Ultimate Reality which impels them to move beyond their own cultural limitations, and that precisely is what gets them into trouble. Mystics are seen as belonging to the whole human race, and so are the greatest of scientists.

Good practising scientists with strong experimental/research involvement relate easily to the language and experiments of those practising other specialties in science. Some of the best among them also develop mystical tendencies. Hence from the side of science as much as religion, occasional science-mysticism dialogues could be really valuable, particularly for purifying ideas about "God" when conveniently manufactured to human's own image and likeness rather than the other way around.

Those who wish to engage in such dialogue do not need to furnish valid, prior claims for being themselves good scientists or gifted mystics. All one really needs is the humility to strip oneself of preconceived ideas and ideologies. An open mind and a willing heart suffice to learn from the sayings and writings which genuine scientists and true mystics have provided for all human beings irrespective of nation, culture, religion or geographic location.

Regarding the mystics, one's learning takes place by symbiotic osmosis even though the mystic will speak from her/his own background. If we go deep enough we will encounter the common springs which can fundamentally slake our thirst for Total Reality. Fritjof Capra offers a useful analogy: Mystics tend to understand the Roots of the Tree of Reality, while scientists can understand better the Branches. Human beings with a genuine interest in all of Reality need both. And, let me add, they may additionally need, in varied degrees, the religious systems by which they feel nourished.

Coming now to molecular biology(MB), I would like first to offer an operational definition. MB attempts to understand and explain phenomena in biology by linking them to the chemical structures, 3-dimensional conformations and behaviour of molecules - mostly large molecules such as DNA, RNA and proteins. I am aware that all researchers may not define MB in an identical way, but for our purpose the definition offered is accurate enough.

Earlier findings about the structure and function of smaller entities such as metal ions, water, triglycerides, vitamins or ATP are accepted and incorporated into MB, together with the various laws of chemistry, physics and quantum mechanics. But MB respectfully transcends all of them, much the way mystics do with their own religions.

Right down the ages, many cultures have - each in their own way - shown an awareness of the connected hierarchy in what we experience as human beings. The higher levels include but transcend the lower levels. To get back to Wilber's ideas on "The Great Chain of Being," there are at least five major levels beginning at the bottom with physics/chemistry, followed by a sequential movement upwards through biology at level 2, psychology at level 3, religion at level 4, right up to mysticism at level 5. It will have been noticed that this paper has been touching on all of these five levels in different ways.

Since MB examines biological phenomena through molecules, it basically works in the fertile, symbiotic space bridging levels 2 and 1. Hence any science-religion dialogue in the 21st century would do well to face a new situation: The advent of MB must require a movement upwards and away from the danger of an exclusive preoccupation with the "hard sciences" such as physics and chemistry.

For understanding and dealing with strictly biological phenomena such as ingestion, metabolism, mitosis, reproduction, motor functions, membrane transport and the like, the insights of chemistry/physics are useful but clearly insufficient. That, for instance, is why science went in for biophysics and biochemistry. All the same, no branch of science today brings out the extremely complex but fantastically coordinated patterns evident in life processes more clearly than MB. With the help of a few examples, that claim will be further illustrated later on.

Many of the brightest young minds in the world today find themselves more attracted to MB - and other fields closely related to MB - than they are to mathematical physics, particle physics, string theory or cosmology. Those "other fields" include genetic engineering, nanotechnology, biocomputers, immunogenetics and neurobiology.

Intelligent, educated persons will not, however, find it too easy to come to terms with the coordinated complexities of MB. In contrast, the general public has greatly benefited from the many-sided, successful attempts to popularize the "new physics". Less successful attempts in regard to MB have begun to appear but much still remains to be done before the curious seeker can feel at ease with MB. Moreover, most of our undergraduate biology programmes in India do not as yet give to MB the importance it deserves.

It is therefore a pleasure to strongly recommend an outstanding, recent publication making waves in the West. This is "The Hidden Face of God" (subtitled : Science Reveals the Ultimate Truth) by Gerald Schroeder, an

M.I.T.-trained, Israeli scientist well versed in both physics and MB. Schroeder has a great gift for pointed, persuasive writing and popularizes without falling into the trap of oversimplification. In fact he himself admits that his book is not easy to read or assimilate. Still, anybody familiar with the difficulties of MB has to admire Schroeder's teaching skills. To my mind, it is a book which the majority of interested non-specialists will, with some effort, appreciate and even enjoy.

The book is also very useful for believers keen on dialogue. Antony Flew was till recently one of the world's best known atheists. According to some circles in the U.S.A. it was Schroeder's ideas which finally moved Flew to publicly admit that the only satisfying way to explain the extraordinary complexity and order in living things was to postulate that "God" had to exist. It seems significant to me that for Flew all the earlier arguments for "God" based on physics, chemistry, astronomy and cosmology had been ineffective. The inexplicably complex order pointing to "God" stood out best with MB.

However, it appears that Flew remains unconvinced even from the evidence of MB that this "God" really cares for what "He" has made. Fair enough! One step at a time...Let me therefore, in what follows immediately here, offer a few personal observations to meet the situation of those who may be having difficulties similar to Flew's. What is the next step? ? That for me would be to accept that caring implies love - and love pertains to the heart rather than to the reasoning mind. Let us consider reason first and then love. Centuries ago, Nicholas of Cusa, noted mathematician and mystic, had pointed out that the door to the wall surrounding God's Paradise was guarded by "the proud spirit of Reason and unless he is vanquished, the way will not be open". For me that translates to: One who wishes to enter Paradise is well advised to give Reason an honoured place and leave it there.

It used to be said by Nobel Prize winning quantum physicists that nobody could claim to understand quantum theory. But, heh!, it works, doesn't it?

Well, today anyone who thinks he really understands what goes on in a single living cell can, on grounds of pure reason, be considered either blind or crazy. But the cell does get along fine on the principles of MB, doesn't it? Otherwise, as I hope soon to convince you, my cells would not allow me to be here writing about the little we do understand.

And coming next to love: who believes that love is rational? Human lovers gladly, if intuitively, accept Blaise Pascal's: "The heart has its reasons which the mind knows nothing about". And let it be noted that Pascal is a recognized mathematical genius whose power for rational thought cannot possibly be doubted except by the irrationally prejudiced.

But then Pascal was once gifted with a "mind-blowing" mystical experience that left him stunned. The awareness of God he thereby gained remained for him rationally inexplicable, and he has left a powerful written record of that experience. So he was granted something he did not deserve but could neither rationally explain nor doubt.

That apart, if God has given us human beings the loving hearts we so deeply cherish then something akin to human love must be present in God even if that be in some manner totally beyond our ability to comprehend. Would it be unreasonable for me to argue that way?

Genuine love transcends reason without being unreasonable. Genuine mysticism transcends religion without being irreligious. Genuine biology as practised by living things transcends all of physics and chemistry in an altogether charming way. Nothing is deader than the equations of physics but lively butterflies flit through the skies obeying the very equations they go beyond.

In his book, right in the midst of a perfectly rational account of the wonders of the cosmos as well as the human brain, Schroeder writes of experiencing something like a shudder of the Divine. The accompanying rush of emotion unites him to the "single consciousness, an all-encompassing wisdom (which) pervades the universe".

A few added details about "The Hidden Face of God". There is true novelty in the way Gerald Schroeder uses the idea that "INFORMATION" is embedded in all that exists. In his view, scientists can have no difficulty in accepting a rational approach based on "information". He is enthusiastic about the suggestion of John Wheeler, the eminent physicist, that EVERYTHING WE SEE ABOUT US IS THE EXPRESSION OF CONDENSED INFORMATION. Stated more technically, the "bit" (binary digit of information) precedes and gives rise to the "it" (of matter).

Here is a brief summary of Schroeder's book: We live in an era of information which lies at the base of both molecular biology and computer science. Both molecular biology and computers rely on a phenomenal ability to process and manipulate information. The unique contribution of molecular biology is to reveal the perplexing depth and breadth of the complex underlying information which, when processed and manipulated, makes the behaviour of living things possible and to us more understandable. It is that latent underlying information waiting to be expressed which represents "the hidden face of God". Chance or natural selection working over vast, immense stretches of time are unacceptable as explanations for the presence of that embedded information which molecular biology has revealed with such great clarity.

Let me add that there seems to be no end just now to the process of uncovering this information, which just sits there very quietly - like precious stones - waiting to be brought to light and incorporated into the joyous sense of being alive. The more information we dig out, the more remains to be discovered. We are stopped not by exhausting the embedded information but by the inability of our instruments and experimental techniques to go deeper.

For Schroeder the old saying remains relevant: "God is in the details". His book came out in 2001. But already four years later, I discover that new research has come up with fresh findings that improve on what he presented. That only strengthens his line of thinking, doesn't it? The contours of a mysterious hidden face merely continue to be clarified. Some experts in MB from among my former students - who I gladly admit now know far more of the topic than I ever did - assure me that, for some aspects of what goes on inside the cell, the amount of information available today is twice what it was as recently as 12 months ago!

In the rest of this Section I want to be a courageous clown and attempt to present the enormous treasure of MB in its barest outline - and do that with special reference to human beings. The spirit of Schroeder will hover over what I say but I may not make much use of his thinking directly. My presentation will also be reflecting ideas from other authors as well as my own personal insights. Any deficiencies the reader may detect will almost certainly be mine - except that there exists an immense difficulty beyond my control, because MB betrays links to the extraordinary features of a Divine Intelligence far beyond our limited mental capacities.

To quote the noted physicist Freeman Dyson who also functions as a stimulating speaker: "God is what mind becomes when it has passed beyond the scale of our comprehension". If then I do not succeed in providing some indications that in MB one encounters something totally fantastic which lies beyond our imagination and mental grasp, I will have failed in a big way. Good MB makes mysticism more credible.

MB must be seen against the background of large numbers like trillions and of tiny dimensions like microns. We take up the numbers first. The one thousand we know is written as the number 1 followed by 3 zeros: 1,000. Similarly, one million has 6 zeros (1,000,000) - which means that one billion, trillion, quadrillion have respectively 9, 12 and 15 zeros. If we say one hundred billion, it works out to 1 followed by 11 zeros.

Not many perhaps are aware that the human brain has as many as one hundred billion "axons" and as many as one quadrillion "dendrites" - i.e. 100,000,000,000 and 1,000,000,000,000,000 respectively. These numbers are of the kind which boggle my own imagination but maybe the biological terms could first be explained a little.

The AXON is the MESSAGE TRANSMITTER REGION of the nerve cell and that region can end in a bush of terminals quite capable of stimulating simultaneously whole groups of targets such as muscle fibres - as may be necessary, via the generated "action potentials", if one wishes to return a smash in tennis or a fast ball in cricket. (About cricket, the reader can look forward to something to chuckle over at the end).

The DENDRITE is the MESSAGE RECEIVER REGION of the same nerve cell and that region can have numerous fingerlike extensions to receive the messages coming in from the axons of other nerves. A single dendrite may be at the receiving end of several thousand axon terminals.

Together, axons and dendrites ensure that every single nerve cell is massively interconnected to the others. In practice it also makes possible the kind of "parallel processing" so important to chess players and so frustrating to the rest of us engaged in trying to make nice, clear decisions in unpleasant circumstances.

The unflappable Schroeder has the bright suggestion for making realistic the number quadrillion - as for the dendrites in the brain: Try to count 1,2,3...97,98...23,684...1,735,269 etc. right up to 1,000,000,000,000,000, at the rate of one number a second. The job, he says, would take about 30 million years to finish. This would be true, it seems to me, even if I did not indulge in a quick shower to celebrate Christmas each year.

As human beings we began life when an egg in our mother's womb - about the size of a "full stop" on this printed page - was united to a sperm about as big as one-fortieth of a "comma". That allowed the DNA of father and mother to merge. The powerful information imprinted in this extremely tiny bundle of merged DNA, with help from the egg's cytoplasm, eventually gave rise to blood, flesh, bones, muscles, sense-organs and the one hundred billion axons and one quadrillion dendrites of the nervous system - not to mention the kind of hair, nose and skin-colour betraying our ancestry.

"Its" from "bits" in Wheeler's terminology. Who or what could be THAT, which has so mysteriously masked "information-as-wonder-this-awesome" - and then been content to permit that wonder to lie quietly hidden till our own times? And where is all this going to end? As surely as has happened in our dazzling present, there is much more to come in the centuries ahead...

Next, we proceed to deal with the other end of the scale from huge numbers by looking briefly at a few more examples of tiny, minuscule dimensions.

The human body has in all about 75 trillion cells of all kinds of shapes and sizes, but it would not be unreasonable to consider 30 MICRONS to be the average size of a cell. The double-helical DNA inside that cell is like a "ball" condensed into less than 5 MICRONS.

Now, a micron is a millionth of a metre. Try to take that in by looking at what one millimetre is on the school "foot-ruler" and then visualizing what one thousandth of that millimetre would be like.

Interestingly, the DNA has been condensed from an original length of 2 metres (hence 2 million microns) to a "ball" of 5 microns so as to fit into a cell of 30 microns - the hidden face of the " modern science of packology" and an enormous encouragement to all those trying to pack a million things into a small bag for a big journey.

But there is worse to come! Within the tiny space of 30 microns in a single cell, hundreds of amazing events proceed at high speed every second without any "mix-ups". To a sensitized person the dance of the molecules can be far more exciting than any ballet performance.

The "ball" of helical DNA is unwound bit by bit, its message "read" and then "translated" into various proteins (a little more about this soon), forming them at the rate of about 2000 proteins per second. Molecules of exactly the right kind, because screened with care at various points, move merrily in their thousands into and out of the cell. By one estimate there are, within those 30 microns maybe something like 10,000 intersections for the traffic - in three dimensions, as in superhighways, complete with entry and exit points. So no "mix-ups". The information includes traffic control.

Additionally, when the time is ripe, the entire cell duplicates itself by mitosis and produces a perfect copy of itself without interrupting the dance. Now dancers are not exactly duplicated in a short time by even the best ballet companies - at least on the stage. The "bits", however, double the number of "its" with ease.

Earlier, I had offered the reader an operational definition of MB as involving large molecules such as DNA, RNA and proteins. For a cell to express the informational blueprint stamped into the DNA situated in the nucleus, that blueprint will need to be converted in the cytoplasm - via RNA - to the cell's characteristic proteins. Those characteristic proteins play crucial roles in virtually all the biological processes of the cell.

The kind reader will excuse me for restating that because it is a point needing emphasis in different ways. The essential sequence is: DNA blueprint to RNA message converted in turn into the many thousands of characteristic proteins essential for the numerous jobs to be done in the cell. For our purposes it is not necessary to explain further that RNA functions, for instance, in at least three forms - as messenger RNA, transfer RNA and ribosomal RNA. The bottom line is to finally have at hand those proteins which really get the work done.

The "NA" in DNA and RNA is for NUCLEIC ACID, while "D" is for the sugar Deoxyribose and "R" for its cousin Ribose. Both DNA and RNA are constructed from closely related sub-units called NUCLEOTIDES.

The proteins on the other hand are POLYPEPTIDE CHAINS constructed from sub-units called amino-acids. These amino-acids differ a good deal from each other and very considerably from nucleotides.

So the conversion of DNA to its messenger RNA is like changing from a language to its dialect and the process is called "transcription". But the transition from RNA to the entirely different language of proteins is like changing from Chinese to Hindi and is therefore called "translation".

It helps just now to focus on MB as it works out in the cells of HUMANS, even though all living things show strong parallels between the basic routes to obtaining their own distinctive DNAs, RNAs, and proteins. For instance, the "genetic code" in DNA based on A,G,C,T (adenine, guanine, cytosine, thymine) is common to all living things. Similarly, all living things use the same 20 amino-acids in constructing their polypeptide chains. How these commonalities and similarities are used to produce so many types and varieties of living things is a fascinating matter which we can merely hint at here. Personally, I have doubts that MB will ever be able to provide a final answer.

There is, however, one general point that must be made. The way a given protein behaves depends on the 3-dimensional conformation it acquires from spontaneous folding of its polypeptide chain - which in turn depends on the sequence of the 20 amino-acids in that chain. Also a single polypeptide chain may contain a few hundred of the same 20 amino acids, but the precise number and sequence of those amino-acids are special to that chain.

Thus far we have looked into MB as it was known about 40 years ago - till, say, around the mid-sixties of the previous century. During the next 20 years or so after that - till the mid-eighties - the dominant operational role of proteins to effect and affect almost everything going on in the cell became increasingly appreciated. Naturally the associated roles of DNA and RNA were also clarified.

For example, regarding proteins, the following list from around the mid-eighties gives some idea of their importance:

1. As sensors controlling the flow of energy and matter, proteins monitor growth and differentiation at many levels in the cell. To take just three areas : the sequential and orderly transcription and translation of the DNA blueprint, the formation of neural networks serving the brain, the coordinated activity of cells in a human being (many hormones are proteins).

2. Nerve impulses in the neural networks are generated and transmitted with the help of receptor proteins.

3. As enzymes, proteins in the cell speed up the rate of chemical reactions often by a millionfold or more! Also, several thousand different enzymes have become known.

4. Proteins are involved in the coordinated contraction and movement of muscle filaments and in the tails of sperm moving towards the egg - our lives began that way.

5. As antibodies, proteins protect against foreign substances and disease-producing invaders.

6. The high tensile strength of skin and bone is due to the presence of collagen, a fibrous protein.

7. Proteins transport small molecules such as oxygen both in muscle and in red blood cells - or, as happens in the liver, they store metal ions.

To sum up. The more the details of body-functioning at the level of MB came to be known, the more the all-embracing role of proteins became evident. And all this protein activity is made possible by the thousands of different shapes arising spontaneously from the varied sequences of just 20 amino-acids! The sequences of amino-acids in turn are generated, via RNA, from the sequences of just 4 nitrogenous bases (A,G,C,T) in the DNA blueprint.

Maximum creativity from minimum material - as in classic musical compositions from just 12 notes (22 in the Indian system) or great paintings from a few brush strokes by a Picasso.

The MB research of the last 30 years reveals that still more information sits within the DNA waiting to be recognized. It seems more than likely that much information in there remains to be grasped by our scientists. We are, for instance, aware of several biological features manifested by the common living things of our daily experience, including human beings, which we need to understand better. And all that still leaves us far from applying MB to tropical fish and coral reefs and uncommonly strange new organisms which grow at high temperatures and pressures deep down in the oceans, where the plates supporting the continents rest precariously perched on a sea of fire.

Against that kind of background the inadequacy of the "chance alone" hypothesis to account for the existence and variety of living things becomes crystal clear.

For instance, current mathematical calculations show that, over the 13.8 billion years or so during which the universe is thought to have existed, there is not enough time for "chance alone" to produce EVEN ONE SINGLE ENZYME. And here we are today knowing for sure that there are not only several thousand enzymes already characterized, but that these numerous enzymes work closely together with an even larger number of non-enzymatic proteins - in human beings 90,000 proteins in all - to make our lives possible.

There are authors of bestselling biology books on evolution today who continue to insist on "chance alone" as sufficient explanation for the origin and rich variety of living things. To me that is difficult to accept in the face of hard thinking applied to the obvious facts, especially those revealed by MB. And if these authors say instead that we need to hold to "natural selection operating over vast stretches of time" as a sufficient explanation for living things, it changes nothing. Natural selection is only a more interesting and refined way of re-stating the "chance alone" hypothesis and so does not require to be handled as if it were something radically new.

I consider Darwin to be an outstanding genius who lived in the era before MB and always remained faithful to the data he was aware of in his time. Given modern evidence, I have grave doubts about whether he would reach the same ideological conclusions as his present followers.

What is more, I think that EVOLUTION HAS INDEED OCCURRED. The quarrel is over mechanism.

It is also regrettable that good biology teachers in India today spread these weak notions of "chance alone" or "natural selection" as an acceptable mechanism without batting an eyelid. One wishes they were able to reflect adequately and with an open mind about what MB is making so obvious. If I took time earlier to discuss the case of Antony Flew, it was in the hope that others would be as honest, well informed, and intelligent as Flew has shown himself to be.

We have reached a point where - in the interest of intelligent dialogue - I can now offer to the reader a personal set of four propositions which summarize where we find ourselves in 2005 especially when MB is taken into consideration.

ONE. With all due respect, "chance alone" is simply out of the question as an adequate explanation for life in all its rich variety. Still, I would refuse to actually pour scorn on those who stick stubbornly to "chance alone". Religious believers used to be much ridiculed in former times for their beliefs. Things have changed and the temptation for believers to now pay back in kind must be resisted. Humour might work better. As Max Planck realized a century ago, entrenched positions are not really given up - their defenders die. Compassion and good manners are to be preferred by us religious believers - joined to a readiness to give up entrenched, irrational positions of our own (before we die, please!). However, what is beyond reason in religious matters is not necessarily against reason.

TWO. If, as scientist, a person is willing to offer an alternative explanation, I am ready to listen and to analyze the pros and cons. At the same time, if I find that alternative explanation unconvincing, I would also not hesitate to point that out gently. As a scientist, one needs to take care not to drag God unnecessarily into scientific experiments, which in practice means that one is entitled to search for convincing alternative explanations based on science alone. But as a thoughtful human being, I may have to talk in a different way, and I am entitled to that also. Science is not the only way to truth.

THREE. If any person, as a thoughtful human being - which most scientists I know also are - says that MB points to "the hidden face of God", I would agree that it is a reasonable conclusion for me too.

FOUR. If any thoughtful human being jumps from a statement asserting that MB points to "the hidden face of God" to the rather different statement that the face of the God in question is the one described by her/his own religion, I would politely disagree - the mystics of that religion, as we shall soon see, may be a quite different matter. I would go on to explain that, for me, MB suggests the face of a Divinity of immense, subtle energy linked to the astonishing creativity of an exquisitely controlled intelligence. I would also add that such a face is a great stimulus and encouragement to me as a convinced Christian believer, but that the reasons for my Christian convictions do not originate in MB.

It is not unlikely that most readers will find the above four propositions fairly acceptable. But I would be grateful if they would be willing to examine in the next paragraph a deeper insight, which could be more challenging.

The God whose hidden face seems embedded in MB manifests features close to the God experienced by the mystics of various religions, East and West. I feel that we are confronted in MB by a God that is sheer, pure, naked RADIANCE beyond all telling and thinking and imagining. What is more: I think we need the blinkers of our carefully controlled, scientific experiments to protect ourselves from being blinded - for we are blinded as much by light as by darkness.

To recall a parallel situation: we humans rightly value very much the beautiful realities we experience with our five senses, forgetting perhaps that those sense-experiences are also protecting us from being really overwhelmed by the Total Wonder of the Underlying Hidden Reality. Are the glories of MB protecting us from a blinding Radiance?

Even before the advent of MB, science classes in high schools and colleges routinely exposed students to the biological phenomena found in human beings: mitosis, meiosis, muscle contraction, the cell cycle, the two-way traffic between nerves and brain, how human life begins in the womb, and so on.

What specific contribution has MB made to the understanding of these well-known phenomena? Well, MB has traced them back to their roots in the chemical structure, 3-dimensional conformation and behaviour of DNA, RNA and proteins. Thereby we have been made aware of the nature of such phenomena as an astonishing, information-based UNFOLDING and a wonder-filled orderly FLOW into the FULLNESS of life's possibilities.

Some are helped by thinking of DNA as an integrated book of life in which these phenomena represent various chapters. The metaphor helps to convey the idea of each phenomenon as the expression of a different section of the "genome" - the "genome" being the entire complement of genetic information available in the DNA. That's fine, as long as the sense of a dynamic flow is not thereby lost or downplayed.

MB throws light on these phenomena starting from the first primordial cell, where the DNA of sperm and ovum join forces within the nurturing environment provided by the cytoplasm of the maternal egg. From there on development moves sequentially through birth, growth, adolescence, parenthood, old age and death. All these stages have an honoured place in the unfolding and flow of a life.

At each stage the molecules express hidden, imprinted programmes as the primordial cell multiplies and diversifies into an amazing, interconnected pattern of cell-types, tissues and organ-systems. As always, watching from the outside, it seems that the molecules know exactly what they are supposed to do and where they are going. So much for "NATURE".

With time, "NURTURE" enters to work along with nature, so that mother, family, education, friends, life-experiences and personal decisions can all serve as influences for moulding a unique individual to be gifted to our world. What astonishes me, however, is the flexible capacity of nature's cell-systems not only to interact with and adapt to any information coming in from the outside, but also then to proceed to make it part of the molecular information within the cell-systems. That is true even if the first cell and its DNA, RNA, proteins and cytoplasm eventually operate through what has become adult skin, muscles, blood, bones, heart, brain, hormones and the like. All these realities which appear later in the course of sequential development are, after all, flows and partial unfoldings from the first cell to serve the needs of the human being as a connected whole.

The magnificent development of a human being flowing out from one primordial cell is more factually based and far better researched than the emergence of our astonishing, expanding universe from the postulated primordial atom. I have to confess in all honesty that - even apart from any religious considerations - MB makes clear to me that it is AN UNACCEPTABLE HORROR to kill or maim or destroy the dignity of ANY, SINGLE HUMAN BEING. Despite all our so-called civilized ideas and supposedly deep religious convictions, too many of us may still in practice continue to live by the laws of the jungle...

To speak less passionately: Anyone not dazzled by what MB reveals to us about the wonder of our humanity is suffering from a handicap far worse than anything purely physical.

My own awful handicap is a mischievous streak which now and then produces an exciting temptation which alas! I am quite powerless to resist. This time it is to use the religion of cricket as a parable to explain how MB can transform watching the game into a mystical experience. I hope to be forgiven the tongue-in-cheek humour while trying to convey a serious message - sometimes that could be the best way! So, here goes...

The dialogue between East and West has produced a great world religion called cricket. It originally arose in England (the West) and was carried by missionaries to Australia and New Zealand (the farthest East).

However, it is in the Eastern nations of India and Pakistan that the religion of cricket can boast of its most fervent followers, these being distinguished by strong beliefs in the death and rebirth of their teams. Players from these two countries, full of true sporting spirit, cooperate in fostering those beliefs by indulging in frequent, dramatic collapses. The Australians, on the other hand, are not so sporting. In fact, they are deeply resented and bitterly fought against because of their contrary faith in eternal victory for their teams.

In this part of the world, the religion of cricket has thrown up gods with strange names like Sachin Tendulkar and Shoaib Akhtar. Like the mythological characters of old, these famous worthies are full of magnificent, superhuman deeds and - when least expected - equally heroic failures. The devotees occasionally respond to these deeds and failures by violence in the public stands and heart attacks on the couches at home. Religion, as we know, is a force not to be trifled with.

As a theologian with decades of training in watching cricket with immense devotion, I feel personally empowered to explain how MB has allowed me to transcribe and translate the watching of cricket into a mystical experience that makes the soft bone marrow within me dance. And that takes me through the religion, but beyond the religion, into mysticism.

You do not believe me? O.K., let's see if we can do a small scientific experiment: First, quieten your mind and lay aside all profane non-cricketing thoughts by breathing deeply for a few minutes and repeating the name Sachin, Sachin, Sachin many times like a mantra - till you can almost see the god in front of you.

That done, try to imagine, as vividly as possible, the phenomenon of Sachin Tendulkar making the split-second decision to execute a superb cover-drive dispatching to the boundary a barely visible, high speed, red missile fired at him by Shoaib Akhtar.

Now it may be true, dear reader, that the Divinity behind this Universe could be a Mathematician, an Artist, or a Dancer as some quantum physicists and their followers suggest. I let that pass. What MB makes clear to me is that this Divinity has the hidden face of an adoring Cricketer who worships the game - why else would the Tendulkar cover-drive have been made at all possible?

Allow me to put aside for the moment a discussion of the NURTURE behind that cover-drive - coach, press, adoring public, advertising revenues etc. Instead let me concentrate on his NATURE.

The NATURE, as we know, started in a tiny egg and now - given the rapidly approaching missile - requires from Tendulkar the INSTANTANEOUS, COMPLEX COORDINATION OF his visual pathways from eye to back of brain, (AND) OF millions of his axons firing at maybe 1,000 times a second, (AND) consequently, OF numerous "action potentials" travelling at more than 100 metres a second inside him - thereby inducing entire groups of muscles in his arms, legs and trunk to contract and move into action. All this in a split second. Wow!

Externally, what the millions of religious devotees - in public stands or glued to TV sets worldwide - merely notice is that Tendulkar lifts his bat lazily, and then a loud "THWACK!" is heard, and the red bullet is dispatched like greased lightning to the boundary. Using, in a creative personal way, the accepted hand-signal, one of the two high priests - present in a white coat - solemnly confirms that it is so.

The crowd dutifully erupts into loud cries of religious ecstasy. And I, watching quietly at the TV set at home, whisper the "Alleluia" appropriate to a Jesuit under remote control.

So, dear reader, as I have been pointing out, mysticism goes through religion beyond religion. Even better, mysticism is the source of a quiet, abiding joy - and it does not really matter how much we have to suffer when life is so full of "action potentials" permitting Love to fill our emptiness.

Endnotes

[1] Translation by Coleman-Barks.

[2] Lancy Pereira, *The Enchanted Darkness* (Anand: Gujarat Sahithya Prakashan, 1995).

[3] See Lee Smolin," Einstein's Lonely Path,"*Discover*, Sept. 2004.

[4] The four known forces are the gravitational, electromagnetic, weak nuclear and strong nuclear forces.

[5] Gordn Kame, "The The Dawn of Physics Beyond the Standard Model," *Scientific American*, June 2003.

[6] Roger Penrose, *The Road to Reality - A Complete Guide to the Universe*, (London: Jonathan Cape, 2004).

[7] Stephen Hawking, *A Brief History of Time* (New York: Bantam, 1988).

[8] Jean-Claude Carriere.

Inner Net of the Heart

The Fractal Nature of Consciousness

Will Keepin

At the cutting edge of science today, there is a cross disciplinary theme that is emerging in field after field: in biology, physics, nonlinear dynamics, artificial life, brain physiology, complexity theory, etc. This new idea is that beyond the physical realm, there exist invisible patterns and principles that somehow organize what we observe and experience. This development is highly auspicious, because it points western science in an unprecedented direction toward the existence of a realm beyond the observable, material, empirical world. Science is discovering that something transpires behind that which appears.

This 'something' is explored below in a metaphorical journey that takes off from hard science, cruises aloft through heights of consciousness and spirit, and lands, eventually, in love. In this manner, the paper articulates a fundamental connection between science and mysticism, and for this purpose we step somewhat beyond traditional scholarly formulations to give free rein to the intuition in weaving the threads of this vision. The story begins at the cutting edge of physics, moves through its cosmological and consciousness implications, and then formulates a simple, integral model of the cosmos. Finally we bring it all together in the "inner net" of the heart, which links all beings in love through the vast, invisible doorway of our own hearts. We conclude with a few reflections on how science and western society might be different if mystical consciousness were viewed as fundamental to reality, rather than an epiphenomenon of physical existence.

Toward a Science of Consciousness: Beyond $E = mc^2$

We begin on the solid ground of science, by summarizing the work of physicist David Bohm (1917—1992). Bohm was a colleague of Einstein's at Princeton University, where the two began a promising collaboration on the theoretical foundations of quantum theory, on which they shared similar views. But then Bohm suddenly lost his job at Princeton and had to leave the United States because he refused to testify in the McCarthy hearings against Robert Oppenheimer, with whom he had gotten his doctorate at Berkeley. Despite being born and raised an American citizen, Bohm was effectively exiled. He went to Brazil and later Israel, and ended up at the University of London for the last 35 years of his life.

Bohm was driven by a deep passion to understand the nature of the Universe. He felt this was the true purpose and spirit of science — a quest for truth. He was disturbed by the fact that many scientists regarded science primarily as a pragmatic discipline for prediction and control of natural systems. In contrast, Bohm, like Einstein, felt that the true purpose of science was a kind of spiritual quest, a form of *jnana* yoga that seeks to know the true nature of existence.

In Bohm's own work, he not only delved deeply into modern physics — where he made major contributions — but he also carried his quest into other disciplines, quite beyond science itself. He explored art, for example, to try to understand the nature of order in art. He also had extensive dialogues with leading spiritual masters, including a twenty year dialogue with Krishnamurti, the Indian sage. He had many conversations with the Dalai Lama and other masters, and eagerly explored their epistemologies of inner inquiry — their other ways of knowing. In addition to applying the scientific method, Bohm wanted to explore these other epistemologies so that he could "triangulate," so to speak, on the nature of reality, taking into account the broadest possible range of data and methods of inquiry.

Bohm had noticed a fundamental contradiction in modern physics and was puzzled that it didn't seem to trouble most physicists: The twin pillars of modern physics, Quantum Theory and Relativity Theory, were contradictory at their foundation. Quantum Theory required the nature of reality to be discontinuous, nonlocal, and noncausal. In contrast, Relativity Theory required reality to be continuous, local, and causal. So here were these two foundational theories whose implications for the nature of reality were in utter contradiction.

Pondering this, Bohm asked "What do these two branches of modern physics have in common? What is unifying here?" And the answer emerged: *wholeness*. Both theories proposed that the universe is an integral whole, and that the laws of physics apply everywhere, from the microscopic to the macrocosm. So, he surmised, let's start with wholeness itself, and build a theory from that foundation which is consistent with the data of both Quantum Theory and Relativity Theory.

And what he came up with after decades of rigorous scientific work was the proposal that the essence of the universe is what he called the *holomovement*. "Movement" meant that the nature of existence is a process of continual change, and "holo" meant that it has a kind of holographic structure, in which each part contains the whole. To quote Bohm precisely, "The cosmos is a single, unbroken wholeness in flowing movement." Notice that the holomovement is similar to a synthesis of two ancient spiritual principles: (1) the Buddhist teaching of impermanence — the notion (also from Heraclitus) that the nature of manifest existence is perpetual change, and (2) the microcosm is the macrocosm, as characterized for example in the Hindu mythological image of Indra's Net, where reality is represented as an infinite lattice of glistening jewels, each of which reflects all the others in its own facets. So for Bohm the nature of the cosmos is a single, unitive process — an unbroken, flowing wholeness in which each part of the flow contains the entire flow. Each *part* of the flow replicates the *totality* of the flow — a structure analogous to "holons" as Aldous Huxley dubbed them, which are utilized extensively in the work of Ken Wilber and others.

The Implicate Order

Bohm proposed that there are two fundamental aspects to the holomovement: the *explicate order* and the *implicate order*. Now why, after we've just said it's a single unbroken wholeness, are we breaking it into two aspects? Does this mean we are creating a duality from what is actually a oneness? No, because the explicate and implicate order only *appear* as distinct — although convincingly so, because of our perceptual limitations. Human beings have five fundamental senses plus the thinking mind, and the subset of the wholeness that is directly perceived by these human faculties constitutes what Bohm calls the explicate order. *Everything* else —that which we don't directly see, hear, taste, feel, touch, or think — constitutes the implicate order. Human perception is limited and so there needs to be this distinction between what is directly perceptible and what isn't.

To illustrate the relationship between the implicate and the explicate order, consider the following example that Bohm himself articulated. Take two concentric cylinders, one larger than the other, and fill the annular column between them with a thick transparent liquid like glycerine. Now place a small droplet of ink on the top surface of the glycerine, and begin rotating the inner cylinder (while the outer cylinder remains fixed). As the rotation continues, the ink droplet gets stretched out and becomes longer and thinner, and ever fainter. Eventually, it disappears altogether. At this point, the natural conclusion to draw is that the *order*, or organization, of the original ink drop has been lost — rendered chaotic — and the ink appears to be randomly distributed throughout the glycerin in microscopically small particles. However, if you now rotate the inner cylinder in the opposite direction, the ink structure will begin to reappear very faintly, and as you keep rotating, it gets stronger and thicker and eventually comes all the way back; the ink droplet reconstructs itself completely.

Bohm used this example to illustrate the relationship between the explicate and implicate order. Before rotation begins, the ink drop is plainly visible, its order is *explicate*, or "unfolded." After sufficient rotation, the ink drop disappears, yet its *order* is still preserved, albeit hidden. The order is now "enfolded" in the glycerine, or *implicate*. The key point is that the order may not be visible, but it is there nonetheless. In an analogous fashion, Bohm posits a vast realm called the "implicate order" that lies beyond what we directly perceive in the physical universe. Indeed, throughout science, oftentimes we see certain processes that we don't understand, or in which we don't see any order, or where we observe what we call "random" behavior. But this is no guarantee that what we're observing actually *is* random. There may be an underlying hidden order, which may (or may not) by some means become an explicate order perceptible to our scientific instruments. In Bohm's eloquent words, the key lesson is that "a hidden order may be present in what appears to be random."

At first blush, it's natural to suppose that the implicate order is some kind of secondary, ethereal reality floating around somewhere in space, whereas the primary reality is the physical universe as our senses perceive it and science describes it. However, for Bohm, precisely the opposite is the case. The implicate order is the *fundamental* reality, and the explicate order is secondary. The explicate order is akin to the foam on the waves of the ocean, and the implicate order is the ocean itself. This is reminiscent of what God (Krishna) tells the warrior Arjuna in the Bhagavad Gita: "I support this entire cosmos with a tiny part of my Being." The implicate order is profoundly vast — a kind of interpenetrating field of conscious information and presence that far transcends the known physical universe.

The implicate order thus extends throughout space and time, but also way beyond space and time. This is very important. Space is not some giant vacuum through which matter moves. For Bohm, matter and empty space are intimately interconnected, and they are both part of the explicate order. The implicate order is beyond space and time altogether, although it's accessible at every point in space time. It is present everywhere, but visible nowhere. You can think of the implicate order as a synonym for the Unseen, for that which is neither manifest nor accessible to our mind and five senses — in short, a synonym for the spiritual realm. We don't directly perceive it, except through inner intuitions and contemplative forms of spiritual practice.

Of course, Bohm underpinned his theory with a mathematical foundation, which is beyond the scope of this paper. But it's important to know that he showed how these ideas are consistent with the data of modern quantum and relativistic physics, and various remarkable corollaries like Bell's Theorem and quantum nonlocality. Bohm and his colleagues analyzed the Schroedinger equation, the central equation of quantum theory, in a remarkable yet natural way, which revealed a mathematical formulation for an unmanifest realm that Bohm originally called the "quantum potential," which later evolved into his concept of the implicate order. Bohm called his theory an ontological interpretation of quantum theory.

Matter, Energy, and Consciousness

Another vital aspect of Bohm's thinking is that the nature of reality has three fundamental components. Science has generally dealt with only two of them: matter and energy. These two are equated in the famous equation from Einstein: $E = mc^2$. This equation essentially affirms that energy and matter are different forms of the same thing. Bohm insists that there is a third element, which he called "meaning," which is a synonym for consciousness. For Bohm, meaning is as significant as matter and energy, and he proposed a tripartite structure to reality: matter, energy, and meaning. Moreover, each of these basic notions enfolds the other two. Thus, "energy" consists not only of explicate energy, but also includes implicate matter and implicate meaning. Put another way, energy "enfolds" both matter and meaning. Similarly, matter enfolds energy and meaning. And finally, meaning enfolds both matter and energy. Bohm reaches a powerful conclusion: "This implies, in contrast to the usual view, that meaning is an inherent and essential part of our overall reality, and is not merely a purely abstract and ethereal quality having its existence only in the mind." What we call the evolution of consciousness is basically the unfolding of meaning as it becomes manifest in the explicate order.

Figure 1

Thus meaning, or consciousness, includes all the invisibles of life—purpose, yearning, intention, love, despair, all of the intangibles of life—

which are no less real for being intangible. They are just as real as matter or energy, but they cannot be measured in the scientific laboratory. Indeed, scientific instruments are nothing but technological extensions of our five sense perceptions. Microscopes and telescopes are just bigger eyes. Microphones are bigger ears. What Bohm says is that these instruments operate only in the explicate order, and so they perceive only a tiny fraction of the totality of existence. Conventional science misses the implicate order altogether. Yet this is where the vast realm of consciousness dwells, and science is finally beginning to open itself to this domain of inquiry.

The other major characteristic of the model of reality of Bohm, which for our purposes is crucial, is its holographic structure. To illustrate, consider an example from mathematical physics — fractal geometry — called the Mandelbrot set as shown in Figure 1.

The remarkable structure of a fractal illustrates the holographic nature of consciousness. If we were to zoom in on this figure to observe its structure more closely, by magnifying the portion near the center left hand edge of Figure 1., and then repeat this process and zoom in on the center portion of that portion and continuing thus, zoom in on the center of each figure to generate the next figure, we would discover something very remarkable: there is a complete replica of the original structure we started off with back in Figure 1. We have come full circle; back to the original structure: the part contains the whole! And there are billions of other miniature replicas embedded throughout the set in each successive selection if we keep zooming in. This intricate structure is called a fractal, and it mimics the holographic nature of consciousness.

Moreover, if we keep going with this magnification process, we find further embedded miniatures of the original set. In fact, there are billions of them, embedded throughout the Mandelbrot set, and no two are exactly alike. In science, this holographic phenomenon is a recent discovery known as fractal geometry, which is characterized by "nested sets of self similar structures." Yet this insight has been known to the mystics down through the ages: "As above, so below." The fractal is thus a modern scientific discovery of an ancient alchemical principle, which can also be stated: "As within, so without." The key insight is that deeply embedded within universal structures are a series of complete replicas of the original, on vastly smaller scales. The microcosm replicates the macrocosm.

The Fractal Nature of Consciousness

To pursue the spiritual implications of these ideas, let us now take a flight of fancy — and this is where things start getting interesting. Let us invoke our imagination to construct a simple model of the cosmos, using this Mandelbrot set. Now the equation which gives rise to the Mandelbrot set is this: $Z_{n+1} = Z_n^2 + Z_0$. Again, the reader *need not* understand the mathematics here!—(s)he need only understand that the Mandelbrot set doesn't come out of thin air, it comes from a very particular equation, which is itself a principle of mathematical ordering.[1] An equation doesn't live in the physical dimension, you can't *see* it, it's not possible to weigh it, smell it, or hold it in your hand. It doesn't exist in the manifest realm, but you can see its manifest effects, which are revealed in the Mandelbrot set, whose nature is entirely determined by this particular equation. So in Bohm's terminology, the equation represents the *implicate* order; it is the invisible ordering principle that actually creates the set. And the Mandelbrot set itself represents the *explicate* order, it is the manifest structure that results from the creative process of the implicate order. So the implicate order is the agency of creation, and the explicate order is what gets created. In this case, the equation (implicate order) creates the Mandelbrot set (explicate order).

Now back to our model of the cosmos. Imagine that the Mandelbrot set represents the entire physical universe — which is the explicate order, or matter-energy realm. This is the domain of traditional science. And the equation $(Z_{n+1} = Z_n^2 + Z_0)$ represents the implicate order, which is the realm of consciousness. Taken together — matter, energy, and consciousness — we have a model of the entire cosmos. Notice that in this model consciousness creates the matter-energy realm, not the other way around. The forms of matter and energy are projected from the implicate order into manifestation in space and time.

So in this model the physical universe is represented in Figure1. Now imagine yourself, a single human being in this huge universe. Deeply embedded within the universe, billions of times smaller, there you are— a single human being with a yearning heart — as represented by the miniature Mandelbrot set in Figure 1. On the face of it, you are such a tiny speck amidst this vast expanse. Now, imagine that you explore your true nature, using perhaps meditation and other spiritual methods of inquiry, and through these practices you discover your true identity. You unveil the fundamental process that gives rise to your existence. In this metaphorical model, that would mean that you discover the underlying equation, or process, that created you and your particular form. Hence you discover that your interior essence — the truth of who you are — is not the tiny speck you thought you were, rather it is this mysterious process in the implicate order: $Z_{n+1} = Z_n^2 + Z_0$. This is the source that created your being; it gave you all the awareness and knowledge you have, and sculpted your particular size, shape, and form. And then suddenly, you have a breakthrough realization, a major "Aha!" You realize that this fundamental truth of who you are (namely, $Z_{n+1} = Z_n^2 + Z_0$) is *absolutely identical* to the fundamental truth of the entire cosmos (namely, $Z_{n+1} = Z_n^2 + Z_0$). The process that creates you, and is *your* true identity, is none other than the very same process that creates the entire cosmos, and is *its* true identity. You and the cosmos are one!

As the mystical poet Rumi describes this realization, "The secret turning in your heart is the entire Universe turning!" Of course on the physical plane — the explicate order — your outer form is indeed a tiny speck, but even there, your form is a miniature version of the cosmos — "you are made in the image of God." And on the consciousness level — the implicate order — your interior essence is one with the essence of the cosmos. So your outer form is a tiny speck, but your inner essence is the vast cosmos itself. And this is true not only for you, but for every other being as well. Our hearts are bigger than the universe.

The doorway to this universal consciousness is through our hearts, and the implicate order that links us all together can therefore be called the "inner net of the heart." The homonymic similarity to "internet" is intentional, because the computerized internet may be seen as a technological manifestation of this fractal principle in the explicate order. For every computer has access — apart from electronic firewalls that cordon off domains of cyber security — to the entirety of information on the internet. Any part of this vast cyberspace is only a few clicks away. Indeed the very existence of the internet is a consequence, in the explicate order, of a pre-existent and far more refined parallel principle in the implicate order. Just as every computer can access the entire universe of cyberspace through the internet, every heart can access the entire cosmos of consciousness through the inner net of the heart.

Of course, this model is only metaphorical, but it does reflect the character of spiritual realization in different traditions. For example, in Hinduism, the "Atman" represents the spiritual nature of the individual (sometimes called the Self), and "Brahman" is the spiritual nature of the cosmos. The fundamental enlightenment experience is the realization that Atman *is* Brahman — the two are identical. Or in the Bhagavad Gita, we "see the Self in every creature, and all of creation in the Self." Similarly in the Christian Gospels, "All that is mine is yours and all that is yours is mine" (John 17:10), and "The Father and I are one" (John 10.30). The Christian mystic Julian of Norwich tells us: "We are all in Him enclosed, and He is enclosed in us." In Islam, Allah says: "Heaven and earth are too small to contain Me, but I fit easily inside the heart of my beloved devotee." In Zen, the great master Dogen says: "We study the self to forget the self, and when we forget the self, we become one with the ten thousand things." Here, the self we forget is just our physical and conditioned forms — our body, personality, ego, thoughts, family, vocation — all the attributes that characterize our manifest, temporal form. In the example above, it's represented by the tiny Mandelbrot structure in Figure 1. And when we forget this self, we become one with the "ten thousand things" because we become one with that which gives rise to all of existence. Similarly, according to the gnostic Gospel of Thomas, Jesus said: "When you make the two one, and when you make the inner as the outer and the outer as the inner and the above as the below, you enter the Kingdom." And finally, in Tantric Buddhism, the scholar Ajit Mukerjee says unequivocally: "The entire drama of the universe is replicated in the human body. When you come to know the truth of the body, you come to know the truth of the cosmos." And this is meant literally, but at a consciousness level, not a physical level. If you explore the nature of consciousness, you discover in your own being everything that goes on at the cosmic scale. As transpersonal psychologist Stanislav Grof emphasizes, "Each of us is everything."

Only on the physical level — the space-time plane — are you anything less than the whole of existence. If you identify with your form and attributes, you are but a speck in the cosmos. If you identify with your

Being or essence, the whole of the Divine is merged into you, in all its depth and splendor. Your true identity is thus oneness with God. As Meister Eckhart put it, "Nothing is hidden anymore in God which has not become manifest or mine. I become all things, as He is, and I am one and the same being with Him . . . so entirely that 'He' and this 'I' become one 'is,' and act in this 'isness' as one."

Intention and will in the implicate order

Thus far this model embodies a significant limitation in the way it's presented: it is static, like taking a snapshot of an evolving cosmos. But imagine now that the implicate order is changing over time, and the resulting explicate order also unfolds in time. And the two are coupled, so that each affects the other. Hence there is a coevolution of the implicate and explicate order.[2] This implies that by working in the implicate order, by working with spiritual laws in the invisible realms of consciousness, you can actually affect what takes place in the explicate order. This suggests that if you connect deeply to your core essence, and your actions are inspired from there, then not only does this shape your own destiny, but you may become an instrument for a profound impact on a much larger scale. The leaf can heal the tree. This holds because you are working on the plane of your essence identity, which transcends scale, so when your work translates back into the manifest plane, it does so on every conceivable scale.

This holds because you are working directly with the single, unitive process that underlies all of creation. "God is a simple essence," as Meister Eckhart put it. The process of creation takes place in consciousness first, and subsequently manifests in outward form. So if you want to make a change in your life or in the world, you work with it deeply in consciousness first, before anything "happens." In practical terms, you hold an intention or engage in a disciplined contemplative practice, and as you focus your attention and will in this way, it tends toward manifestation. In this model, when you focus your will and deep yearning of the heart in this way, you're effectively 'sweeping' the implicate order and concentrating it, drawing it together to serve what it is you are seeking to manifest. As this energetic field becomes increasingly concentrated, there comes a point where suddenly it "condenses" out of the implicate order into explicate manifestation. If our physical eyes could see the implicate order, we could observe this dynamic process, but from our normal explicate point of view, the manifestation often appears to be quite sudden and magical. Note this also shows why faith is so important — faith defined as inherent trust in the unknown — because we must maintain the intention and work with the practice in our consciousness, despite the lack of observable evidence that it is making any difference. But if we could see into the implicate order, we would observe this energetic field of intention; how it gathers and intensifies and then becomes ever denser and more focused, until eventually it "pops" into explicate manifestation.

Implications of a Fractal Model of Consciousness

Of course this is a simple model, and our purpose is just to illustrate heuristically how science is beginning to embrace consciousness as fundamental to reality, and also how consciousness radically transcends certain laws of matter, energy, space, and time. The physical universe is dwarfed by the consciousness universe, and science itself is opening to the possibility that consciousness may be fundamental. What are the implications of this?

First, consciousness has a fractal or holographic structure. This means that your consciousness is fundamentally one with the consciousness of the entire universe, and it is possible to access that universal consciousness. This is not a dreamy, poetic metaphor — it is a literal truth of consciousness. Mystics have known this for ages. As Rumi put it in the 13th century, "Let the drop of water that is you become a hundred mighty seas. But do not think that the drop alone becomes the Ocean. The Ocean, too, becomes the drop." It is our birthright to discover this "inner net of the heart" within ourselves, and live from that vast interior foundation of Being.

Second, this model points to the transformative power of serving the world from a spiritual foundation. When our actions are led by the larger wisdom of universal consciousness, and we serve the explicate world from our inner roots in the implicate order, then our work can become profound and transformative. This is what Gandhi, Mother Teresa, Martin Luther King, Aung Sang Su Kyi and other spiritual activists understand so deeply in their implementation of the spiritual law in the secular world. This doesn't necessarily mean you have to become a Gandhi to make a difference, just as you don't have to be an Einstein to be a good scientist. The transformative principles for social change and cultural evolution that

Gandhi and King applied are accessible to us all, by transforming our selves through inner disciplines of consciousness, thereby becoming the instruments for a larger wisdom.

Third, this model also implies that there is an amplified power of consciousness that operates in groups or communities who work with consciousness practices together through the inner net of the heart. Zen master Thich Nhat Hahn has said that the next Buddha will emerge not in the form of an individual, but rather in the form of a community of people living in loving kindness and mindful awareness. This is because such a community — people working together with their hearts and minds in alignment around a shared intention of the highest integrity — creates an amplified field of intentionality, like a laser beam of coherent consciousness that harnesses tremendous power from the implicate order. Taken far enough, this can tap into the core of the implicate order and begin working directly with the creative process of love itself. This dramatically increases the power and possibilities for manifestation in the explicate order.

Fourth, we are witnessing the dawning of a new science of consciousness and profound interconnection, or perhaps we should call it intercommunion. Thomas Berry observes that the universe is not a collection of objects, but a *communion of subjects* — a beautiful synonym for the inner net of the heart. However, before mainstream science can fully embrace the rich promise of these new developments, it will have to loosen its grip on cherished doctrines of materialism and rationalism, which excessively restrict both its epistemology and ontology. Physicist Ravi Ravindra has observed that, "the greatest discovery of modern science is the discovery of its own limitations." Yet sadly, many scientists today still live as unwitting inmates in the conceptual prisons of a narrow orthodox worldview. As Mark Twain aptly sums up the consequences, "It ain't what you don't know that gets you into trouble, it's what you *think* you know that ain't so."

A brief thought experiment may shed some light in this regard. The following vignette overstates the case, but illustrates the problem — one that equally afflicts many fields beyond science as well. Imagine that the sum total of all scientific truth is represented by a complex conglomeration of sophisticated gears, pulleys, valves, pipes, switches, wires, computers, etc. — a huge machine of sorts, with myriad interconnections, each one accurately representing some aspect of a proven scientific fact. Now imagine this giant machine is floating in empty space somewhere, and that it's covered on all sides with mirrors. Then from anywhere inside, it appears that this complex structure extends to infinity in all directions. In other words, it appears from *within* science that the truths of science span the entirety of the universe. Whereas in fact, the mirrors — put in place by the mind—create a two-fold delusion: first, the compelling appearance that scientific truth exhausts all possible truth, and second, a blindness to other forms of truth, because they are totally eclipsed. Fortunately in recent years, these mirrors are slowly being removed, exposing the limitations of science, and unveiling the vast cosmos that lies beyond it.

What if mystical consciousness were viewed as fundamental?

We conclude with several reflections on this question:

First, if mysticism or consciousness were viewed as fundamental in our culture, then our primary work as human beings would be with consciousness. This means that we would focus on developing, purifying, deepening our consciousness as the first and foremost task in life. What are traditionally called "spiritual" laws or mystical truths are really laws or principles of consciousness. We would learn these and apply them directly in our lives. Rumi tells us: "There is one thing you must do, and if you remember this and forget everything else, there's nothing to worry about. But if you forget this, and remember everything else, your life will be utter waste." That one thing is to connect to the deepest core of our being — to return to the truth of who we are, and live from there. This is a task of transforming consciousness, and it is accomplished through contemplative disciplines that work with and through our consciousness.

Second, we would realize instinctively that, as Meister Eckhart put it: "What is received in contemplation is given out in love." Martin Luther King, Gandhi and Mother Teresa all lived this truth. Each of them achieved first in their individual consciousness the profound integration, love, and liberation which was later manifested through their work on a much larger scale in the world. The liberation of consciousness wrought in the heart of one individual was thereby transformed into a conscious liberation for many. This is the fractal of consciousness in action — the leaf can heal the tree. It's an application of "As above, so below" in reverse: As below, so above.

Third, we would move away from mistaken identity with our own thoughts. We would recognize the limitations of thought, and the crippling debilitation of incessant thinking all the time. As Bohm observed, "Thought creates structures, and then pretends they exist independently of thought." We lead our lives within these thought structures as if they were immutable laws of nature. If consciousness were primary, we would see through thought itself to the subtle consciousness that underlies and creates it. Then our conceptual frameworks would appear as they are, elaborate (though often useful) props in the vast cosmic drama of life. We would then regard thought as just one powerful modality of consciousness, within a vastly larger, more subtle and ultimately more nourishing expanse. As Rumi puts it, "Thought gives off smoke to prove the existence of fire. The mystic sits within the burning."

Fourth, we would become increasingly free of our false selves. Einstein himself remarked that "the value of a human being is determined primarily by the measure and the sense in which he has attained liberation from the self."[3] If consciousness were primary, there would be a natural progression away from identification with one's own personal selfhood, and an expanded alignment with the larger conscious purpose of life itself.

Fifth, there would be a greater plurality of voices in our society. Diversity in all its forms would be valued, as an explicate expression of the endlessly rich textures of consciousness in the implicate order. To give just one example, there would be more women's voices in this very book.

Finally, and most important, we would love more. Eknath Easwaran has observed that in a healthy society, there is a natural tendency "to love people, and use objects," whereas in a materialistic society, there is a reverse tendency — "to love objects, and use people." Our society has certainly erred in the latter direction. Yet as we connect more deeply to consciousness, love inevitably comes to the fore. As our consciousness becomes emptied of our selves, love rushes in to fill the void. "By love has appeared everything that exists," Shebastari tells us, and "By love, that which does *not* exist, appears as existing." Love is indeed the greatest power in the universe. And divine love is the most powerful form of love. If we give ourselves to the transforming fire of this love, with its attendant demands of radical humility and spiritual surrender, our entire lives begin to burn with longing for the Divine, regardless of the path or tradition we approach it from. This takes us directly into the implicate order, where we reconnect with the Source of all life. At the core of the implicate order is the creative power of love, which initiates us into a mysterious alchemy that opens, from the inside, the inner net of the heart, the gateway to the Infinite.

In closing, there is of course the question of whether any of this could ever be "proven." My guess is probably so, in various forms, but this is not the point. The mystic has nothing to prove, and has moved beyond the need for proof in terms palatable to the rationalist and the skeptic. Rather than living by their proofs, mystics prove by their living. As Rumi put it, "If you are in love, that love is all the proof you need. If you are *not* in love, what good are all your proofs?"

Epilogue: The epistemology of mysticism

Eastern mystics have long maintained that the mind is a power of ignorance. How can we dispel ignorance with the very instrument that creates it? We cannot, say the mystics. We must go beyond the mind to escape the clutches of illusion. We must go beyond thought to come to truth.

A few pioneering scientists have also recognized this. David Bohm tells us: "Thought creates structures, and then pretends they are objective realities independent of thought." Indeed, in Bohm's view, despite being a brilliant thinker himself, he maintains that "thought is really a very tiny little thing. But thought forms a world of its own in which it is everything. It reifies itself and imagines there's nothing else but what it can think about . . ."

The requisite task of the scientist who wishes to truly explore mysticism is to employ epistemologies that go beyond thought. Indeed, a major obstacle to the next great leap for science is the failure to recognize the limitations of the principal epistemic instrument of scientific inquiry: the human mind. Science will begin to make major strides forward when it takes seriously the fundamental limitations of human reason and intellectual knowledge.

Mysticism Must Be Practiced, not Merely Studied

Study and research of mysticism does not, by itself, cultivate mystical wisdom. Just as "musicologists" are those who study music but are often not musicians themselves, so we might give the name "mysticologists" to those who study mysticism, but who may not be mystics themselves. Mysticism must be practiced to be known —it is not an intellectual body of information, but a practical path of *trans*formation. Just as theoretical science would be meaningless speculation if it were not grounded in laboratory experimentation, so the inquiry into mysticism is meaningless unless it is grounded in mystical practice.

What might be called the "mystical hypothesis" is the affirmation that beyond the realms of the mind and physical senses, there exists an altogether different reality which is at least as real, if not more real, than the physical reality accessible to our senses and scientific instruments (the latter being technological extensions and refinements of the physical senses). In short, mystics assert that there is another reality beyond the shores of our mental and physical understanding, and this mystical realm can be directly known and experienced.

The proper scientific response to this claim is to find a suitable vessel, enter the water, and start rowing to reach that other shore. To do otherwise is to fall short of the true spirit of scientific inquiry and epistemology, because it means we are unwilling to undertake the empirical mystical experiment ourselves. Unless we perform the actual experiment, how can we legitimately claim to be taking a scientific approach to mysticism? We must do the mystical experiment; otherwise we are just "mysticologists" - those who study mysticism but don't practice it.

Nor can mysticism be known by delving into the fascinating parallels between mysticism and science about the nature of reality. Such comparative analyses have their place and serve to inspire us, but they are no substitute for actually taking the mystical journey. Mysticism has to be *experienced* on its own terms to be known — it cannot be known by thinking, analyzing, or speculating about it.

As Thomas Kuhn emphasized, new paradigms in science entail new practices that disclose new data. The scientific inquiry into mysticism therefore requires that we take up mystical practices, which will in turn bring forth new kinds of empirical data. And as we approach these new disciplines of consciousness, transpersonal researcher Roger Walsh counsels us: "we need to first become aware of our own (usually unrecognized) assumptions and beliefs in order to begin to recognize their possibly distorting and biasing effects." . . . [We must] "be open to the possibility that these disciplines may represent systems and paradigms that, although different, are as sophisticated as our own. . . . Investigators, therefore, need to examine both the literature *and practices* of these disciplines." (emphasis in original).

If we do not engage in mystical practice ourselves, then even if we feel sympathetic to the mystical hypothesis, we are at best rather like naïve fans of Galileo, who celebrate his wonderful discoveries but refuse to look through his telescope. This is not the stance of genuine scientists.

Closing reflections from the pioneering work of Peter Kingsley

The recent groundbreaking work of mystical philosopher Peter Kingsley suggests that limiting our epistemology to thinking and intellectual analysis is a fatal flaw in the entire western philosophical tradition, including science. In his books *Reality* and *The Dark Side of Wisdom*, Kingsley maintains that western philosophy was derailed from its true purpose long ago, beginning with the schools of Plato and Aristotle, and that both philosophy and its brainchild science have yet to recover and make course corrections.

Grounding his insights in scholarly research on the work of Parmenides, Empedocles, and Socrates, Kingsley maintains that the true purpose of philosophy is the pursuit and love of wisdom. Yet beginning with the schools of Plato and Aristotle, philosophy was transformed into a pursuit of *talking and arguing about* the love of wisdom. Since that time, the talking and arguing have pushed everything else out of the picture, and we are left with an intellectual enterprise that is profoundly cut off from its source in wisdom. "Philosophy is a travesty of what it once was, no longer a path to wisdom but a defense against it."[4]

To summarize Kingsley's work in a few paragraphs would be near impossible, but we can outline some key highlights. The early pioneers of western philosophy —Socrates, Parmenides, Empedocles, Zeno — all saw through the limitations of the mind, and looked beyond it for truth. They worked "to challenge the mind only to undermine it; to paralyze it, silence it, bring it face to face with stillness."[5] And in this stillness, truth would reveal itself, on its own terms. Theirs was an essentially mystical epistemology.

In the case of Parmenides, for example, often called the father of logic, his teachings came as revelations received through a specific contemplative practice called incubation. He would spend hours or days at a time lying absolutely motionless in a cave, similar to the meditative practices of the eastern mystics. Parmenides' revelations were remarkably deep and expansive; something divine, a gift from the gods. Then "Plato took this 'logic' and put it in everyone's hands: encouraged people to think and argue for themselves. This required all sorts of distortions, falsifications, obscurations, which his successor, Aristotle, was soon pursuing to perfection."[6]

In essence, the effect of Plato's and Aristotle's work was to reduce these profound early western mystics to mere thinkers, and to relegate their revealed wisdom to mere ideas — all the while promoting the vast illusion that "the way to get to the truth in these ideas was not through entering some other state of consciousness, but through thinking"[7] "Plato was quick to realize that such slick definitions could be endless sources of amusement, and he enjoyed making humorous use of them in his dialogues. It was Aristotle, though, who — disarmingly superficial, disastrously influential — converted the playful trivialities into serious statements of doctrine."[8] The belief that truth could be reached through thinking and reason took deep root. Philosophy's empirical offspring, science, followed in precisely these same footsteps, and remains to this day embroiled in the same quagmire.

Kingsley goes on to show that the crucial point Aristotle failed to grasp is that the faculty of reasoning he placed his faith in, is in fact a power of infinite trickery and illusion. Believing reality to be the truth is the ultimate deception. Illusion is inherently ingrained in reality, similar to the concept of Maya developed by Shankacharya and the eastern mystical traditions. Moreover, "our rationality, our proud belief in the ability to argue our way to the truth, is an essential part of the deception."[9] "The greatest deception of all is to tell the truth, and . . . the greatest truth is to deceive."[10] For deception is inherent in the nature of reality. "To try not to be deceived is far more foolish than to be deceived." In the end, the only protection against deception is to surrender to being deceived. "Talk about truth and you lose sight of it. Understand illusion and you find truth right in the middle of it. Create great philosophical schemes about reality [e.g. science!] and you fall straight into deception. Appreciate the power of deception, and you come face to face with reality. Run away from deception, try to avoid it, and you are deceived."[11] We are led, eventually, to a place no longer burdened by knowledge. As a mystic from India once observed, the opposite of ignorance is not knowledge, but rather knowledgelessness. "You can at last afford to relax and know nothing — in the quiet knowledge that whatever needs to be known will make itself known to you at the appropriate moment."[12]

In the end, the journey leads to a startling awakening that mystics have long proclaimed: "All of a sudden we become aware that, instead of our being born into the world, this world has been born in us.... Everything is inside you now. However huge any scientists choose to make the age of the cosmos, you are more ancient. However far into the distances of outer space they claim it reaches, you reach further...."[13]

Endnotes

[1] This equation is the simplest form of what is called a non-linear iterative process, which is a technical term for complex evolving systems in which the future state of the system depends on its current state. Mathematical structures like these are used to model a wide range of natural phenomena.

[2] This is oversimplified but suffices for our purposes. In refinements to his theory, Bohm proposed a hierarchy of several "superimplicate" orders. For Bohm, time is a particular type of explicate order that is unfolded from its own implicate order, which Bohm called the "eternal order." The eternal order unfolds into a succession of events that we experience as "time" in the explicate order. Bohm regards all of time to be enfolded in each particular moment of time, in alignment with mystical understanding of time. Eternity is present in each moment of time.

[3] Albert Einstein, *Ideas and Opinions*, Crown Publication 1954.

[4] Peter Kingsley, *Reality*, Golden Sufi Center, 2003, p.156.

[5] *Reality*, p.304.

[6] *Ibid.*, p.305.

[7] Idem.

[8] *Ibid.*, p.456.

[9] *Ibid.*, pp.481-482.

[10] *Ibid.*, p.461.

[11] *Ibid.*, p.495.

[12] *Ibid.*, p.531.

[13] *Ibid.*, p.559.

Pathway To Reality

N.V. Kulkarni

The Road

The pathway to Reality starts from its quest. Can we take anything about our universe, about ourselves for granted - some fundamental as a starting point for the explanation of everything else? It is not easy to find such a 'still point.' Therefore the quest begins with a leap of faith.

The quest begins with one's certainty of one's own existence. It continues with his/her mind's eye view of the universe, ends with the discovery of objective truth with distillations carried out by the senses. What makes one think that one can start here and finish there, when the ultimate objective truth is in one's mind view?

It is faith – faith that truth does exist in a way that is independent and 'other' from everyone, unchanged whether or not studied by scientists or anyone else, and not affected by how it is viewed in anyone's mind's eye.

A most pertinent example of faith in search of the Ultimate Reality which comes to my mind often is that of Stephen Hawking – a man of extraordinary genius, condemned to live out his years locked in a useless body without movement or speech, whose sheer courage nevertheless allows him to be one of the pre-eminent physicists of our time as well as an international celebrity.

The three chief types of approaches to the problem of the Ultimate Reality in the history of philosophic thought are the cosmological, the theological and the psychological. Dr. Caird has said that by the very constitution of the human mind, there have been only three ways of thinking open to a human being. "He can look outward upon the world around him, he can look inward upon the Self within him, and he can look upward to the God above him, to the Being who unites the outward and inward worlds, and who manifests himself in both."[1] We will first look at the cosmological approach and leave the other two till we come to mysticism proper.

Cosmological Approach

One begins by trusting some ideas about the universe that have never been proved, may never be proved, and might turn out to be wrong. So it boils down to the assumption that one exists and is sound in mind in the Cartesian fashion. This is the basic assumption – the faith, which cannot be proved by science, but well founded to provide a springboard for all scientific investigations.

The starting point of the scientific method is belief in the cause-effect relationship. Some scientists maintain that the Law of Cause and Effect is not a law but an article of faith. It cannot be proved to operate in all cases. We all know that in the quantum realm we cannot pin down any event with an unbroken history of cause and effect leading up to it.

Some articles of faith, basic assumptions about the universe, which continue to underlie the practice of science, are rationality, accessibility, contingency, objectivity and unity, as put forth by Kitty Ferguson.[2]

(i) **Rationality**: The universe is rational. It has a pattern, symmetry and predictability. Effect follows cause in a dependable manner.

(ii) **Accessibility**: The book of Nature is open for us.

(iii) **Contingency**: Things could have been different. There would have been no observers. Whether this contingency was brought about by chance and/or choice, one can observe, test and know.

(iv) **Objectivity**: There is something definite, some raw material out there for us to study, which does not change in response to our opinions, perceptions, preferences, beliefs or anything else.

(v) Unity: The universe operates by underlying laws that do not change in an arbitrary fashion from place to place, from minute to minute or even millennium to millennium. There is a unity at the deepest level.

Roger Penrose would add two more articles of faith to the above list – beauty and miracles.

If God/Creator was made responsible or otherwise for the above five assumptions, the seventeenth century scientists could have had it both ways without risking charges of contradiction. Today God/Creator has been divorced from them.

Is it really so? John Watkins defines Normal Science in which there is not really any testing of theories as genuine science. Extraordinary science in which genuine testing of theories occurs is so abnormal, so different from genuine science, that it can hardly be called science at all.[3]

"Consider a theological scholar working on an apparent inconsistency between two biblical passages. Theological doctrine assures him that the Bible, properly understood, contains no inconsistencies. His task is to provide a gloss that offers a convincing reconciliation of the two passages. Such work seems essentially analogous to 'normal' scientific research as depicted by Kuhn; and there are grounds for supposing that he would not repudiate the analogy. For *The Structure of Scientific Revolutions* contains many suggestions, some explicit others implicit in the choice of language, of a significant parallelism between science, especially Normal Science, and theology. And when Kuhn discusses the personal process of repudiating an old paradigm and embracing a new one, he describes it as a 'conversion experience,' adding that 'a decision of that kind can only be made on faith.'"[4]

For Kuhn the scientific community is analogous to a religious community and science is the scientist's religion. For this reason he elevates Normal Science above Extraordinary Science. Extraordinary Science corresponds, on the religious side, to a period of crisis and schism, confusion and despair, to a spiritual catastrophe – the dark night of the soul. Karl Popper admits, "I admit that an intellectual revolution often looks like a religious conversion. A new insight may strike us like a flash of lightning."[5]

Yet it should be noted, as Pearce Williams observes, that the views with regard to the structure of science of both Kuhn and Popper are based on the History of Science, and he considers that in the absence of enough historical knowledge it would be dangerous to erect a philosophical structure.[6] And, as Imre Lakotos emphatically states, "one cannot understand the history of science without taking account of the interaction of the three worlds, for the rationally reconstructed growth of science takes place essentially in the world of ideas, in Plato's third world."[7] In a similar tone Paul Feyerabend articulates: "According to Lakatos the apparently unreasonable features of science occur only in the material world and the mental world; they are absent from the third world of ideas. It is in the third world that the growth of knowledge takes place and that a rational judgment of all aspects of science becomes possible."[8]

The numerous deviations from the straight path of rationality which we observe in actual science may well be necessary if we want to achieve progress with the brittle and unreliable material (instruments, brains, etc.) at our disposal.

Let us glance at these three worlds. The first world we know most directly is the world of our conscious perceptions. Yet it is the world we know least about in any kind of precise scientific terms. It contains happiness, pain, perception of colours, earliest childhood memories, love, understanding, ignorance, revenge, knowledge of various facts, and fear of death. It contains mental images of chairs and tables, and where smells and sounds and sensations of all kinds intermingle with our thoughts and our decisions to act.

The second is what we call the physical world. It contains actual chairs and tables, automobiles and T.V. sets, human beings, human brains, actions of neurons. It is the world of the sun, the moon and stars, so also clouds, hurricanes, rocks, flowers, butterflies and, at a deeper level, molecules and atoms, electrons and photons and spacetime, cytoskeletons, tubulin dimers and super conductors. The connection of the world of our perception with the physical world is mysterious.

There is also one other world — the Platonic world of mathematical forms. It contains Lagrange's theorem, Euclidean geometry's Pythagorean theorem, natural numbers, Gassmann product, non-Euclidean geometries, infinite numbers, non–computable numbers, recursive and non – recursive ordinals, Maxwell's and Einstein's equations, mathematical solutions of chairs and tables as would be made use of in virtual reality, simulations also of black holes and hurricanes. The Platonic world contains other absolutes, such as the Good and the Beautiful. Its existence rests on the profound timeless and universal nature of these concepts.

This brings us to the question of beauty and miracles. "Beauty in physics similarly has to do with a falling-into-place that appears little short of miraculous. It implies simplicity, elegance, and mathematical consistency and creativity. These are the qualities that make such theories as superstring theory and wormhole theory appealing and convincing, not the fact that anyone has ever observed a superstring or wormhole or that anyone hopes to in the foreseeable future."[9]

"Occasionally, however, something can arise, in research into mathematical theories of the physical world, which has a much more powerful impact on such choices than mere mathematical elegance, and this is what I refer to as a 'miracle.'"[10]

The Unfolding of Reality

The reality we observe is the evolving of matter in its arena, space and time, the very fabric of the cosmos. How much do we know about space and time? The question has many dimensions.

(i) No single sense modality can be made responsible for their intuition in our minds.

(ii) Kant calls them a priori.

(iii) Regarding space Leibniz has made some interesting arguments. He argued that if space really exists as an entity, as a background substance, God would have to choose where in this substance to place the universe. What is the location of the universe within space? If the universe were to move as a whole, say, ten feet to the left or right, how would we know? If we are fundamentally unable to detect space, or changes within space, how can we claim that it actually exists? The size of the visible universe today is estimated to be about 3×10^{27} cm.

Let us focus on the nature of space in the context of some of the latest grand unification theories.

String Theory

Depending on how hard one thinks, this theory is either intuitively pleasing or thoroughly baffling. Since we speak of the fabric of spacetime, the suggestion is that spacetime is stitched out of strings, much as a shirt is stitched out of thread. We picture strings as vibrating in space and through time, but without the spacetime fabric that the strings are themselves imagined to yield through their orderly union, there is no space or time. In this proposal, the concepts of space and time fail to have meaning until innumerable strings weave together to produce them. Thus to make sense of this proposal, we would need a fully spaceless and timeless formulation of the string theory in which spacetime emerges from the collective behavior of strings.

But the string theory has other ingredients. The brane world scenario brings this question into sharp relief. Now there can be one brane, two branes, p branes. The answer is in Matrix theory with zero branes. Matrix theory, if found true, might then solve strings, branes and perhaps even spacetime.

If this way of seeing things is from one end, the loop quantum gravity is the other end from which reality is being approached. These are elementary loops of spaces. The researchers have calculated the allowed areas of such surfaces of space. These happen to be one square Plank length, two square Plank lengths, but no fractions are possible. This is a proof to show that space also comes in discrete, indivisible chunks like the electrons.

Let us now come to time. Once Einstein said to Rudolf Carnap, that "the problem of now worried him seriously. Because the experience of now means something special for man, something essentially different from the past and the future, but that this important difference does not and cannot occur within physics. That this experience of a fundamental quality of time that the human mind embraces as readily as the lungs take in air, cannot be grasped by science seemed to him a matter of painful but inevitable resignation."[11]

As a movie projector illuminates film after film, in the intuitive way of thinking about time, moment after moment comes and goes. However, scientists have been unable to find in the laws of physics, any mechanism that singles out moment after moment to be momentarily real – to be the momentary now – as the mechanism flows ever onward toward the future. Reality embraces past, present, and fture equally, and the flow that we envision is illusory.

In this grand arena, enticing and baffling at the same time, humans have been groping into the book of Nature. With their constant endeavour they have been peeling out layer after layer of knowledge to reveal deeper knowledge. The human march on this pathway to reality made it discover many wonders of nature and formulate worldviews at those times. The sequence of the human encounter with the Reality can be presented as follows.

Classical Reality

Galileo Galilei, Rene Descartes and Isaac Newton were some of the early pioneers of modern scientific thought, and argued that happenings in the universe are explicable and predictable when observed correctly. Humans were then trying to discover harmonies in nature. They were atuning their ears to the rhyme behind the rhythm and sought reason behind regularity. Many sung and unsung heroes contributed their mite to the rapid and impressive progress of science. But Newton stole the show. Newton crystallized many a physical phenomenon in a handful of mathematical equations. To him space and time supplied an invisible scaffolding as absolute and immovable entities rendering shape and structure to the universe.

Not that Newton's ideas were not criticized. But the power in his equations was so tremendous that for the next two hundred years they ruled the scientific scenario absolutely. Even today Newton's conception of space and time, though flawed, works wonderfully well at the slow speeds and moderate gravity of our daily life.

Relativistic Reality

Newton's equations included the force of gravity. They described natural phenomena mathematically which fitted with common experience. Classical physics provided a rigorous ground for human intuition. In 1860 Maxwell extended the field of classical physics to take account of electrical and magnetic forces. Maxwell knew that electric and magnetic fields could be visualized as force fields that permeate all space. He further stated that these fields could vibrate in precise synchronization, so that they generate a wave that could travel by itself in space without assistance.

Maxwell's theory predicted that a clock placed on a moving rocket ship should beat slower than a clock placed on the earth. The scientists failed to realise this. For half a century, however, scientists overlooked this strange prediction of Maxwell's equations. It was only in 1905 that a physicist finally understood this profound distortion of space and time that was implied in Maxwell's equations. The physicist was Albert Einstein. He created the special theory of relativity, which changed the course of human history.

But when Einstein learned Maxwell's equations at the Polytechnic, he was surprised to find that they do *not* admit stationary waves as solutions. In 1905, Einstein finally solved the puzzle of Maxwell's theory of light. In the process, he overturned the notions of space and time that had survived for several thousand years.

"In hindsight, however, we realize that Einstein was able to take Maxwell's theory further than anyone else because he grasped the principle of unification, understanding that there was an *underlying, unifying symmetry* that linked seemingly dissimilar objects such as space and time (as well as matter and energy). Like Newton's seminal discovery that terrestrial and celestial physics could be united by his universal law of gravitation, or Maxwell's discovery of the unity of electricity and magnetism, Einstein's contribution was to unite space and time. This theory demonstrated that space and time are manifestations of one entity, which scientists call "spacetime." However, the theory not only united space and time, it joined the concepts of matter and energy."[12]

However, Einstein was still not satisfied. In the theory there was no reference to gravity. He considered that only light could travel the fastest. Gravity could not catch up with light. Therefore, Newton's theory of gravity must be wrong, since it had no reference to the speed of light. Einstein presented his solution to this puzzle, in 1915, in the form of the theory of general relativity, explaining gravitation as the marriage of space-time and matter-energy.

Once again, this was greeted with scepticism. The digestion of the fact that we live in a four dimensional continuum was still incomplete when the jolt that this continuum is warped by the presence of matter-energy hit.

In reality, things take their own course. On May 29, 1919, Einstein's general theory of relativity was tested and found correct. A total solar eclipse in Brazil and Africa showed that the path of light from a distant star was bent as it passed by the sun. The sun's vast matter-energy did this deflection. The relativity revolution was at the threshold to overthrow the classical conception of space, time and reality.

Quantum Reality

Einstein's masterpiece was general relativity, which begins to answer such questions as:Whether time has a beginning and an end? What is the end point of the universe? What lies beyond this point? What happens at creation?

By contrast Heisenberg and his colleagues, such as Erwin Schrodinger and Neils Bohr, were probing the opposite questions – What is the smallest object in the universe? How far can matter be divided into smaller pieces? Their questioning created quantum mechanics – the most weird manifestation of reality to us.

We have to imagine the effects of Einstein's theories. Even after a hundred years, even professional physicists do not feel relativity in their bones. Our senses are under no evolutionary pressure to develop a relativistic acumen. We have to employ our intellects diligently to fill in the gaps left by our senses.

The weirdness of relativity arises because our personal experience of space and time differs from the experience of others. It is a weirdness born of comparison. We are forced to concede that our view of reality is but one among many. Quantum mechanics is different. Its weirdness is evident without comparison. It is harder to train our mind to have a quantum mechanical intuition, because it shatters our own personal, individual conception of reality.

Special and general relativity pointed out important subtleties of the clockwork metaphor that there is no single preferred moment that constitutes now. Newton and Einstein agree, in principle, concerning the use of the laws of physics to predict everything about the universe arbitrarily far into the future or past, given the present position and velocity of every particle at this instant.

Quantum mechanics breaks with this tradition. We can't even know the exact location and exact velocity of even a single particle. It presents a frontal assault on our basic beliefs as to what constitutes reality.

Quantum mechanics shows that the best we can ever do is to predict the probability that an experiment (to find the position or the velocity of a particle) will turn out this way or that. It further manifested that a single electron moving separately exhibits the characteristics of waves. These are called probability waves. No one has ever directly seen a probability wave, and no one ever will as per conventional quantum mechanics reasoning. Mathematical equations are used to figure out what the probability wave should look like in a given situation. Moreover, there is no universally agreed upon way to envision what quantum mechanical probability waves actually are. It is still debated, for example, whether the probability wave of an electron is the electron itself, or is associated with it, or is a mathematical device (artifact) to describe the electron's motion, or is the embodiment of what we can know about the electron.

It must be noted that Nature has a built-in limit on the precision with which such complementary features can be determined (e.g., the position and velocity of an electron). And further, the uncertainty principle applies to everything, and not only to the electron. Also, according to quantum mechanics, every probability wave extends throughout all of space, throughout the entire universe.

"In many ways, these two theories appear to be opposites. General relativity concerns the cosmic motions of galaxies and the universe, while quantum mechanics probes the subatomic world. Relativity is primarily a theory of force-fields that continuously fill up the space. (The force field of gravity, for example, can be compared to gossamerlike tendrils that extend to the outer reaches of space.) Quantum mechanics, by contrast, is primarily a theory of atomic matter, which travels much slower than the speed of light. In the world of quantum mechanics, a force field only appears to fill up all space smoothly and continuously. If we could examine it closely, we would find that it actually is quantized into discrete units. Light, for example, consists of tiny packets of energy called quanta or photons."[13]

Neither theory by itself provides a satisfactory description of nature. Efforts to merge the two theories have occupied scientists for the past half century. A possible synthesis of both theories is now in view in the form of the superstring theory.

Cosmological Reality

From our rapid march through the history of physics, it might seem that physics has amply justified its role of explaining the elements of reality we actually experience. However, nature has not unfolded all its mysteries. The greatest mystery is yet unresolved, - the Arrow of Time, as the great physicist Sir Arthur Eddington calls it. Why don't eggs unbreak? Why do things happen in one direction and not in the other?

Known and accepted laws of physics treat direction in time forward and backward without distinction. Nothing in the equations of fundamental physics shows any sign of treating one direction of time differently from the other. Special physical conditions at the universe's inception (a highly ordered environment at or just after the Big-Bang) may have imprinted a direction on time. Thus eggs break and do not unbreak – because of conditions at the birth of the universe some 13.82 billion years ago.

The puzzle of the search is now shifted to the realm of cosmology, the study of the origin and evolution of the entire cosmos vis-a-vis an explanation for the arrow of time.

After the publication of Einstein's theory of general relativity, both he and others applied it to the universe as a whole. Within a few decades, their research led to the tentative framework for what is now called the Big-Bang theory. The theory was successful, yet had significant shortcomings, like: (i)Explaining the overall shape of space revealed by astronomical observations. (ii) The uniformity of the microwave radiation temperature.

In the 1970s and 1980s these issues inspired the inflationary cosmology, which modifies the Big-Bang theory by adding an extremely brief burst of astoundingly rapid expansion during the universe's earliest moments.

The use of quantum mechanics is necessary to explain accurately the behaviour of small objects, viz., our universe when it was a mere fraction of a second old. When equations of general relativity commingle with those of quantum mechanics, they break down entirely, preventing all further investigations.

"It's not an overstatement to describe this situation as a theoretician's nightmare: the absence of mathematical tools with which to analyze a vital realm that lies beyond experimental accessibility. And since space and time are so thoroughly entwined with this particular inaccessible realm – the origin of the universe – understanding space and time fully requires us to find equations that can cope with the extreme conditions of huge density, energy and temperature characteristic of the universe's earliest moments. This is an absolutely essential goal, and one that many physicists believe requires developing a so-called unified theory."[14]

The Unified Reality

A harmonious merger of the large and the small is leading to the superstring theory (required for explaining the end of collapsing stars and the origin of the universe.)Every particle is supposed to be a string composed of a tiny filament of energy, some 100 billion billion times smaller than a single atomic nucleus. The strings vibrate in different patterns producing different particle properties. The superstring theory's proposed fusion of general relativity and quantum mechanics is mathematically sensible in 10 dimensions of space and one dimension of time (for M theory).

However, we are not able to see these extra dimensions. Thus, we have had glimpses of a meager slice of reality. Who knows, even those features of the cosmos that we have thought to be readily accessible to human senses need not be so!

Past and Future Reality

This is our dream to break free from the spatio-temporal chains with which we have been shackled for millennia. We hope that the M theory as it develops will deepen our cosmological insights, will give a grasp of the true nature of space and time – the silent, ever present markers delineating the outermost boundaries of human experience.

The Lamppost in the Way

The pathway to reality is strewn with lampposts, to indicate the road covered so far. Sufi mystics call them wine shops where the weary pilgrim is cheered and refreshed by a draught of wine of divine love. We can conclude from the history of science that the scientist arrives at certain truths, destinations. He may or may not obtain recognition for it.

We are listing some critical destinations reached in the scientific quest by Indian sages from the Vedic period. The point we wish to stress is that in the Pathway to Reality such landmarks exist, which are reached by humankind from any age/culture/period. These landmarks exist as ideals in Plato's third world.

Creation of Matter

According to the Samkhya theory, the visible manifested universe evolved out of an invisible, unmanifested, formless, undifferentiated, infinite, indestructible primordial growth called *prakriti*, which is eternal without a beginning or an end. Prakriti is made up of three basic real entities or gunas. The gunas are again indeterminate and incapable of independent existence, but they do possess certain characteristics/ properties. These are:

(i) **Tamas** – matter with the property of inertia.

(ii) **Rajas** – energy to do work.

(iii) **Satvik** – essence with the property to manifest something to the senses.

All these gunas exist in uniform diffusion and equilibrium in prakriti. The tendency of the energy to do work is counteracted by the inertia of the matter, and so the unmanifested nature of prakriti is maintained.

Professor J. R. Oppenheimer in his Reith lectures has said, "The answer to the question, where do the particles come from would be that they come out of the universal primordial matrix of quiescent energy."[15]

Many of today's physicists strongly believe that there is yet one more field. This has never been experimentally detected. But it has played a pivotal role over the last couple of decades both in modern cosmological thought and in elementary particle physics. It is called Higg's field and is responsible for many properties of the particles that make up the entire visible cosmos.

Purusha through his transcendental effect causes a disturbance in this state of equilibrium of the gunas; the energy gets disturbed first and begins to vibrate – the process of creation is set into motion.

Modern day physics' answer to the ancient Greek question about the makeup of matter is the electron, its two heavier cousins, six kinds of quarks, and three kinds of neutrinos. However, according to the string theory, there is only one fundamental ingredient, the string, giving rise to different particles according to the different vibrational patterns that a string can execute.

And where do the vibrations come from? "The quantum uncertainty ensures that the micro world is a turbulent and jittery realm. The electromagnetic field, the strong and weak nuclear force-field and the gravitational field all are subject to frenzied quantum jitters on microscopic scales. In fact, these field jitters exist even in space that you would normally think of as empty, space that would deem to contain no matters and no fields."[16](Higgs field is present in empty space)

This example is to show how metaphysics provides a hypothesis to work on and carry out laboratory experiments. Indian philosophers did not find it necessary to test the hypothesis in the laboratory. But the quest of Reality leads to parallel metaphysical thoughts.

Astronomy

The Rgveda hymns 1.164.11 and 1.164.48 mention a year to have twelve months, 360 days and divided into four quarters of 90 days each. This observation being rough, it must have been noticed that seasons do not coincide with the months. Vedic Aryans solved this problem by adding a full complete month of 30 days to a period of 5 years of 360 days each, making an average of 366 days in a year. This provided better correlation of the months with the seasons.

Constants of Nature

(i)   Speed of Light

A medieval text by Sayana (1315-1387 AD), prime minister in the court of Emperor Buleka—I and his successors of the Vijaynagar Empire, and a Vedic scholar, commenting on the fourth verse of the hymn I-50 of the Rgveda on the sun, says

tatha ca smarayate

yajananam sahasre dve dve sate dve ca yojane

elcena nimisardhena kramamana[17]

(Thus it is remembered; O Sun, you who traverse 2202 yojanas in a half nimesa.) The same statement occurs in the commentary on the Taittiriya Brahmana by Bhaskara in the 10th century. Since a nimesa is 16/75 seconds, and a Yojana is 9 miles, this comes very close to the figure of 186000 miles/second, and obviously does not refer to the speed of the sun but refers to the speed of its rays. However, the credit of discovering the speed of light goes to Roemer in 1675.[18]

Rain Water Measurement

Varahamihira has presented the theory of rain water measurement in Drona and Adhaka systems in 5th century A.D.

Coins and Metallurgy

Coins were prevalent in India in the Vedic Age. Cunningham has suggested coinage around 1000 BC.[19]

The Yajurvedic period shows advancement in metallurgy. In Rudracarakoprasna mention is made of gold, silver, lead, tin, steel, iron and alloys. Gold and iron were known to Rgvedic people.

Mathematics

Yajurveda (xvii 24,25) gives arithmetic progression of odd numbers starting from 1 and ending in 33, with a common difference of 2. Yajurveda also gives even numbers progression. Higher numbers up to 10^{140} were known.[20] Square roots, cube roots were known. In Pingala's *Chandah–sutra* (200B), a symbol for Zero is mentioned. It says:

(Place) two when halved

when unity is subtracted then

(place) zero.[21]

A small list of mathematical theorems discovered by Indians is given below.

Newton Sterling Interpolation

Newton Gauss backward Interpolation

Taylor Series

Lhuiler formula

Tycho Brahe reductions.

Mysticism – Its Nature and Meaning

"There is hardly any soil, be it ever so barren, where Mysticism will not strike root; hardly any creed, however formal, round which it will not twine itself. It is, indeed, the eternal cry of the human soul for rest; the insatiable longing of being wherein infinite ideals are fettered and cramped by a miserable actuality; and so long as man is less than an angel and more than a beast, this cry will not for a moment fail to make itself heard. Wonderfully uniform, too, whether it comes from the Brahmin sage, the Persian poet, or the Christian quietist, it is in essence an enunciation more or less clear, more or less eloquent of the aspiration of the soul to cease altogether from self and to be at one with God."[22]

Prof. Ranade, one of the greatest mystical philosophers of the 20th century, defines mysticism as "that attitude of mind, which involves a direct, immediate, firsthand intuitive apprehension of God."[23] Mysticism is the most vital element in all true religions. It has its doctrines, but it is not a philosophical system. It is the yearning of the human soul, an attitude of the mind, not falling in the ken of reason, seeking to know God firsthand. It believes that God is not an object but has to be experienced. God's immediateness is felt whereupon the self and the world are forgotten. It is the presence of the highest and fullest truth in which the mystic gets intoxicated. Its main characteristic is that the soul possesses a faculty of which Saint Augustine speaks, which can perceive, crossing the barriers of matter, Light Unchangeable.

This faculty is intuition. Intuition, though a gift to every individual, in the spiritual seeker when aroused by the practice of a 'supersensual drill,'[23] as Underhill calls it, is capable of receiving direct revelation and knowledge of God as if through the senses, but not through the senses.

Secondly, to know Reality, the self has to be real. The 'If and only if' condition applies in this case. Mysticism, irrespective of space and time, has assumed that God Himself is the ground of the soul. Every soul is a divine spark of the Eternal Flame.

The process of unification with the Infinite is a *progressus ad infinitum* – an eternal march towards perfection. However, the path is like an ascending spiral, with alternate sunshine and shade.

Universal Nature of Mysticism

Underhill states, "It is hardly an extravagance to say, that those writings which are the outcome of true and firsthand mystical experience may be known by the power of imparting to the reader one's sense of exalted and extended life." "All mystics," says Saint Martin, "speak the same language, for they come from the same country."[24]

Nowhere do we observe the essential solidarity of humankind more clearly than in the history of mysticism because the mystic act prescribed by any tradition consists in the gradual development of an extraordinary faculty of concentration, a power of spiritual attention.

The condition of all valid seeing and hearing, upon every plane of consciousness, lies not in the sharpening of the senses, but in a peculiar attitude of the whole personality; in a self-forgetting attentiveness, a profound concentration, a self-merging which brings about a real communion between the seer and the seen – in a word in contemplation. How much more acute this contemplation has to be when the seen is the Divine!

We will be examining the 'country' from where mystics come, as we proceed further. But at this stage we will put forth the findings of a qualitative study undertaken as regards to intuitive experiences among advanced practitioners of spiritual disciplines by Mr. Peter Conil Battis. The details are taken from his thesis submitted to Boston University in 1981.[25]

Mr. Battis selected a number of willing spiritual practitioners with extensive experience in the Christian, Buddhist and Hindu contemplative traditions. About intuition Battis says: "Intuition is a useful name for a human faculty,... which takes many different forms. It is also typical that the knower cannot verbally express, or does not know, how it is that he knows."[26]

This definition is one which is inclusive of a variety of phenomena including some forms of creative thought, sudden insights, some acts of unconscious inference from minimal cues, a number of phenomena usually classified as extrasensory perception, and mystical insights experienced in the superconscious state. It ranges in intensity from the vague hunch which proves to be correct to an experience of total certainty: from states of reduced awareness (dreaming, hypnosis), to states of heightened awareness (religious and peak experiences). It is distinguished from imagination by virtue of the fact that it yields information which is true, verifiable by one or another form of investigation. (This would include knowledge in mystical states which can be verified by others who pursue the same discipline.).

The main observations/conclusions arrived at after interviewing the subjects are given below:

The first question was whether the appearance of intuition was under volitional control or entirely spontaneous. The unanimous answer was that its appearance was spontaneous – given by God according to the necessity of the occasion. Further, it was observed that intuition is more likely to occur in response to a genuine need, but in highly developed subjects it can operate in all kinds of circumstances. Surroundings are helpful for its arousal. However, it is internal calmness which matters rather than external conditions. Further, the particular physical state of the subject was not seen as an important factor. What mattered was one's overall training and developed sensitivity. Practice of stillness (attention control) and detachment (beyond emotions) are important factors in both the development and arousal of intuition. With practice the reliability of the experience increases since discriminative powers increase. By proper cultivation, intuition can be present at all levels and in all states of consciousness.

The famous Marathi Saint Jnanadeva, as well as St. Augustine's mother, had God's vision in all the states of consciousness, namely, waking, dreaming, sleep or half-sleep.[27]

It was asked whether intuitive knowledge came in words or without words, sequential or simultaneous, in a sudden flash or gradually. Intuition is usually wordless, sudden and simultaneous. It is non-discursive, an experience of knowing all at once. There are many different levels.

However, one has to remember that it is the divine guiding hand which leads the mystics to their destination through visions, auditions and similar experiences.

The subjects were asked whether intuition brings a sense of certainty. The unanimous answer was that it was unerring, unfailing. There was definitely a sense of certainty and immediacy about it.

To the question whether reason was used to make further sense of the insight, all respondents agreed that intuitions were frequently 'filled out' by means of an intellectual process. The two faculties are intertwined especially in practical matters. Meditation becomes an ongoing experiential laboratory for the teachings one receives from teachers and books, and on that one thinks further about experiences from meditation. Intuition does not contradict reason and is above intellect.

The subjects viewed intuition as a universal and natural capacity, the perceptive faculty of the soul. The intuitive experience happens because the ego's defenses are down for a moment. Intuition at work is the urge toward moral action, whether conscious or unconscious. It is concerned with the needs of the whole, the good of all beings. It is a subtle faculty which in its present form is an omniscient self-awareness. But of course, when Grace is added, there is not only the natural state but the supernatural state as well.

Finally, Mr. Battis concludes: Just as there are aspects of reality which can only be detected through the use of complex instruments, there are dimensions which can only be detected by a transformation of consciousness. The basic aspect of intuition is basic knowing according to Deikman, and I find it in some way a religious sense, a sense of awe or reverence. The essence of the various spiritual traditions seems to me to be much the same, founded upon intuitive experience. The spiritual experience is to a large degree universal in nature, the various paths having a common goal.

Genesis, Varieties and Necessity of Religious Experience

Louis Dupre says:"The concept of the soul as an image of God determines the development of Christian mysticism as much as the notion of the Atman determines the Vedic vision."[28]

Weigel (1533-1588) considered the human being as a microcosm, bestowed with a soul having three faculties for obtaining knowledge. The faculties are sense, reason and understanding. The senses bring in the knowledge of the objective world, science and art fall under the jurisdiction of the reason, while understanding, which he calls the spark, sees the invisible and the divine. The eye of the understanding perceives the divine. The divine image lies in the centre of the soul. When we obtain knowledge of the objective world, it is without the object's participation and cooperation. Similarly, the divine comes in when we are absolutely passive, the mind's activity stilled as if dead. Yet, this knowledge is from within. His spirit and word are within us. With this eye He sees Himself. It is not that we know him. It is God in us who knows Himself. We are only an instrument.

This is the crux of mysticism, and William Law describes it very succinctly in these words: "If Christ was to raise a new life like His own in every man, then every man must have had originally in the inmost spirit of his life a seed of Christ, or Christ as a seed of heaven, lying there in a state of insensibility, out of which it could not arise but by the mediatorial power of Christ."[29]

St. John of the Cross says:

If God is to move the soul and to raise it from the extreme height of His loftiness, in Divine union with Him, He must do it with order and sweetness and according to the nature of the soul itself. Then since the order whereby the soul acquires knowledge is through forms and images of created things, and the natural way wherein it acquires this knowledge and wisdom is through the senses, it follows that, if God is to raise up the soul to supreme knowledge, and to do so with sweetness, He must begin to work from the lowest and extreme end of the senses of the soul, in order that He may gradually lead it, according to its own nature, to the other extreme of His spiritual wisdom, which belongs not to sense.[30]

We will now cite a few parallel thoughts from mysticism in the Indian tradition.

(i)   **Mystical phenomena in which the supernatural knowledge is obtained where God is both the subject and the object at the same time.**

This aspect is discussed by King Janaka with the sage Yajnavalkya in the Brihadaranyakopanishad and commented upon by Prof. R. D. Ranade. King Janaka asked Yajnavalkya what the light of man was. Yajnavalkya first said that the light of man was the sun. It is on account of the sun that man is able to see and move about, go forth for work and return. "When the sun has set, O Yajnavalkya," asked King Janaka, "what is the light of man?" Yajnavalkya said that then the moon was the light of man. For, having the moon for light, man could see and move about, and do his work and return. "When both the sun and the moon have set," asked King Janaka, "what is the light of man?" "Fire indeed," said Yajnavalkya, "is man's light. For, having fire for his light, man can see and move about, do his work and return." "When the sun has set, when the moon has set, and when the fire is extinguished, what is the light of man?" asked Janaka. "Now verily," says Yajnavalkya, "you are pressing me to the deepest question. When the sun has set, when the moon has set, and when the fire is extinguished, the self alone is his light." Yajnavalkya is here clearly positing what Aristotle called "theoria", the act of pure self-contemplation in which the self is most mysteriously both the subject and the object of knowledge.

Yajnavalkya says that it is possible for the knower to know himself. In fact self-knowledge or self-consciousness is the ultimate category of existence. The Self can become an object of knowledge to himself. We see here how boldly Yajnavalkya regards both introspection and self-consciousness as the varieties of experience. Introspection is a psychological process corresponding to self-consciousness as a metaphysical reality. Self-consciousness is possible only through the process of introspection. The self is endowed with the supreme power of dichotomising himself/herself. The empirical conditions of knowledge are inapplicable to the self. The self can divide himself/herself into the knower and the known. "The answer of Yajnavalkya is that self-consciousness is possible, and is not only possible, but alone real."[31]

(ii) Christ lying in our spirit as a seed of heaven in a state of insensibility.

This process amounts to the ignition of an inner spark in our soul, and separating it from the organic bonds of the body. The great masters of Nimbargi Sampradaya used to say that while initiating a person into spiritual life, they used to separate his/her soul from its organic bondage. Prof. Ranade states that the principal function of a spiritual master is to separate spirit from matter just as a swan separates water from milk. Kabir in one of his Dohas[32] describes this act:

Kshira rupa Sat nama hai,
Neera rupa bevahar,
Hans rupa koi sadh hai,
tat ka chhananhar

The meaning of the Doha is that a master like the swan separates the mundane from the spiritual, like water from milk. Now milk here is Divine Name in its aspect of Ultimate Reality.

Now that the inner spark has been ignited, the novice commences introversion, the characteristic art of a mystic for achieving movements of his/her consciousness to higher levels – towards the final goal of apprehending the Absolute which is the innate capacity of the spark of the soul. For this the aspirant is called to undertake an education. This education consists largely in a humble willingness to submit to the discipline and to profit by the lessons of the past. Tradition runs side by side with experience. Each new and eager soul rushing towards the only end of Love passes on its way the landmarks left by others upon the pathway to Reality.

In its early stages the practice of introversion is voluntary, difficult and deliberate. This point needs a little more elaboration, and we turn to the *Cloud of Unknowing*, a work of the fourteenth century. "Even though it may be quite worthwhile to think of certain conditions and deeds of some special creatures, nevertheless in this work it is of very little help, or none at all. And to the extent that anything is in your mind other than God, you are that much further from God."[33]

The 'cloud' further advises to pierce the darkness above us with determination and love. This cloud of unknowing must be pierced with a dart of longing love. For this purpose he asks to take but one sharp word of single syllable – such as the word GOD or LOVE, and clasp the word in our bosom. "This word shall be your shield and your spear whether you ride in peace or in war. With this word you shall strike down thoughts of every kind and drive them beneath the cloud of forgetting. After that, if any thought should press upon you to ask you what you are seeking, answer him with this word only and with no other words."[34]

A psychological explanation for the Cloud's recommendation is called for and best available in Krause's words: "From finite reason as finite we might possibly explain the thought of itself, but not the thought of something that is outside finite reasonable beings, far less the absolute idea, in its contents infinite, of God. To become aware of God in knowledge we require certainly to make a freer use of our finite power of thought, but the thought of God itself is primarily and essentially an eternal operation of the eternal revelation of God to the finite mind." But though we are made in the image of God, our likeness to Him only exists potentially. "The Divine spark already shines within us, but it has to be searched for in the innermost depths of our personality, and its light diffused over our whole being."[35]

In the Indian tradition the spiritual master imparts a divine name to his disciple on which he has to meditate. The divine name so imparted is God-in-posse and facilitates perceiving God-in-esse, or as Underhill puts it, "Contemplation is the way in which (the soul) makes those discoveries, perceives the supra-sensible over against itself."[36] These discoveries are in the form of vision, voice, touch and so on, made by the mystical consciousness and presented to the surface mind. According to Scaramelli, "As the body has its exterior senses, with which it perceives the visible and delectable things of this life, and makes experience of them, so the spirit with its faculties of understanding (which is verily intuition) and will, has five interior acts corresponding to these senses, which we call seeing, hearing, smelling and delectable things of Almighty God, and makes experience of them."[37] In a similar vein the great Patanjali of Indian mysticism says: "*Tatah pratibha-sravana-vedanada-rasa-asvada-varta jayante,*" which means "Then the intuition of the yogi gets the intuitive experience of (supersensuous) sound, touch, sight, flavour and fragrance." We will validate Scaramelli's as well as Patanjali's statement with the experiences of Christian and Indian mystics.

Auditory/Phonic Experience

We turn to St. John of the Cross. It happens in the development of the inner life that we experience "substantial words," that is, words which do not come from our own activity, but are completely formed in us all of a sudden and are efficacious by themselves. "Substantial words produce vivid and substantial effects upon the soul…. Only such a word is substantial as impresses substantially on the soul that which it signifies. It is as if Our Lord were to say formally to the soul: 'Be thou good', it would then substantially be good." This is called a "word," because it is, as it were, heard; it implies consciousness. It is qualified as "substantial" because it affects the interior substance of man, his central reality, which it transforms for the better. The two aspects of "inner transformation" and of "consciousness" are joined here.[38] "God draws us," says Tauler, "by this voice in the soul, when an eternal truth mysteriously suggests itself, as happens not infrequently in morning sleep."[39]

This can also come in the form of music: Prof. Ranade, while citing the example of Richard Rolle (13th century), says: "It was Rolle who among all the mystics was peculiarly characterized by his experience of God as music and he tells us how the burning Love for God is later on changed into Divine song."[40]

Photic (Light) Experience

River of Light: Beatrice's experience as narrated by Dante:

And light I saw in fashion of a river
Fervid with its effulgence' twixt two banks
Depicted with an admirable spring.
Out of this river issued living sparks
And on all sides sank down into the flowers
Like unto rubies that are set in gold
And then, as if inebriate with the odors

They plunged again into the wondrous torrent
And as one entered issued forth another.[41]

Mechtild of Magdoburg considered Deity as a "flowing light." Blessed Angela of Foligno apprehended the Divine Beauty as "shining from within and surpassing the splendor of the sun."

Morphic Experience (experience of form)

Blessed Angela of Foligno's vision of two eyes shining in the Host, then again her vision of Christ: "I saw Him most plainly with the eyes of the mind," she says, "first living, suffering, bleeding, crucified; and then dead upon the cross." She continues further, "Another time I beheld the child Christ .... He appeared beautiful and full of majesty. He seemed as a child of twelve years of age."[42] St. Catherine of Siena always saw a ring upon her finger. It is an instance of true corporeal vision. St. Teresa says, "On one occasion when I was holding in my hand the cross of my rosary, He took it from me in His own hand. He returned it, but it was then four large stones incomparably more precious than diamonds. He said to me that for the future that cross would so appear to me always, and so it did. I never saw the wood of which it was made, but only the precious stones. They were seen, however, by no one else."[43]

Tactile Experience

Saint John of the Cross states, "When God Himself visits it (the soul)... it is in total darkness and in concealment from the enemy that the soul receives these spiritual favours of God. The reason for this is that, as his Majesty dwells substantially in the soul, where neither angel nor devil can attain to an understanding of that which comes to pass, they cannot know the intimate and secret communications which take place there between the soul and God. These communications, since the Lord Himself works them, are wholly divine and sovereign, for they are all substantial touches of divine union between the soul and God."[44]

Flavour Experience

St. Teresa in the Interior Castle calls her prayer of quiet, which is a form of supernatural contemplation as insisted by Augustine Baker, as the tasting of God.[45] Jacopone do Todi states that all the perceptions of the mind have gone forth "to gaze ... and contemplate that Beauty which has no likeness.... It feels that which it felt not, sees that which it knew not, possesses that which it believed not, tastes, though it savors not ... it has received in abundance that Imageless God."[46]

Parallels in Indian Mysticism

We will cite examples from the writing of Jnaneswara, the greatest mystic of Maharashtra of the 13th century. He is compared to great philosophic-mystical luminaries of the West like Plotinus, Augustine and Eckhart, as pointed out by Prof. Ranade.[47]

Colour Experience

Jnaneswara tells us, "The abode of God is the thousand petal cavity in the brain, where is the source of spiritual bliss. One sees the red, the white, the blue and the yellow colours - one sees the black, the blue and the tawny colours. The dark-complexioned husband is the source of bliss."

Form Experience

Jnaneswara says, "Beautiful indeed is that pearl which sheds light through all its different eight sides .... What work indeed has to be accomplished who has not investigated the nature of circle ? The circle is indeed a void. When the void and the non-void are both lost, there is the form of self. Now my eye tries to penetrate my eye. The eye sees the eye in the eye."

Light Experience

Jnaneswara says, "The dawn breaks and the light of the sun spreads forth ... There is moonlight without the moon ... the sun shines by night the moon by day ... and it is wonderful that that light is neither hot nor cold ... and beyond indeed that light of God who remains transcendent."

Sound Experience

The unstruck sound fills the whole universe, the mystic does not know whence it comes and whither it goes.

Experience of Bliss

"As I went to see God, my intellect stood motionless, and as I saw Him, I became Himself.... As a dumb man cannot express the sweetness of nectar, so also I cannot express my internal bliss."

Words and Music Experience

The great spiritual masters of Nimbargi Sampradaya heard various divine names from all religions which they imparted to their disciples from various religions while initiating the latter into spiritual life. Mirabai used to hear 36 Ragas mystically.

Post-ecstatic Monologue

"Him who eats all food, I eat as food," utters a sage of Taitariya Upanishad.[48] In a similar tone Ruysbroeck cries, "To eat and be eaten! This is union!"[49]

We have seen that Jnaneswara speaks about the circle. Almost all the Indian mystics speak about circle or ring. Kabir says, "I have found the great God behind the tiniest thing like sesamum."[50] Boehme says, "If thou conceivest a small minute circle, as small as a grain of mustard seed, yet the heart of God is wholly and perfectly therein."[51] Once Suso's spiritual daughter asks him to give her a figure or image of the self-evolution of the Trinity, and he gives her the figure of concentric circles, such as appear when we throw a stone into a pond.[52] Suso further continues to his daughter, "It is said by a learned doctor that God, in regard to his God-head, is like a very wide ring, whose centre is everywhere and circumference nowhere.... From out the great ring... there flow forth...little rings, which may be taken to signify high nobility of rational creatures."[53]

One is here reminded about Leibnitz's monads. Monads are all independent and have no direct relationship with one another. All monads are bound to the central monad Monas Monadum. Relationship with other monads is through the central monad which is indirect through God. God thus becomes the Vinculum Substantiae. The disciple of Allamprabu, a great Kannada mystic, says in one of his poems about the vision of a spiritual seed (monad) which he compares to the seed of a Babul or Sandal tree. The seeds are with a circle within a circle and sweet and fragrant.[54] Prof. Ranade, while commenting on the poem says: "Spiritual experience very often may be said to begin with a vision of spiritual seed. Experience of flavour and taste accompanies with the vision. Further the conjecture whether there may not be an infinity of circles round about a circle is not ruled out. But for our small intellects and small experiences one circle or another is enough, though ultimately it is infinite."[55]

So much for the circles or rings. We will now see that 'Necessity' is a criterion of mystical experience. Mystical experience is a priori cognition, "This feeling of reality, the feeling of a 'numinous' object, objectively given, must be posited as a primary immediate datum of consciousness."[56] Such cognitions according to Kant are clear and certain for themselves, independently of experience, i.e., they are not borrowed from experience as in a posterior or empirical experience, and at the same time have the character of inner necessity.[57] Prof. Ranade tells us that if we follow a definite path, it will lead to necessary consequences; therefore if we follow spiritual path its necessary effect, namely spiritual experience, will be a logical consequence.

Necessity can be seen from a different angle. Mysticism involves a movement of consciousness towards higher levels, movement of the whole person to higher levels of vitality, movement to high levels of liberty. According to Aristotle, each motion therefore presupposes two things: a moving element and a moved. If a moving element moves itself, these two factors must be divided between different elements in it, such as body and soul in a human being. The moving element can only be the actual- the form, the moved only the potential - matter. The former operates on the latter in that it impels it to move towards a definite form or reality, for matter has from its very nature (in so far as every predisposition involves a demand for its activity) a desire for the form as something good and divine ... It moves because it is desired.

Some Paradoxical Statements of Mystics and Their Explanation

Unity of Apperception

The visionary Saint Martin's statement, "I heard flowers that sounded and saw notes that shone," may seem strange and apparently insane. We have similar expressions from Indian Mystics. For instance, "Eyes have become thirsty (for the vision of God) and speech has become fragrant." Similarly, there are reports of "luminous sound and sonorous light."

William James once suggested a consideration of the changes which would be worked in our ordinary world if the various branches of our receiving instruments exchanged duties, if, for instance, we heard all colours and saw all sounds. It is a well known fact that each sense is capable of discriminating the specific differences of the objects proper to it. The sight discriminates between white and red, taste between sweet and bitter, and so on. For this discrimination of objects a single faculty is necessary. William James' suggestion was as a useful exercise for young idealists.

This experience of a sensation coming from outside is recorded in the brain as two sensory modalities simultaneously. The most common experience seems to be seeing colours when hearing sounds. This phenomenon is a most obscure medical condition, and is called synesthesia, affecting only one in a million people. Synesthesia means feeling together. When synesthetics 'see sound' they do in fact use areas of the cortex dedicated to higher visual functions. This cross modality lasts during the lifetime of the individual so that a given sound or word always leads to the perception of the same colours.[58]

So much then about the empirical realm. What about the spiritual realm? The experience of mystics? We turn to Prof. Ranade's explanation. He states, "From the point of view of ordinary psychology, it would be a truism to say that he who is able to see is unable to speak, he who is able to say is unable to see. Each organ is independent in its sphere. Each is unique and each is opaque to the other. From the point of view of (spiritual) experiences (which are super-sensuous), however, all these functions are related to the unity of apperception. It is not the eye that sees, says the Upanishad, but the Self. It is not the ear that hears, but the Self. There is an inter-communicativeness in super-sensuous functions, which is denied in the sensuous sphere (normally). This exchange takes place on account of the unity of apperception, which lies at the back of all super-sensuous functions, or, if we prefer to use a physiological expression, the "apperception masse (William James) which may be regarded as responsible for vicarious functions in the super-sensuous sphere."[59] It was for this reason that mystics see singing flowers and shining notes, their eyes become thirsty and their speech emits fragrance.

Contradictory Statements about God

We sometimes meet with contradictory qualities attributed to the Divine as,

> "Thou comest not, thou goest not,
> Thou wert not, wilt not be."[60]

Again, the Upanishads say, "soul is smaller than a grain of mustard and is greater than the sky, greater than all these worlds." One can give two plausible explanations. (1)The mystic may experience the Divine either in tiny form or as the Infinite Cosmic Vision, which Arjuna saw as depicted in Bhagvadgita, Chap. 11. (2) No parameters of the phenomenal world like length, depth, etc., are applicable in the spiritual realm.

Dark Night of the Soul

When the seeker begins his/her spiritual journey, he/she finds him/herself composed of a perishable body and a soul with an everlasting spirit. He/she gives up the bodily cravings and subjugates them to the ultimate goal of uniting with the Eternal Flame. Now, suppose the seeker has trodden on this path for a long time and still the Eternal Flame, the supreme Spirit, has always eluded the seeker's grasp, he/she starts realizing utter helplessness. The seeker develops total contempt for the ever-dancing sensual images. Practically, in this pursuit the self loses itself, of which Saint Paul speaks, "I live, but not I," and of which Christ has said "Blessed are the poor in spirit."

The loss of the self is not a simple event. "During the time in which the illuminated consciousness is fully established, the self, as a rule, is perfectly content, believing that in its vision of Eternity, its intense and loving consciousness of God, it has reached the goal of its quest. Sooner or later, however, psychological fatigue sets in, the state of illumination begins to break up, the complementary negative consciousness appears itself as an overwhelming sense of darkness and deprivation. This sense is so deep and strong that it inhibits all consciousness of the transcendent, and plunges the self into the state of negation and misery which is called the Dark Night (of the Soul), or mystic death."[61]

In this state the power of contemplation seems not to exist. What the soul had earned through travails and turmoil of body and mind, of nature and society, seems to have vanished. A vantage point is no more available to sit upon for gazing at the Divine. It feels impotent, forlorn and blank. Even the capacity to introvert disappears. There is complete absence of the Divine.

Here it is where the final price has to be paid. Complete self-surrender is called upon. Through hours and days of anguish and torture the soul has to take its lessons in lovelessness for the sake of love, nothingness for the sake of all, without the hope of finding to learn to lose, without the hope of living to learn to die. "It sees with amazement the most sure foundations of its transcendental life crumble beneath it, dwells in darkness which seems to hold no promise of a dawn."[62] An overwhelming yet impotent conviction of something supremely wrong spreads out in the consciousness. It has the following characteristics: (1) For those mystics for whom the absolute took the form of a sense of divine companionship and for whom the objective idea of 'God' had become the central fact of life, it seems that God, having shown Himself, has withdrawn never to appear again. (2) Mystics for whom "Moral Perfection" was utmost for uniting with the Divine, now being overwhelmed by the Divine perfection and purity, feel the least atoms of their imperfections as though they were enormous sins, because of the infinite distance there is between the purity of God and the creature. (3) A sort of "aridity" sets in, perhaps due to emotional fatigue, and the very desire for and interest in God grows cold. (4) Emotional stagnation has its counterparts in the stagnation of the will and intelligence. As regards the will, there is a sort of moral dereliction, the self cannot control its inclinations and thoughts. The lower impulses and unworthy ideas which have long been imprisoned below the threshold upsurge into the field of consciousness. Teresa says that in that "spirit of bad temper I think I could eat people up!" (5) Some mystics, given to rapid oscillations between pain and pleasure, are seized with an abrupt invasion of a wild and unendurable desire to "see God" which can only, they think, be satisfied by death.

This state of pain is well expressed in the life of Henry Suso, a German mystic born in 1300 AD, whose ardent impressionable and poetic nature reached every aspect of the contemplative experience, every mood and fluctuation of the soul, which he has told firsthand in his singularly ingenuous autobiography. Suso's personalistic mysticism is very comparable with that of Tukaram, the famous mystic of Maharashtra born in 1598 AD.

In one of the extraordinary trials which the Servitor had to bear, a malicious woman accuses him of being the father of her child. The story is long and painful. Poor Suso, living in another place, hears that both the Master general of the whole Order and the Master of German Province have come to the town in which the wicked woman had slandered the pious Servitor. "When the poor man, who was living in another place, heard this news, his heart died within him utterly, and he said to himself: If perchance the Masters give credence to the wicked woman against thee, thou art dead; for they will condemn thee to such a penitential prison that it were better for thee to die. He remained under the weight of this anguish twelve days and nights continuously, and during this time he was in constant expectation of this agonising penance, as soon as they should arrive there."[63] "Alas ! O everlasting God, what is Thy purpose with me? Where is now thy detachment and that evenness of soul in weal and woe which thou hast so often and so joyously counselled to others, whilst thou didst lovingly point out to them how entirely a man should abandon himself to God, and hold fast to nothing ?"[64]

To this he answered with many tears: "Askest thou me where my detachment is? Rather do thou tell me where is God's unfathomable pity for His friends? For in spite of it I am waiting here in utter desolation, like a man condemned to forfeit his life, property and honor. I had fancied that God was kind. I had fancied that he was a good and gracious Lord to all who ventured to abandon themselves to Him. Woe is me! God has failed me!"[65]

Tukaram got married in 1613 AD and had two wives. Soon he lost his parents. He suffered a loss in trade. Dire famine set in. One of his wives died for want of food. He lost his son in this famine. Overcome by tremendous grief he gave himself up to spiritual reading. He met his guru in a dream and was initiated in 1619 AD. He had two great enemies who did not lose a single opportunity for making fun of and ill-treating him. His living wife was a Xantippe and often quarreled with him. Her main complaint was that Tukaram did not work to earn a livelihood and maintain his family (five children from the second wife), but only performed Bhajans with his colleagues and friends. He composed many poems. We will see the various difficulties and his passing into the centre of indifference and everlasting 'No' from his poems.

From the everlasting yea, he now began to pass through the centre of indifference. "How long shall I wait," he asks, "I see no sign of God's presence. It seems to me, O God, that Thou and I shall have now to part. How long shall I wait? I do not see the fructification of Thy promises."

Tukaram thought that he was ruined both externally and internally. His family life was a failure, and it seemed that his spiritual life was equally so. He went up and down as if caught in a whirlpool. He was incessantly going up and descending down the mountain of thought.[62]

Tukaram did not stay for a long time in the centre of indifference. He saw no help coming. He began to call in question the omnipotence of God. He thought that even his Fate was more powerful than God. He said, "God's impotence is now proved," He further says, "I feel my life to be a burden. In my opinion God does not exist. My hopes are shattered and I shall now commit suicide."[66]

The Unitive Life

"La forma universal di questo nodo." The mystics have now seen the key of the universe. They have reached their goal of participating in the creative energies of the Divine Nature. They are in union with the Divine. Though they live this unitive life in the world, are never of it. They are on another plane of being, move securely upon levels unrelated to our speech, and hence elude the measuring powers of humanity. We from the valley can only catch a glimpse of the true life of these elect spirits. They are far away, breathing another air; we cannot reach them. Yet it is impossible to overestimate their importance for the race. They are our ambassadors to the Absolute. Miguel de Molinos, a Spanish priest who published in Italian his spiritual guide, a mystical treatise of great interest, calls them spiritual directors. "They vindicate humanity's claims to the possible and permanent attainment of reality."[67]

The unitive life passes through five successive stages and can be compared to an ascension on a Spiritual Ladder. Prof. Ranade has depicted this ascent of a mystic as projected in the Upanishads in his internationally acclaimed work, *A Constructive Survey of Upanishadic Philosophy, Being a Systematic Introduction To Indian Metaphysics.*[68] Alongside we will see these stages as described by Christian mystics.

Stage I

The first stage consists in realizing the Self, in mystically apprehending the Self within us, as though we were distinct from it.

"Atma va are drashtavyaha (Verily the Self should be realized)"[69] The realization comes about when we perceive intuitively our own form as if reflected in a mirror, but without lateral inversion. At this point a person starts repaying the debt. Eckhart indicates this spiritual burden on us in these words, "Our Lord says to every living soul, 'I became a man for you. If you do not become God for me, you do me wrong.'"[70] The first stage is therefore the first step on the right path in sublimating the wrong.

We can see a parallel in Christian mysticism. The incidence appeared in the case of a beginner, and is reported in Suso's autobiography. "Once when the Servitor was preaching at Cologne with great fervor, there sat among his hearers a beginner in the spiritual life, who had been recently converted to God. Now while this beginner was attending diligently to the preacher, he saw with the eyes of his soul, that the preacher's face began to be transfigured with a ravishing brightness, and three times it became like the radiant sun when his splendor is at the highest; and the face, moreover, was so pure, that the beginner saw himself reflected in it. This vision brought him very great consolation in his sufferings, and confirmed him in a holy life."[71]

Stage II

Here the Being which calls itself the 'I' within us, must be identified with the Self hitherto realized. "We must experience that we are really the very Self, and that we are neither the bodily, or the sensuous, or the intellectual, or the emotional vestures; that we are in our essential nature entirely identical with the pure Self."[72]

"Atmanam vijaniyadayamasmiti purushaha (man knows the Self as 'I am it.'"[73] Ruysbrock says: "For what we are, that we intently contemplate, and what we contemplate, that we are".[74]

Stage III

The mystic's consciousness transforms to Divine consciousness. Here comes about the identification of the Atman (Self) with the Brahman (Absolute). No difference is perceived by the mystic between the Self and the Absolute.

"Ayamatma brahma (This Self is Brahman)."[75] Delacroix says, "[The mystic's] states of consciousness free from the Self, lost in a vaster consciousness, may become modes of the Infinite, and states of Divine Consciousness."[76] Starbuck says, "The individual learns to transfer himself from a centre of self-activity into an organ of revelation of universal being."[77]

Stage IV

Here 'I' is identified with the Absolute. Also 'Thou' comes to be identified with the Absolute.

"Aham brahmasmi (I am Brahman.)"[78]

"Tatvamasi (That Thou art)."[79] Eckhart says, "The eye with which I see God is the same as that with which He sees me."[80] Emerson says, "I become a transparent eyeball.... I am nothing. I see all, the currents of the Universal Being circulate through me."[81] Or as Tauler in his sermon for the fifteenth Sunday after Trinity says, "The kingdom is seated in the inmost recesses of the spirit. When, through all manner of exercises, the outward man has been converted into the inward reasonable man, and thus the two, that is to say, the powers of the senses and the powers of the reason, are gathered up into the very centre of the man's being, - the unseen depths of his spirit, wherein lies the image of God, - and thus he flings himself into the Divine Abyss, in which he dwelt eternally before he was created; then when God finds the man thus firmly down and turned towards Him, the Godhead bends and nakedly descends into the depths of the pure waiting soul, and transforms the created soul, drawing it up into the uncreated essence, so that the spirit becomes one with Him. Could such a man behold himself, he would see himself so noble that he would fancy himself God, and see himself a thousand times nobler than he is in himself, and would perceive all the thoughts and purposes, words and works, and have all the knowledge of all men that ever were."[82] Suso and the German Theology use similar language.

Stage V

The ultimate consummation : Now, 'I' is absolute, and 'thou' is also absolute, i.e., subject and object are Absolute, "then it follows that everything we see in this world, Mind and Nature, the Self and the not-Self, equally constitute the Absolute. Whatever falls within the ken of apprehension, equally with whatever we are, goes to make up the fulness of the Absolute." [83] As the *Chhandogya Upanishad* says: "Sarvam khalvidam brahmam "(Verily, all this universe is Brahman.)"[84] The process of deification is thus described by Ruysbroek and by Tauler. The former writes: "All men who are exalted above their creatureliness into a contemplative life are one with this Divine glory – yea, are that glory. And they see and feel and find in themselves, by means of this Divine light, that they are the same simple ground as to their uncreated nature. Thus they arrive at the eternal image after which they were created, and contemplate God and all things without distinction, in a simple beholding, in Divine glory. This is the loftiest and most profitable contemplation to which men attain in this life."[85]

This is perhaps the best place to take note of the mystical treatise of James Hinton entitled *Man and His Dwelling-place*. He says, "Suppose that all human beings felt permanently to each other as they now do occasionally to those they love best. All the pain of the world would be swallowed up in doing good. So far as we can conceive of such a state, it would be one in which there would be no 'individuals' at all, but a universal being in and for another; where being took the form of consciousness, it would be the consciousness, it would be the consciousness of "another" which was also "oneself" – a common consciousness. Such would be the 'atonement of the world.'"[86]

Having reached to such giddy heights to Absolute Monism, is this the end of the mystic's career, or what is in store for him/her further? We will see the answer to this problem in Kabir's words. In one of his Doha's, which is a cryptic couplet containing great meaning, he dwells on this theme. Prof. Ranade has styled this Doha literature, as 'Epigrammatic Mysticism.'

The Doha now under consideration is –

Had had par sab hi gaya, behad gaya na koy, behad ke maidan me rame Kabira soy (Many have gone up to the boundary. No one has ventured beyond the boundary. But Kabir is relishing his stay, in this region.)[87]

Underhill aptly calls this boundary as the sorting house of the spiritual life. Here we part from the "nature mystics," the mystic poets, and all who shared in and were contented with the illuminated vision of reality. Those who go on are the great and strong spirits, who do not seek to **know,** but are driven to be...."[88]

Christian mystics call it 'immense wilderness without limits.' It is a vast solitude where no creature can come, and this solitude is the more delicious, sweet and lovely, the more it is deep, vast and empty. "This abyss of wisdom now lifts up and enlarges the soul, giving it to drink at the very sources of the science of love."[89]

Let us now see Prof. Ranade's commentary on the Doha of Kabir. "The conception of the Apeiron in Anaximander, which stands for the Unitary and Divine Being, marks out Anaximander from a number of other Greek and modern philosophers, who vainly bear the badge of a 'philosophos.' Kabir's conception of Behad is exactly like that of Anaximander. This infinite, and Incomprehensible Beyond in which Kabir lives is exactly the Infinite, the Unitary, and the Divine Being of Anaximander – to Theion."[90]

Conclusion

Religious experience's texture is rich, though it is not available for public scrutiny. Human experience is the ground where science, religion, art, music and literature find their roots, thrive and grow. But one is not able to share other's experience. Knowledge, of whatsoever it be, finds its entry at the level of human experience.

The same assumptions underlie science and religion. These are unprovable and cannot be defended logically. One such assumption is the authenticity of human experience. Since the emergence of the scientific method, science has relied heavily on human experience. Also it is our experience which can decide the existence of God. Yet, there is no proof for the authenticity of our experience. Nevertheless, we are staunch believers in our experiences. After Aquinas had an experience of God's presence, he said that all his intellectual debate in his *Summa Theologica* was just like straw.

While reconciling science and mysticism, John Horgan writes, "Dyson has calculated that consciousness – albeit in the form of clouds of charged particles rather than flesh and blood – might resist entropy and sustain itself forever in an eternally expanding universe through shrewd conservation of energy." Dyson was piqued into making these calculations by Steven Weinberg's comment: "The more the universe seems comprehensible, the more it also seems pointless." Dyson retorted, in effect, that no universe with conscious life is pointless. Other scientists have imagined how consciousness might endure even if the universe eventually stops expanding and collapses into an infinitely dense "Omega Point." I call suppositions such as these "scientific theology," because they are little more than theology – speculation about ultimate ends – clad in flimsy scientific garb. "Scientific theology nonetheless demonstrates that science can imagine futures at least as hopeful and open-ended as those of religion."[91]

Endnotes

[1] R.D. Ranade, A Constructive Survey of Upanishadic Philosophy (Mumbai: Bharatiya Vidya Bhavan, 1968), p.182.

[2] Kitty Ferguson, The Fire in the Equation (London: Templeton Foundation Press, 2004), p.49.

[3] Imre Lakatos and Atan Musgrave, ed.,Criticism and the Growth of Knowledge (Cambridge: Cambridge University Press, 1999 reprint), p.29.

[4] *Ibid.*, p.33.

[5] *Ibid.*, p.57.

[6] *Ibid.*, p.50.

[7] *Ibid.*, p.179/80.

[8] *Ibid.*, p.218.

[9] Roger Penrose, The Road to Reality (London: Jonathan Cape,2004), p.61.

[10] *Ibid.*, p.40.

[11] Brian Greene, The Fabric of the Cosmos (New York: Allen Lane, 2004), p.141.

[12] Michio Kaku and Jennifer Thompson, Beyond Einstein (Oxford, Oxford University Press, 1999), p.26.

[13] *Ibid.*, p.37.

[14] *Ibid.*, p.15.

[15] O. P. Jaggi, The Dawn of Indian Science: The Vedic and Upanishadic Period, Vol.II, p.71.

[16] *Ibid.*, p.330.

[17] Quoted by Max Muller (London: Oxford University Press,1890).

[18] See Annals of the Bhandarkar Oriental Research Institute, 1999, Pune,p.114.

[19] *Ibid.*, p.125.

[20] See Asankhyeya.

[21] *Ibid.*, p.132.

[22] Richard Woods, ed., Understanding Mysticism (New York: Image Books, 1980), p.30.

[23] R. D. Ranade, Mysticism in Maharashtra (Delhi: Motilal Banarasidas), p.1.

[24] Evelyn Underhill, Mysticism (London: University paperbacks, 1960), p.299.

[25] Peter Collin Battis, "Intuitive Experience among Advanced Practitioners of Spiritual Disciplines – A Qualitative Study, 1981 (UMI Dissertation Services, Michigan).

[26] *Ibid.*, p.2.

[27] H. Suso, The life of Blessed Henry Suso (London: Burns, Lambert and Oats, 1865), p.300.

[28] *Ibid.*, p.453.

[29] U. R. Inge, Christian Mysticism (New York: Living Age Books, 1956), p.287.

[30] Woods, *op.cit.*, p.453.

[31] Ranade, 1968, p.200.

[32] R. D. Ranade, Paramartha Sopan (Nimbal: Shri Gurudev Ranade Samadhi Trust, 1997), p.296.

[33] The Cloud of Unknowing, tr. R. Ira Progoff (New York: Delta Books, 1957),p.71.

[34] *Ibid.*, p.77.

[35] Inge, *op.cit.*, p.7.

[36] Underhill, p.299.

[37] Woods, p.464.

[38] George H. Tavard, The Inner Life (New York: Paulist Press, 1976), p.88.

[39] Inge, *op.cit.*, p.180.

[40] Ranade – Mysticism in Maharashtra, p.485.

[41] Dante, The Divine Comedy, tr. H. W. Longfellow (London: George Routledge and Sons Ltd), p.591.

[42] Underhill, *op.cit.*, p.288.

[43] *Ibid.*, p.241.

[44] Understanding Mysticism, p.456

[45] Underhill, *op.cit.*, p.308.

[46] *Ibid.*, p.375.

[47] See Ranade, pp.170-172.

[48] Ranade, Upanishadic Philosophy, p.257.

[49] Underhill, p.425.

[50] R. D. Ranade, Pathway To God in Hindi Literature (Nimbal: Shri Gurudev Ranade Samadhi Trust, 1997), p.278.

[51] Underhill, p.100.

[52] Inge, Christian Mysticism, p.179.

[53] Suso, pp.313 and 314.

[54] R. D. Ranade, Pathway to God in Kannad Literature (Mumbai: Bharatiya Vidya Bhavan, 1960), p.218.

[55] See Idem.

[56] Rudolf Otto, The Idea of Holy (Oxford: Oxford University Press, 2nd edition, 1952), p.81.

[57] Immanual Kant, Critique of Pure Reason (Cambridge: Cambridge University Press, 1998), p.127.

[58] There are two excellent books on this matter. K.E. Cytowic, The Man Who Tasted Shapes (Cambridge, Mass: MIT Press) and Lyall Watson, Gifts of Unknown Things.

[59] Underhill, p.375.

[60] Inge, p.166.

[61] Underhill, pp.381-382.

[62] *Ibid.,* p.397.

[63] Suso, *op.cit.,* p.207.

[64] *Ibid.,* p.208.

[65] Idem.

[66] *Mysticism in Maharashtra,* pp.282 and 291.

[67] Underhill, p.414.

[68] Upanishadic Philosophy, p.202.

[69] *Brihadaranyaka Upanishad* (Madras: Shri Ramkrishna Math, 1951), p.144.

[70] Underhill, p.420.

[71] Suso, p.71.

[72] *Upanishadic Philosophy,* p.202.

[73] *Brihadaranyaka Upanishad,* p.367.

[74] Inge, Christian Mysticism, p.170.

[75] *Brihadaranyaka Upanishad,* p.177.

[76] Underhill, p.172.

[77] Idem.

[78] *Brihadaranyaka Upanishad,* p.59.

[79] *Chhandogya Upanishad* (Madras: Shri Ramkrishna Math, 1956), p.453.

[80] Inge, p.157.

[81] Richard Geldard, The Vision of Emerson (Massachusetts, 1995), p.14.

[82] Inge, pp.189-190.

[83] *Upanishadic Philosophy,* p.203.

[84] *Chhandogya Upanishad,* p.217.

[85] Inge, p.189.

[86] *Ibid.,* p.315.

[87] Ranade, Pathway to God in Hindi Literature, p.441

[88] Underhill, p.383.

[89] St.. John of the Cross.

[90] Pathway to God in Hindi Literature, p.443.

[91] John Horgan, Rational Mysticism (Boston: Houghton Miffin Company, 2003), p.222.

Mysticism and
East-West Dialogue on Darwinism

T.D. Singh

Introduction

It has been the ageless human endeavour to understand life and its various manifestations. Darwin's portrait of life, commonly known as Darwinism, has left a great influence on western minds. His account of life, based on 'evolution' and 'natural selection', has significantly affected our worldview. The East, however, because of its strong spiritual foundation, has always found it difficult to imbibe Darwinism. In the eastern tradition, especially in Vedanta, there is an entirely different conception about life. In this view, life is much more than the morphological structure of living organisms (animated bodies). This view puts emphasis on the evolution of consciousness, and life and matter are regarded as entirely separate realities.

In the following pages, we will survey these two views, and will attempt to draw possible means for a synthesis of these approaches for a more holistic view of life. Thus a dialogue between the West and the East or science and religion is called for in this paper. Mysticism, being a common experience both in scientific discoveries as well as in religious experiences, will help in laying the foundation for this dialogue.

Mysticism in General

"I think there are many things in the universe that we cannot perceive or penetrate and that also we experience some of the most beautiful things in life in only a very primitive form. Only in relation to these mysteries do I consider myself to be a religious man. But I sense these things deeply ... the most beautiful and most profound religious emotion that we can experience is the sensation of the mystical. And this mysticality is the power of all true science."

Mysticism is a direct experience of the divine. It is the pursuit of achieving communion with ultimate reality, or the divine, or God through direct, personal experience (intuition or insight) beyond rational thought. A 19th-century scholar, Otto Pfleiderer, defined it as "the immediate feeling of unity of the self with God; it is nothing, therefore, but the fundamental feeling of religion, the religious life at its very heart and centre."[1] Evelyn Underhill in *Practical Mysticism* defines it as: "Mysticism is the art of union with Reality. The mystic is a person who has attained that union in greater or less degree, or who aims at and believes in such attainment."[2]

Mysticism involves an experience beyond sense perception – a window to subtle and deeper realities, which are central to our being, but are beyond our ordinary sense perception. It is universal and unites not only various religions, but also provides a vital ground for the synthesis of scientific and religious wisdom. It is a genuine and important source of knowledge both in scientific discoveries as well as in spiritual insights.

Mysticism in Science

Increasing knowledge in the natural sciences seems to have resulted in greater skepticism about the existence of a reality that can neither be experienced through our senses nor described in mathematical formulas. Phenomena are being studied today that cannot be directly experienced through our senses. It seems that these developments have moved natural sciences closer to mysticism. Some of the examples are outlined below:

The Mysterious Quantum World

Quantum physics, at its elementary foundation, points out that the components of real things are not real in the same way as those that we commonly perceive through our senses. Elementary entities like electrons, protons, neutrons, or atoms and molecules exist in states which appear like waves when they are not observed, and like particles when observed. Local order is affected by non-local, faster-than-light phenomena. The deterministic processes alternate with expressions of choices in creating the visible order of things. An observation creates reality, and mind-like properties are discovered in the quantum world.

Each of the above statements is a violation of common sense, which is entangled with the visible properties of things. A whole new mode of abstract 'thought' is required to be able to even approach these notions. Scientists, like mystics, have had to resort to symbols, imagery, and metaphors in their attempts to describe what cannot actually be experienced with our five senses.

Imaginary numbers

The imaginary numbers, which are now routinely used by mathematicians, engineers and physicists, and without which many applications of mathematics would be unthinkable, are a mystery to us. They are extremely useful tools to solve countless new problems and questions, which could not even have been raised in the context of real numbers alone.

Imaginary numbers were first known in 1545 when the Italian Jesuit mathematician Girolamo Cardano was trying to come up with a general solution to the cubic equation.[3] For some 350 years from the time that these numbers were introduced through the works of Cardano and Bombelli, complex numbers were perceived to have purely a mathematical role.[4] There was no reason to expect that the physical world should be concerned with them. However, it came as a great surprise, according to the physics of the latter three quarters of the 20th century, that the laws used to define the behavior of the world, at the tiniest scales, include the complex number system.

Roger Penrose, a world-renowned mathematical physicist from the University of Oxford, says that the imaginary number is the mystery number one for him. He astonishingly said to me in a discussion last year, "Just one number, square root of minus one, ... can solve many different kinds of equations, which we never believed we would be able to solve. It has many different kinds of roles, which are completely miraculous. It almost looks like magic, you see. For a long time people called this "Mathematical Magic" because we don't see complex numbers in the real world. They simply don't exist in reality. When we measure distances we use real numbers, not imaginary ones. Then Quantum Mechanics comes along, and suddenly you see that they have a universal role to play in the behavior of the world at the quantum level.[55]The mathematical description of the wave function includes a mixture of both ordinary ("real") numbers and imaginary numbers. The basic nonrelativistic equation of wave mechanics, Schrödinger's Wave Equation (1926), expresses the behavior of a particle in a field of force. The time dependent equation describing progressive waves, applicable to the motion of a free particle includes the imaginary number 'i'. They are out there in the real world. Some parts of that are in the mental world or the Platonic world, and suddenly, we see they are in the physical world. This is the part of the mystery I am talking about."[6]

He writes further about it in his recent volume, *The Road to Reality*, although the "mystical quantity "-1, usually denoted by 'i'x 'i,' was first encountered in the 16th century, but treated for hundreds of years with distrust, the mathematical utility of complex numbers gradually impressed the mathematical community to a greater and greater degree, until complex numbers became an indispensable, even magical, ingredient of our mathematical thinking. Yet we now find that they are fundamental not just to mathematics: these strange numbers also play an extraordinary and very basic role in the operation of the physical universe at its tiniest scales. This is a cause for wonder ... the magic of complex numbers ... is a miracle well worth appreciating."[7]

Mystery behind Physical Constants

Scientific progress has explained many of the physical phenomena. But the awe in the fine-tuned workings of the universe will remain. A sunset has lost none of its magnificent beauty, even though we may now explain that what paints the sky red each evening is the preferential scattering of the blue end of the visible light spectrum, and it is the greater penetrating power of the longer red wavelengths that pushes the red photons of light through the atmosphere to the cones of our eyes.

Physicists explain that the physical constants of our universe like the speed of light, Planck's constant, the gravitational constant, etc., are unique.[8] If the value of these physical constants had been slightly different, the universe would have been completely different. Even the electrons and the protons are arranged in such a way that nature is very fine-tuned. Explaining the mystery in the precision of the masses of electrons, protons and neutrons, Prof. George Wald, a Nobel Laureate in Biology from

Harvard University, states: "The great disparity in mass between nucleons and the electrons is one of the necessary conditions for life. Almost the entire mass of an atom is in the nucleus and it is thought to maintain its position regardless of how the electrons are moving about it. That is the only reason why anything in the universe stays put. If the protons and neutrons were close in mass to the electrons – whether light or heavy they would rotate around one another (about their common center of mass). All the matter in the universe would be fluid."[9]

The existence of the four forces – gravity, the electrostatic force, and strong and weak nuclear forces, which are said to help us to have a user-friendly universe filled with order and stability, is a mystery. Take for example, gravity. If we hold a heavy object out at arm's length, we feel the downward pull. What is causing this pull? We say, gravity. But what produces gravity? We may say, gravitons, of course. But what are gravitons? We do not know. They are totally imperceptible.

Similarly, both the magnetic and the electrostatic forces are theoretically carried by a single type of entity, photons, totally invisible and massless, observed only in their effects, as iron is drawn to a magnet. But what exactly produces the photon in the magnet that reaches out to the iron, or in the nucleus of an atom that sends it hurtling off toward the orbiting cloud of electrons? Perhaps we are encountering the mysterious subtlety hidden beyond the physical.

Mystery in Biological Systems

As we journey even through the simplest forms of life, one can only wonder how and from where the complex order of life arose. We decide to pick a pen and then start writing. But to accomplish this simple act, millions of cells and billions of atoms acting simultaneously on command are required. It seems so straightforward, just like starting the computer – pressing the power button. But we know that a myriad of hours were required to design the circuits and components so that one simple act of pressing the power button will activate the billions and billions of atoms in the needed correct sequence. If we could see what is happening inside living systems as we see what is happening outside of them, every aspect of existence would be an unfolding encounter with awe – almost a mystical experience.

The human body acts as a finely tuned machine, a magnificent metropolis in which, as its inhabitants, each of the 100 trillion cells, composed of more than 10^{27} atoms, moves in symbiotic precision. Going inside the body and then inside the cell is a journey to wonderland.[10]

If we could walk inside a cell, our first task would be to keep from getting bowled over. We would be faced with a myriad of microsized vessels moving in all directions.[11] It has been estimated that there may be as many as some 200 trillion molecules in a single cell, all executing thousands of coordinated actions and reactions with precise timing and function. To get a scale for the rate of activity, consider on average, each cell in our body forms 2000 proteins every second.[12]

A protein is a string of several hundreds of amino acids, and an amino acid is a molecule having twenty or so atoms. Every cell in our body is selecting right now approximately five hundred thousands amino acids, organizing them into pre-selected strings, joining them together, checking to be certain that each string is folded into specific shapes, and then shipping each protein off to a site, some inside the cell and some outside. Our body is a living wonder. We are so embedded in the biosphere that the marvel of its organization has become lost within its commonness.

The entrance to a living cell is marked by a passage through a membrane functioning to keep the bad stuff out, while letting the good stuff in. Membrane design is absolutely brilliant. A myriad of portals provide entry, but only if signaled to open and allow entrance. Some of these ports are gated or opened by subtle changes in voltage differences across the membrane. Others open when a molecular key comes and unlocks them, allowing another molecule to pass. The cues come from within the cell if it is a call for the building blocks needed in protein replication, and from outside if, for example, it's a nerve cell coaxing a neighboring cell into action. A vast number of factors are woven in a simple act of signaling a membrane port to open. And we are so immersed that we project to identify life and consciousness with these chemical messengers.

To meet the energy demanded for every molecular move, every cell has within it the machinery to take glucose from the food we eat and to combust it, storing the released energy in a power-packed molecule called ATP (adenosine triphosphate), a sort of biochemical battery that makes itself available to whatever power-hungry molecule it might encounter. All living systems use ATP as their power package – it is nature's global battery. But the subtlety in ATP production is another mystery.[13]

Digestion in the mouth and stomach degrades the large carbohydrate molecules into more manageable-sized glucose, which is able to pass through the intestine wall, diffuse into the adjacent bloodstream, and be swept by the blood flow to some glucose-hungry cell. But glucose is a highly polar molecule and so it cannot cross the non-polar barrier of the cell membrane. Along comes the glucose carrier protein called insulin, which attaches itself to the glucose. With insulin on site, the membrane gates fly open and the glucose enters the cell. Here, in a complex multi-step process in which a dozen intermediate molecules are formed, free-floating enzyme proteins change the glucose into a substance called pyruvate and then, within the cell's many sausage-shaped mitochondria organelles, oxidize the pyruvate into the end products, carbon dioxide and water plus copious amounts of energy-rich ATP. The first two stages of this process are energy intensive and so require an energy source of ATP to power them. But this whole process is designed to make energy-rich ATP, and yet just to get the process started we need ATP. It is again a mystery, a chicken-and-egg problem, as biologists and chemical evolutionists encounter in the mystery of the origin of life.

Let us try to have a glimpse of the mystery of the brain. Through the dedicated work of many scientists, we have discovered how and where in the brain each of our sensations is processed and stored. But take, for example, sound. How do we hear sound? The waves of sound impinge upon my eardrum and in a beautifully complex path become converted to bioelectrical pulses that are chemically stored in the cortex of our brain. Up to and including the storage of the data in the brain, it's all biochemistry. But we do not hear biochemistry. We hear sound. Where's the sound generated in my head? Similarly the vision, the smell? How these stored biochemical data points are recalled and replayed into sentience remains an enigmatic mystery.[14] We swim in a stream of consciousness and accept it without even noticing it.

And all the above is but a tiny glimpse of the magnificent mystery hidden beneath our complex living systems. There is much more to cover here in this short paper: from the cell's DNA code to the startling design of our eye, from the cell's mind-boggling mitotic and meiotic divisions to brain's mysterious functions.[15] Undoubtedly, the scientific inquiry of nature has exposed a metaphysical reality hidden beneath the physical. But for certain, physicality is in the scheme of the divine. We have a physical body. Linking the physical with the spiritual is the goal – the lesson of mysticism.

Mystery of Time

We drift in a river of time. It is an intrinsic, ubiquitous quality of our universe, irrespective of whether or not we measure its passage. But what is time? We all live with time and we use it all the time in scientific research, but we do not still really understand what its nature and origin are.

When it comes to the nature of time, physicists are pretty much at as much of a loss as the rest of us who seem hopelessly swept along in its current. The mystery of time is connected with some of the thorniest questions in physics as well as in philosophy. "Time is really difficult," said Dr. Cumrun Vafa, a Harvard string-theorist. "We have not made much progress on the emergence of time. Once we make progress, we will make progress on the early universe, on high energy physics and black holes."[16]

It has eluded history's most magnificent minds. From the imaginative designs of Galileo to the soaring discoveries of Einstein, we go on to the latest debates and into the farthest reaches of modern thought on the nature of time. Along the way, me meet Ptolemy, Newton, and Stephen Hawking – plus many others whose study and struggle, feuding and folly, have played a part in the story. Dr. Bousso, an expert on holographic theories of space-time, said, "There is a lot of mysticism about time. Time is what a clock measures. What a clock measures is more interesting than you thought."[17] St. Augustine of Hippo wrote: "What, then, is time? If no one asks me, I know. If I wish to explain it to one that asketh, I know not. My soul is on fire to know this most intricate enigma."[18]

In short, time is a mystery. In this connection attention may be drawn to the words in the *Bhagavadgītā* (11.32)—*kālo 'smi loka-kñaya-kåt* meaning, "Time I am, the great destroyer of the worlds." This very verse was uttered by J. Robert Oppenheimer when the first atom bomb was tested in Los Alamos, New Mexico, USA, on July 16, 1945.

Mystery behind Scientific Discoveries – The role of inspiration and intuition in scientific discoveries

From the earliest discoveries of fire and gravity to today's technology-trained insights like the discovery of PCR (polymerase chain reaction), scientific breakthroughs are not always results of logical and rational steps. Rather some of the greatest discoveries in science were made through mysterious inspiration or intuition. It is echoed by mathematician Bark Kosko when he expressed, "There is no shame in admitting to what extent scientific progress depends on intuition. This needs to be taught in schools as much as mathematics."[19] Many renowned scientists, mathematicians, artists, poets, etc., report their experience of inspiration. In our day-to-day activities we can feel a seemingly inexplicable guidance. This guidance is something more than mere algorithmic process. This happens often when we are deeply pondering over a problem like a mystic contemplating on the Lord in the heart. And the solution comes like a flash without any connection to the line of thought that we have been contemplating. But where does this inspiration come from? Charles H. Townes, Nobel Laureate in Physics who discovered the laser and the maser, explains: "In religion, people talk about revelations. In science you find many revelations, too. It's just that people don't talk about them that way. When the idea for the laser came to me, I was sitting on a park bench thinking, now, why haven't I been able to do this? Suddenly a new idea comes to me, a new creation. Where did it come from? Did God give me this idea? Who knows? I didn't suddenly have a view of God's face, if that's what you mean. In science we just don't talk about it much. You say, well, I had an idea. In the religious world people talk about revelations. They are not so basically different."[20] Briefly, some of the salient features of inspiration or intuition are:

1. Happiness or a happy mood

This is one of the fundamental qualities which enables one to have and capture insights, thereby making one creative. When the mind is disturbed, new thoughts will not come. Only when we are joyful and enthusiastic and seeking the truth do creative and visionary thoughts appear. Consider, for example, the experience of the famous composer Mozart: "When I feel well and in good humour, thoughts crowd into my mind as easily as you could wish. Whence and how do they come? I do not know and I have nothing to do with it.... Once I have my theme, another melody comes, linking itself with the first one, in accordance with the needs of the composition as a whole.... Then my soul is on fire with inspiration, if however nothing occurs to distract my attention. The work grows: I keep expanding it, conceiving it more and more clearly until I have the entire composition finished in my head though it may be long .... It does not come to me successively, with its various parts worked out in detail, as they will be later on, but it is in its entirety."[21]

2.   Deep contemplation

Often, one receives insights when one is deeply contemplating a problem. As Charles Townes explained his discovery: "I will recount my own experience in the invention of the laser and the maser. I had been working hard to get shorter wavelengths. Specifically, I was thinking about it for a long time and tried many ways but could not succeed. I was the chairman of the national committee for trying to find out the possibilities. We were having the last meeting. I woke up early that morning. I was upset at the thought that we were so far not successful. We tried many ways. Suddenly the idea came - that it is possible by using non-thermal molecules. If instead of having thermal equilibrium, if more molecules are in the higher state than in the lower state, one can obtain an inversion condition. And we can amplify this way. Then I wrote it down. That was the moment of inspiration. Yes, true! Where did the idea come from? I had thought and tried hard to get a broad idea. Then suddenly it occurred and I would like to say that the inspiration came from God."[22]

3.   Openness and the mood of humility

These conditions facilitate the receiver to obtain inspiration or insights. Wislawa Szymborska, who received the Nobel Prize in literature in 1996, described inspiration in his Nobel lecture as, "Whatever inspiration is, it's born from a continuous 'I don't know.'"[23]

4.   The element of surprise

This guidance comes in a flash, in a fraction of a second, so to say. For example, the famous mathematician Gauss said, "Finally two days ago, I succeeded, ... like a sudden flash of lightening, the riddle happened to be solved." Similarly, we have the well-known example of the discovery of the structure of the benzene molecule: Friedrich Kekulé, the 19th century

German chemist, reaching an impasse studying the structure of the benzene molecule, dozed off in front of a fire. We could ask now "Why did he doze then? What was the meaning of that?" And then he had a vision of a snake biting its tail, and in a flash he realized that the molecular structure was characterized by a ring of carbon atoms. This dream vision directed him towards his future so-called objective research.

5.   A holistic picture

The guidance comes as a whole and reveals a complete answer to the aspirant's riddle. It is something more than a mere algorithmic process.

6.   A feeling of great satisfaction

The receiver of the inspiration or intuition experiences a feeling of great satisfaction at the time of discovery. 'I am overcome by intense joy, a wild pleasure,' noted biologist François Jacob, whilst chemist Michael Polyani spoke of the "feeling of extreme exaltation that a scientist can feel at the moment of discovery."[24]

As is evident, the above shown mysteries are a tiny fraction of enormous mysteries with which we are surrounded. In a way the whole universe, including life, is a total mystery. We live with mysteries every day. The Czech-born mathematician Kurt Gödel has ensured, through his famous Gödel's Incompleteness Theorem, that we will always have to remain with mysteries – providing a fundamental and eternal place for mysticism in our life.[25]

In the Vedic tradition there is a notion, which in Sanskrit is called *acintya*. It means something very mysterious, inconceivable and beyond our ability to comprehend or think.[26] In this ancient tradition, this word *acintya* is an attribute given to God. God has innumerable inconceivable attributes, *acintya-guna-svarupam*. These attributes are visible everywhere in quantum physics and in biological sciences. In fact, the long road to reality will be segments of mysteries. Hence, we can say that there are not only mathematical mysteries, but there are also cosmological mysteries, artistic mysteries and so on. The small part that we can understand or comprehend will be extremely insignificant compared with the vast ocean of unknown things. Newton was right when he said that the vast ocean of knowledge lies beyond.

Einstein also expressed it, "We are in the position of a little child entering a huge library filled with books in many languages. The child knows someone must have written those books. It does not know how. It does not understand the languages in which they are written. The child dimly suspects a mysterious order in the arrangement of the books but doesn't know what it is. That, it seems to me, is the attitude of even the most intelligent human being towards God. We see the universe marvelously arranged and obeying certain laws, but only dimly understand these laws."

Roger Penrose also expressed it thus, "Yes, I frankly admit that there are many things in Nature that we do not understand. There is something really deep, very deep. It is 'mysterious' if you like to use that word."[27] We are a minuscule speck, floating in the seemingly endless darkness of the night sky.

Mysticism in Religion

Mysticism represents a spiritual tendency which is universal; a fundamental tendency of the soul to have an intimate union with the divine. As E. G. Browne, an eminent oriental scholar has put it: "It is, indeed, the eternal cry of the human soul for rest; the insatiable longing of a being wherein infinite ideals are fettered and cramped by a miserable actuality; and so long as man is less than an angel and more than a beast, this cry will not for a moment fail to make itself heard. Wonderfully uniform, too, is its tenor: in all ages, in all countries, in all creeds, whether it comes from the Brahmin sage, the Greek philosopher, the Persian poet, or the Christian quietist, it is in essence an enunciation more or less clear, more or less eloquent, of the aspiration of the soul to cease altogether from self, and to be at one with God."[28] The aim of the mystic is to establish a conscious relation with the Absolute, in which he/she finds the personal object of love. As A. B. Sharpe has put it, mystics seek, "the supernatural union of likeness, begotten of love, which is the union of the human will with the Divine. They seek to realize the unfelt natural presence of God in creation – by entering into a personal relationship with the concealed presence which is the source of being."[29] Mysticism, thus, is spiritual and transcendental in its aims, and holds that the object of its quest, the Absolute, is also the beloved.

Mysticism maintains that we must be a partaker of the divine nature, if we are to know the divine. Only if the self is real can it hope to know reality. So every creature is by nature akin to the Creator, i.e., there is within every living being a divine spark, soul, that which seeks re-union with the divine.[30]

There must be inner sense, or spiritual senses of the soul, by means of which one can receive direct revelation and knowledge of God, by which one perceives things hidden from reason, through which one is brought into a conscious fellowship with God. As Ralph Waldo Trine (1866-1958) expressed in one of his most famous writings, *In Tune with the Infinite*, "It is a spiritual sense opening inwardly, as the physical senses open outwardly, and because it has the capacity to perceive, grasp and know the truth at first hand, independent of all external sources of information, we call it intuition. All inspired teaching and spiritual revelations are based upon the recognition of this spiritual faculty of the soul."[31]

Mysticism maintains that one has to undergo purification of the self to attain the knowledge of God. Mystics both in the East and the West have maintained that the stripping from the soul of selfishness and sensuality is essential for the beholding of the vision of God. This is essential for all those who would approach the Absolute. The Greek philosopher Plotinus presented it amicably when he said that as the eye could not behold the sun unless it were itself sun-like, so no more can the soul behold God unless it is Godlike. Only when all images of the earth are hushed and the clamour of the senses is stilled and the soul has passed beyond thought of self can the eternal wisdom be revealed to the one who seeks that high relationship with the Lord.[32]

In this tremendous journey towards God the mystic receives two-fold guidance: the instructions from the spiritual guide and love with the divine. E. Underhill attempted to define this term 'love' of the mystic as, "it is to be understood in its deepest, fullest sense; as the ultimate expression of the self's most vital tendencies ... the deep-seated desire and tendency of the soul towards its source .... Love, to the mystic, is the active expression of his will and desire for the Absolute and also his innate tendency to that Absolute."[33]

It is accompanied by unusual feelings such as awe, wonder, reverence, mystery, inconceivability and ecstasy. The stages of the mystic, to a large extent, are threefold: At the beginning of all must be the awakening or the conversion of the mystic, who becomes aware of what he/she seeks, and sets his face towards the goal. But a long preparation is needed before he/she can expect to attain it, and the discipline of the purgative life must be endured. With this, the external life has been brought into accordance with the good and now the struggle is transferred to the inner life. All the faculties, feeling, intellect and will must be cleansed and brought into harmony with the Lord's will. As described by Underhill, "the complete surrender of man's personal striving to the overruling will of God and thus the linking up of all the successive acts of life with the Abiding."[34] The presence of God is now an experienced reality, not simply a concept of the imagination.

The final stage is in which one is joined to Him in a progressive relationship, a relationship which is a fact of experience consciously realized. Plotinus, one of the most influential philosophers in antiquity after Plato and Aristotle, speaks of it as, "Beholding this Being – resting, rapt, in the vision and possession of so lofty a loveliness, growing to Its likeness – what beauty can the soul yet lack?"[35] Similarly, the Franciscan concept of the vision: "A rapture and uplifting of the mind intoxicated in the contemplation of the unspeakable savour of the divine sweetness, and a happy, peaceful and sweet delight of the soul, that is rapt and uplifted in great marvel – and a burning sense within of that celestial glory unspeakable."[36]

Mysticism is active and practical. The mystic is not simply to take delight, but to throw him/herself into action leading the active life of service of inspiring humanity, living life in God, deified in all his being and so in all his acts to be only the instrument of God. As the Supreme Lord Sri Krishna confirms in the *Bhagavadgétä, yat karoñi yad açnäsi yaj juhoñi dadäsi yat yat tapasyasi kaunteya tat kuruñva mad-arpaëam*, meaning, "Whatever you do, whatever you eat, whatever you offer or give away, and whatever austerities you perform —do that, O son of Kunté, as an offering to Me." (Bg. 9.27) And further Lord Krishna proclaims, *ya idaà paramaà guhyaà mad-bhakteñv abhidhäsyati bhaktià mayi paräà kåtvä mäm evaiñyaty asaàçayaù na ca tasmän manuñyeñu kaçcin me priya-kåttamaù bhavitä na ca me tasmäd anyaù priyataro bhuvi*, meaning, "For one who explains this supreme secret to the devotees, pure devotional service is guaranteed, and at the end he will come back to Me. There is no servant in this world more dear to Me than he, nor will there ever be one more dear." (Bg. 18.68 & 18.69)

Darwinism and its Limitations

Darwin began his voyage around the world in 1831. He studied plants and animals everywhere he went, collecting specimens for further study. After his return from the Voyage of the Beagle in 1836, he spent the next 22 years in research on gathering evidence and arguments on the origin of species. In 1859, he published his account of life in the form of a book, *The Origin of Species*.

The gist of Darwin's conception can be put as "Evolution by Natural Selection." He theorized that there is evolution of all species and the main mechanism causing the evolution is natural selection. A single species is transformed through the following evolutionary process. Small, random, heritable differences among individuals result in different chances of survival and reproduction – success for some, death without offspring for others – and this natural culling leads to significant changes in shape, size, strength, color, biochemistry, and behaviour among the descendants. Excess population growth drives the competitive struggle. Because less successful competitors produce fewer surviving offspring, the useless or negative variations tend to disappear, whereas the useful variations tend to be perpetuated and gradually magnified throughout a population.

The second part, called speciation, is the process whereby new species are formed. Genetic changes sometimes accumulate within an isolated segment of a species, but not throughout the whole, as that isolated population adapts to its local conditions. Gradually it goes its own way, seizing a new ecological niche. At a certain point it becomes irreversibly distinct – that is, so different that its members can't interbreed with the rest. Two species now exist where formerly there was one. Darwin named that splitting-and-specializing phenomenon the "principle of divergence."

Darwin used mainly four branches of biological sciences – paleontology, biogeography, embryology and morphology - to support his idea.[37] Darwin argued that closely allied species – that is, similar creatures sharing roughly the same body plan – succeed one another in time, as well as living nearby in space, because they are related through evolutionary descent. He further argued that the number of shared characteristics between any one species and another indicates how recently those two species have diverged from a shared lineage.

The modern version of Darwinism, the synthesis of Mendelian[38] genetics and Darwinism, is called Neo-Darwinism. Darwin knew very little about the mechanism of variation. Modern genetics is said to provide the insight into the means by which variation in biology may originate. Neo-Darwinism postulates that natural selection acts on the heritable (genetic) variations within individuals in populations and that mutations (especially random copying errors in DNA) provide the main source of these genetic variations.

Chance mutations affect one or a few nucleotides of DNA per occurrence. Bigger changes come from recombination, a genetic process in which longer strands of DNA are swapped, transferred, or doubled. These two processes, mutation and recombination, create new meaning in DNA by lucky accidents.[39]

Darwin tried to explain life's journey without invoking God. The term 'natural selection' could be thought of as the mystical element in Darwin's concept. Nature selects. But what does it mean to say 'nature selects'? Since when do the lifeless atoms and molecules become so clever to have their own ideas and make a selection? What is behind 'nature' and 'natural selection'? The ancient Indian writings of Vedanta proclaim that behind nature there is the divine hand. In other words, in Vedanta, nature works under the direction of the Supreme Lord, *mayädhyakñeëa prakåtiù süyate sa-caräcaram hetunänena kaunteya jagad viparivartate*, meaning, "This material nature, which is one of My energies, is working under My direction, O son of Kunté, producing all moving and nonmoving beings. Under its rule this manifestation is created and annihilated again and again." (Bg 9.10) Thus the role of God and the presence of the soul cannot be excluded in the Darwinian theory of evolution.

Vedanta further explains that many life forms manifest simultaneously. In other words, genetic variation is already within a cosmic plan. It is not that natural selection and random mutation will be the cause of biodiversity. The observation of Werner Arber, Nobel Laureate in Biology from the

University of Basel, Switzerland, that genetic mutation is not due to error or mistake, corroborates the Vedantic conceptions. He says, "Evolution does not occur on the basis of errors, accidents or the action of selfish genetic elements. Rather, the evolution genes must have been fine-tuned for their functions to provide and to replenish a wide diversity of life forms."[40]

Besides, on the human level there are so many subtle traits of personality, for example, humility, stability and self-control, honesty, tolerance, responsibility, cleanliness, love and so on which are beyond any molecular mechanisms. The marvels of life are enormous and the theorists of evolution cannot even think of touching these points. Darwin himself encountered insurmountable difficulty in conceiving how an eye could evolve. The fine, intricate details of the colorful feather in a peacock's tail were also impossible for him to explain. He thus remarked: "I remember well the time when the thought of the eye made me cold all over, but I have got over the complaint, and now small trifling particulars of structure often make me very uncomfortable. The sight of a feather in a peacock's tail, whenever I gaze at it, makes me sick."[41]

Even though Darwinism presents enlightening accounts of some aspects of life, by no means does it provide us a holistic picture of life.[42] Darwinism leaves out a lot and cannot tell us many mysteries of life.

The author has presented a glimpse in section 2.1 about the amazing and startling discoveries in physics and biology during the past few decades which have given us the tools to gain scientific insights into the mystical underpinnings of our world. As we journey through these newly discovered marvels of the cosmos and life, we need to reexamine our concepts concerning the origins, evolution and essence of this wonderful world in which we live. Perhaps mysticism or *acintya* could be a fundamental element in our search for the ultimate meaning of life and the universe.

4.   Mysticism – A Meeting Point of East-West Dialogue

"In India there is much more union between the two (science and spirituality) than there is in the west. I think that the western scientists are coming back to that point of view – what the universe is all about. A few scientists are interested and their number is increasing."[43] Life is a mystery. Even after Darwin's *The Origin of Species* in 1859, the question of life remained unsolved. Eighty-five years

later, Erwin Schrödinger published his famous monograph *What is life?* (1944) in an attempt to probe the mystery of life. Later, Watson and Crick discovered the structure of the DNA molecule in 1953. It was a great triumph in scientific achievements and many scientists thought that now they had deciphered the code of life. Scientists spend their life decoding what is life. But life's mystery seems to deeper at every step. Peering into life's innermost workings serves only to deepen the mystery. As Max Planck said, "Each hilltop that we reach discloses to us another hilltop beyond."[44] DNA is nothing less than a blueprint – or, more accurately, an algorithm or instruction manual – for building our physical forms. We share this wonderful molecule with almost all other life forms on Earth. From fungi to flies, from bacteria to bears, organisms' physical forms are sculpted according to their respective DNA instructions. Each individual's DNA differs from others in the same species (with the exception of identical twins), and differs even more from that of other species. But the essential structure – the chemical makeup, the double-helix architecture – is universal. That makes many feel that we have now decoded lifes mystery. But the explanation of life requires something in addition to normal physical and chemical forces. Scientists still can't quite put their finger on *exactly* what it is that separates a living organism from other types of physical objects. Available biochemical information points strongly that life is beyond mechanism.

Spiriton – Particle of Life beyond the Genetic Code

According to Vedanta, a divine spark or soul or as the author has coined it 'spiriton,' animates our physical body. Consciousness, free will and many other qualities of life such as humility, love, etc., which are beyond our present scientific understanding, are defined as characteristics of this spiriton. This conscious divine particle of life, spiriton, is the missing element in Darwinism.

As physicist Paul Davies observes: "Living creatures literally have a life of their own. It is as if they contain some inner spark that gives them autonomy … Even bacteria do their own thing in a restricted way."[45] The secret of life comes from this spiritual domain.

William Phillips, Nobel Laureate in Physics from the University of Maryland, USA, also states quite strongly: "At least for me, we are defined creatures, we have a soul and we have responsibilities. Research won't change the fundamental truth that we have souls and that those souls connect with the divine."[46]

Vedanta describes that due to the presence of 'spiriton' the body is animated and active and undergoes six types of transformations.[47] It takes birth, lives for some time, grows, produces some offspring, gradually dwindles, and at last vanishes into oblivion.[46]

When the spirit soul, spiriton, goes away, i.e.,at death, the body can no longer be animated in spite of the fact that all the molecular machineries that make up the body are still intact. The symphony of life decays to street noise-like chaos once the forces of life cease. Dead bodies decay.

The *Bhagavad-Gétä* mentions about 'spiriton' being different from matter: "Earth, water, fire, air, ether, mind, intelligence and false ego — altogether these eight constitute My (Lord Krishna's) separated material energies. Besides these, O mighty-armed Arjuna, there is another, superior energy of Mine, which comprises the living entities (spiritons) who are exploiting the resources of this material, inferior nature."[48]

According to Vedanta, the science of the soul or spiriton (*ätman*) is the sublime essence of spirituality. The *Bhagavad-Gétä* refers to this science as—*räja-vidyä räja-guhyaà pavitram idam uttamam pratyakñävagamaà dharmyaà su-sukhaà kartum avyayam*, meaning, "This knowledge is the king of education, the most secret of all secrets. It is purest knowledge, and because it gives direct perception of the self by realization, it is the perfection of religion. It is everlasting, and it is joyfully performed."[49] The ultimate purpose of human life is to find our real spiritual identity and our relationship with the Supreme.

Consciousness is a fundamental quality of the 'spiriton.' Thus it is purely spiritual and transcendental to matter. Matter is the inferior energy of the Supreme Lord. It is inferior because matter, however complex it may be, will never have conscious symptoms. On the other hand, the living entities are the superior energy of the Supreme Being. They are superior because they have consciousness.

All living beings, microorganisms, birds, animals, etc., possess different degrees of consciousness. Thus microorganisms too possess consciousness, though very little. The nervous systems of insects are not nearly as complex as ours, and insects probably do not have as rich an experience of the world as we do, but they nevertheless possesses consciousness.

Vedantic science describes evolution as the journey of the innumerable conscious particles of life (souls or spiritons) in time and space as they travel from one form of body to another under the laws of *karma* (cause and effect). Each living entity's degree or level of consciousness, *guëa* (quality) and *karma* (activity) will determine the direction of its evolutionary path.

Thus consciousness evolves, not bodies. It reminds us of the enlightening words of the well-known quantum physicist Erwin Schrödinger: "What happens is not that I am created for the first time but that I slowly awaken as though from a deep sleep."[50] Darwin's mistake was that he could not conceive the existence of consciousness or a spiritual soul.

If spiriton is a reality and the fundamental ingredient of life, what is its nature? Does it have a form? What is its fundamental constitution? How does it interact with matter and get captured by it? How does it interact with God? Mysteries will never end. Mysticism has an eternal role in our life. As Henry Poincare put it, "Truth resides in a deep well and we shall never get to the bottom."[51] But we will be on a new road to the journey of life. Perhaps we will then be the modern scientific mystics.

We have seen that one of the most important features of mysticism is the presence of a divine spark or soul or 'spiriton' in each of us, which longs to connect with the divine, God. Whereas the East has always emphasised, even today, the spiritual aspects of life, spiriton and God, the West has mainly focused on the physical aspects of our being. Since mysticism is common to both the East and the West, it could be a fruitful platform for a synthesis of scientific and spiritual domains or in other words for the East-West dialogue on Darwinism. I am sure, if alive today, Darwin would have approved it.

I end with a quote from Max Planck: "It is a land of mystery. It is a world whose nature cannot be comprehended by human powers of mental conception; but we can perceive its harmony and beauty as we struggle towards an understanding of it."[52]

Endnotes

[1] *Understanding Mysticism*, Ed. Richard Woods, 1980, NY, p. 20.

[2] E. Underhill, *Practical Mysticism*, New York, 2003, p. 10.

[3] Philip J. Davis & Reuben Hersh, *The Mathematical Experience*, Harmondsworth: Penguin, 1983.

[4] Roger Penrose, *The Road to Reality*, London, Jonathan Cape, 2004, p. 73.

[5] The mathematical description of the wave function includes a mixture of both ordinary ("real") numbers and imaginary numbers. The basic nonrelativistic equation of wave mechanics, Schrödinger's Wave Equation (1926), expresses the behavior of a particle in a field of force. The time dependent equation describing progressive waves, applicable to the motion of a free particle includes the imaginary number 'i.'

[6] *Science, Spirituality and the Nature of Reality*, A Discussion between Sir Roger Penrose and Dr. T. D. Singh, Bhaktivedanta Institute, Kolkata, 2005, p. 34.

[7] Roger Penrose, *The Road to Reality*, London, 2004, pp. 67-74.

[8] For a larger list of the physical constants, see *Savijanam – Scientific Exploration for a Spiritual Paradigm*, Vol. 2, 2003, p. 79.

[9] T. D. Singh and R. Gomatam, eds., *Synthesis of Science and Religion: Critical Essays and Dialogue*, Bombay, 1987, pp.10-11.

[10] See Gerald L. Schroeder, *The Hidden Face of God: Science Reveals the Ultimate Truth*, 2001, p. 49.

[11] Please note that in the diagram generally given in the biology textbooks, only representative organelles are shown. In an actual cell, most of those components are present by the thousands, filling the interior space with activity.

[12] *Ibid.*, p. 62.

[13] *Ibid.*, pp. 66-68.

[14] *Ibid.*, p. 6.

[15] See Gerald L. Schroeder.

[16] Dennis Overbye , "Remembrance of Things Future: The Mystery of Time," The New York Times, June 28, 2005. web: http://www.nytimes.com/2005/06/28/science/28time.html

[17] *Ibid.*

[18] *Ibid.*

[19] *RTD info* – "Magazine for European Research," Special Issue, March 2004, p. 19; web: http://europa. eu.int/comm/research/rtdinfo/special_as/ article_815_en.html.

[20] Charles H. Townes, "What I've Learned?" Interviewed by Scott Carrier, Esquire, December 2001, Volume 136, Issue 6.

[21] J. Hadamard, T*he Psychology of Invention in the Mathematical Field.* Princeton: Princeton University Press, 1949, p.16.

[22] *Savijanam , Scientific Exploration for a Spiritual Paradigm*, Vol. 2, 2003, pp. 13-14.

[23] Wislawa Szymborska, "The Poet and the World," *Nobel Lecture*, December 7, 1996. web: http://nobelprize.org/literature/laureates/1996/szymborska-lecture.html

[24] Royston M. Roberts, *Serendipity: Accidental Discoveries in Science*, 1989, NY, USA, pp.75-82.

[24] *RTD info* – "Magazine for European Research," Special Issue, March 2004, p.19; web: http://europa. eu.int/comm/research/rtdinfo/special_as/ article_815_en.html

[25] Gödel Incompleteness Theorem states that if 'A' is a mathematical system which involves the natural numbers 0, 1, 2, 3, … then there are questions in 'A' which cannot be answered using the axioms of 'A'. In order to answer a question of this kind, one could expand the set of axioms by adding a new one. But the new system will again be subject to Gödel's theorem and there will be other questions that cannot be answered. Thus, Gödel's theorem ensures that there will always remain unanswered questions.

[26] Cinta - thoughtfulness, cintya – that which can be thought about; acintya– that which cannot be thought about.

[27] *Science, Spirituality and the Nature of Reality*, p.36.

[28] Edward Granville Browne, *A Year Amongst The Persians – Impressions as to the Life, Character, & Thought of the People of Persia*, First published by Messrs A & C Black Ltd 1893; New Edition published by the Cambridge University Press 1926; Reprinted 1927.

[29] A.B. Sharpe, *Mysticism: Its True Nature and Value*, London, 1910.

[30] Richard Woods, ed., *Understanding Mysticism*, 1980, NY, p.21.

[31] R. W. Trine, *In Tune with the Infinite*, p.40.

[32] See *Understanding Mysticism*, Ed. Richard Woods, 1980, NY, p.21.

[33] E. Underhill, *Mysticism*, pp.101ff.

[34] E. Underhill, *Man and the Supernatural*, p.246.

[35] Plotinus, *The Enneads*, translated by Stephen MacKenna and John Dillon. London: Penguin, 1991.

[36] *Little Flowers of St. Francis*, tr. T. W. Arnold, pp.290-91.

[37] Biogeography is the study of the geographical distribution of living creatures. Paleontology investigates extinct life-forms, as revealed in the fossil record. Embryology examines the revealing stages of development that embryos pass through before birth or hatching Morphology is the science of anatomical shape and design.

[38] In 1866 Gregor Mendel (1822-1884), a monk in Brün, Moravia, published a paper on the inheritance of attributes ('characters') in the garden pea. His work remained in obscurity for more than three decades, but in it he showed that characters were transmitted as units. Each higher organism had a pair of units (which we now call 'genes') for each inherited character. A particular gene (for example for blue eyes) may be expressed or lie dormant, but it is not simply diluted out as Darwin feared.

[39] Current ideas on evolution are usually referred to as the 'Modern Synthesis' which is described by Futuyma as: "The major tenets of the evolutionary synthesis, then, were that populations contain genetic variation that arises by random (i.e., not adaptively directed) mutation and recombination; that populations evolve by changes in gene frequency brought about by random genetic drift, gene flow, and especially natural selection; that most adaptive genetic variants have individually slight phenotypic effects so that phenotypic changes are gradual (although some alleles with discrete effects may be advantageous, as in certain color polymorphisms); that diversification comes about by speciation, which normally entails the gradual evolution of reproductive isolation among populations; and that these processes, continued for sufficiently long, give rise to changes of such great magnitude as to warrant the designation of higher taxonomic levels (genera, families, and so forth)." – Futuyma, D.J. in *Evolutionary Biology*, Sinauer Assocites, 1986, p.12.

[40] T. D. Singh & W. Arber, "Dialogue on Life and its Origin", *Savijänam – Scientific Exploration for a Spiritual Paradigm*, Vol.1 Kolkata, 2002, p.12.

[41] N. Macbeth, *Darwin Retried: An Appeal to Reason.* Boston: Gambit, 1971, p. 101.

[42] The author has attempted to provide more details about the limitation and difficulties of Darwinian concept of life in his upcoming book, Life, Matter and their Interactions.

[43] Charles H. Townes, *Nobel Laureate in Physics.*

[44] Max Planck, Where is Science Going? p.83.

[45] Paul Davies, *The 5th Miracle: The Search for the Origin and Meaning of Life*, 1999, p.33.

[46] Dialogue between T. D. Singh and William Phillips, National Institute of Standards and Technology (NIST), Gaithersburg, USA on June 11, 2005.

[47] We should note that some religious traditions do not accept the existence of the soul and some others proclaim that the soul is present in human beings only.

However, ancient Vedic science of India does not accept such statements and states very firmly that all living entities have spirit souls. 46 Bhagavad-Gétä As It Is, verse 2.20 purport, *Ibid.*

[48] *Ibid.,* verses 7.4-5.

[49] *Ibid.,* verse 9.2.

[50] Erwin Schrödinger, *My View of the World*

[51] Henry Poincare, *Science and Hypothesis,* p.XX.

[52] Max Planck, *Where is Science Going?* p.106.

Science and the Sacred, Silence and Service

Towards a Dialogical Enrichment between Eastern and Western Mysticism

Kuruvilla Pandikattu

In this paper I want to go beyond the popular stereotypes of the spirituality (and therefore, mysticism) of eastern and western traditions. Then I want to broadly categorise the mysticism of the western tradition as a "Mysticism of Service" which may be complemented by the "Mysticism of Silence," of the eastern tradition. I draw two examples (Raimundo Panikkar and Bede Griffiths) to illustrate these approaches. Finally, I plead for a mystical orientation for today which respects and interfaces both these traditions.

Beyond the Stereotypes of the East and the West

It has been assumed that eastern spirituality and mysticism is intuitive, feminine and receptive.[1] These three form the basic stereotypes of the eastern tradition. Out of it we can trace a culture in the East that is deeply spiritual and vibrantly religious. Without much exaggeration we can say that we "breathe" spirituality in India. It is a part of life, and no aspect of human being escapes the touch of religion. The people just live their religion, and vibrate a sense of oneness with the world. Coupled with it there is a profound philosophical (intellectual) depth connected with the Indian tradition.

The general stereotypes of the West are that they are rational, assertive, masculine and so predominantly materialistic than the East. Unlike the East, the western men and women seem to be more in control of themselves and of their environment by their technological prowess. They manipulate and dominate the rest of the world and claim their superiority over others. Therefore they are much more pragmatic in dealings, resulting in the attitude of "use and throw." This has led to tremendous technological advancement without moral convictions. Theirs is therefore, "progress without depth (profundity)" and leads to a uni-dimensional growth.

Though these stereotypes are of a general nature, it must be admitted that they contain some grain of truth, but not the (whole) truth. To some extent, they are pointers of the way of living. Though at times they may be exaggerations of the reality, they have a heuristic function of comparison. So though we must be careful in taking these claims at their face value, we can still learn some things from these generalized stereotypes. They could be treated as "points of departure," rather than the "dwelling place" of the truth. They are lame imageries needing refinement and nuances. But they also play significant functions, though at times totally inadequate.[2]

For our purpose even after affirming the limited usefulness of such stereotypes, we need to go beyond them, in order to facilitate the process of mutually beneficial cross-fertilization. In the background of the cultural differences between the East and the West we need to assert the need to have a deeper appreciation of the differences in our ways of living and of praying. Drawing from the postmodernists, we need to have a deeper appreciation *of the superficial.* Further, we need to affirm the significance of science, liberal education and enlightenment in the growth of our spirituality including mysticism. So today we cannot be satisfied by a spirituality/mysticism for the elite. Postmodernism and modern sensibility urge us to respect the world and matter. We need to affirm unashamedly that "materiality matters." Therefore science is important not only for its technological benefits, but also for its spiritual insights. And religion and spirituality have to learn to be vibrant and flexible like science. So the warning of the world famous mathematician Alfred North Whitehead can only be ignored at the peril of religion itself: "Religion will not regain its old power until it can face change in the same spirit as does science."

This makes the contemporary people sensitive to the sacred and luminous dimensions of our day to day life.

Mystical Strands of Today

The very term "mysticism" provokes various responses. Though not many seem to have clear definitions of this term, almost everyone seems to have an opinion about it. For this paper, I want to leave the term ambiguous, so that hopefully we may be able to gain a better and deeper clarity about it towards the end of our discussion.

These differences (in mysticism) won't go away because they can't go away: they're ineradicable, here to stay. So don't think we can ever finally get to, or give voice to, the one mysticism behind all the different mystical voices. Just as there is no one language behind all our different languages, there is no one, identifiable mysticism beyond all our different mystical experiences. Yes, we can all be trying to say the same thing in our different languages, or in our different religious experiences, but we will never find the one language to do so. To speak, we have to speak German or English or Japanese. To have a mystical experience, we have to have it in a particular religious language. There can never be a mystical Esperanto.

Mysticism of Service

Though mysticism has various strands, we may generalize the western approach to mysticism in terms of service. Along with service for fellow human beings, one of the strong points of western (Christian, Jewish, Islamic) traditions is agape, expressed variously as love, care and concern. Such an agapeic love urges the believer to find God in humans and to discern the will of God in the world around us. So helping others is helping God. The Christian tradition is unambiguous that serving the neighbour is the highest spiritual activity, and is equal to serving God.

The best example of such a mysticism (spirituality) is Mother Teresa. She found God in serving the "poorest of the poor," and has been the classical case of a spirituality that reaches out to the poor. In the self-gift (kenosis) of her own comforts and conveniences and in the self-forgetting of her own ego and in the renunciation of her own ambitions, she has served her fellow human beings. This has been rightly considered the highest form of spirituality in western circles.

From such an understanding of mysticism as service, it follows that matter is sacred. If matter is sacred, then the study of matter, science is equally sacred. Closely related is the significant Christian affirmation that the human body is noble. It is the temple of God. The fundamental Christian dogmas of incarnation and resurrection do not make any sense apart from such a noble understanding of the human body. If matter and body are important, it follows without doubt that the world here and now is significant. This world has to make a significant contribution in the realization of human beings and in the final unfolding of our own destinies.

This urges the western traditions to focus on technological advancements as a very serious matter, a sacred duty. The world is not *maya,* and therefore its importance is not confined to the *vyavaharika* (practical) level only. The world has an independent existence, and contributes profoundly to the spiritual growth and mystical intuitions of the religious believer.

Therefore from a Christian perspective, the Kingdom of God (Ramrajya) is related to material prosperity! They are neither identical nor distinct! The material well-being is related to the spiritual well-being. So the Christian traditions seek to have a unified perspective. It further focuses on the "I-Thou" relationship of Martin Buber, as opposed to the "I-It" relationship. The former is the domain of genuine relationships, and includes one's interaction with fellow human beings and God. The latter is at the realm of the interaction with the material objects. Though this latter is definitely inferior, it too constitutes the totality of human interaction. Further, the other (fellow human beings and God, who is "The Totally Other") does not merely limit me. They define me and constitute me. I am what I am, in terms of the interaction with the other. So human relationship counts a lot in one's self-realisation, as well as spiritual fulfillment. From this perspective reality is essentially relationship and God is Love. God as Love interacts with us and enables us so that we can be ourselves in the all embracing divine presence.

From these considerations it follows that for a Christian the most pertinent question is raised by John in his Epistle: "If I do not love my brother whom I can see, how do I love God whom I do not see?" Without serving our fellow human beings (including the enemies), there is no way we can be spiritual. Service of the world and love for fellow human beings are constitutive of our mystical experience. So the Christian extrovert mysticism tends to embrace the material world without belittling the spiritual realm.

Mysticism of Silence

In contrast to the western mystical tradition as primarily one of service, the eastern mystical tradition can be termed as of "silence." The focus of the eastern tradition is to discover silence as the source of one's profound mystical experiences. The silence in the eastern tradition enables one not only to concentrate but also to focus on the essentials and to get in touch with one's own depth. The silence of the eastern tradition is not merely the absence of words or activities, but the pregnant fullness of being and bliss. The silence into which the mystics descend is the silence of fullness – *nirvana* – where the ephemeral external sounds and activities are transcended to reach the depth of the absolute.[3]

The *maunavrata* that many of the Eastern ascetics regularly practice is a symbolic representation of such a "silent" way of life. The *maunavrata* and the stress on interior silence are meant to lead one from the absence of words to the absence of ego and of self. Only when one realizes the absence of one's ego can one be totally one with the whole reality in its ultimate destiny. Such spiritual practices (flowing from physical asceticism and mental perseverance) have enabled many gurus to develop tremendous paranormal physical and mental powers. Such exercises and experiences put them in touch with their own deepest self, with their own unconsciousness or subtle selves, enabling the flow of extraordinary powers.

Thus the awareness of the solitude coupled with the power of detached observation makes the eastern mystics compassionate people. It helps them to integrate their limited action with their deepest contemplation. The *nishkama-karma* (self-less action) that stems from such contemplation is in harmony with the rhythm of the universe.

Thus the attention on solitude leads them to the awareness of *nirvana* (which is both the total fullness and at the same time the total absence of the ego). The positive understanding of *sunyata* (void or null) can be understood as extinguishing the fire of the ego (*ahamkara, samsara,* etc.) which necessarily leads to the fullness of being. Therefore unlike the

Aristotelian understanding of the philosophical quest ("Know Thyself") the eastern traditions attempt just to "Forget One's Self." The mysticism of silence and solitude is the best means for such an enterprise of total self-annihilation, leading to the realization of one's fullness in the Ultimate (that is Being, Bliss and Consciousness). Thus the one good representative of this tradition of mysticism is Shirdi Sai Baba, who completely detached himself from the affairs of the world, and discovered the depth of his being. An enlightened man, he has attracted countless millions of people to himself and provided them with solace and strength. His active spiritual exercises of meditation and contemplation were first achieved by sustained effort. They later gave way to a peace that comes from effortless silence.

In the eastern tradition the role of a guru (spiritual master) is imperative for self-realisation. When passing through the various spiritual stages there is every danger that one gets lost. When the disciple gives himself undividedly to the guru, it is also symbolic of his self-denial. The guru helps the disciple to choose the path fit for him/her to attain the total unity with the Brahman.

So the mystic arrves at an ecstatic union where he/she realizes the fullness of *sat-cit-ananda,* and in the process loses himself/herself. He/she realizes the truth of the great sayings, *(Mahavakya) Aham Brahmasmi; Tatvam asi.*[4] Thus the initial silence and detachment from the world leads a mystic necessarily to get himself totally absorbed into the fullness of reality.

So the focus of the mysticism of silence is to realize one's total union with the whole, to forget oneself to attain the Ultimate. The innermost quest for one's own depth leads one to discover the depth of the cosmos that is the *Paramatman.* Hence running away from the world and from the activities of the world is primarily to get to the root of it and to realize one's fullness there.

Two Illustrative Examples

After having seen the broad outlines of two different approaches to mysticism, we are in a position to see if these two strands can converge at least sometimes. For this purpose I have randomly picked up two contemporary "mystics" who have, in my opinion, succeeded admirably in fostering the creative interaction between these two streams: Raimundo Panikkar and Bede Griffiths.

Raimundo Panikkar (1918-) was born of a Spanish mother and an Indian father. Till his death recently he used to spend his time between India and Spain. Though a practicing Christian, he has opened his vision to embrace the larger Hindu tradition. His opus magnum, *The Vedic Experience*, is a subtle interpretation of the classical advaitic tradition for contemporary times. His cosmo-theandric vision of reality is the crucial response to the contemporary problems of abject poverty, environmental disaster and religious fanaticism. Holder of three doctorates, he was in the forefront in inter-religious dialogue. Once he claimed that for the contemporary times, "inter-religious dialogue is a necessary religious activity."

Bede Griffiths (1903-93) was an Englishman who made India his home. After his initial struggles with faith, he embraced Catholicism, became a monk and came to India. Well-versed in the ideas and traditions of Hinduism, he opened his heart totally to Christian *advaita*. He was a compassionate mystic who was open to all forms of knowledge (including science, atheism, philosophies). Author of more than 20 books and 400 articles, he has had a profound impact on the Christian Ashram movements in India. His own formulation of Christian *advaita* is a metaphysical key to those undertaking interreligious dialogue.

Mystical Orientations for Today

After having seen the two mystical traditions, and how two great contemporary mystics have personalized it, we go beyond and formulate for ourselves the mystical orientations for today. In this process we draw from both the streams so as to come up with a mysticism that responds truly to the concerns of contemporary men and women. Our treatment in this section may be subjective, but we try our best to be fair and just to both the traditions without being one-sided.

For this purpose we draw three insights from the service traditions: Margins, Marketplace, Materiality. Similarly we draw three insights from the silence traditions; Basics, Bottom, Beyond! This calls for a true dialogue between the various mystical traditions. In such a mystical dialogue that includes both silence and service we can deepen the spiritual unity of our religious communities and at the same time, further the worldly well-being of all creatures.[5]

Along with the postmoderns, we see the need to take the ordinary and everyday life seriously. Without agreeing with postmoderns ideologically, we can very well appreciate the concern to experience the deeper life of the superficial. Modern science and liberal education have enabled today's people to open their mind wider and to understand reality better. Knowledge, which was once a privilege of a few, is made accessible to the vast majority of people. Accessibility to the Scriptures and availability of religious practices are all indicators in this direction. Thus spirituality, and even mysticism, has to move from the elite to the ordinary. Contemporary human persons with their quest for God-experience cannot be satisfied today with a spirituality for the elite.

Mysticism of the Margins

The people on the margins may be naïve, superficial. They may be considered as insignificant by the powers that be. They may not have had much spiritual experience. But the daily life that they lead has taught them to be humble to others and open to God. Therefore, today's situation demands a spirituality of the margins that does not limit mysticism to the esoteric and exotic.

From this perspective the spiritual depth is to be related to spiritual breadth. When one goes really deeper into oneself, one discovers the breadth and width of human religions. So for the contemporary humans, "To be deeply religious is to be broadly religious"[6]

These sentiments are very clearly discerned in Christianity, which was essentially a religion of the slaves and the downtrodden. Furthermore, the Beatitudes ("Blessed are the poor"), the basis of Christian Ethics can be understood only within a context of the poor and the oppressed.

Further, Jesus who is the embodiment of self-emptying can only be understood from the perspective of the poor, the anawim of Yahweh. The "sign of contradiction" that early Christianity was, can only be experienced as a commitment to the poor and marginalized.

Therefore the spirituality for today, responding to the needs of the poor and under-privileged, sees mysticism not as an exercise of elitist piety, but of unconditional surrender to the loving Father (and Mother). It is a gift and not one's right, a gift given freely and gratuitously, given not because one deserves it, but because one is unconditionally loved. Thus reference to the margins implies a mysticism of and by the poor.

Mysticism of the Marketplace

Similar to the concern for the poor, today's spiritual sensibilities urge us to experience the divine touch in ordinary events, things and people or in the marketplace of ordinary place and locale. Only when one sees the ordinary in the extra-ordinary, can we experience the loving God, who is both very ordinary and at the same time extraordinary.

This urges spirituality to take the normal concerns of the people seriously. This invites the spiritual people to seek God also in the ordinary human experiences of hunger, thirst, suffering, justice and love. Unless spirituality understands and speaks the language of ordinary people, it cannot respond to the concerns of ordinary humans. So the mysticism for today is one that also encounters the holy in the ordinary, the divine in the mundane and the sacred in the most insignificant.

Such a spirituality of the market place goes beyond a new age spirituality for the elite, where the elite are given instant (spiritual) gratification, provided they can pay for it! Thus the transformation from genuine mysticism comes not from the New Age of today's fashionable elite, but by rational, responsible and open minded dealings of the ordinary people. So Ken Wilber can rightly claim: "In fact, at this point in history, the most radical, pervasive, and earth-shaking transformation would occur simply if everybody truly evolved to a mature, rational, and responsible ego, capable of freely participating in the open exchange of mutual self-esteem. *There* is the 'edge of history.' There would be a *real* New Age."

Similarly, the contemporary Catholic theologian Karl Rahner called for a new day in Christianity. He affirmed that "the devout Christian of the future will either be a 'mystic' ... or he will cease to be anything at all." Thus following Rahner today's mysticism needs to reinvent a mysticism of every day things and a "theology of everyday things"

Mysticism of the Materiality

Further the service traditions urges us to give real spiritual importance to this world and to our bodiliness. It invites us to reflect and experience the significance of being human, being bodily, being-in-the-world (Dasein).

If we take incarnation and resurrection seriously, we can never disdain the world and materiality. At the same time this tradition listens to the wise teachers and relativises the material world. This implies that our body, our world and our worldly concerns are sacred, though we do not absolutise them. This implies that our being involved in this sacred world has necessarily implications for a life that is larger than this life. So we are called "to find God in all things," as St. Ignatius of Loyola says.[7]

Back to the Basics[8]

The first thing we can learn from the silence tradition is to go back to the basics. Spiritual teachers of all ages have always insisted on the need to relativise (at least some) reality. It is the basic Hindu insight that the world is maya.[9] As spiritual persons, we need to set priorities in life. We need to be open to the whole, but we cannot be carried away by everything. There is need for real discernment of the spirit. We need to discern the real from the unreal, the life-giving from the death-promoting. While giving importance to this world, we need to set our priorities properly so that the spiritual realm of total joy may be experienced by us. To enjoy both material joy and spiritual bliss we need to have a framework that distinguishes the necessary from the accidentals, the basics from the unimportant.

Get to the Bottom

Only when we can get into the depth of being (without sacrificing the superficial), can we really enjoy the fruit of our work. If we are ceaselessly carried away by every fad, we just cannot grow roots. Without rootedness and belongingness, we just cannot be spiritual persons. The mystics of today must be unwavering when confronted with the ever changing craze of our times. They need to be rooted and grounded in the reality of being, without being authoritarian and absolutist.

Only those who dare to reach the bottom can really soar high and enjoy the vast sky. Only those who have developed the taste for the deepest spiritual level can fully cherish the material that lies all around us. Without the anchor of God's love we cannot be connected to the whole.

Be Beyond

After tracing the basics and getting to the bottom the mystics of today are called to go beyond themselves. Unless they dare to cross the narrow limitations of their own culture and religion, they cannot be genuinely open. Unless they can go beyond every bond (bodily, mental and spiritual), they cannot reach the Infinite, who is boundless. The longing for the infinite, which is the primary concern of the mystics cannot be realized if they do not let themselves go and dare to transcend all boundaries: including the boundary of their own lives and selves.

In this sense contemporary mystics are truly "pilgrims" on the way . As pilgrims their permanent dwelling place is not here, though they may feel totally "at home" here.

In this manner they dare to worship God who is beyond all names and forms. They reach out to the Unconditional who is beyond the concepts and categories that we humans are capable of. Such a God is even beyond our imagination. He/She is the "Totally Other" who invites them to Himself/Herself and urges them to cross all barriers and boundaries.

Conclusion: Dialogue as Way of Life

Thus the challenge of today is to enter into dialogue with our different mystical traditions. But, in such a dialogue of service, we will also become aware of our differences. For although there is one voice calling us to serve, each of us – Buddhists, Christians, Muslims, Hindus, Jews – will have different views of how to respond to suffering, how to confront injustice, how to deal with hatred and violence, how to change society and the world. But, as has been my limited experience, these real differences between us will usually turn out to be more complementary than contradictory. We will learn from our differences. Why? Because what is animating and guiding us in this dialogue of service is not the desire to prove that our view is more true or better than yours, but how we can all help the victims who have called us together – how we can help the children who are about to fall into the well. This further calls for deepest experiences of the compassion, love and respect that stems from the Ultimate experiences of the divine.

So the Ultimate is beyond our conception and is beyond ourselves. The clear challenge before us is: "Either be mystics or perish." Confronted with the unenviable challenges of the world, we are faced with our own collective destruction and common experience of mysticism.

So the mysticism of today demands a silence that leads to serenity, peace and calm. "Unattached observation" and "choiceless awareness" are its features.[10] It prevents us from clinging to anything other than God for our well-being. It frees us from all inordinate attachments and enables us to abandoning ourselves unconditionally and lovingly to God who is greater than ourselves. Such a lifestyle leads to serenity, serendipity and active social commitment. Concern for the environment and commitment to the unfortunate ones are integral dimension of such a mystical way of life.

Such a mystical experience of oneness with God, with other human beings and reality makes dialogue imperative: dialogue between science and religion, between religious traditions and between mystical ways. Such a dialogical encounter between humans, world and God helps to create collectively a new world, a new horizon, a new spirituality. Only in such dialogue, will humans become what they are. The basic feature of such a way of life is respect: for oneself, for the other and for God.

Thus the mystic of contemporary times has both "feet" and "wings." Grounded on his/her feet, he/she is rooted to the whole. Therefore, he/she is "at home in the universe." He/she is basically open to others, sensitive to the poor and ready to embrace the whole reality. He has the wings that takes him/her to dimensions totally beyond to the realm of the Transcendental (God, the Wholly Other)! In such a mode of life, the mystic leads a life that is blissfully pure, transparent, simple and full.

Endnotes

[1] For the purpose of this paper I limit the eastern tradition to that of the Indian subcontinent. However, it seems to me that these ideas are very much applicable to the other eastern regions like China, Japan, Korea etc, with some nuances.

[2] It may be noted that some of the authors like Fritjof Capra, Deepak Chopra and Ken Wilber have popularized these notions. Their books have tremendously influenced the popular audience. The now powerful New Age Movement also has contributed to the affirmation of these stereotypes.

[3] This is the mystical practice that most of us are familiar with – silence, retreat from the world, withdrawal into the cave of the heart, "contemplation." It is the conviction that we find in all mystics - that the Reality they are experiencing or searching for can be found only in silence; though our experience of it begins with language, the Divine lies beyond all language. And so we have the many different mystical practices that all urge us to stop talking, and even to stop thinking: zazen, centering prayer, raja yoga, counting the breath, mindfulness, the Jesus Prayer, the Namu Amida Butsu, the dance of the whirling dervish. All of these exercises seek to turn off, as it were, the constant flow of words and thoughts that fill our mouths and minds; they try to move us beyond discursive thinking into that realm where we just "are" and where we can feel what it is like simply to be. For it is in such silence that we can hear the wordless voice of Mystery, of what Ibn-Arabi calls "the really Real."

[4] This means, "I am Brahman," or "That Thou Art.

[5] But I am urging that such dialogue of silence, already practiced, be balanced also by a dialogue of service. In this dialogue, we not only sit in meditation together, we act together. Such action begins first with identifying the forms of suffering – human as well as ecological – that are calling each of us. Who or where, in our own context or in our own world, is the child about to fall into the well whom we all want to help? And then we will deliberate together about what can or must be done. Then, we will roll up our sleeves and act together, struggle together as we try to listen to and work with the victims of this world. In such acting and struggling together, we will become aware of the bonds that unite us as brothers and sisters; we will hear the same Voice that is calling us in the voices of the victims.

[6] The abover quote is ascribed to Paul Knitter.

[7] This worldly mysticism of St. Ignatius, as it may be called, is not at all different from the basic Christian teaching that Christ brings God into our midst and the gift of the Spirit brings God into our deepest selves. God is very much in the world and in particular in all human beings. And our love of God must be manifested in our love of one another so that we love not only in word but also in deed. We Jesuits believe that our worldly spirituality, at its best, has touched many who have passed through our schools or who have made the Spiritual Exercises or have had Jesuit friends or known a Jesuit working in their own so-called secular world. We Jesuits may be less present in the future to "lay occupations," and perhaps a valuable witness will thus be lost because lay persons cannot as easily publicly declare themselves both as committed disciples of Jesus Christ and as astrophysicists, artists, or cardiac surgeons, as Jesuits in these fields are able to do.

[8] The following three orientations are borrowed mainly from the Silence tradition of Hindusim.

[9] The term *maya*, illusion, may definitely be understood positively and not necessarily nihilistically.

[10] J. Krishnamurthi is popularised these terms.

Self-Organizing Systems
and Final Causality
Joseph Bracken

Introduction: The Mechanistic Worldview and Its Impact on Teleology

At the beginning of the 17th century in Western Europe, a dramatic change of worldview took place which enormously facilitated the development of modern natural science. Pioneering individuals like Galileo Galilei basically set aside the medieval worldview which laid such heavy emphasis on teleology, the logical order of all things in this world, both to one another and to God as their transcendent Creator, and focused their attention on physical phenomena in dynamic interrelation according to mathematical laws and thus in quantifiably measurable terms.[1] In this respect Galileo and his contemporaries were, at least in some measure, returning to a very old worldview which preceded the philosophy of Plato and Aristotle, the world of philosophical atomism propagated by the Greek pre-Socratic thinkers like Leucippus and Democritus. According to this latter view, physical reality is simply matter-in-motion within an all-encompassing void, a universe of inert bits of matter (atoms) which over time aggregate and then disperse to form the enduring objects of ordinary sense experience.[2]

The inevitable consequence of this approach to physical reality, of course, is that final causality no longer plays any significant role in the relations of material entities to one another and to God. For there are no innate principles of activity or "natures" within the things of this world, guaranteeing that they will act one way rather than another. Everything is reduced to the contingent workings of efficient causality under the conditions of space and time. That is, the atoms constituting the things of this world are in themselves inert and lifeless and are moved in one direction rather than another simply through the impact of external forces. The most influential philosopher of that period, Rene Descartes, proposed that only the human mind as a "thinking substance" was exempt from the laws of mechanical interaction; all other things in this world, including the human body, were to be regarded as machines, nothing more than the sum of their interrelated parts.[3]

So great was the influence of this mechanistic approach to physical reality in terms of physics and astronomy that it likewise had a significant impact upon the philosophical assumptions governing the newly emerging life sciences in the 18th and 19th centuries. Charles Darwin, for example, set forth his principle of natural selection along basically mechanistic lines. Evolution takes place by chance rather than by design. Minor changes in the physical makeup of plants and animals can lead over time to a distinct environmental advantage for certain individual organisms within a given species and for entire species in competition with still other species in the ongoing effort at survival. Thus there is no grand design or divine plan for creation at work here. Still less is there any sign of purposeful adaptation on the part of individual organisms and species in the ongoing struggle to survive and propagate in a hostile environment. It is pure chance whether the individual organism or species is unexpectedly better equipped by nature to prosper rather than to undergo extinction. Behavioral patterns for coping with the environment, in other words, are not passed on from generation to generation through sexual reproduction but have to be worked out all over again by each new generation. Only inherited changes in body structure can be transmitted from one generation to the next.

Darwin's principle of natural selection, of course, was eventually further modified and explained in terms of gene mutation and the novel combination of genes through sexual reproduction, the so-called "modern synthesis." But even here the tendency among professionals in the life sciences has been to think of evolution in terms of the gradual accumulation of very small changes in bodily structure for the organism or species. Thus the organism or species is basically passive under the influence of external forces rather than actively engaged in promoting its own survival.[4] There are scientists, to be sure, who resist the idea of evolution as based exclusively on small incremental changes; Stephen Gould and Niles Eldridge come to mind with their theory of "punctuated equilibrium," namely, periods of rapid change followed by even longer periods of relative non-change among existing species.[5]

But they too tend to think of evolution in largely mechanistic terms. That is, any notion of final causality or teleological orientation operative within individual organisms or species is customarily dismissed as an uncritical return to an outdated understanding of physical reality from earlier times. But there are some hardy individuals who have braved the ridicule of their peers to set forth their own understanding of teleology operative within Nature and thus to challenge some of the reigning assumptions of the "modern synthesis." Two of these individuals are Michael Polanyi and Rupert Sheldrake. In the remainder of this paper I will summarize their understanding of what they call "morphogenetic fields" and indicate how this new approach to a developmental teleology within Nature might be further legitimated by my own rethinking of Whiteheadian metaphysics. In addition, this neo-Whiteheadian approach to reality seems to exhibit some unexpected affinities to classical Eastern conceptions of Ultimate Reality, as I shall make clear at the end of this paper.

Michael Polanyi and Rupert Sheldrake

In his classic work *The Tacit Dimension*, Michael Polanyi set forth a heuristic approach to human understanding whereby human beings tend to organize the world of their experience in terms of tacitly known holistic structures or patterns of behavior. Calling it the "from–to" structure of human knowing,[6] he noted how we first intuit a pattern in a set of empirical data and then organize the data to fit the pattern. Sometimes, of course, the pattern proves to be illusory and we start all over again in our hunt for an organizational principle. But his basic point was that epistemologically the whole or totality does not so much arise out of the study of the parts in their dynamic interrelation but rather precedes the organization of the parts as a heuristic principle by way of a logic of discovery. While many academic colleagues conceded Polanyi's point about the heuristic character of human knowing, they nevertheless balked at his further postulate that Nature itself seems to be governed by a logic of achievement structurally akin to the logic of discovery within the human mind. That is, deliberately prescinding from the organization of inanimate Nature, Polanyi argued that the gradual evolution of living organisms toward greater complexity and ultimately toward consciousness is governed by what he called "morphogenetic fields," holistic structures that condition how the individual entities within the field relate to one another over time more and more coherently.[7] In the opinion of his critics, Polanyi was here covertly reintroducing a basically Aristotelian approach to final causality in Nature which is at odds with the presuppositions of modern natural science, in particular, with contemporary biology as based on the principle of natural selection.

Some years later, to be sure, Rupert Sheldrake renewed the debate over the notion of morphogenetic fields with the publication of his book *A New Science of Life*. Calling his theory "the hypothesis of formative causation," Sheldrake proposes:

Specific morphogenetic fields are responsible for the characteristic form and organization of systems at all levels of complexity, not only in the realm of biology, but also in the realm of chemistry and physics. These fields order the systems with which they are associated by affecting events which, from an energetic point of view, appear to be indeterminate or probabilistic; they impose patterned restrictions on the energetically possible outcomes of physical processes.[8]

In answer to the question where these field-structures come from, Sheldrake replied that they are derived from previous morphogenetic fields associated with previous similar systems: "A plant takes up the form characteristic of its species because past members of the species took up that form; and an animal acts instinctively in a particular manner because similar animals behaved like that previously."[9] Hence, the world is made up of structured fields of activity which interlock and are hierarchically ordered through both space and time.

Morphogenetic Fields of Whitehead

Once again outrage was expressed by more conservatively oriented colleagues who resented this affront to the standard presuppositions of modern science in which notions of final causality in Nature had for several centuries been effectively ruled out. In this paper, however, I will offer a neo-Whiteheadian interpretation of the notion of morphogenetic fields which may mediate between the theories of Polanyi and Sheldrake on the one hand, and the objections of their critics on the other. In brief, I will make clear how an understanding of Whiteheadian "societies" as structured fields of activity for their constituent actual occasions seems to provide both for "bottom-up" and for "top-down" causation at the same time. In this way one can argue that final causality is indeed at work in the gradual evolution of Whiteheadian societies but only in and through the ongoing interrelated activity of their constituent actual occasions. The structure or form of the field is at one moment generated by the constituent actual occasions "from below," and yet in the next moment that same "common element of form" is active "from above" in conditioning the next set of constituent actual occasions. What results then is the notion of a developmental rather than a fixed entelechy as the governing insight in the concept of morphogenetic fields. In addition, I will indicate how, given this understanding of Whiteheadian societies, one has at hand a new and interesting way to think about the God-world relationship, that is, how God "informs" the cosmic process without altering the normal operation of secondary causes within Nature.

In his book *A Social Ontology*, David Weissman claims that Whiteheadian actual occasions are "atomic and self-contained: each one comes into being from nothing, only to be annihilated when the sensible endowment of its creation has been organized in accord with its feelings, thoughts, and aims."[10] As a result, he develops an alternate vision of reality based on interlocking and hierarchically ordered "systems" which "derive their coherence or integrity from the reciprocal causal relations of their parts."[11] While I agree with Weissman in much of his critique of the latent atomism within Whitehead's thought, I have for many years now believed that a rethinking of Whiteheadian "societies" could convert the latter's philosophy into a more fully consistent social ontology while at the same time preserving other key insights (e.g., actual occasions as "the final real things of which the world is made up."[12]) Systems thinking, after all, runs the risk of reducing reality to the interplay of impersonal forces and mechanisms with too little attention paid to the particular contributions of individuals to the existence and activity of the group in question.[13]

Maintaining that self-constituting subjects of experience are the ultimate constituents of all socially organized realities keeps in focus the conviction that systems exist for the well-being of individuals and not vice-versa.

In any event, my own line of thought for many years now has basically run as follows. Whiteheadian societies, since they correspond to the relatively stable persons and things of common sense experience, must be more than just aggregates of analogously constituted actual occasions. For, as such, these aggregates would come into and go out of existence as rapidly as their constituent actual occasions. Hence, as I see it, Whiteheadian societies should be treated as "environments" or "structured fields of activity" for those same actual occasions.[14] The structure within the field is, to be sure, ontologically dependent upon the interrelated activity of successive actual occasions (or sets of actual occasions in the case of Whiteheadian societies extended in space as well as time). But the field endures as these actual occasions or sets of actual occasions come and go. Furthermore, the structure embedded in the field by reason of the activity of previous actual occasions or sets of actual occasions, heavily conditions the self-constituting activity of the present actual occasion or set of actual occasions.

The net effect of this arrangement is that there is indeed a form or organizing principle within every Whiteheadian society at any given moment. But the form is not active as an Aristotelian substantial form is active with respect to its material components. Rather, the form is passive, both because it originated in virtue of the self-constituting activity of an antecedent actual occasion or set of actual occasions and because it is simply "prehended" by the next actual occasion or set of actual occasions. Like an Aristotelian substantial form, therefore, it is ontologically prior to the material components which it here and now "informs." But, unlike an Aristotelian substantial form, it "informs" its components not in virtue of its own inherent activity but simply by being there as an object of prehension or activity on the part of the next actual occasion or set of actual occasions. Furthermore, unlike an Aristotelian substantial form, the form or pattern of existence and activity within a Whiteheadian society is, as a result, seldom exactly the same from moment to moment. It undergoes, at least within organic compounds, a slow but steady transformation as a result of new actual occasions or new sets of actual occasions constituting themselves in slightly different ways from their predecessors, and thus collectively achieving a new "common element of form." It thereby serves as an entelechy or organizing principle for a Whiteheadian society, but it is strictly a developmental entelechy passively dependent upon the activity of its material parts or members, namely, its constituent actual occasions from moment to moment.

As I see it, this line of thought allows me to liken a Whiteheadian society to a morphogenetic field as conceived by Polanyi and Sheldrake but without the theoretical limitations traditionally attributed to Aristotelian final causality. The morphogenetic field, in other words, possesses an immanent principle for the organization of its material components at any given moment. But, insofar as this immanent principle is passive rather than active with respect to those same components, and insofar as this immanent principle is itself in process of change or development in virtue of the activity of those same material components, then one cannot give ontological priority to the immanent principle over the material components as Aristotle gave ontological priority to form over matter. Rather, it would be the morphogenetic field as a whole which undergoes gradual change in virtue of the interrelated functions of the material components and their immanent principle of organization from moment to moment (in the language of Whitehead's philosophy, interrelated actual occasions and their "common element of form)." Furthermore, since the material components, the actual occasions, are by definition self-organizing and thus open to change in various ways (e.g., through external environmental influences and, as we shall see below, through what Whitehead calls "divine initial aims"), this scheme amply provides for "bottom-up" as well as "top-down" causation in the explanation of evolution. Neither of the two forms of causation by themselves, but only the two in combination, fully explain how higher-order systems of organization can emerge over time out of lower-order systems.

Here it might be useful to cite the work of Niels Henrik Gregersen in a pair of articles published in *Zygon* some years ago.[15] His understanding of "autopoietic processes" both within certain inanimate compounds (so-called "dissipative structures") and in organic compounds or living systems seems in my judgment nicely to parallel my above-stated understanding of Whiteheadian societies as structured fields of activity or morphogenetic fields for their constituent actual occasions. For, as Gregersen makes clear, "autopoiesis is less than self-constitution, but more than self-organization."[16] That is, whereas the term self-organization "usually suggests that the elements of a system remain self-identical and that they are only synthesized differently in different self-organizing systems, the idea of autopoiesis suggests that the elements themselves are produced and reproduced *within the local systems themselves.*"[17] Not only are the elements within a given system differently arranged as a result of self-organization; rather, in "autopoiesis" new elements or new component parts arise so as to make up a higher-order system which has thus emerged out of a lower-level system or set of such systems. Initially, this proposal might seem to stand in opposition to Whitehead's concept of actual occasions as self-constituting subjects of experience within any and every societal configuration. But if, as noted above, these actual occasions are capable of gradual growth in complexity over time as a result of interaction with a common element of form, itself in process of change and development, then Gregersen's stipulation that autopoietic processes involve the production of new elements, and thus higher-order systems, seems to be unexpectedly confirmed from a Whiteheadian perspective.

Whitehead himself, for example, explicitly allowed for four "grades" of actual occasions: "First, and lowest, there are the actual occasions in so-called 'empty space;' secondly, there are the actual occasions which are moments in the life-histories of enduring non-living objects, such as electrons or other primitive organisms; thirdly, there are the actual occasions which are moments in the life-histories of enduring living objects; fourthly, there are the actual occasions which are moments in the life-histories of enduring objects with conscious knowledge."[18] All these "grades" of actual occasions, to be sure, exist here and now simultaneously; but in terms of cosmic evolution they must have emerged successively as their societal configuration became more complicated. That is, the higher-order "grade" of actual occasion came into being precisely when higher-order, more complex societies (structured fields of activity) emerged out of lower-order, less tightly organized societies (fields of activity) through a process akin to what I described above.

The key idea here is, as indicated earlier, the dynamic inter-relation of the constituent actual occasions and their "common element of form" constituting them as a society rather than a simple aggregate. The occasions are self-constituting; that is, they each "prehend" both the structure and the feelings pertinent to antecedent actual occasions and integrate these physical and conceptual "prehensions" into their own self-constitution here and now. But the single strongest influence on their self-constitution is presumably the pattern of relation existing among their predecessors a moment ago and preserved in their common field of activity. Yet, as already indicated, since the constituent actual occasions are genuinely self-constituting, they are not bound simply to repeat the pattern of the past in their own interrelation here and now. They can make a very modest but still significant change in that "common element of form" by their own dynamic interrelation. In this way, a new structured field of activity or morphogenetic field will slowly begin to take shape with constituent actual occasions to match in the following moment as they prehend this new "common element of form." Thus, when the new structure within the field and the altered self-constitution of the constituent actual occasions are once again in full alignment with one another, we have a new ontological reality or higher-order level of being which has emerged out of its predecessors in the same line of development or evolution.[19]

A New Perspective on God-world Relationship

Earlier I mentioned that this rethinking of Whitehead's notion of society could also shed light on our human understanding of the God-world relationship. One of the persistent problems in the contemporary religion and science debate is the following: if God exists and is active in this world, how can God exert causal influence on the direction of the cosmic process without suspending, or otherwise interfering with, the laws of Nature familiar to scientists. Yet, if we concede that "the final real things of which the world is made up" are actual occasions or momentary self-constituting subjects of experience, and if we stipulate with Whitehead that each actual occasion is guided in its self-constitution by what Whitehead calls a "divine initial aim,"[20] then God can "inform" their self-constitution in each case without physically coercing it and thereby interfering with the normal operation of natural processes. Formal causality, in other words, is non-energetic and immaterial; it provides information to the newly concrescing actual occasion without physically overpowering it or making it happen in terms of brute force.[21]

All this is standard Whiteheadian doctrine. Through the ongoing integration of the "primordial nature" and the "consequent" nature within God, God "is the poet of the world, with tender patience leading it by his vision of truth, beauty, and goodness."[22]

Where I differ from Whitehead is in my further proposal that God creates or empowers the actual occasion as well as gives it a "lure" toward its proper self-actualization. For, in terms of my own Neo-Whiteheadian understanding of the God-world relationship, creativity is not a metaphysical "given" (as in Whitehead's scheme) but the nature of the triune God, the inner principle of existence and activity whereby the three divine persons exist for one another as one God.[23] Thus, as I see it, through initial aims to their creatures at every moment, the divine persons communicate to those same creatures a share in their own divine power of existence and activity. Thereby the divine persons empower their creatures both to be themselves and to respond without coercion to the divine initiative in their regard. In my judgment, this is what is (or at least should be) meant by God's primary causality as opposed to the secondary causality of creatures. There is, in other words, genuine spontaneity at work here, both on God's part and from the side of the creature. Hence, primary causality is not a unilateral exercise of divine power upon a purely passive created reality but the creation of an intersubjective relationship with a creature, with God as primary cause taking the initiative and the creature as secondary cause responding. Otherwise, the relation between primary and secondary causality remains obscure. For, how does the secondary cause (e.g., an axe in the hands of a woodsman) serve as anything but the passive instrument for the achievement of the goal set by the primary cause (e.g., the woodsman cutting down a tree)? Only if both the primary cause and the secondary cause are subjects of experience in dynamic interrelation as indicated above is there a *bona fide* exercise of spontaneity by both the primary and the secondary causes in the action at hand.[24]

In effect, then, at every moment of the cosmic process, the three divine persons and all their creatures exercise both efficient and final causality, albeit in inverse proportion.[25] That is, on the one hand the divine persons empower the created actual occasion to make its own self-constituting decision. Thereby the divine persons exercise some limited efficient causality but the created actual occasion is primarily responsible for its own self-constitution and for its immediate impact upon later actual occasions. On the other hand, the created actual occasion exercises only a limited form of final causality in fashioning its subjective aim and achieving "satisfaction" as the goal of the process of concrescence.

But the divine persons exercise far more final causality in incorporating the "decisions" of all contemporary actual occasions into their consequent nature and in communicating still another set of initial aims to the next generation of actual occasions. In the end, therefore, creatures are primarily responsible for what happens here and now, whether for better or for worse. But the divine persons are primarily responsible for the overall directionality of the cosmic process. The divine persons cannot reverse or otherwise negate the "decisions" of their creatures. But, as Whitehead implies in *Process and Reality*,[26] they can save "what in the temporal world is mere wreckage" by incorporating it into a larger context still in process of completion.

Whitehead and Classical Eastern Views

One further point should be noted before concluding. As I proposed some years ago in a book entitled *The Divine Matrix*,[27] I believe that this neo-Whiteheadian understanding of the God-world relationship allows for an unexpected affinity between conceptions of Ultimate Reality or the Transcendent within the major East Asian religions (Vedanta Hinduism, classical Buddhism and Taoism) and a trinitarian understanding of the God-world relationship. For, if Whiteheadian Creativity be understood not simply as a metaphysical given as with Whitehead but rather as the inner principle or ground of the divine being, whereby the three divine persons co-exist in dynamic relationship both with one another and with all their creatures, then one can legitimately affirm a non-personal or trans-personal as well as an interpersonal dimension to the reality of God. The full reality of God is then non-personal or trans-personal as well as inter-personal, and one can make suitable comparisons with the notion of *Brahman* in Vedanta Hinduism, with the notion of Dependent Co-origination or Absolute Emptiness in classical Buddhism, and with the notion of the Tao in the *Tao te Ching*. But, to elaborate at greater length on this point, would presumably be a distraction or diversion from the principal focus of the present paper.

Conclusion

To sum up, then, in my presentation I have tried to vindicate Michael Polanyi's and Rupert Sheldrake's controversial appeal to immanent teleology within cosmic evolution in virtue of what they call morphogenetic fields. As I see it, if these morphogenetic fields are conceived as Whiteheadian societies in the sense defined above, that is, as structured fields of activity for their constituent actual occasions, then one has at hand an explanatory mechanism for both "bottom-up" and "top-down" causation at different levels of existence and activity within Nature. At one moment the constituent actual occasions by their dynamic interrelation are giving shape to the "common element of form" for the society. But in the next moment that same "common element of form" heavily conditions the next set of self-constituting actual occasions. Through this dialectical interplay between the structured field of activity and its constituent actual occasions, the society in question can undergo a gradual transformation in a given direction. Above all, if one then factors in the influence of the three divine persons of the Christian doctrine of the Trinity through their ongoing "initial aims" to concrescing actual occasions, then one can reasonably affirm some form of directionality to the cosmic process. This is not to claim, of course, that the course of cosmic evolution is predetermined in every detail but it should allow one to reject with some confidence the counter-claim that cosmic evolution is "a direction-less process going nowhere slowly."[28]

Endnotes

[1] See,e.g., Ian G. Barbour, *Religion and Science: Historical and Contemporary Issues* (San Francisco: HarperCollins, 1997), pp.9-11.

[2] See *The Book of the Cosmos: Imagining the Universe from Heraclitus to Hawking* (Cambridge, MA: Perseus Books, 2000), pp.23-30.

[3] Barbour, *Religion and Science*, pp.11-13.

[4] *Ibid.*, pp.221-23.

[5] *Ibid.*, pp.223-24.

[6] Michael Polanyi, *The Tacit Dimension* (New York: Doubleday, 1967), p. 10.

[7] Michael Polanyi, *Personal Knowledge: Towards a Post-Critical Philosohy* (New York: Harper Torchbooks, 1964), pp.382-90, 398-400.

[8] See Rupert Sheldrake, *A New Science of Life: The Hypothesis of Formative Causation* (Los Angeles: J. P. Tarcher, 1981), p.13.

[9] *Ibid.*

[10] David Weissman, *A Social Ontology* (New Haven, CT: Yale University Press, 2000), p.98.

[11] *Ibid.*, p.1.

[12] Alfred North Whitehead, *Process and Reality: An Essay in Cosmology,* Corrected Edition, eds. David Ray Griffin and Donald W. Sherburne (New York: Free Press, 1978), p.18.

[13] See here Bracken, *The One in the Many: A Contemporary Reconstruction of the God-World Relationship* (Grand Rapids, MI: Eerdmans, 2001), pp. 65-68, where I review Jurgen Habermas's efforts to restore interpersonal accountability within highly organized contemporary society through his ideal of "communicative rationality." (cf. Jurgen Habermas, *The Theory of Communicative Action,* 2 vols. trans. Thomas McCarthy [Boston: Beacon Press, 1984 & 1987]).

[14] Whitehead, *Process and Reality*, p.90: "Every society must be considered with its background of a wider environment of actual entities, which also contribute their objectifications to which the members of the society must conform. Thus the given contributions of the environment must at least be permissive of the self-sustenance of the society."

[15] Niels Henrik Gregersen, "The Idea of Creation and the Theory of Autopoietic processes," *Zygon* 33 (1998), 333-67; "Autopoiesis: Less than Self-Constitution, More than Self-Organization: Reply to Gilkey, McClelland and Deltete, and Brun," *Zygon* 34 (1999), 117-38.

[16] Gregersen, "Autopoiesis," p.119.

[17] *Ibid.*

[18] Whitehead, *Process and Reality*, p.177.

[19] See here Sheldrake, *A New Science of Life*, pp.76-77, where he indicates how a morphogenetic field gradually evolves under the influence of what he calls a "morphogenetic germ" or subsystem within the overall morphogenetic field. I basically agree with this hypothesis although I would likewise insist that the morphogenetic germ or subsystem within the larger morphogenetic field will not necessarily succeed in transforming the entire field into its own pattern of existence and activity. It may just as readily die out, if the actual occasions within the other subsystems of the field negatively prehend its pattern of activity. Sheldrake may be too Aristotelian here in his surmise that the morphogenetic germ infallibly represents the pattern of future development for the field as a whole (see also on this point Bracken, *Society and Spirit: A Trinitarian Cosmology* [Cranbury, NJ: Associated University Presses, 1991], pp.74-88).

[20] Whitehead, *Process and Reality*, p.244.

[21] See here John F. Haught, *God After Darwin* (Boulder, CO: Westview Press, 2000), pp.69-77, esp. p.70: "Though it is not physically separate, information is logically distinguishable from mass and energy. Information is quietly resident in nature, and in spite of being nonenergetic and nonmassive, it powerfully patterns subordinate natural elements and routines into hierarchically distinct domains.

[22] Whitehead, *Process and Reality*, p.346.

[23] See, e.g., Bracken, *Society and Spirit*, pp.123-29; The One in the Many, pp.120-30.

[24] See here William R. Stoeger, S.J., "Describing God's action in the world in light of Scientific Knowledge of Reality," *Chaos and Complexity: Scientific Perspectives on Divine Action*, eds. Robert John Russell, Nancy Murphy and Arthur R. Peacocke (Notre Dame, IN: Notre Dame University Press, 1995), pp. 239-61, esp. p. 260:"God has created it [the creature, presumably a human being] and is creating it, but at the same time is radically setting it free to become itself, to discover itself, to become conscious of itself, to become free and to become independently personal and social, to discover its roots and its ultimate origin, to respond freely to the invitation to enter into relationship with the community and society of persons which is God, its source and origin." What Stoeger envisions as the pattern of God's relationship with human beings is within my scheme, of course, the basic pattern of God's action with all created actual occasions since one and all are subjects of experience in an inter-subjective relationship with the triune God of Christian belief.

[25] See also Joseph A. Bracken, "A New Look at Time and Eternity," *Theology and Science* 2(2004), 77-88.

[26] *Ibid.,* p.346.

[27] Joseph A. Bracken, S.J., *The Divine Matrix: Creativity as Link between East and West* (Delhi: Motilal Banarsidass, 1997), pp.75-140.

[28] Michael Ruse, "A Darwinian Naturalist's Perspective on Altruism," *Altruism & Altruistic Love: Science, Philosophy, & Religion in Dialogue*, eds. Stephen G. Post, Lynn G. Underwood, Jeffrey B. Schloss, and William B. Hurlbut (New York: Oxford University Press, 2002), p.164.

The Theory of Evolution

Input for a Teilhardian Mysticism

Kathleen Duffy

Introduction

Pierre Teilhard de Chardin (1881-1955) was well positioned for his pioneering efforts in the science and religion dialogue that has recently been gaining momentum. As a geologist and paleontologist, he was in direct contact with the evidence for evolution contained both in the strata of rock that he explored and in the fossil record that he helped to expand. As a Jesuit, he was conversant with the intricacies of Christian theology. And as a person living in an era when evolution was beginning to shake the very foundations of religious belief, he experienced its conflict. Teilhard was able eventually to resolve this conflict for himself and to integrate the science of evolution with the mystery of Christ and the Incarnation. This integration was not only the fruit of his mystical experience, but also its continuing impulse. In this paper, I examine Teilhard's unique approach to mysticism.

Perhaps the best way to understand Teilhard's mysticism is to listen to the story of his spiritual awakening, as he tells it. We are fortunate to have several essays in which he relates details of his life and of his struggle to develop and articulate his mystical vision. Chief among these is his autobiographical essay "The Heart of Matter."[1] Written about five years before his death, this essay contains many intimate memories of his blessed, though difficult, path to integration.

Teilhard's Story

The young Teilhard had a scientist's temperament. Having grown up among the beautiful volcanic hills of central France as the son of an amateur naturalist, he developed a deep love for rock. It was not simply the beauty of the Puys that fascinated him. Rather, it was rock's relative hardness. He tells us that even as a young child, he was baffled, perhaps frightened, by his own mortality. He relates an incident that probably initiated this concern. One day when he was about five or six years old, he was sitting by the fire having his hair trimmed. The sight and smell of a lock of his hair burning in the fire caused him an existential shock. This encounter with his own mortality started him on a search for something more permanent, more immutable, more consistent. He began to collect what seemed to him hardest – iron, stone, and rock – and to wonder about what holds everything together. Eventually, he even considered studying physics so that he could explore the theory of gravity, a topic that he thought might give him some clues.

During his youth, he often found himself drawn by nature, or, as he would maintain at a later date, by something shining at the heart of matter.[2] This stirred in him a sense of the cosmos, a sense of the whole. Later in life he would still vividly recall the power that Nature exerted over him. Reflecting on his days in Hastings, England, as a student of theology, for instance, he remembers: "The extraordinary solidity and intensity I found then in the English countryside, particularly at sunset, when the Sussex woods were charged with all that 'fossil' life which I was then hunting for, from cliff to quarry . . . .. There were moments, indeed, when it seemed to me that a sort of universal being was about to take shape suddenly in Nature before my very eyes."[3] Teilhard's love for Nature finally lured him into the study of geology and paleontology, and supported his lifetime work in the field.

Teilhard was also a very religious child. He credits his mother with his early devotion, especially to the Sacred Heart of Jesus. The example of the Jesuits who staffed the boarding school that he attended deepened his desire to love and to serve God so strongly that a few days before his 19th birthday, he entered the Jesuit order, was ordained a priest at age 30, and finally professed at age 37. As a young Jesuit, he was as serious about his religious life as he was about his science, and over time continued to develop a deep love for Christ.

While still a Jesuit novice, Teilhard was often disturbed by what appeared as conflicting feelings: his love for Earth and his love for God. On the one hand, his innate mystical sense was urging him to become wholly united with nature; on the other hand, his religious sense was inviting him to love God with his whole being. He found this confusing. And, although his novice master encouraged him to continue to develop both of these passions, his dilemma was not so easily resolved. Like a Zen koan, this question persisted in the background of his being, while he waited patiently for inner enlightenment.

He began to see the light while studying theology in Hastings. During a year of intense lecture, discussion, and study, his scripture professors focused primarily on a verse from St. Paul's letter to the Colossians referring to Christ, "All things hold together in Him."(Col. 1:17b). This verse provided him with an alternative way to look at consistence and launched within him a reversal from his early focus on the hardness of rock and the attractive power of gravity to the integrating power of spirit. At the time, he had also been reading Henri Bergson's *Creative Evolution*. When Teilhard juxtaposed the verse from Colossians against the theory of evolution, a deeper meaning emerged. Eventually, in what he would later call "an explosion of dazzling flashes,"[4] a unique and powerful mysticism was born. It would take years to develop it fully, to articulate it clearly, and to grapple with its implications. But, at that moment, science and religion became inextricably coupled for Teilhard in a way that he would never be able to separate.

Mysticism

Mysticism is a universal phenomenon in that it manifests itself in every religious tradition, though with different emphases in each. Traditionally, it is thought of as a spiritual quest for union, one that proceeds gradually through successive stages of illumination. Teilhard would concur. He understands mysticism as "a feeling for . . . the total and final unity of the world, beyond its present sensibly apprehended multiplicity."[5] For him, mysticism is "the need, the science and the art of attaining, and each through the other, the universal and the spiritual."[6] Thus, the mystic is not only dedicated to "the search for the One behind the multiple,"[7] but is also, at the same time and by the same act, gradually becoming one with the All.

Teilhard's path to mysticism consisted of three phases. In his earliest essay, "Cosmic Life,"[8] he characterizes them as "a communion with God, and a communion with the earth, and a communion with God through the earth."[9] The first two phases, "communion with God" and "communion with the earth," represent the partial and seemingly incompatible solutions of his youth. The final phase, "communion with God through the earth," describes, in a nutshell, his final synthetic approach.

The apparent conflict between communion with God and communion with the earth that plagued his early religious life began to resolve itself during his study of theology. Several passages from Paul's epistles, read through the lens of his evolutionary understanding of the universe, shed new light on the Incarnation giving it a cosmic nature. These passages made it possible for Teilhard to link Evolution and Incarnation into a single cosmic vision.

Both the evolutionary portrait of the cosmos and the Incarnation of Christ offer us profoundly powerful views of reality. Each suggests its own path to union. On the one hand, evolution discloses a material universe of enormous extension and cohesion, a cosmos filled with elements that continually form new stars and galaxies, a planet on which life species adapt and emerge and where the human mind has become conscious of itself. The world of our experience is unfinished, in process of becoming something new as it continues to find new ways of adapting to its changing environment.

This view has mystical overtones. The space-time history of each and every element in the universe establishes our basic oneness with the rest of the cosmos: we are interconnected with and related to all life forms throughout space and time; we are constituted from the elements produced in the stars; we share a common destiny. The interactive history of these elements establishes the critical role of relationship in the cosmic picture: it is only through interaction that things come into being. The primitive matter that was once scattered throughout the early universe now continues to complexify with time and to weave the intricate fabric of space-time.[10]

The Christian mystery of the Incarnation proposes a view of ultimate reality that seems at first very different from the evolutionary view. This mystery has traditionally been focused on the spiritual, and concerned more about the salvation of the human person than with the fate of the larger cosmos. Christians pray to a triune God, Father, Son, and Spirit, who is intimately involved in the world. The Father sends his Son to dwell with us as the visible sign of his love. Christ manifests this love by becoming one with us, even dying for us to save us from the power of sin. He then ascends to his Father, sends his Spirit to be with us until the end of time, and takes on the role of merciful and just judge who will bring us into one with the Father.

At first glance, it might be difficult to see any true connection between these distinctly material and spiritual views, between an evolving universe and a personal God. Can they speak to one another? And, if they can, what light does evolution shine on the Incarnation and vice versa? Teilhard was able to gain much fruit from his reflection on these questions. He found that evolution deepened his understanding of the Christian message and that John's gospel and Paul's letters expanded his understanding of evolution. Eventually Evolution and Incarnation became interlocked and provided a single view of reality.

First of all, the evolutionary picture of the cosmos necessitates a new understanding of the Incarnation, one that is universal, dynamic, and process-oriented. Teilhard realizes that for Christ to be immanent, to be present in all things at all times, he must first have descended into the disorganized and disparate matter and energy at the beginning. In order to create, he had first "to immerse himself in the multiple, so that he [could] incorporate it in Himself."[11] In other words, "the Redeemer could penetrate the stuff of the cosmos, could pour himself into the life-blood of the universe, only by first dissolving himself in matter, later to be reborn from it."[12] Thus, Christ is inoculated into matter at the beginning itself, there to remain its unifying principle and guide.

Furthermore, for Christ to be the principle of evolutionary unification, he must also be transcendent. Teilhard's reading of the verse from Paul's letter to the Colossians, "All things hold together in him," (Col. 1:17b) satisfies this imperative. The Cosmic Christ who resides up ahead of creation, in the future, drawing all things forward becomes the force behind evolution. He is the impetus for the complexification that has been occurring over billions of years. The Cosmic Christ is the one who effects an eventual unity within the mass of cosmic space-time fibers. As Paul pictures so graphically in his letter to the Romans, all of creation is groaning as it awaits the coming of Christ, (See Romans 8: 22) as it gradually advances from inert matter, to life, to thought, and, ultimately, to ultra-personhood, as it gropes toward wholeness, as it forms the Body of Christ. Like the mystic, the cosmos experiences "a continuum of progressively more centered experiences"[13] as it wends its way forward.

Through the lens of evolution, Paul's metaphor of creation as the body of Christ becomes a reality. Teilhard's understanding of the theory of evolution suggests that there is something more profound happening at the heart of matter than any of the mystical currents have been able to observe. Christ who permeates all of creation is drawing all things into cosmic unity. God is not only present in all things, but is also at work in them, drawing them forward, encouraging them into greater novelty and complexity. Within this framework, the Incarnation takes on new meaning. Teilhard discovers "a God who makes himself cosmic and an evolution which makes itself person."[14]

The three major Christian mysteries, Creation, Incarnation, and Redemption, have generally been considered logically independent from one another, three separate functions of the Godhead. By considering them in the light of evolution, Teilhard is able to view them as one. Since each of the three represents a phase in the formation of one single thing, the Body of Christ,[15] they simplify for Teilhard into a single integrated mystery that he calls Pleromization, that is, a "synthesis of the created and uncreated in the Mystical Body of Christ."[16] Embedded within the cosmos from the beginning, Christ, the Incarnate God, suffers with creation as it encounters the failure, evil, and death that must accompany a cosmos in process of unification,[17] and guides creation from within as it ascends from one critical point to another along its path to integration.[18] This final synthesis of all the elements of the world is the Cosmic Christ who, through the power of his Incarnation, leads the entire cosmos back to God.[19]

In all of his writings, Teilhard emphasizes the kenotic cycle that Paul articulates so beautifully in his letter to the Philippians.(Phil 2: 5-8). "The power of the Word Incarnate penetrates matter itself; goes down into the deepest depths of the lower forces."[20] Christ immerses himself in things, by becoming 'element.' Then after sinking down into Earth's depths, Christ reaches up to the heavens[21] in order to bring all things back to the Father.

Unlike those who find themselves unbelievers in the face of evolution, Teilhard discovers that the theory of evolution actually enhances his faith. It illuminates for him the mystery of the Incarnation, intensifies the role of the Cosmic Christ in the ongoing development of the cosmos, and solidifies his already vibrant cosmic sense.

Teilhard's Mysticism

In the 16th century, Ignatius of Loyola founded the Jesuit order for members who would choose to follow Christ in a life of integrated prayer and action rather than to spend a life in the silence and isolation of the monastery. To prepare those who wished to embrace such a life, he introduced them to a type of mysticism more relevant to an active life. The goal of this religious practice is to enable the mystic to see God in all things. To guide the mystic on this spiritual path, Ignatius devised a method called the Spiritual Exercises. Through an intense prayer life and devotion to the incarnate Christ, followers of Ignatius learn to identify with Christ in their activity.

Teilhard was schooled in the Ignatian Exercises from at least the time that he entered the Society. It is not surprising then to see what a major role the Exercises play in his development as a mystic. His treatise on mysticism, *The Divine Milieu*, is written in a format that follows rather closely the divisions of the Ignatian Exercises,[22] exercises that he personally repeated yearly at the time of his annual retreat. The Ignatian Exercises act as a template for his own mysticism.

However, grounded in the evolutionary cosmos, Teilhard propels Ignatius' Exercises one step further, appropriating them in a very personal way. It is not only for the grace to see God in all things that he prays, but, even more basically, for the grace to see God at work in the continuing creation and for an ardent desire to participate in its ongoing creative process.

Teilhard writes *The Divine Milieu* not for the traditional mystic but for the religious waverer, especially for the person who would initially be touched more by the theory of evolution than by Christian doctrine. His aim in writing is to share his mystical insights with a larger audience, convinced that mysticism is a gift available to many more persons than is usually considered possible.

Teilhard emphasizes that mysticism is the ability to see things as they really are, to see deeply and clearly into the heart of reality, to see both the inner and outer aspects of reality. He considers this ability to see ever more clearly a fundamental component of human development, one that is extremely crucial if the human race is to survive and develop as a species. His formula for greater being, "to be more is to be more united,"[23] depends critically on the potential to become increasingly aware of the nature of reality and of the true interconnectedness of all things in the universe. It depends also on an awareness of the inner dynamics at work both in oneself and in the cosmos as a whole. And, for Teilhard, the ability to see is nurtured by mysticism.

But, he stresses, the ability to see is also nurtured by science. Teilhard places great value on the scientific endeavor. Science provides him with the raw data and the lens for the mystical act of seeing things as they truly are. It provides him with imagery to describe God's action in the world. The explanatory power of evolution allows him to visualize more clearly Christ at work in the cosmic unfolding.

Teilhard's approach to mysticism is informed not only by his love for Earth and his evolutionary understanding of the cosmos, but also by his scientific practice. For Teilhard, faith is never simply a matter of accepting doctrines on the word of an authority. Instead, it relies as much on scientific and religious experience as on solid theological understanding. Religious doctrine, he argues, is not in itself an effective starting point for a lively faith. On the contrary, doctrine must be seen through the lens of experience and within a cosmic context where it tends to display a much deeper integrating power. Otherwise, he claims, faith is lifeless.

Teilhard demonstrates for the would-be mystic how to approach faith like a scientist. Armed with a religious intuition in one hand (the Incarnation) and a life experience that might at first seem at odds with this intuition in the other (the fossil record), he spends time with both impressions, allowing them to interact with one another. Although at first they might seem diametrically opposed, after some contemplation, the two perceptions begin to shed light on one another. When an insight arises he forms a hypothesis, a plausible assumption based on previous experience that makes sense of what seemed at first a paradox. He continually tests his hypothesis against his own religious and scientific experience. As evidence for their integration increases, the experience of enlightenment tends to draw him more deeply into the mystery being contemplated.[24] On the other hand, if the insight is not fruitful, it remains barren, a sure sign that it is not useful. Teilhard insists that this contemplative method is the only one capable of producing a truly living faith.

Teilhard considers every attempt at unifying to be a holy act. This includes the hypothesis, the attempt to unify knowledge. In fact, he calls a hypothesis the "supreme spiritual act by which the dust cloud of experience takes on form and is kindled in the fire of knowledge."[25] Since a hypothesis makes possible the integration of disparate facts, its formulation draws the knower into God's own act of knowing.[26]

Philosophy of Mysticism

In an early essay, "The Mystical Milieu,"[27] Teilhard describes the roots and stages of his mystical growth in terms of expanding circles. Stepping through these circles one by one, he moves gradually and logically from an awareness of a Divine Presence in all things to the radiance of a loving, cosmic Person.

Teilhard's vibrant mystical life begins, in the first of these circles, the Circle of Presence. He becomes aware of a Presence that asserts itself in the simple yet aesthetic details of his life: a song, a sunbeam, a glance, three seemingly small yet cosmic "vibrations" that are rarely sensed but once noticed penetrate to the depths of the soul. These simple encounters stir in Teilhard a deep desire to become one with the cosmos or, as he puts it, to be "immersed in an Ocean of matter."[28] They foster in him "an insatiable desire to maintain contact . . . with a sort of universal root of being."[29] The mystic, he says, is born to give first place to this Presence, to strive to hear the heartbeat of a higher reality.[30] Teilhard's faith and mysticism flow from his awareness of this presence. They are the very ground of his belief. As he gives himself over to nature's allurement, its beauty reverberates at the very core of his being[31] and draws him out of himself. He becomes aware of the immensity, the potential, and the fruitfulness of this super presence diffusing itself throughout the cosmos.

Teilhard's encounter with the beauty of creation fills him with "an impassioned awareness of a wider expansion and an all-embracing unity"[32] and affects him profoundly. As every lover comes to learn, openness to the other is primary to the practice of any kind of mysticism or love. Before true union becomes possible, the chains that keep the self from forming bonds with the other must be broken. Teilhard's encounter with this Presence shatters his ego. The more deeply the beauty of a line of music, a brilliant sunset, or a loving face touches his emotions, the more it tends to break up his sense of autonomy leaving him free to experience true union.[33]

Teilhard's sense of the brilliant Presence that fills the universe with glory lures him further along the mystical path. The radical separation generally assumed between the subject and object in any act of knowledge begins to break down.[34] He, the mystic, is now able to pass through the object known. He senses that All is One. As he moves beyond this first circle, *Reality becomes transparent*. Space becomes holy.

Vibrantly aware of the presence of the Real filling the whole cosmos, Teilhard's mystical encounter leads him into the next circle, the Circle of Consistence. There he begins to discern a universal substrate of relationships within the cosmic fabric. The All that he once saw reflected from matter and refracted through the crystalline transparency of things begins to reveal itself holding all things together in a single Whole. He finds the consistence that he was seeking no longer in rock or in the gravitational field as he did in his youth. Something greater than gravity is holding all things together at the depths of the visible world. What had seemed like separate material and spiritual entities are now woven together into a single unity. The Presence of the first circle becomes internal Coherence in the second. Matter is filled with an integrating spirit. *The world has become solidly enduring.*[35]

Despite the deep joy that fills his soul, Teilhard is mindful of the suffering that accompanies any life or movement toward greater growth and the roadblocks that impede its progress. In an evolutionary world, suffering is no longer a punishment for wrongdoing or expiation for sin. Rather, it is the consequence of the work of development, the price paid for living in an unfinished world.[36] Thus suffering, like evil of any kind, must be overcome with great determination until it becomes fairly certain that this suffering is unyielding. Only then is surrender an appropriate response. Despite the many obstacles that Teilhard encounters during his lifetime, he finds that suffering and death can no longer touch the core of his being or destroy it. The Divine Presence that had become so powerfully real to him in the first circle holds all things together.

Yearning to be possessed by this Sacred Presence, Teilhard continues on his mystical journey. As he steps through the third circle, the Circle of Energy, he encounters the Divine as Creative Action, at work in every corner of the cosmos. Teilhard becomes aware of the vibrant nature of the cosmos. Earth is alive; the biosphere and the noosphere seethe with activity. He realizes his own need to participate in this great work, to become creative action, and to be guided by the divine influence in which he is embedded. This insight counteracts any temptation to excessive passivity or inertia. Instead, Teilhard is motivated to work in resonance with the divine, to trust that his own action is effective because the work that he does is a creative act of cosmic novelty and beauty.

The way we see the world affects the way we act in the world. The way we act, in turn, affects the future of the planet and the cosmos.[37] For Teilhard, this is mysticism's great social importance and evolutionary value. In fact, as Ursula King notes, "few contemporary writers have seen the importance of spirituality and mysticism for today with such great clarity."[38] Mysticism is "the only power capable of synthesizing the riches accumulated by other forms of human activity,"[39] of providing the psychic energy needed for the further evolution of humankind,[40] the only force capable of uniting the peoples of the world so that they can assume the task of building the Earth. Teilhard claims: "The only human embrace capable of worthily enfolding the divine is that of all men and women opening their arms to call down and welcome the Fire. The only subject ultimately capable of mystical transfiguration is the whole group of humanity forming a single body and a single soul in [love]."[41]

The possibilities that lie within evolving humanity are tremendous: "The greater we humans become, the more humanity becomes united, with consciousness of, and mastery of, its potentialities, the more beautiful creation will be, the more perfect adoration will become, and the more Christ will find, for mystical extensions, a body worthy of resurrection . . . To desire [this], all we have to do is to let the very heart of the earth . . . beat within us."[42] In the third circle, *the world is filled with divine Energy. It is alive!*

In order to enter into the fourth circle, The Circle of Spirit, Teilhard reverses his direction and reexamines the details of the evolutionary process. He notes that the mystical milieu to which he is drawn is not static. Thus the Truth that he finds in one era can be preserved only if he allows it to become continually enlarged by exploring the details of the cosmic process.[43] Thus, Teilhard's scientific work enables him to advance the growth and development of the universal Spirit that is in continual process of becoming.[44] The fact that no fragment of his work will be lost gives him comfort.

Teilhard is critical of a mysticism that is disconnected from daily practice, and rejects any mysticism that does not make full use of the power of the human to love. He bemoans the fact that for many mysticism is an escape from the world. In contrast, he cites responsibility for the ongoing creation as a critical component of any mysticism. Teilhard emphasizes the value and persistence of our work. The goal of life and work is to cooperate with the Cosmic Christ who is drawing all things into unity. The mysticism of union means that he and Christ work hand in hand with others and always in the direction of great unity. In this fourth circle, Teilhard sees that, through his action, *the world is becoming.*

Teilhard is propelled onward into the fifth and final circle, the Circle of Person, toward an elusive Something shining ahead of him.[45] Once inside this circle, the full awareness of the nature of the mystical milieu becomes apparent. Not only does the Divine Presence impregnate, sustain, and energize all things. It also draws both matter and spirit into a single unity. The Divine Presence reveals itself to Teilhard as Person, a person he recognizes as the Cosmic Christ, the Omega Point of all creation. It is in the heart of this cosmic Person that all things live and move and have their being (See Acts 17:28). It is the Body of the Cosmic Christ that is being made through the evolutionary process. All things converge into Christ. Yet, convergence does not mean conflation. "In the powerful embrace of the omnipresent Christ, souls do not lose their personality."[46] Mystical "union does not confuse the beings it brings together."[47] Instead, true union differentiates. Entities that unite become more themselves as they come together.

The coincidence of Christ with Omega opens Teilhard's eyes "in an explosion of dazzling flashes."[48] He is amazed by "the organic and cosmic splendours enclosed in its universal Christ."[49] Now it is possible to love the universe as Person. He notes that in the end, "creation, totally dominated by Christ, will be lost in him and through him within the final and permanent unity, where . . . 'God will be all in all.'"[50] "Like a vast tide, Being will have engulfed the shifting sands of being."[51] The Universe is "ablaze with the fire of divine love, suffused with the elements of a presence which beckons, summons and embraces [humanity]; a world intimately united with God in all its fibres and phases of development."[52]

Once Teilhard realizes who it is who draws him, he is able to surrender, to allow himself to be totally grasped by God whom he sees at the heart of matter. There is now no need to be distressed by his love for the earth. It is God's alluring presence that draws him to the heart of matter. He says:

Now the earth can certainly clasp me in her giant arms. She can swell me with her life, or take me back into her dust. She can deck herself out for me with every charm, with every horror, with every mystery. She can intoxicate me with her perfume of tangibility and unity. She can cast me to my knees in expectation of what is maturing in her breast. But her enchantments can no longer do me harm, since she has become for me, over and above herself, the body of him who is and of him who is coming: The divine *milieu*.[53]

The world has become Person.

The Three Mystical Currents
It is interesting to consider how Teilhard's mysticism compares with Eastern mysticism. In an essay entitled "How I Believe,"[54] Teilhard contrasts the basic approach to mysticism pursued by what he considered the three major currents of his time: Eastern religions, humanist neopantheisms, and Christianity. He presents each tradition in a somewhat stereotypical form, highlighting its strong and weak points. He lauds Eastern mysticism

for its sense of the universal and of the organic unity of the cosmos, but is wary of its tendency toward fusion with an impersonal All, its rejection of knowledge, personalization, and earthly progress.[55] The humanist pantheisms such as Marxism are similarly critiqued. He applauds their drive for progress, those "unlimited efforts to conquer time and space,"[56] but he is concerned by their failure to investigate the immortality and personality of their efforts. Finally, he congratulates Christianity for its serious belief in the immortal spirit and in a personal God, but regrets its lack of concern for earthly progress and its resistance to any reference to the organic unity of the cosmos that is so evident in the evolutionary picture. Although he finds each of these currents wanting for one reason or another, he notes the richness that each is capable of sharing with the other. In fact, he looks forward to a more holistic approach to mysticism constructed from a common synthesis of these age-old traditions.

Whether these stereotypes are faithful to the actual traditions can be easily contested. Despite more than 20 years of intimate contact with the East, for instance, it is not clear that Teilhard fully understood the Eastern religions. Though always interested in the East, he was certainly not a serious student of their mysticisms. He did live in China for more than 20 years, traveled to both India and Indonesia on paleontological expeditions, and was influenced, at least indirectly, by his contact with these cultures. However, during his extended stay in China, he lived a life more or less isolated from the mainstream Chinese culture, and never pursued a deep study of any form of Eastern mysticism.

He was, of course, more conversant with the Christian tradition than with either of the others. Of the Eastern traditions, Teilhard refers most often to Hinduism expressing interest in certain of its components. He says, "My own individual faith was inevitably peculiarly sensitive to Eastern influences; and I am perfectly conscious of having felt their attraction . ... The East fascinates me by its faith in the ultimate unity of the universe."[57] However, he never explored these traditions in depth, never made suggestions regarding how they could enrich his own vision,[58] and certainly did not take the historical diversity and pluralism of the East into account.[59] In fact, as Beatrice Bruteau, scholar of both Sri Aurobindo and Teilhard, notes, some of the Hindu insights might have proven quite helpful to Teilhard[60] since the Eastern mindset was not so static as was the Western.

Teilhard goes on to insist, "The fact remains that the two of us, the East and I, have two diametrically opposed conceptions."[61] The main thrust of this criticism is directed at his understanding, rightly or wrongly, that the East had succumbed to what he considered his own elementary mystical temptation – to become fused with an impersonal All, rather than to interact with a personal God.

Yet, according to Teilhard scholar Ursula King, "the experience of the East and its religions both influenced and enriched his fundamental vision."[62] Although Teilhard's mysticism is "firmly rooted in the Christian tradition," King claims, "without the experience of the East, his thought would not have developed in the way it did. It would never have reached the same perspectives of unity, universality, and convergence, searching for a spirit of one earth which ultimately transcends both East and West."[63]

Conclusion

In modern society where specialization reigns, only the poet, the philosopher, and the mystic, it seems, are capable of weaving strands of knowledge together to form a coherent whole.[64] Yet, as humans, we have an affective and spontaneous need for this form of intellectual synthesis.[65] Teilhard's carefully structured philosophy of mysticism[66] relies on the same sort of profound feeling for the Whole that fertilizes poetic genius[67] and so fulfills this need. Based on the complex and increasingly convergent process of unification[68] at work at the very heart of the cosmos, it consists of a series of progressively more centered experiences of integrating and correlating one's outer activity with one's inner life.[69] However, Teilhard's mysticism of unification is not simply concerned with the personal enlightenment of the mystic. In fact, the universe itself is experiencing this same centering as it gradually forms the Body of Christ. It is to participating in this work that the mystic is called.

Teilhardian mystics living in a dynamic and future-oriented framework draw not only to the heart of the universe, but also to the heart of Christ, the focal point of the attractive force exerted on the universe. Ever striving to be in tune with the lure of the Divine, they become ever more capable of sharing in the divine act of creation. Perhaps the process character of Teilhard's mysticism is its most unique contribution.

Teilhard likens the future of mysticism to a large river into which the currents of the major religions flow. His own mysticism is "a curious blend of Hindu 'totality,' Western 'technology,' and Christian 'personalism.'"[70] His mystical experience integrates what he considers the best of these three worlds: the notion of a personal God, a cosmic sense, and a drive for progress. His synthesis continues to beg for attention as a model of synthesis that takes seriously the profound religious insights of the centuries as well as the continuing breakthroughs of modern science. In order to help Christians expand their consciousness of the divine and to welcome non-Christians into his vision, Teilhard uses the name, Omega, for the Divine. Focused on Omega, a universal and personal presence, whose features are illuminated by the mystical insights of the many religions, the universe is slowly but surely converging into the Mystical Body of this personal God. In the end, it "will blaze out like a flash of lightning in the storm clouds of a world whose slow consecration [will be] complete."[71]

Endnotes

[1] See Pierre Teilhard de Chardin, *The Heart of Matter*, tr. Rene Hague (New York: Harcourt Brace Jovanovich, Inc., 1978), pp.15-79. Hereafter this book will be referred to as HM.

[2] See HM, p.17.

[3] HM, p.25.

[4] HM, p.50.

[5] Pierre Teilhard de Chardin, *Towards the Future*, tr. Rene Hague (New York: Harcourt Brace Jovanovich, Inc., 1975), p.209. Hereafter TF.

[6] TF, p.199.

[7] Sion Cowell, *The Teilhard Lexicon* (Brighton: Sussex Academic Press, 2001), p. 122. Hereafter Cowell.

[8] Teilhard de Chardin, *Writings in Time of War*, tr. Rene Hague (New York: Harper & Row, Publishers, 1967), pp. 13-71. Hereafter W.

[9] W, p.14.

[10] See Kathleen Duffy, "The Texture of the Evolutionary Cosmos: Matter and Spirit in Teilhard de Chardin," in *Teilhard in the 21st Century: The Emerging Spirit of Earth*, Ed. Arthur Fabel and Donald St. John (Maryknoll, NY: Orbis Books, 2003), pp.138-153.

[11] TF, p.196.

[12] Pierre Teilhard de Chardin, *Science and Christ* (New York: Harper & Row, Publishers, 1968), p. 60. Hereafter S.

[13] Ursula King, *Towards a New Mysticism: Teilhard de Chardin and Eastern Religions*, (London: Collins, 1980), p.195. Hereafter U. King.

[14] Pierre Teilhard de Chardin, *Activation of Energy, tr. Rene Hague* (New York: Harvest Book, Harcourt, Inc., 1978), p.381. Hereafter AE.

[15] See Pierre Teilhard de Chardin, *The Divine Milieu*, tr. Sion Cowell (Brighton: Sussex Academic Press, 2004), p.106. Hereafter D.

[16] Cowell, p.159.

[17] See Pierre Teilhard de Chardin, *Christianity and Evolution*, tr. Rene Hague (New York: Harcourt Brace Jovanovich, Inc., 1971), pp. 182-183. Hereafter CE.

[18] See CE, p.75.

[19] See D, p.84.

[20] D, pp.61-62.

[21] See S, p.64.

[22] See Kathleen Duffy, "The Spiritual Power of Matter: Teilhard and the Exercises." *Review for Religious*, 63.2, 2004, pp.192-203.

[23] Pierre Teilhard de Chardin, *The Human Phenomenon*, tr. Sarah Appleton Weber (Brighton: Sussex Academic Press, 1999), p.3.

[24] See Thomas King, "An Explosion of Dazzling Flashes: Teilhard's Unity of Faith and Science," *Zygon*, vol. 30, no. 1 (March 1995), pp. 105-115.

[25] AE, p.9.

[26] See Thomas King, *Teilhard de Chardin* (Wilmington: Michael Glazier, 1988), p.17. Hereafter Teilhard.

[27] See W, pp.115-149.

[28] HM, p.25.

[29] HM, p.20.

[30] See W, p.119.

[31] See W, p.117.

[32] W, p.118.

[33] See W, pp.117-118.

[34] See Thomas M. King, *The Mysticism of Knowing* (New York: The Seabury Press, 1981), p.67.

[35] See W, p.124.

[36] See W, p.71.

[37] See U. King, p.217-18.

[38] U. King, p.16.

[39] *Letter to Henri Breuil*, 9 September 1923, *Lettres Inedites*, p. 143. Quoted in Cowell p.122.

[40] See U. King, p.34.

[41] D, p.108.

[42] D, pp.117.

[43] See W, p.140.

[44] See W, p.137.

[45] See W, p.138.

[46] CE, p.74.

[47] S, p.137.

[48] HM, p.50.

[49] S, p.150.

[50] CE, p.75.

[51] S, p.85.

[52] U. King, pp.22-23.

[53] D, pp.118.

[54] See CE, pp.96-132.

[55] See CE, p.122.

[56] CE, p.124.

[57] CE, p.122.

[58] See U. King, p.99.

[59] See U. King, p.197.

[60] See Beatrice Bruteau, *Evolution toward Divinity: Teilhard de Chardin and the Hindu Tradition* (Wheaton, Ill: The Theosophical Publishing House, 1974), p.106.

[61] CE, p.122.

[62] U. King, p.16.

[63] U. King, p.88.

[64] See CE, p.60.

[65] See CE, p.57.

[66] See Teilhard, p.13.

[67] See CE, p.59.

[68] See U. King, p.198.

[69] See U. King, p.217-18.

[70] Pierre Teilhard de Chardin, *Letters to Two Friends, 1926-1952.* (New York: Meridian Books, World Publishing, 1969), p.113. 71S, p.84.

Mysticism as Re-Enchanting the World

Teilhard de Chardin and Albert Einstein

Sarojini Henry

Introduction

Mysticism belongs to the core of almost all religions and philosophies and is variously defined. No definition, however, can be comprehensive enough to include all the experiences described as mystical. Mysticism is basically a belief in a transcendent reality with which one can communicate by direct experience. Traditionally, mysticism is understood as the inner state of consciousness characterized by a unitive experience with the divine. In a broader sense, mysticism is taken to be a belief in the existence of realities beyond perceptions or intellectual apprehensions that are central to being and directly accessible to subjective experience.

The mysticism of Teilhard de Chardin and Albert Einstein was both realistic and active. Both Teilhard and Einstein understood mysticism as immersing oneself in the world of science, awed by a sense of wonder and by taking delight in the glorious things of this earthly existence. Their mysticism was one of involvement, not withdrawal from the world. Both viewed nature in a unique way; the universe with its deep mystery formed the basic foundation for their mystical sensibilities.

Before the modern era of the Enlightenment period, the world was an enchanted world. It was a holistic tradition in which rocks, trees and clouds were all seen as wondrous, and people felt at home in the world.

The story of the modern period, however, was one of progressive disenchantment. It was a mechanical philosophy, in which humans believed that they could know the natural world only by distancing themselves from it.

The word re-enchantment is a spin off from the word disenchantment. This paper will, therefore, begin with a brief description and history of disenchantment. While the disenchantment of the Enlightenment period expelled God from ordinary events in nature and history, re-enchantment will be suffused with aesthetic and spiritual sensibilities. A re-enchanted world would also be grounded in an intimate connection between humans and nature. Such a re-enchanted worldview, it is hoped, will penetrate into the various dimensions of our life, inviting us to re-invent ourselves and the world we live in.

The Enlightenment Ethos: Disenchantment of the World

Commenting on the supremacy of science at the time of the Enlightenment, Max Weber, the most profound sociologist of the twentieth century, pointed out: "The fate of our times is characterized by rationalization and intellectualization and above all by the 'disenchantment of the world.'"[1] Following Friedrich Schiller who spoke about the 'de-divinization' of the world, Weber employed the term disenchantment of the world, which, in his view, resulted with the rise of the rational and the secular impulse and scientific exploration of the world. According to Weber, the "tension between religion and intellectual knowledge definitely comes to the fore whenever rational empirical knowledge has consistently worked through to the disenchantment of the world and its transformation into a causal mechanism."[2] Weber is emphatic that the disenchantment of the world steadily grows with the progress in science. He concludes: "Precisely the ultimate and the most sublime values have retreated from public life."[3]

Thus the elimination of the transcendent and the sublime from life became a matter of great importance to the people of the early nineteenth century. Some philosophers and scholars were skeptical of religious sentiments and often presented a hostile critique of religion. The German philosopher Ludwig Feuerbach (1804-72), an interpreter of Hegel's philosophy, argued that God was the product of a sad and lonely human mind. Karl Marx (1818-83), asserted that religion mythically justified a fundamental social frustration. In this sense he called religion the opium of the people dulled by the pain and tragedy of life. The founder of psychoanalysis, Sigmund Freud (1856-1939), opined that religion was an illusion and that people accepted religious ideas simply because they wanted them to be true. God accordingly becomes a wish fulfillment.

The implication is that the rationalism of the eighteenth century modern science, while liberating humans from several needless superstitions, had at the same time left the world drained of meaning, hope and divinity. As people achieved more matter-of-fact orientation, their religious fervour waned. In his much-quoted poem "Dover Beach," written in 1851, Matthew Arnold describes the receding tide of faith:

The sea of Faith
Was, once, too, at the full and round earth's shore
Lay like the folds of a bright girdle furl'd.
But now I only hear
Its melancholy, long withdrawing roar
Retreating to the breath
Of the night wind, down the vast edges drear
And naked shingles of the world

In such a disenchanted world, some poets began to sense that scientists could not feel the warmth of nature and that they employed cold-blooded methods to convey their findings. These poets address the sharp separation between disciplined research and human sentiments. For example, William Wordsworth writes:

Sweet is the lore which nature brings;
Our meddling intellect
Misshapes the beauteous forms of things
We murder to dissect.

Some poets were of the opinion that the rationalization of science deprived humans of the sense of wonder and awe at the grandeur of creation. The familiarity and the ordinariness of the things of the world seemed to hide the splendour and the beauty of existence. For example, John Keats felt cheated when the mystery of the rainbow was scientifically explained.

According to Keats, Newton had destroyed the poetry of the rainbow by explaining its origin and reducing it scientifically to its prismatic colours.

Newton had indeed made a private rainbow in a dark room. He first admitted a sunbeam through a small hole; then along the path of the sun beam, he placed his famous prism. The sunbeam, once it penetrated the glass prism displayed its seven colours. In 1820 in his long poem 'Lamia', Keats wrote:

Do not all charm fly
At the mere touch of cold philosophy?
There was an awful rainbow once in heaven
We know her woof, her texture; she is given
In the dull catalogue of common things
Philosophy will clip an Angel's wings,
Conquer all the mysteries by rule and line
Empty the haunted air and gnomed mine —
Unweave a rainbow.

In Keats's view, the rainbow was meant to lift the human imagination above the earthly realm to something beyond. Keats had no fundamental problem with scientific explanation as such. He was only against the tendency of the rational arguments to diminish the mystery of nature, in seeking to bring it under the purview of the human mind. In his excitement to exalt human emotion over reason and the senses over the intellect, Keats was anxious that the arid intellectualism of the scientific enterprise did not rob human life of purpose and meaning.

Integration of Thought and Feeling for Re-Enchantment

Philosophers of science argue that the disenchantment during the modern period has been fuelled by the dichotomy between thought and feeling, mind and the heart. It was mainly because of the separation of feeling and thought that the scientific method at the time of the Enlightenment was able to quickly claim complete superiority. The fear was that feeling would mar the objectivity of rational thought. Thus philosophers claim that disenchantment grew partly because of the belief that the reasoning power is the only way to obtain knowledge. Thus the Enlightenment reason has not only expelled God from ordinary events, but also ejected other means of knowing. According to philosophers of science, there are other modes of attaining knowledge, namely, intuition, and experience.

In contemporary times, philosophers feel that personal feeling and involvement are integral to rational thinking. Thomas Kuhn, for example, claims that scientific theories are dependent on the prevailing paradigm of a scientific community. He pointed out that science is not the self sufficient and steady accumulation of objective knowledge as it was once believed, but comes through a paradigm shift in thinking, a transformation of vision and conversion almost. Being culturally dependent, science becomes also observer-dependent.

Michael Polanyi's (1891-1976) main theme is the personal participation of the knower in all forms of knowledge. Polanyi, a scientist-turned philosopher, also emphasizes that belief is the source of knowledge. He reiterated, "All truth is but the external pole of belief and to destroy all belief would be to deny all truth."[4] A recurring motif in Michael Polanyi's seminal book, *Personal Knowledge*, is the intimacy between beauty and truth. Polanyi points out that scientists approach their work with intellectual passion and with beliefs inherent in their passion. He claims: "The affirmation of a great scientific theory is in part an expression of delight. The theory has an inarticulate component acclaiming its beauty, and this is essential to the belief that the theory is true. No animal can appreciate the intellectual beauties of science."[5]

Charles H. Townes, a Nobel Laureate, points out that thought and feeling or truth and beauty are not separated in the mind of a scientist; often they converge harmoniously in the scientist's thinking. Referring to Keats who wrote, "Beauty is truth, and truth beauty," Townes continues, "We scientists, seeing a simple relationship that seems beautiful, intuitively think it likely to be true. Both scientists and theologians give themselves to the truth that transcends and invites us." He further argues that for a scientist, "The vastness of the apparently limitless reaches of outer space combined with the intriguing complexities of the smallest microscopic things elicit an aesthetic response in the human soul. Nature communicates meaning; and science can actually facilitate this communication."[6]

It is significant that the lives of both Einstein and Teilhard de Chardin were constantly moving freely around the two poles of thought and feeling, truth and beauty. For both, the physical world was a setting for a profound mystic vision of the ultimate reality. Their immense fascination and wonder about the natural world was accompanied by a deep sense of a transcendent presence welling up from the world . We shall show that for both Teilhard and Einstein, it is the scientific vision of the world that contributed much to their religious sentiments.

Teilhard de Chardin: Love for God and the World

Pierre Teilhard de Chardin (1881-1955) was a paleontologist, philosopher and a scholar of extraordinary breadth and originality who wanted to reconcile the theory of evolution with Christian faith. He lived to witness the two World Wars, the growing significance of Darwin, Marx and Freud and, at least six papacies, including that of Pius XII. Because of the controversial nature of his writings, Teilhard came to be considered a threat to the strong orthodox Catholic faith. It was only after his death in 1955 that his books and essays were published. It was probably his radical thinking that set the stage for the new trend of thought that came within Catholic circles at the time of the Vatican Council II.

Teilhard was born in the central part of France, the fourth child in a family of eleven children. The family lived in a manor house from the top of which the rolling hills in the locality could be seen. Teilhard attributes to his mother all that was 'best in his soul'. It was from his father that Teilhard learnt the love of nature. As a child he was attracted to the minerals and was fond of collecting rocks because of their durability. This fascination for the essence of things probably evoked deeper questions for Teilhard about the mystery of nature, as it did for the poet William Wordsworth who writes:

> *The sounding cataract*
> *Haunted me like a passion: the tall rock,*
> *The mountain, and the deep and gloomy wood,*
> *Their colours and their forms, were then to me*
> *An appetite, a feeling and a love.*

At age eighteen, Teilhard entered the Jesuit novitiate. Teilhard's aim was to begin a career of teaching in the areas of geology and paleontology. The World War I disrupted his plans as he was conscripted for military service. The four years spent in the trenches of the war evoked a myriad of feelings in the young Teilhard's mind; he pondered over the meaning of the senseless killing of so many people, and the role of God in the misery caused to the people. These years of warfare and isolation from the rest of the world brought all his different experiences into a single process of spiritual transformation.

After the war, Teilhard became a professor of geology at the Catholic Institute in Paris. In 1923 he moved to China where he stayed for more than twenty years. It is here that Teilhard wrote his magnum opus *The Phenomenon of Man* and his spiritual treatise *The Divine Milieu*. After the Second World War Teilhard returned to France and from there went over to the United States. Death came to him at the age of seventy-four, when he fell down at a concert he was attending on Easter Sunday after mass at St Patrick's Church in the city of New York.

Teilhard's scientific studies had already convinced him of the validity of evolution as a paradigm fundamental to the understanding of human existence. He considered evolution as a working out of God's purposes in the world. Teilhard was influenced by Henri Bergson, who propounded a non-mechanistic portrait of evolution propelled by an inner vital impulse. Using this as a theoretical tool, Teilhard wanted to reconcile evolution with Christian faith, and this led him to envision evolution as directional, meaning that it is oriented towards the human person, and will move toward the Omega Point where all consciousness will converge.

The relation between God and the world was central to Teilhard's thinking. Can a Christian love the world and God at the same time? Is it possible to hold the crucified Christ before our eyes while still being passionately devoted to human enterprise? But then in Teilhard's thinking there is no separation between the sacred and the secular. Teilhard, who loved the earth, found it a fount of energy in which God can be found. In fact, Teilhard's experience of God was always mediated through nature. While scientists normally consider nature as providing only the raw material for their research, Teilhard affirmed the natural world itself as a source of mystical illumination, and saw God's presence emanating from within the world.

Teilhard was sure that scientific knowledge contributes to our vision of the world, and plays an important part in shaping our religious experience. According to him, one of the important factors that science has bequeathed to theology is the idea of the interconnectedness of all things. Teilhard pointed out that everything in the world is influenced by its being a part of the space-time continuum of the whole of reality. Contemplating on human beings as to where they come from, Teilhard pointed out that our ancestors are not just our grand parents but also the animals and the plants that emerged billions of years ago. All life on earth is genetically related through the evolution of the chemical structures and processes. Teilhard rightly claims, "In each of us through matter, the whole history of the world is in part reflected."[7]

In his quest to make sense of all that was going on around him, Teilhard referred to many convergent forces: the rapid pace of technological growth, the multiplying knowledge coming from the sciences, and the remarkable technological leaps in communication. Writing in the early years of the computer, Teilhard was able to envision electronic communication in a network of interconnected consciousness, a global layer of thought called the noosphere. The word noosphere coming from the Greek word *nous,* meaning mind, is understood as integrating vision, and it refers to a layer of mind , thought and spirit within the biosphere.

Teilhard was sure that a new spirituality intimately connected with the physical universe will emerge, and that people will experience God in and through this relation. People will aspire for an integrative unity not only with God, but also for the unity developing in every sphere of our lives whether physical, personal, or social. Teilhard calls this new mysticism, the 'road to the West' because it is based on Christian principles. In this mood he pointed out clearly that we have no value in ourselves, save for that part of ourselves that passes into the universe. He writes, "Nothing is precious save what is yourself in others, and others in yourself."[8]

Teilhard's entire life was mystical and this mysticism was rooted in contemporary scientific research. Teilhard confidently makes the claim that "without mysticism, there can be no successful religion; and there can be no well-founded mysticism apart from faith in some unification of the universe."[9]

His mysticism was firmly wrapped with the act of knowledge. It was a mysticism where holiness is understood as wholeness. The mysticism was grounded in love for the earth, for the people and for God.

One of Teilhard's aims was to show how science and religion mutually influence each other and can be in harmony. Teilhard begins with his conviction that scientific knowledge helps to shape religious experience. He was also sure that theology needs a scientific foundation. He takes passages from the scriptures, particularly from the letters of Paul, to show that scientific knowledge and Christian revelation are in accord, and that religion provides ultimate meaning for scientific research into the nature and evolution of the universe. Teilhard indeed had the courage to take scientific data as a major component for his theological treatise *The Divine Milieu*.

It was in the year 1927 that Teilhard wrote *The Divine Milieu*, which he called 'a little book on piety.' This book is a spiritual masterpiece and is a genuine record of Teilhard's faith experience as a Catholic priest. The title suggests the theme of the book, namely, that the natural world is the setting for a vision of the ultimate. Teilhard was convinced that it is in the world, seen through the insights of science, that the working of God is apparent. Precisely for this reason the earth becomes a holy place worthy of our appreciation and respect.

In his contemplation Teilhard was able to realize the mystery of the incarnation, God's presence in the universe holding all things together. Because of the incarnation, nothing is profane and there is no separation between the sacred and the secular. As a priest committed to Christ, he identified the Omega Point, where all consciousness meet, with the consummation of the cosmos in Christ. This led him to envisage the Christ Omega as the Cosmic Christ. It is with the Cosmic Christ, that the divine purpose to unite all reality will come to fruition. And Teilhard would affirm, "All endeavor cooperates to complete the world in Jesus Christ."[10]

In this spiritual journey Teilhard prayed for three things: purity, faith and fidelity. Further, he began to contemplate on the evolution of the universe which, in his view, is becoming more complex and more beautiful. The evolutionary paradigm greatly modified his understanding of the whole universe, its sacredness and God's involvement with the world. It is significant that along with the evolution of matter and spirit, Teilhard also wrote about the evolution of love. Herein lies the basis for Teilhard's spirituality, as expounded in his words: "To begin with, in action I cleave to the creative power of God. I coincide with it; I become not only its instrument but also its living prolongation. And since there is nothing more personal in a being than its will, I merge myself, in a sense, through my heart, with the very heart of God."[11]

Albert Einstein: Keeping Alive the Sense of Wonder

Albert Einstein comes in the long line of Jewish scientists of the nineteenth and twentieth centuries, all bearing witness to the spectacular part Jewish scholarship has played in the field of science, often displaying exemplary courage in the face of anti-Semitism. For Einstein himself, his quest for spiritual truth had played a prominent part both in his personal life and in his scientific research.

Banesh Hoffmann, Einstein's assistant in 1937, calls Einstein a creator and rebel, and rightly summarizes Einstein's philosophy in the following words, "The essence of Einstein's profundity lay in his simplicity; and the essence of his science lay in his artistry — his phenomenal sense of beauty."[12] Einstein had indeed captured the world's imagination with his exceptional blend of a profound aesthetic sense, an insatiable curiosity about the secrets of the universe and a rare ability to grasp mentally the structure of all there is. But vanity was no part of Einstein. He retained his simplicity, his love of music, his passion for sailing and an extraordinary sense of humour.

Albert Einstein was born in a Jewish family on March 14, 1879, in Ulm, a city in southwest Germany. Shy and introverted as a child, Einstein grew up as an independent young man who was popular with his colleagues and students but always remote, letting no one get close to him. All his life, he resisted authority and resented orthodoxy. To a stranger in a train who asked Einstein his profession, Einstein replied "I am an artist's model."[13] In his later years, with his pipe in one hand and a violin case in the other, Einstein was indeed a cartoonist dream come true.

The year 1905 was Einstein's *annus mirabilis*; while still working at the Bern Office, he published five papers in the *Annalen der Physik,* which proved to be revolutionary. One of them titled, "On the Electrodynamics of Moving Bodies," outlined Einstein's Special Theory of Relativity. A few years later, Einstein would propose the General Theory of Relativity, where gravity is described not as a force like other forces, but as the consequence of the fact that space-time is warped by the distribution of mass and energy in it.

From the year 1914, he moved to Berlin, the citadel of European Physics, as professor at the illustrious Royal Prussian Academy of Science. Here and in later years fellow scientists were highly impressed with Einstein's exceptional talent to penetrate into the heart of any problem, and to grasp its significance immediately. To the students Einstein was a friendly teacher who could logically articulate complex theoretical problems. They were particularly delighted with his artistic sense which gave them immense aesthetic pleasure.

Because of the rising anti-Semitic attitude in Germany, Einstein moved to America in 1931 having been invited by the Institute of Advanced Study in Princeton. Einstein soon came to be a well-known figure in the university campus due in no small part to the shock of white hair, and his total absorption in scientific problems. Two years before his death he wrote to the Queen Mother of Belgium: "The strange thing about growing old is that the intimate identification with the here and now is slowly lost; one feels transposed into infinity, more or less alone, no longer in hope or fear, only observing."[14]

What aided Einstein in his experiments was the sense of wonder at the beauty and intricacies of the universe. It was the spectacular view of the universe and his sense of marvel and awe that opened the gate to the scientific experiments that was to be an important part of his life. In his autobiographical note, Einstein refers to the idea of wonder as something that comes to scientists in their search for beauty and elegance. He asks, "For how, otherwise, should it happen that sometimes we 'wonder' quite spontaneously about some experience? This 'wondering' seems to occur when an experience comes into conflict with a world of concepts which is already sufficiently fixed in us."[15] Einstein then referred to the first wonder of the compass he received as a child. When Einstein was about six, his father gave him a pocket compass to play with, and the effect it had on the child's life was both prophetic and dramatic.

One of the free creations of the mind which made Einstein famous was his General Theory of Relativity. This theory was not based on any collection of experimental research, but arose from the creative imagination which could unfold the universe as it really is. The complete General Theory of Relativity was a marvelous act of creative insight. Perhaps no one except Einstein could have dared to describe gravity as a geometrical phenomenon and as a bending of space-time. It would have been another few decades before another scientist worked out the concepts and the mathematics of general relativity.

Cosmic Religious Feeling

Einstein's mysticism can be seen in the way he defines his religion as a 'cosmic religious feeling.' Einstein confidently writes: "The most beautiful thing that we can experience is the mysterious. It is the fundamental emotion which stands at the cradle of true art and true science. Whoever does not know it and can no longer wonder, no longer marvel, is as good as dead.... It was the experience of mystery ... that engendered religion." Accepting that he is religious, Einstein adds, "I am satisfied with the mystery of the eternity of life and with the awareness and a glimpse of the marvelous structures of the existing world together with the devoted striving to comprehend a portion, be it ever so tiny, of the Reason that manifests itself in nature."[16]

Einstein described his religious feeling as a "rapturous amazement at the harmony of natural law which reveals an intelligence of such superiority that, compared with it, all the systematic thinking and acting of human beings is an utterly insignificant reflection."[17] This 'rapturous amazement' in Einstein's thinking inevitably leads to a craving on the part of the human person to experience the universe as a single significant whole; and Einstein calls it 'cosmic religious feeling.' Einstein in his scientific adventure was motivated by a profound artistic conviction that beauty was there in the cosmos waiting to be discovered.

Einstein often acknowledged that he believed in Spinoza's God who reveals Himself in the orderly harmony of the universe. Like Spinoza, Einstein regarded the idea of a personal God as an anthropomorphism. Einstein considered God as an absolute entity in accordance with the biblical command not to make graven images. But he was emphatic that "every one who is seriously involved in the pursuit of science becomes convinced that a spirit is manifest in the laws of the Universe - a spirit vastly superior to that of man, and one in the face of which we with our modest powers must feel humble."[18]

For Einstein God can be known through nature, not because nature is God, but because the pursuit of science in studying nature leads to religion. The success of his scientific endeavour aroused in him a deep conviction of the rationality of the universe to which he gave the name 'cosmic religious feeling.' He was convinced that "the cosmic religious feeling is the strongest and noblest motive for scientific research."[19] With such a conviction Einstein would point out that the serious scientific workers are the only profoundly religious people.

Teilhard Chardin and Einstein: Toward Re-enchantment of the World

Science has dramatically disclosed to us the grandeur of an elegant universe consisting of billions of stars and galaxies. Somehow most of us have lost sight of the beauty of the universe. We seem to believe that the universe has been created for our use and manipulation, and fail to appreciate the exquisite beauty around us. For too long, the world has been chained to the mechanistic worldview of the Enlightenment period. We need to move away from this dispassionate, disenchanted and manipulative culture of the modern era to a new world re-enchanted by contemporary science suffused with aesthetic and spiritual sensibilities.

Any re-enchantment of the world includes a new attitude towards nature and the whole environment. While Einstein was fascinated by the grandeur of the universe and its laws, Teilhard saw God's presence welling up from within the universe. Both affirmed the material world; Einstein developed a sense of awe and wonder about the universe, whereas for Teilhard, nature was the repository of mystical illumination. For Einstein, understanding the universe was an exquisite joy, and the acquisition of scientific knowledge a prerequisite for life. Most of Teilhard's writings seem to be the outcome of a personal encounter with life. For both, the physical world was a setting for a profound mystic vision of the ultimate reality.

Such an assessment is not meant to overlook the crucial differences between Teilhard and Einstein. Whereas Teilhard was filled with love of the world and for the humans, Einstein was a loner. To a fellow scientist, Einstein remarked: " I'm not much with people. I am not a family man. I want my peace. I want to know how God created this world. I am not interested in this or that phenomenon."[20] Further, while Einstein was not a practicing Jew, Teilhard was a dedicated religious priest seized by Christ in the depth of his being. Teilhard was certainly more of a mystic than Einstein.

In their scientific adventures, however, Teilhard and Einstein have been extraordinarily creative, and they have revealed many fascinating marvels about our world. With their innovative contributions to the scientific enterprise they have opened our eyes to deeper realms of mystery. Their unique intellectual engagement in the scientific field has fundamentally changed and deepened our physical and philosophical conception of the universe. And we can be sure that scientific research will be adding more to the wealth of intellectual joy and mystery all the time.

Endnotes

[1] H. H Gerth and C. Wright Mills, eds. and trans. Max Weber: *Essays in Sociology* (New York: Oxford university Press, 1946), p.155.

[2] *Ibid.*, p.350.

[3] *Ibid.*, p.155.

[4] Michael Polanyi, *Personal Knowledge: Towards a Post–Critical Philosophy* (London: Routledge & Kegan Paul, 1958), p.286.

[5] *Ibid.*, p.133.

[6] Charles H. Townes, "Logic and Uncertainties in Science and Religion," in *Science and Theology: The New Consonance*, ed. Ted Peters (Colorado: Westview Press, 1998), p.44-45.

[7] Pierre Teilhard de Chardin, *The Divine Milieu* (New York: Harper& Row, 1960), p.59.

[8] Pierre Teilhard de Chardin, *Hymn of the Universe* (New York: Harper & Row, 1965), p.62.

[9] Pierre Teilhard de Chardin, *Toward the Future* (New York: Harper & Row, 1975), p.40.

[10] Teilhard de Chardin, *The Divine Milieu*, p.56.

[11] *Ibid.*, p.31.

[12] Banesh Hoffman, *Albert Einstein: Creator and Rebel* (New York: Penguin, 1972), p.3.

[13] See Banesh Hoffman, *Albert Einstein: Creator and Rebel*, p.4.

[14] See Banesh Hoffman, *Albert Einstein: Creator and Rebel*, p.261.

[15] Albert Einstein, "Autobiographical Notes," in *Albert Einstein: Philosopher-Scientist*, ed. P.A. Schilpp (Evanston: Library of Living Philosophers, 1949), p. 9.

[16] Albert Einstein, *Ideas and Opinions*, ed. Carl Seeling trans. Sonja Bargmann, (1954 Reprint, New Delhi: Rupa & Co, 2002), p.11.

[17] *Ibid.*, p.40.

[18] See Max Jammer, *Einstein and Religion: Physics and Theology* (Princeton: Princeton Press, 1998).

[19] Albert Einstein, *Ideas and Opinions*, p.39.

[20] See Ronald W. Clark, *Einstein: The Life and Times*, p.37.

Islamic Perspective on Mysticism and Modern Science

Yusuf Amin

Mysticism and Islam

Mysticism or *Tasawwuf* (Sufism), as it is called in Islam, is not explicitly mentioned in the Qur'an. It took nearly three centuries to crystallize and acquire its name. Yet, except for the minor school of Ahlal-Hadith and some present-day Islamic Movements, the Ummah accepts it as a part of Islam. Thus the position and orthodoxy of mysticism in Islam is lesser than in Hinduism and greater than in Christianity.

The form mysticism takes in Islam is quite different from the focus that modern thought puts on it. The latter approaches it mainly as a psychological phenomenon, or studies its final unitive experience, while Islam, though concerned with the unitive experience averred by it, shows greater interest in its multifarious cognitive fruits. Its form in Islam is better indicated by the sister-term Esoterism, which lays stress on the spiritual efficacy of 'insights' obtained in mystical journeys and the explication and application of these insights, while mysticism hurriedly passes them towards the goal of union. But even Esoterism uses mystically obtained doctrine only for direct spiritual realization, while in Islam it is extended to inform philosophy, science, practical ethics and even social and political engineering, so characteristically expressed in Shah Wali Allah's treatise on the entirety of thought and practice based on a Sufi worldview, *"Hujjat Allah al-Baligha."*[1]

Shah Wali Allah avowedly uses extra-scriptural occult knowledge, along with scriptural and empirical data, to present an Islamic cosmology, epistemology, eschatology, theology, history, sociology, proto-science and technology, economics and political science, including the blue-print for a revolutionary, ethics-directed reconfiguration of social relations and structures. In this he makes a most satisfactory demonstration of the uniquely Islamic trait of wedding mystical pursuits with cognitive and practical concerns.

The reasons for the emergence of this knowledge-oriented mysticism are Islam's stand that Knowledge is central to human Felicity, its stress on the unity of Reality and the knowability of all its degrees. Thus, it is placed at the highest degree, i.e., God could be known and this knowledge would be relevant to the understanding of all aspects and degrees of Reality ranging from the angelic realms to the subtle and material Nature as well as ethics and aesthetics, etc. This descending arc that affords the vision of God-centred Self and Universe is complemented by an ascending arc which – obviously - is the final aim of Knowledge, and in which the God-centred vision of Reality provided by the descending arc is transformed into Gnosis and takes humans back to God in a fulfilled manner.

Before proceeding further, the incontrovertibility and the orthodoxy of the claim that with Islam Felicity rests on Knowledge needs to be demonstrated. The Islamic dogma that Felicity and Deliverance ultimately depend upon Iman (Believing the Truth) is well known. However, Iman being basically a cognitive operation is seldom appreciated in non-Muslim circles. A Hadith of the Holy Prophet (Peace be upon him): *"Qulu la ilaha illa'Llah wa tuflihu* (say, i.e., know, there is no divinity but the Divine and be delivered" amply illuminates the matter. The second point will be made when we move onto science.

Having seen the form that mysticism takes in Islam it is time to discuss its place in this religion. The undeniable seeds of mysticism are present in the Qur'an and Hadith. The Qur'an unequivocally avers the primacy of the inward. The Islamic practice, e.g., the five daily canonical prayers are conducive to an inner life. The Qur'an, despite its legalistic dimension, on occasions unexpectedly rises to castigate Particularism.

It is not righteousness that ye turn your faces towards East or West; but it is righteousness – to believe in God and the Last Day, and the

Angels, and the Book, and the Messengers; to spend of your substance, out of love for Him, for your kin, for orphans, for the needy, for the wayfarer, for those who ask, and for the ransom of slaves; to be steadfast in prayer, and practise regular charity; to fulfil the contracts which ye have made; and to be firm and patient, in pain (or suffering) and adversity, and throughout all periods of panic. Such are the people of truth, the Allah-fearing.[2]

Finally, as some would say the twin canons of Islam have statements that can have none but mystical meaning: "He is the First and the Last, the Evident and the Immanent: and He has full knowledge of all things."[3]

Thus, its pro-mysticism character is similar to that of Hinduism, though less explicit and not in the least detrimental to Exoterism. The search for foreign sources of Sufism is, therefore, not of crucial importance. For instance, there is no need for tracing the origin of the central sufi practice of *Zikr* to christian litany as the phenomenon and term of *Zikr* is explicitly present in the Qur'an itself. Though Sufism's history does exhibit successive stress on *makhafah* (fear), *mahabbah* (love) and *ma'arifah* (gnosis), yet all three elements have been constantly present in it. These considerations show that Sufism is an Islamic entity, both phenomenologically and historically.

Al-Ghazali, an authoritative spokesman of Sufism, once and forever declared the ultimate separateness of humans and God. But this served to unshackle rather than stonewall mystical realization and philosophisation, as hence none of its subtle products would ever be misconstrued as total identity of humans and God. Thus, despite the predominance of the *wujudiyyah* type (misleadingly translated as pantheistic), Islamic mysticism is protean in nature with a big segment amounting to the *shuhudiyyah* (duality emphasizing) type.

The winning of orthodoxy for Sufism by Al-Ghazali saved it from alienation and tremendously helped it to actualize its balance and positivity vis-a-vis other dimensions of human thought and practice, to whom it provided not a negation but a sure footing and productive direction, as accessibly exhibited in *"Hujjat Allah al-Baligha."* Thus Sufism became intimately related to science in Islamic Civilisation and helped it to develop quantitatively and qualitatively, to acquire its distinctive Islamic character.

Thus Ibn Sina, the qualitatively 'average' Muslim scientist, wrote *Al-Qanoon*, the magnum opus of medicine, that talks of *Quwa* and *Arwah* (non-Formal 'Faculties' and subtle 'Pneuma') as the basis of Human Physiology; *Al-Shifa*, the metaphysical compendium whose cosmology includes the angelic realm and "The Oriental Recitals," the books on mysticism.

Islam and Science

Before taking up the second part of our inquiry, viz., Islamic perspective on Modern Science, we have to see what we mean by the adjective 'Modern'. It may be taken to mean many things, but any exercise in seeking a positive relation between Mysticism and Science can give to it only one essential meaning, to wit, the centrality of Physical Nature as the 'object' of study and of the empirico-rational method as the means of getting knowledge. Most would agree that this detailing of 'Modern' is enough to include all necessary aspects of 'Modern' Science. Any other gloss on 'Modern,' such as agnosticism regarding the spiritual-intuitional as the object-method of study, though justifiable in a sense, would foreclose all discussion of Mysticism-Science relationship. We have adopted the former meaning of Modern Science in the present inquiry.

Given the unawareness of traditional Muslim scholars about western civilization, including its Modern Science, there is very little direct Islamic discourse on it. As expected from the world-affirming genius of Islam, the Neo-Modernists, e.g., Afghani, Maudoodi, Iqbal, etc., who were the first to encounter Modern Science as it developed and exists in western civilization, welcomed it per se, with riders about the error of its materialist worldview.

On the other hand the Neo-Traditionalists, led by the Muslim, European Esoterists Guenon[4] and Schuon, who had a deeper insight in Western Modern Science and its terrible errors, and who were free of the pressure on Muslimdom to prove its virility by mastering Modern Science, unequivocally condemn Modern Science *as* it has developed in the West, while affirming the empirico-rational approach as *an* element of the grand method of obtaining knowledge. But they don't have much to say about the desirability of knowing the Physical Level of Reality, both in itself and in its continuations with higher levels of Being.

However, Modern Western Science per se, in isolation from its worldview, scale, some of its results, etc., is, on the whole, similar to *a* segment of science, as it was and to a small extent is, e.g., Islamic Medicine, which still thrives as a living science in the Islamic civilization. Thus, the traditional Islamic attitude to science can be extrapolated – with necessary adjustments – to Modern Science. So, we will not restrict the inquiry regarding Islam's attitude towards Modern Science, as we now know it (in other words science as it has developed in the Modern West), to a perusal of the views of contemporary Muslim scholars, but will explore the Canons and History of Islam to get our answer.

Islamic Tradition definitely denies Scientism, i.e., the view that all aspects of Reality, or whatever is knowable, can be known only by what Modern Science holds to be the Scientific Method, i.e., observation and reasoning. What is less well appreciated is that it also denies Modern Science's claim that the Scientific Method, in the sense of being the Method of studying Nature, is limited only to observation and reasoning. Other methods too can have a role in the study of Nature. But Islamic Tradition is neither hostile to nor even oblivious of observation and reasoning as part of the method of obtaining knowledge, particularly of Nature. So, whatever traditional Islam, pre-dating both Neo-Modernist and Neo-Traditionalist Islamic view, says about science predicates observation and reasoning too, albeit as a part of a larger whole. Hence, it is not totally at a tangent with Modern Science. It is the attitude of this Traditional Islam which we will use to understand Islam's attitude to Modern Science.

In Islam, science does not hang in the air, so to speak, as it does in Modern West, but finds a clear locus in the hierarchy and vista of Knowledge. This brings us to the second basic point we promised to make. It is the descending arc of Knowledge that provides justification, locus and character to science, and indeed to all other cognitive systems such as Theosophy, Philosophy, Philology, etc. The descending arc of Knowledge, starting with the knowledge of God (or the Absolute) unfolds at every lower level of Being to envelop the knowledge of the objects at that level. The fact of science being embedded in this descending arc of Knowledge is the key to understanding not only Islam's attitude to science but also to the delineation of the Islamic vision of science, with its similarities as well as differences from Modern Western Science.

Progressively descending knowledge systems, including science, are not of course ends in themselves but a preparation for embarking on the ascending arc of Knowledge, i.e., attainment of Gnosis by seeing everything with God.

We will now discuss the Islamic elements that lead to the development of that aspect which is common to Modern Science and Traditional Sciences. Together with the stress on the Unity of Reality and the knowability of all degrees of Reality, a most unambiguous inclusion of Nature among objects worthy of study is probably the biggest impetus to science.

The homogeneity, stability, regularity and harmony of Nature implied in Unity, and explicitly mentioned in the Qur'an, have a more direct bearing on science. "Who hath created seven heavens in harmony. Thou canst see no fault in the Beneficent One's creation; then look again: Canst thou see any rifts?" Then look again and yet again, thy sight will return unto thee weakened and made dim."[5] "It is not for the sun to overtake the moon, nor doth the night outstrip the day. They float each in an orbit."[6]

However, the Qur'an doesn't sacrifice the Life (animation) and alterability of Natural entities for these purposes. "And We subdued the hills and the birds to hymn (His) praise along with David."[7] "They said: Fear not! and gave him tidings of (the birth of) a wise son. Then his wife came forward, making moan, and smote her face, and cried: a barren old woman! They said: Even so saith thy Lord. Lo! He is the Wise, the Knower."[8]

Further, the Qur'an holds Observation to be a means of Knowledge: "Do not follow what you do not know. Surely the *hearing, sight* and *heart* – about all these (you) shall be questioned."[9]

Thus, science gets not only the means of physical study, but the commission to make *a posteriori* discovery. Though not at all considered to be the only or even the primary method of obtaining knowledge, observation is given much greater importance by Islam as compared to other traditional civilizations. This difference is reflected even in the sciences arising in these civilizations. For instance Islamic Medicine (known as Unani Medicine in the Indo-Pak Subcontinent) conceives diseases not only in terms of general symptoms but also as structural abnormalities, while Ayurvedic pathology is more or less restricted to the first perspective.

Now we come to those aspects of Islamic Science which make it as well as other Traditional Sciences different from Modern Science. Going back to the Qur'anic Verse XVII:36 it can be seen that, along with Observation, Islam simultaneously accepts Intuition and Reason (subsumed in 'Heart'), as means to knowledge. The metaphysics and cosmology arising from the intuitive vision of higher levels of Reality and their reasoned elaborations and systematization give to science a sound perspective (larger Reality and its corner in it), controlling values, the very charter of its existence (by confirming the reality and knowability of its object, i.e., Nature as well as the truth of its method of study, including observation, mathematics, etc.). Metaphysics and cosmology also give axioms and even infra-axiomatic concepts to science, with which it orders itself and which it also uses as the means of *a priori* discovery. It even gets data from these sources.

The above discussion shows that Islam provides a distinct ontology (study of material level of Being) and epistemology (observation, etc.) to science that distinguishes it from other types of knowledge, say for instance, metaphysics, which has its own ontology and epistemology. But there is no watertight compartmentalization. We have seen how metaphysics and cosmology provide to science not only justification and perspective but also principles that enter into the very body of science. Thus, differentiation of science from metaphysics etc., in ontology and epistemology is balanced by integrative influences too. This not only allows a more direct and intimate perspectivisation of physical study within the larger, non-material milieu, but also allows science to pursue objects above their physical level to study subtle natural phenomena, e.g., Vital Principles and even Ideal (pertaining to the Platonic Realm of Ideas) and higher extensions and correspondences of material and subtle, natural phenomena. The differentiation-integration dialectic gives science independent existence but freedom to draw on any level of Reality, either as object or as subject (i.e., the consciousness and method of study pertaining to a particular level of Reality).

"The interesting point here is the fact that Ibn Sina the scientist, and al-Ghazali the theologian, both maintained that ontologically speaking there is a basis for accepting the reality of the hidden or occult sciences, although they might have questioned the pursuit of some of these sciences on ethical and moral grounds."[10]

The history of Islamic civilization reveals a remarkable consensus on the nature of science. It is considered a part of philosophy, below metaphysics, mathematics, etc. Mysticism and the higher and kindred phenomenon of Prophecy-Revelation, in their interpenetrations with metaphysics are considered the highest form of Knowledge. The impact of this positioning in the totality of Reality has been examined above.

There is greater diversity with regard to methodology. Although there is nearly universal consensus on *"Burhan"* (Demonstration) as the method of obtaining new and certain knowledge from known premises, there are differences regarding the premises as well as the structure of the *"Burhan"* to be used in science. The choice in premises range from observation to intuited entities, and within the latter there is choice on the basis of the level of intuition, namely, sensory, formal, mystical, revelational, etc. The options in the type of *Burhan,* i.e., logical operations also range from deductive, inductive, dialectical, mathematical and symbolical/analogical. For instance, Al-Kindi chiefly uses mathematics, Ibn Rushd is partial to the empirical method, while Jabir bin Hayyan and *Ikhwan al-Safa* mainly take to metaphysical-symbolic means. This, along with the extent to which the scientist chooses to go from the material to higher levels of Reality, is responsible for the plurality of sciences in Islamic civilization; with *Ikhwan al-Safa's* science being exotically Pythagorean, despite its unquestionable scientific efficacy, Al-Biruni's science lying very close to Modern Western Science, but with clear acceptance of the larger Reality left unexplored, and Ibn Sina's Medicine recognizable to modern scientists, traditional Hindu scientists and ancient Greek scientists in equal measure.

Views regarding the aims and role of science show the greatest differences. The Qur'an speaks of both gnostic and worldly-welfare benefits of contemplating / studying Nature. "We shall show them Our portents on the horizons and within themselves until it is manifest unto them that it is the Truth."[11] "And We subdued the hills and the birds to hymn (His) praise along with David. We were the doers (thereof). And We taught him the art of making garments (of mail) to protect you in your daring. Are ye then thankful?"[12]

Al-Ghazali justifies science by the latter, while the Ikhwan al-Safa use it for the former. The Peripatetics like Ibn Sina believe that the study of science helps in the perfection of the soul and the achievement of felicity.

"Al-Ghazali maintains that the mathematical sciences are purely quantitative or exact sciences which 'do not entail denial or affirmation of religious matters'.... The *Ikhwan al-Safa* took a different intellectual stand. For them numbers and geometrical figures, when seen as qualities and symbols, are not neutral with respect to spiritual truths but rather lend support to them."[13]

As claimed above, the traditional Islamic attitude to science is relevant to figuring out Islam's stand on Modern Western Science. However, since the traditional scholars were not conversant with Modern Western Science, this stand is only implicit. It was left to the Neo-Traditionalists, who have a good grasp of Traditional Islam and also have first-hand understanding of Modern Western Science, to state Islam's judgment explicitly.

The Neo-Traditionalist Islamic critique of Modern Western Science indicts it for claiming to be the sole method of knowing, thereby causing the death of spirituality. Since the Absolute and consequently the Sacred is known by non-scientific revelational-mystical intuitions and analogical reasoning, etc., their denial by Modern Science and its votaries has led to the loss of the vision of Reality's sanctity and to the dysfunctioning of the Human Spirit. This denial of non-scientific knowledge, which we can call Scientism, has also made Modern Science free of higher cognitive or ethical control. The lack of supra-scientific cognitive control has allowed it to concoct and impose *philosophies* in the garb of facts, e.g., Evolutionism. When philosophies are crafted without using the proper method of philosophy, they are likely to be false. So, it is not surprising that these philosophies parading as scientific facts are monstrous falsehoods and perversions. The lack of ethical control has created its own problems. They not only lie in this or that abuse, such as anti-ecological measures, invention of weapons of mass destruction, but in the very scale of Western Science which has assumed cancerous growth, unsustainable internally and detrimental to other aspects of life, such as prayer, contemplation, socialization, aesthetics, literature, etc.

"This criticism of modern science ... is made not on the grounds that it studies some fragmentary field within the limits of its competence, but on the grounds that it claims to be in a position to attain total knowledge, and that it ventures conclusions in fields accessible only to supra-sensible and truly intellective wisdom, the existence of which it refuses on principle to admit. In other words, the foundations of modern science are false because, from the "subjective" point of view, it replaces Intellect and Revelation by reason and experiment, as if it were not contradictory to lay claim to totality on an empirical basis; and its foundations are false too because, from the "object" point of view, it replaces the universal Substance by matter alone, either denying the universal Principle or reducing it to matter or to some kind of pseudo-absolute from which all transcendence has been eliminated."[14]

"Science is supposed to inform us not only about what is in space but also about what is in time ... but as for the second category, which ought to reveal to us what the abysses of duration hold, science is more ignorant than any Siberian shaman, who can at least relate his ideas to a mythology..."[6] "Science, although in itself neutral - for facts are facts - is nonetheless a seed of corruption and annihilation in the hands of man who, in general, has not enough knowledge of the underlying nature of Existence to be able to integrate - and thereby neutralize - the facts of science in a total view of the world.."[15] "Promethean science everywhere runs against enigmas which give the lie to its postulates and which appear as unforeseen fissures in this laboriously erected system."[16] "In fact there is proof in plenty that man cannot support a body of knowledge which breaks a certain natural and providential equilibrium."[17]

Conclusion

It is generally believed that overemphasis on mysticism in Islamic and other traditional civilizations, including pre-Renaissance Christian Civilisation, harmed science by belittling life in the world, the reality of physical phenomena and observation and reasoning. In the light of the above discussion this seems to be far from the truth. The later-day scientific backwardness of traditional civilizations arose from decadence rather than error. In fact mysticism had a crucial role in nurturing and guiding science in Islamic Civilization, and by extension, in all traditional civilizations. So, it will again have a positive effect on science, by providing it justification and another thing which it needs today even more direly, that is, guidance.

Endnotes

[1] Kemal R & Kemal S, "Shah Waliullah" in *History of Islamic Philosophy*, ed. SH Nasr and O. Leaman, (London: Routledge, 1996), pp.663-670.

[2] Qur'an: II-177.

[3] Qur'an: LVII-3.

[4] Clarke A, "Rene Guenon" in *The Encyclopedia of Religion*, ed. Mircea Eliade (New York: Macmillan Publishing Company, 1987), pp. 136-138.

[5] Qur'an:LXVIII-3-4.

[6] Qur'an:XXXVI-40.

[7] *Qur'an*:XLI- 53.

[8] Qur'an: LI-28-30.

[9] Qur'an: XVII: 36.

[10] O. Bakar, "Science," in S.H. Nasr and O. Leaman, op.cit., p.938.

[11] Qur'an:XLI-53.

[12] Qur'an: XXI-79-80.

[13] Bakar p.943.

[14] F, Schuon, in *The Essential Writings of Fritjof Schuon*, SH Nasr, ed., (New York: Amity House, 1986), p.498.

[15] Schuon, F, p.502.

[16] Schuon, F, p.503.

[17] Schuon, F, p.510.

Modern Science, Mysticism and East-West Dialogue: Tribal Perspective

Nirmal Minz

It was an education for me to engage myself in the study of the dialogue between religion and science. I was well acquainted with the dialogue between the major religions of the world - Hinduism, Islam, Christianity, Judaism, etc. Some years of my younger days were spent in attending conferences, seminars, presenting papers and listening to the professors of religion - theologians, missiologists and others. Professionally I felt quite at home among the leading proponents of the dialogue between the major religions. It had been an exciting experience to interact with the scholars like Paul David Devandan, Murray Rogers, Raymond Pannikar and others in the nineteen sixties and seventies. Now I am drawn into the circle of people concerned with the dialogue between religion and science! Having had the intellectual contacts and interactions with the scholars engaged in these two areas of dialogues, i.e., the dialogue between the major religions of the world and the dialogue between religion and science, I have a strange feeling. There is, I feel, the general impression and understanding that the tribal people have neither religion nor science. Therefore the logical conclusion is that this group of people cannot become substantial partners in these dialogues.

As I represent and speak on behalf of the tribal people, I would like to introduce very briefly who the tribals are. Anthropologists, sociologists, Christian missionaries and British government officials have written a lot about the tribals. Some have done it extremely well, and we are grateful to them. But the fact is that all these authors are outsiders and foreigners. We would listen to the insider's views about tribals. An insider writes, "In India, the concept of 'tribe' has undergone a change with the passage of time. During the Vedic period a tribe was a political unit, and could be compared with the present 'state.' Now a tribe indicates a group of people who are backward and poor. The term Scheduled Tribe implies those tribes under article 342 of the Indian Constitution."[1] The outsider's opinion on the tribals is well accepted in scholarly circles, and by the government of India. One of the prominent scholars is Dr. Kumar Suresh Singh. He says, "Any discussions of the tribe of India has to proceed from the assumption that a tribe is an administrative and political concept in India."[2] With his long association with the tribals of Jharkhand and the study of tribals in general, he observes that "Christianity has emerged as the strongest factor of modernization and has given the tribals, as it has done elsewhere, a strong sense of identity."[3]

W.G. Archer, a British government servant, has written on the Oraons and the Santhals of Jharkhand. A relevant point in his books on the Santhals is his perception of the customary law/Santhal law among the Santhals. Since tribal customs are important in our discussions, we should listen to what Archer has to say on Santhal customs. "A custom to be binding must be unaltered, uniform, constant and definite. A custom to be valid must have been continued and acquiesced in and must be reasonable and certain: the ultimate canon in tribal view of what is just. This ideal can be achieved only by a deep respect for previous decisions and traditional practices, and in fact when the village council meets it does not meet alone but sits with ancestors."[4]

In their recent research and publications on the tribal religion, the practicing tribals themselves have very strongly criticized the works of many foreign missionaries. Dr. Ram Dayal Munda says that there is a belief in the highest power (high God) among the tribals in general, besides their worship of benevolent spirits and appeasing the malevolent spirits.[5]

The tribals of India share many similarities of the social structure, political systems, economic practices and the religious observances of the Indigenous people of Asia - the Aborigines of Australia, the Maoris of New Zealand, the Ainu people of Japan, the Bontec, Sagada, Mindanao people of Philippines, the Batak people of Sumatra (Indonesia), the Malays of Malaysia, tribes of Myanmar. The same similarities can also be found among the indigenous people of Europe - Laps of Lapland and all indigenous nations and people of North American, Middle American and South American continents, and those hundreds of tribes in the African continent.

It is highly important to mention about the indigenous people and the similarity in their worldviews since the Indian government has repeatedly denied in the international forums that there are indigenous people in India. Such ideas are misleading, and gives the wrong impression about the tribal people of India while the tribal population in India consists around 100 million. I wish that the scholarly world would recognize the tribals as the indigenous people of India and our identity as a people with a distinct religion, human dignity and self-respect.

There are strong movements of the indigenous people all over the world for their rights of self-determination. The forum for the indigenous and tribal people in UNO has expedited the matter and each country or regions of a continent have formed Indigenous People Councils. The Asian Council of Indigenous People and the Indian Council of Indigenous Tribal People have joined hands with the World Council of Indigenous People to struggle together in their demands for the rights of self-determination in each continent and nation state. This is now with the UN General Council.

The tribal people of India do have their socio, economic, political and religious identity with their territorial identities. It is true that today modern science and technology and the unbridled and inhuman development programmes launched by the modem state powers have tried to disturb the territorial identity. The socio-political and religious identity of the tribals are disrupted, but not completely destroyed. There is still substantial evidence that the traditional socio-political and religious structures and practices continue to operate even today. The modern missionary movements - both the Christian and the Vishwa Hindu Parishad, etc. - have tried to undervalue tribal organizations, structures and beliefs. Yet, even today they do continue to hold credibility for the tribal people.

Tribal/Adivasi/Indigenous People's Worldview

The worldview of any group provides the basic philosophical foundation for organizing, guiding and sustaining their lives. This foundation is nurtured and sustained by people's religious beliefs and practices. Kuruvilla Pandikattu states, "Besides values and vocation, religion endows us with a vision or a worldview. A vision is a way of understanding ourselves, the world and God. It is a way of coping with the exigencies of life, dealing with the difficulties of existence and responding to the challenges offered by daily living. A vision gives a reason to live for."[6]

The tribals/adivasis/indigenous people all over the world have a very strong faith in a supreme power. They hold the view that the mountains, fields, rivers, air, water and fire, i.e., the whole of nature, are God's gift. No king or *jamindar* has owned or created them. As a God given gift, they have to use them gratefully and economically. The tribals/adivasis/ indigenous people have lived close to nature from the very beginning. The trees, plants, animals and every living being are their friends and close relatives. The totem and taboo they observe are the traditional signs of this intimate relationship between human beings and all of creation. The totem is believed to be on line with human beings from the creation in this world. The adivasis/tribals/ indigenous people of Jharkhand and elsewhere forbid marriage between the young men and women of the same *gotra*. This shows their knowledge and understanding that such marriage relationships degenerate the human genes, and therefore must be avoided. Customary law as well strongly objects to such behaviors and practices and considers them punishable. We know that the tribal/adivasi/ indigenous people still practice hunting and fishing for their livelihood. One may be tempted to believe that these people always hunt wild animals and go fishing in rivers and ponds for their food. On the contrary, they do not kill animals and birds and catch fish in an unbridled manner. They know that there is a specific period of the year/month set aside for hunting and fishing. Such practices of hunting and fishing, helps preserve the species in balance. Even the trees of the jungle and the fruits of the forest are not cut or plucked carelessly. Certain trees are cut only in the month of November/December when they don't put on any new leaves and bear fruits or flowers. These are some of the practices by which the tribals/ adivasis/indigenous people have kept the ecological balance intact for hundreds and thousands of years. According to various scholars, all major tribes in Jharkhand have their creation stories. The Santals by P.O. Bodding, Mundas by Fr. Hoffman and S.C. Roy, the Oraons by S.C. Roy, Baigas and Gonds by Verrier Elwin are some of the scholarly works on this account. Traditional creation stories support the idea of a Supreme power, God, who alone creates the earth and the universe. The tribals/adivasis/ indigenous people defy any claim of a king or *jamindar*, even of a democratic government, on forests and rivers. Traditionally the natural resources belonged to the entire community, and the individuals could make use of them as and when they needed. Nature was never exploited by the tribals/ adivasis/indigenous people as modern society, including the scientists, have done. They were used according to the need.

Tribals/Adivasis/Indigenous People and Modern Society: Epistemological Question

The source and method of gaining knowledge is the key to our understanding of the tribals and the modem society. In the West the Christians have nature and the Bible as the source of knowledge. In India and in the other eastern countries, the Hindus have their Vedas/ Upanishads, Sastras and nature for acquiring knowledge. The tribals/ adivasis/indigenous people have had no written Sastras/Bible in their society. They certainly have traditions and customs to transmit knowledge from one generation to another. But their immediate and major source of knowledge is nature. They have learnt many things from working with nature for thousands of years. Their intimate relationship with nature has taught them all knowledge in dealing with life's problems, difficulties and issues in their individual and community life. They learn from the trees that a human being can sit or sleep under a peepal tree day and night as it sends out oxygen day and night. No other trees have this quality for the benefit of the human beings. Though I have tried to find out from the teachers and students of science the reason for this, I have not got a satisfactory answer. This can be a point of research for the scientists. The tribal people/adivasis in Jharkhand know rain is expected within 12 to 24 hours according to the direction of the wind. When they see the black ants (*Loha Chinti*) crossing footpaths/roads from one edge to the other in the morning, they would foretell that there will be rain this day. They have not studied meteorology. But nature has provided them with this knowledge that is useful for their lives.

At this juncture, it is appropriate to mention the kind of reasoning that the tribals/adivasis/indigenous people in general have. There are discursive and intuitive knowledge/reasons. Modern science uses discursive reasoning. There are questions and logical answers to them. The intuitive enquiry is generally used for religious pursuits. The intuitive knowledge is led by intuition rather than reason. The tribals/adivasis/indigenous people are led by an inner power of knowing. They see nature, and intuitively grasp the inner working of nature. At this point we can say they are close to the 'mystic' in the ordinary sense. As they are led by an inner power to know and to grasp the natural laws, their knowledge tends towards religious knowledge rather than scientific knowledge. The tribals/adivasis/indigenous people wonder at the awesomeness of the hills, the mountains and the valleys with the beauty of flowers and fruits on plants and trees. The stone sitting at the hilltop/mountain peaks looks quite mysterious to them. His/her intuitive reason takes him/her to God who only can create the wonders of nature around him/her. Though "wonder can be said to be the starting point of philosophy and science, the tribals/adivasis/indigenous people could not step into the scientific world. They have remained at the philosophical and the religious level of thought. What we need is an epistemology that is capable of dealing with the human person and his/her context as an indivisible unit. Such an epistemology can be termed as 'eco-centric epistemology.' It means that the centre of every spatio–temporal manifestation is within itself. Such understanding of meaning admits co-existence of pluralistic claims together, and it says that there can be different methods capable of giving equally valid knowledge within the context of its eco-centric existence."[7] It may be that this eco-centric epistemology will provide a good instrument in dealing with the dialogue between science and religion.

Mysticism

Mysticism in the classical religious sense is a serious and sincere pursuit of knowing God. In general, in mysticism the *bhakta* places himself/herself before the Supreme Being. He/she enters into *devaloka* and slowly begins to be transformed in *deveswarupa*, and proceeds towards the unity of identity in the Indian religious tradition.

The tribals/adivasis/indigenous people are visionaries, therefore their outlook is more philosophical than scientific. In their own intuitive way they approach the deity/the Spirit. The divine/Spirit overpowers the *bhakta*. He/she gets more ecstatic than mystical experience. He/she is overpowered by the spirit, and becomes completely under the divine control – spirit-possessed. After some time with the humble petition the spirit leaves the *bhakta*. Then he/she comes back to normal senses. There is no experience of *samadhi* in the Hindu sense of a *bhakta's* experience.

The Place of Observation, Experiment and Experience in Tribal/Adivasi/Indigenous People

Modem science has developed within the last two hundred years or so. The scientist's experiment, observation and experience are finally concluded in their laboratories. The tribals/adivasis/indigenous people have observed and experienced the natural events over thousands of years. They have not made any experiment in the modern sense of the term, and arrived at any amazing conclusions. But it is true that they have in their own way tested the workings of nature, and found solutions to some of their problems. Nature's working patterns are understood intuitively in their personal and community experiences, and they respond to it in life. This test may take a life span, one whole generation or more, to find out the final result. In the medicinal practices they find similarity between the shape of a disease and the natural objects. The same plant/leaf/flower/fruit is determined to have the medicinal value to counteract a disease. This is true particularly in case of various kinds of boils, deforms, swellings in the body or part of the body that is watched. Further, in some cases the medicinal value they find in root/flower/fruit of trees/plants are discovered in dreams and he/she begins to treat diseases. Though this seems to be quite unreasonable, this is how they have dealt with diseases and health care in the past. The knowledge about the various species of plants in the jungle among the adivasis is amazingly wide. It is told of a tribal/adivasi boy in Orissa that he could name about two hundred types of plants found in the jungle. This knowledge is gained by their experiences, contacts, observations, listening to traditional stories and by remembering and recognizing them in the course of time.

East-West Dialogue

The concept 'East-West' appears to be an accepted fact in the modern world. But the tribals/adivasis/indigenous people live above the East—

West divide in the human society even in the present world. There is a sense in which they have maintained basic human values in their tradition. Co-operation rather than competition; sharing instead of grabbing money and power; consensus in political and other decision making processes, i.e., an inclusive rather than majority democracy which excludes almost half of the population of the country/nation (51-49=100) and a concept of equality of not only human beings but of all the living beings in our planet are some of the human values existing among the tribal/adivasi/indigenous people of the world. There are various communities occupying the different segments of this earth. Each one has the right of self-determination in all matters for living as humans.

Modern Science and Technology

Modern science and technology are a blessing in general, but they are a bane for the tribal/adivasi/indigenous people. Since tribal people still occupy the unwanted hills, mountains of the country, they sit on the mines and minerals of the nation in the sight of the modern state. The nation states today claim their sovereignty, legal ownership over every inch of the country. They use modern scientific and technological knowledge to extract/exploit and use all natural resources even under people's residential and legal holdings of the land and properties, under the disguise of the "larger interest of the nation." The tribals/adivasis/indigenous people are displaced from their original home and hearth to give place to mining and industries. This so-called national development programme/project is one of the major causes of immense human suffering among the tribal section of human society all over the world. Unfortunately, all the benefits of modern science and technology are used for a small segment of population, compared to the vast majority of people in the villages of India and in other third world countries. Jharkhand, one of the largest mining regions of India (in coal and iron), is very badly treated even in the 21st century. The unbridled vested self-interest of the dominant society has consciously sidetracked the tribals/adivasis/indigenous people, and has kept them outside the circle of benefits of modern science and technology in many pockets of the world even today. Such behaviors and attitudes of certain segments of our society have caused more harm than good through modern science and technology to the tribals/adivasis/indigenous people, particularly in India. The indigenous people's right of self determination is still pending in the office of the United Nations. The General Assembly of the United Nations is not able to show its courage to accord the indigenous people of the world, their right to self determination even in the 21st century. The vested interests of the unbridled self-seeking groups and communities are standing on the way. Without human values, which are traditionally held high by these people, modern science and technology cannot be used for the benefit of the whole human society. Without the human and religious values, modern science and technology may lead to self-destruction of this planet, the mother Earth.

Religion, Myth and Reality

The tribals/adivasis/indigenous people all over the world have a tradition of creation myths. In fact, creation is one of the key concerns in the primal(*Adi*) religions. There is a wrong notion of 'myth' in the modern society. It has been almost discarded by the modern secular writers and those with a scientific bent of mind. However, today many historians of religion have given a new status and meaning to the word/concept myth. Dr. Mircea Eliade has done a great service to all the scholars concerned with philosophy and religions by publishing books like *Myth and Reality* and others. "Myth," according to Mircea Eliade "means a true story and beyond that, a story that is a most precious possession because it is sacred, exemplary and significant."[8] Since it is true, sacred and significant, we must take myth seriously today. It is very important to remember that the tribal/adivasi/indigenous societies value their individual creation myth as it is told and passed on from generation to generation. While defining myth, Dr. Eliade, further adds, "Myth narrates a sacred history: it restates an event that took place in primordial time, the fabled time of the beginnings. In other words, myth tells how, through the deeds of Supernatural Beings, a reality came into existence, be it the whole of reality, the cosmos, or only a fragment of reality - an island, a species of plants, a particular kind of human behavior, an institution. Myth, then, is always an account of "creation," it relates how something was produced, began to be. In short, myths describe the various and sometimes dramatic breakthroughs of the sacred (or supernatural) into the world."[9]

Myth constitutes a knowledge, which is accompanied by a magico-religious power. And to get this power, one must have the knowledge of the origin of a thing, a person, yes, of the world, to be able to deal with the object, a person or a spirit in our day-to-day life. In order to deal with the world, one must relate to the myth of creation handed down in the tradition of his/her people. Religion of any community, indigenous or advanced, without any exception, must relate the creation story. The tribals/ adivasis/indigenous people also hold the creation story very precious and important, the stories differ in details but not in the motif. The main actors in this story are always supernatural beings. These supernatural beings are given names by each society according to its own language and literature. The Oraons of Jharkhand/Chattisgarh call this being - Dharme/ Dharmes and the Mundas Singbonga, and so on.

The tribals/adivasis/indigenous people see nature, the human and the spirit in a continuum. God, the human and this world have their intimate relationship. Interdependence is the very nature of things. In fact adivasis see, understand and hold an organismic view of reality. It is in a dynamic world in which the humans, ancestors, spirits and even God play their respective roles to keep the universe going.

Hence it is quite evident that reality has the physical, moral and spiritual dimension. I think that modern science must accept and explore the mysteries of this universe. But in the search for reality today it should take the tribals/adivasis/indigenous people also into confidence.

Endnotes

[1] R.C. Verma, *Indian Tribes through the Ages* (New Delhi: Publication Division, Ministry of Information and Broadcasting, Government of India. Patiala House, 1990), p.1.

[2] K.S.Singh *The Scheduled Tribes* (Delhi: Oxford University Press, 1994), p.1.

[3] K.S.Singh *Tribal Movement in India*, vol 1 (Delhi: Manohar Publications, 1982) p.xi.

[4] W.G Archer. *Tribal Law and Justice: A Report on the Santal*, (Concept Publishing Company, 1984), Preface, p.1.

[5] See R.D. Munda, *Aadi Dharam* (Chaibasa: BIRSA Institute, 1997).

[6] Kuruvilla Pandikattu, "Dialogue Between Science and Religion for Preserving and Fostering Life" in *Science, Technology and Values*, in Job Kozhamhtadam, ed., Science, Technology and Values, ASSR Series Vol. II (Pune: Jnana Deepa Vidyepeeth, 2003), p.39.

[7] Eliade Mircea, *Myth and Reality* (New York: Harper and Row Publishers, 1963), p.1.

[8] Eliade Mircea, pp. 5-6.

[9] *Ibid.*

Concept of Reality in
Aad Guru Granth Sahib and its Physical,
Metaphysical and Mystical Aspects

Hardev Singh Virk

Introduction

Since the beginnings of culture, humans have been curious about the world in which they live and eager to explain it. The explanations have taken different forms: mythological, magical, religious or philosophical. The world is not presented to the reflective mind as a finished product. The mind has to form its picture from innumerable sensations, experiences, communications, memories and perceptions. Hence the concept of reality or worldview has been changing with the evolution of man.

With the dawn of the modern era in physics, the gap between the physical and metaphysical aspects of reality has almost disappeared. Science must admit the psychological validity of religious experience. The mystical and direct apprehension of God is clearly to some as real as their perception of the external world. It is this sense of communion with the Divine Reality through the practice of *Naam* which is the *summum-bonum* of the Aad Guru Granth Sahib (AGGS). Modern physics is inadequate to reveal the true nature of reality even in the material world, but it has parallels with the mystical philosophies of the East.[1]

Physical Nature of Reality

In the old picture of classical physics, it was assumed that the natural phenomena arise from the interplay of a large number of minute particles, the so-called atoms *(parmanus)*, which are the ultimate constituents of matter. The doors through which Nature imposes her presence on us are the senses. Their properties determine the extent of what is accessible to sensation or intuitive perception. The natural phenomena are the result of the interaction of atoms as experienced through the medium of our senses. This is the reason why classical physics was subdivided into mechanics, heat, sound and light, i.e., concepts determined by the qualities of sense impressions.

But modern physics reveals the inadequacy of this approach in the understanding of the nature of reality.[2] Every student of science knows that our vision is limited to a small part of the spectrum (4000-8000 Angstrom) perceptible to the human eye. We cannot experience the phenomena in the infrared or ultraviolet or in the X-ray region of the spectrum with our eyes. If our eyes were sensitive to X-rays, the whole natural phenomenon would appear to us in an entirely different perspective. Our ears are sensitive to sounds of audible range while the frequencies on both sides of this interval are inaudible to human ear. It has been verified by experiments that bats and dogs are sensitive to ultrasonics, while these sounds are inaudible to human beings. In the flood of invisible light that is accessible to the mental eye of the physicist, the material eye is almost blind, so small is the interval of vibrations which it converts into sensations. Inaudible tones, invisible light, imperceptible heat, these constitute the world of modern physics, cold and dead for those who wish to experience living nature.

Quantum theory presents the penultimate view about the nature of physical reality. It has created new problems in philosophy by introducing consciousness into physics. Knowledge of universal reality demands a much closer integration of our understanding of physical and mental phenomena. In our present scientific thinking either consciousness plays no role at all, or it is brought in as a *deus ex machina* as in quantum mechanics.

According to Heisenberg, "All the information concerning any object is given by its wave function in quantum mechanics. The wave function permits us to foretell with what probabilities the object will make one or another impression on us if we let it interact with us either directly, or indirectly. The impression gained through interaction with the system modifies the wave function and the impression enters our consciousness. Therefore, the consciousness enters the theory unavoidably or unalterably."[3]

The hypothesis of the dual nature of matter, put forward by Louis de Broglie, is an enigma in understanding the physical nature of reality. Elementary particles behave as waves as well as particles. Similarly, a beam of light can be treated as a bundle of waves or particles known as quantas. The important fact to note is that this duality and dichotomy is not exhibited in one and the same experiment.

The idea that it is possible to think about the same phenomenon with the help of two entirely different and mutually exclusive pictures without any danger of logical contradiction is certainly new in science. Bohr's complementarity principle may help to solve fundamental problems in other spheres of life as well.[4] A living creature - plant or animal- is certainly a physico-chemical system. But it is also something more than this. There are apparently two aspects again. The time of materialism is over, and we are convinced that the physico-chemical aspect is insufficient to represent the facts of life, to say nothing of the facts of mind. The processes of life and mind need other conceptions for their description than the physico-chemical processes with which they are coupled.

Bohr introduced the idea of complementarity to express the fact that the maximum knowledge of a physical entity cannot be obtained from a single observation or a single experimental arrangement. The observation of atomic phenomenon needs instruments of such sensitivity that their reaction in making measurements must be taken into account, and as this reaction is subject to the same quantum laws as the particles observed, a degree of uncertainty is introduced, which prohibits deterministic prediction. Therefore, strict determinism is not possible in the microscopic world. The word 'reality' does not connote the meaning 'known in every detail.' The mere fact of observing the phenomenon interferes with its reality.

The old physics assumed that we observed directly real things.[5] Relativity theory says we observe "relations," and these must be relations between physical concepts, which are subjective. But according to quantum theory, we only observe probabilities; future probabilities can be determined, but future observational knowledge is essentially indeterministic. By scientific methods we cannot reveal the intrinsic nature of reality. There seems to be an ultimate impossibility of exact knowledge, a fundamental indeterminacy behind which we cannot go. It looks as though the final limits of human knowledge have been reached.

Metaphysical Nature of Reality

Metaphysics is a systematic and sustained inquiry into the nature of ultimate reality. It is an attempt to know the reality as against mere appearance. Metaphysics is the bridge between science and religion. Religion relies both on reason and revelation in its attempt to study the nature of reality. In the *Mandukya Upanishad* the method of inquiry into the states of experiencing, waking, dreaming and deep sleep is frequently adopted.

To the Indian philosopher experience is the ultimate test of truth.[6] Since reality is trans-empirical, it cannot be known through sense experience in the way in which empirical objects are known. It is known through intuitive experience *(anubhuti)*, it is the experience of the highest level, for it transcends both the rational and the sensory aspects of human experience with which we are normally acquainted.

Since the ultimate reality is trans-empirical, the Hindu philosophers rely on scripture *(sruti)* for obtaining the knowledge of the real. Discursive reasoning functions at the relational level. Since the ultimate reality is distinctionless, reason is not competent to comprehend it. So the proper ground of rational knowledge is immediate experience, which differs from experimentation in science.

The truth which the scripture speaks about is the direct outcome of the intuitive or mystic experience of the ancient seers. It contains what is borne out by their direct and authentic experience. Though the scripture is authoritative, the knowledge which one derives from it is only mediate. The knowledge which is revealed by the scripture must become a matter of experience, only then revelation would have fulfilled its mission. For a person who has realised the integral experience, there is no need to depend on any external authority in the form of a scripture. His wisdom is self-certifying or self-revealed.

According to the *Upanishads,* Brahman orAtman, which isthe ultimate reality, is of the nature of existence *(sat),* consciousness *(cit),* and bliss *(ananda).* It is one only and non-dual. The pluralistic universe is only an illusory appearance of *Brahman* or *Atman* due to *maya* or *avidya.* There are two views of reality in the *Upanishads,* the cosmic view and the non-cosmic view. These two views serve as the bases for the theistic and absolutistic schools of the Vedanta. Hindu Philosophy of the Vedanta considers this world as *maya* (illusion) and lays stress on Reality beyond appearance in the phenomenal world.

Mystical Nature of Reality

Many people feel that science should be able to answer all questions. However, it is probably a narrow view to expect that the scientific method is the only way of learning and knowing. In view of the changes within the field of science itself, a scientist must keep an open mind in these matters. After all, science was invented by human beings and is based on the assumption that there actually is a physical world out there beyond our senses.

Capra,[7] in his book, *The Tao of Physics,* has established parallels between the principal theories of modern physics and the mystical traditions of the East, viz., Hinduism, Buddhism and Taoism. For example, we have no direct sensory experience of the four-dimensional spacetime continuum, and whenever this 'relativistic' reality manifests itself, we find it very hard to deal with it at the level of intuition and ordinary language. A similar situation exists in Eastern mysticism. The mystics seem to be able to attain non-ordinary states of consciousness in which they transcend the three-dimensional world of everyday life to experience a multi-dimensional reality, which is impossible to be described in ordinary language.

Opposed to the mechanistic conception of the world is the view of the eastern mystics,[8] which may be characterized by the word 'organic,' as it regards all phenomena in the universe as integral parts of an inseparable harmonious whole. For the eastern mystic, all things and events perceived by the senses are interrelated, connected, and are but different aspects or manifestations of the same ultimate reality. Our tendency to divide the world we perceive into individual and separate 'things' and to experience ourselves in this world as isolated egos is seen as an 'illusion' which comes from our measuring and categorizing mentality. The division of nature into separate objects is, of course, useful and necessary to cope with the everyday environment, but it is not a fundamental feature of reality. For the eastern mystic, any such objects have, therefore, a fluid and ever-changing character.

The eastern worldview is thus intrinsically dynamic, and contains time and change as essential features. The cosmos is seen as one inseparable reality forever in motion, alive, organic - spiritual and material at the same time.

Mysticism is the art of union with reality.[9] A mystical state has the quality of ineffability. It thus resembles a state of feeling rather than a state of the intellect. The mystical experience is imbued with a noetic quality, a quality of transience and of timelessness. There are many stages of evolution in the life of a mystic. Ultimately, the mystic attains perfect union with God and cries: "I am God - *aham brahm asmi.*" It is a well-known fact that mystics feel that exalted state of ecstasy but fail to describe it in ordinary language. The mystics use the simile of a dumb person who cannot describe the taste of candy. Saith Kabir : "Such state is like the dumb tasting of sugar, which in no way can be described."[10]

Mystics believe in the integral or holistic experience of reality. We need not rest content with the partial truths revealed by astronomy, physics, biology, history: Each true in its own field, none complete in itself, none giving the whole picture. This is the case with the truth of mathematics or the truth of language, which are primarily truths of expression, obeying rules which humans themselves have made. Beyond all these, beyond the contradictions of each separate truth, lies concealed the supreme and final truth.

The realm of mystic experience is a reality beyond the comprehension of our senses. But there is clear evidence in AGGS regarding the transcendental nature of this phenomenon: "In this realm, one sees but without the eyes; one listens but without the ears; one walks but without the feet; one works but without the hands; one speaks but without the tongue; thus attaining life in death. O Nanak, one meets the God after realisation of the divine law."[11]

The Concept of Reality in AGGS

The concept of ultimate reality propounded by Guru Nanak in the AGGS is most scientific. As a consequence, it is also dynamic and precise. The *Manglacharan* (the Commencing Verse of the AGGS) is a philosophic testimony of Guru Nanak's poetic and scientific vision of the supreme reality.[12] Reality is one and non-dual. Hence the *Manglacharan*[13] commences with the numeral 1 before *'Open Oora', which* represents Existence or Being. It is followed by *Satt Naam* which means the supreme reality is True and it is manifested in Truth, Existence and Being. The other features of reality are its transcendence and immanence, creator person, without fear or hatred, beyond time and space, self-existent, transcendental cosmic spirit made manifest by the grace of the Guru. Thus Guru Nanak projects the nature, potentialities and characteristics of the supreme reality or the God of his vision. This concept of reality is unique, scientific and revolutionary and it differs in its connotation from the Vedantic concept. According to Ahluwalia: "This new conception of God marks a qualitative change in the cognition of the Ultimate Reality from Being to Spirit. This evolutionary change, heralded by the Sikh metaphysics in the history of the Indian religious thought, leads to a new conception of time."[14]

The very first sloka[15] after *Manglacharan* elaborates further the nature of the ultimate reality. Reality or God was in existence before the commencement of creation and time *(yugas)* during the epoch of cosmic void. God existed at the beginning of this universe, i.e., creation of space and time. God exists now and will also exist in the future (even when the universe is annihilated). The Nanakian philosophy dialectically unites the ideas of God and the world. Transcendence shows that God is prior to and distinct from the world. Immanence of God represents God's connection with the world. God himself transforms into creation, that is, changing His *nirguna* form into *saguna* form. "The Formless is attributed and un-attributed; and gone into absorption in the cosmic void. Saith Nanak: Himself has made creation, Himself on it meditates."[16]

The *Manglacharan* in the AGGS is an expression of Guru Nanak's intuitive insight into the metaphysical realm, which presents an integrated view of the basic reality that is monistic, but whose manifestation is pluralistic.[17] The conceptual framework of the *Manglacharan* is comprehensive enough to include some of the most significant attributes of the Absolute (supreme reality). Even the manifest aspect of reality, namely, the physical universe, defies measure and count: "Limitless the creation; Limitless the expansion."[18] Perhaps, God alone can contemplate the vastness and totality of cosmic existence. The Guru assures us that the light and grace of the Absolute are ever with humans in their search for the supreme reality. A person of cosmic consciousness *(brahm gyani)* can experience reality and all his/her doubts are dispelled. "He, who receives faith of Lord in himself, his mind is illumined by the Reality of the Real."[19]

Ultimate reality is subtle and incomprehensible but can be realised through the Guru's *sabda* unconsciously. "The Lord is the subtle, unfathomable entity; so how is one to attain Him? It is through Guru's Word that our doubt is dispelled and the self-dependent Being cometh into our minds."[20]

Guru Nanak has combined the symbol *Satt* with *Naam,* which literally means 'Name.' When we refer to the world of names and forms, we refer to the concrete, empirical universe which we know in our ordinary experience and discover through the agency of science. In short *Naam is* Truth, or the knowable aspect of Reality. *Naam* is immanent in the universe and its practice is the only formula prescribed by the Sikh Gurus to realize God. In fact, whatever is created, is *Naam.* "All that is created is His manifestation."[21]

Guru Nanak was always antipathetic to any view of the world which denigrated its reality or made the world illusory. He was, therefore, firm on the principle that the creation is as real as the creator. It includes, besides the material existence, the culture of humans, their thoughts and values. Guru Nanak discards the Vedantic conception of reality in *Asa-di-Var,* and proclaims that this universe is real, not an illusion: "Real are Thy continents; Real is the universe; Real are these forms and material objects; Thy doings are Real, 0 Lord."[22] The Guru calls this vast universe His mansion: "This moving universe is the divine mansion of the true Lord; And the true one lives therein."[23]

Guru Nanak has identified the manifest reality with Nature. "Nanak, the beneficent Lord alone is true and He is revealed through His Nature."[24] God transformed Himself from *nirguna* to *sarguna,* created *Nam(u)* and

Kudrat(i), i.e, Nature. "His-self He created and manifested His Name; And then He created Nature and abiding within it, He revelled in His wonder."[25] The description of Nature by Guru Nanak in *Asa-di-Var* is a new dimension in the history of religious thought. In a way, scientific study of Nature is sanctioned in Nanakian philosophy. "All that is visible is His Nature; All that is heard too is His Nature.... In the nether regions and skies is the manifestation of His Nature; Of His Nature are all the manifestations."[26]

To sum up: the concept of the supreme reality as presented in AGGS is unique, scientific and revolutionary. It is not a mere abstraction. Its realization is possible through the practice of *Sabd* and *Naam.* Guru Nanak was blessed with the vision of God or Reality in Nature. "The Guru hath revealed the Lord's presence to Nanak in the three worlds; in the woods, waters and over the earth."[27]

Endnotes

[1] See Fritjof Capra, *The Tao of Physics* (Berkeley: Shambhala, 1975).

[2] See Niels Bohr, *Atomic Physics and Description of Nature* (Lndon: Cambridge University Press, 1934, 1987 Reprint). H.S. Virk, 1988, "Reality: Physical, Metaphysical and Mystical," in H.S. Virk, *History & Philosophy of Science* (Amritsar: Guru Nanak Dev University, Amritsar, 1988), pp.79-90.

[3] W. Heisenberg, Physics and Philosophy (London: Allen & Unwin, 1963).

[4] Bohr, *op.cit.*

[5] See W. Dampier, Dampier, *A History of Science* (London: Cambridge University Press, 1948).

[6] See T.P. Mahadevan, *Essays on Hinduism,* ed. L.M. Joshi (Patiala: Punjabi University, 1968).

[7] See Capra, *op.cit.*

[8] See Capra, "Modern Physics & Eastern Mysticism," *Journal of Transpersonal Psychology*, (1976), pp.20-40.

[9] F.C. Happold, *Mysticism* (Viking Penguin, 1991).

[10] Aad Guru Granth Sahib, (reprint) (Amritsar: Shiromani Gurdwara Parbandhak Committee, 1983), Kabir, p.334. Aad Guru Granth Sahib will hereafter be referred to as AGGS.

[11] AGGS, M 2, p.139.

[12] Wazir Singh, "Philosophy of Mul Mantra," in *Sikh Concept of the Divine,* ed. Pritam Singh (Amritsar: Guru Nanak Dev University, 1985), pp.143-150.

[13] AGGS, Manglacharan/Commencing Verse, p.114 J.S. Ahluwalia, "Time, Reality and Religion," in *The Doctrine and Dynamics of Sikhism* (Patiala: Punjabi University, 1999), pp.29-50.

[14] J.S. Ahluwalia, "Time, Reality and Religion," in *The Doctrine and Dynamics of Sikhism*, pp. 29-50.

[15] AGGS, Jap. p.1.

[16] AGGS, M. 5, p.290.

[17] AGGS, M. 5, p.250.

[18] AGGS, Jap 24, p.5.

[19] AGGS, M. 5, p.285.

[20] AGGS, M. 3,p.756.

[21] AGGS, Jap 18, p.4.

[22] AGGS, M. 1, p.463.

[23] AGGS, M. 2, p.463.

[24] AGGS, M. 1, p.141.

[25] AGGS, M. 1, p.463.

[26] AGGS, M. 1, p.464.

[27] AGGS, M. 5, p.617.

The Puzzle of Experiential Primacy and Consciousness

Sangeetha Menon

T he major epistemological worry faced by the empirical analyst, the philosopher and the psychologist is based on the central feature of 'consciousness'–'experience.' This worry is commonly described as how to have a theoretical explanation for the mutual influence of neural events and subjective experiences, and which one (neural events/subjective experience) is the defining characteristic of consciousness. Interestingly, any attempt to understand 'experience,' such as simple physical pain or highly complex psychological pain, will have to cross the epistemological barriers of hierarchies and causal relationships, demanding a non-linear path. The classical description of consciousness as 'unitary' has even evolved to accommodate the questions emerging in interdisciplinary dialogues, to present the term 'self' which was once considered metaphysical, as very much available for scientific discussion today. The epistemological transition, however implicit it is, is from a third-person perspective to a first-person perspective.

A distinctive trend in 'consciousness' discussions started with the theory of 'easy problems and hard problem' by David Chalmers[1] which for the first time in the western world made a semantic distinction between 'being conscious' and 'what is responsible for consciousness.' Both experimental and cognitive science took into cognition the strong presence of an 'explanatory gap.'[2] Though the approaches still remained/remain reductionist or at least dualistic in explanations, the complexity of 'consciousness' and its unique nature in contradistinction with any other phenomenon in the lab was largely accepted. This acceptance inspired theories favouring complex cognitive and social functions, neural and subneural structures, system-environment interaction, etc., in order to fill the 'explanatory gap' and place 'consciousness' in its seat.

The views that are currently discussed and debated no more fall into a strict division of reductionist and non-reductionistic approaches. This could be because of the recognition in these approaches of a distinct characteristic of 'consciousness,' namely that it is not strictly linear, and also because of the need for bridging first-person and third-person worlds. One of the prominent views is that there is a distinction between subjective conscious experience and the biological mechanisms responsible for these, and their mutual non-reducibility. This view is based on the position that first-person data cannot be fully understood in terms of third-person data.[3] Biological explanations have also factored a hierarchy of functions in order to explain consciousness. One such view holds that consciousness is a highly complex motor response occupying 'the uppermost echelon of a hierarchy having the primitive reflex at its base' and that which 'arises from the systems' interactions with the environment.'[4]

Approaches to explain consciousness as epiphenomenal, but not in the classical sense of emerging from a physical composite, also take into account that the primary problem for explanation is more than a theoretical divide between the empirical and the subjective aspects of consciousness. Therefore, some of these approaches hold that consciousness 'is formed in the dynamic interrelation of self and the other, and therefore is inherently intersubjective'[5] or that it is a system of interactions between the animal and its environment and that it is not located in the brain.[6] Explanations that address the psychological and social dimensions of consciousness hold that consciousness is 'some pattern of activity in neurons'[7] or that it is best understood in terms of varying degrees of 'intentionality,'[8] and in terms of 'memes' which are the units of cultural evolution.[9]

Yet another school of thought that strongly upholds the need for finding neural correlates for the subjective components of consciousness is interested in the scientific exploration of meditation techniques. This school acknowledges the contribution of Eastern philosophy and wisdom traditions for a very specific role, which is towards understanding and practicing meditational techniques for transcendental and extraordinary states of consciousness and experiences.[10]

It is interesting to see that many of these discussions consider consciousness as a phenomenon to be *understood,* and that it is well within the scope for investigation and dialogue like any other phenomenon. There is a degree of equal balance between two basic explanations/approaches for consciousness such as (i) neural/physical/social correlates (ii) extra-ordinary and meditational (transcendental) experiences mostly validated by neural or other third-person data.

The Puzzle of Experience

The questions we ask about consciousness have their bases on different kinds of experience, whether it is dream, states of mind, memory, pain (physical and mental), etc. But the analysis for these questions is based on segregated information about behaviour or brain events and processes. Therefore, the answers to these questions are given in terms of neural correlates and neural information processing and models thereof. This method focuses on the essential aspect of 'being conscious' or 'consciousness' which is the 'person.' Questions asked as a result of first-person experience are given answers that are founded on third-person information. Essentially, there is a gap between the problematic of conscious experience and the attempts to address it, which I call the 'harder problem.'[11] The standards and criteria that we follow for objective understanding are most often the criteria for third-person information. This method helps us to build technologies and to understand abnormalities transcending individual existences. The first-person qualitative methods give us opportunities to be sensitive to the individual nature, psychology, expressions and uniqueness.

If both methods are important, how could the 'harder problem' be addressed? I do not have a ready answer for this question. But we could attempt a method that will not be mutually converting (information to experience and experience to information), reductionist or solipsistic. Meaning, we should avoid the presumption of the larger picture of consciousness emerging out of solely third-person or first-person methods. The 'harder problem' is not a question, I think, to be answered completely, or a complete theory about consciousness. Rather, it is the ontological essence of 'consciousness' that should always be addressed to whichever method we adopt, that will help us to *see* something more than the third-person information and the first-person experience.

The availability of 'consciousness' for our most intimate experiences and yet our inability to understand it *completely* in terms of third-person information makes us think that 'consciousness' is a complex phenomenon, and that its complexity needs to be addressed. We understand 'complexity' as an intrinsic characteristic of the 'other,' the object of investigation, which we attempt to study. This notion of ours about 'complexity' is to be examined.

When we reduce different expressions and features of a phenomenon to one or two or to some quantity, we have to remember that it certainly is the only possible way of understanding something so multifaceted and simultaneous, and therefore could be called a simple method. But such a method need not be the final and complete method, and not the complete third-person representation of the first-person phenomenon. Complexity could be the characteristic feature needed for the design for providing third-person representation. Maybe, what we distinguish as 'simple' and 'complex' are not the intrinsic characteristics of the object of investigation, but the categories of thinking and understanding we have formed according to the third-person information supplied to us by the tools we have designed. Hence, the question 'should design and tool be complex' becomes important.

Also, therefore, the standard scientific criteria of replicability cannot be applied since the third-person representation cannot be a replica of the complete first-person phenomenon, but only a *representation* of it from a particular framework that follows certain epistemological and empirical/theoretical parameters.

Experiential Primacy

According to the Chalmersian theory of 'easy problems and hard problem' first-person data cannot be subjected to the standard method of reductive explanation. This theory also questions the basic fact of consciousness, that is, why is the performance of neural functions accompanied by subjective experience?

The 'why' question here is pertinent to understand the bases on which we find our primary, secondary and tertiary questions and methods for understanding 'consciousness.' Why 'why'? The 'why' question ('why neural functions are accompanied by subjective experience') assumes:(1) consciousness as a separate 'something' borne or unusual/non-natural,(2) (neural) functions as basically having only mechanistic meanings,(3) subjective experience as not the intrinsic nature of consciousness.

These assumptions that are indirectly upheld by the camp of anti-reductionism stem from the basic conflict between 'experience' and 'cognition.' The normative criteria for establishing 'truth' start from the objective reduction of whatever is posited. Here subjective experience falls out of normative standards for agreeing upon something as valid. So, the why-question as well as the assumptions arises from the conflict we encounter between epistemological necessity and experiential primacy. Both seem to be unavoidable and co-existent in human discourse.

It is difficult, if not impossible, to resolve a conflict if both the components of it are equally important. But the recognition of this unavoidable conflict itself in our theories and models will help us to widen the scope of investigation and prevent de-humanisation of the goals we seek for fulfilment. After all, through both third-person information and first-person experience what we ultimately seek are personal growth and health, co-existence and sharing, and a continuous exploration into the unknown and the unpredictable.

A prologue before we set forth the theorisation and definition of the problem will be helpful for a student of 'consciousness.' This prologue will elucidate the primary division of a set of agenda based on direct first-person experience and the consensus we share on perceived facts. The primary division will be of the meaning and scope of 'awareness of something' and 'awareness by itself.'

What exactly is 'self awareness'? It is awareness of something. It is either the awareness of: (i) the world outside, such as other states of mind, objects, etc., (ii) the world inside, such as 'my emotions', 'my perceptions', 'my body', 'my identity' etc. The 'world inside' cannot be understood without the intervention of self-reflection and self-participation. What is 'awareness itself'? Awareness itself can be seen as (i) uniting discrete thoughts, and the two worlds (inside and outside), (ii) as meta-awareness of the two (inside and outside world) awareness-es, (iii) as pure I-ness.

Unless a clear distinction is made between these different categories of existence for our thinking and analysis, we will end up searching for the needle in the same haystack for centuries without realising that the problem is not just the subtleness of the subject of our inquiry but our own inability to design a comprehensive search. The design of the comprehensive search is important because the way we search for it is going to alter the presence of it in the invincible heap.

Indian Routes for Dialogues

'Consciousness' has become the umbrella term for debating many issues crossing disciplines yet connecting disciplines. This is interesting. Because, given the variety and differences in the themes and ideas for human discourse, to have a common factor in our dialogues seems to be difficult. The route and the possible result of this dialogue is to connect and join various streams of thought, whether empirical or intuitive, experimental or theoretic, in order to map and place consciousness. On a scale of meta-analysis, this is a linear and horizontal approach, essentially because our dialogues start from third-person working definitions we assume (however different they are) of 'consciousness.' Nevertheless, contributions made by dialogues that could be clubbed under the term 'consciousness' are eventful, since they are an attempt to harmonise and integrate otherwise divergent human thinking.

The Eastern wisdom traditions, beginning from the Vedic system of thought, perceived of entities (physical/metaphysical) whose existence is different by being connected with the outside world of objects and the inside world of experiences. There are several verses in the *Brahmanas* that imply the quest for the source of knowledge and experience. Beginning from the origins to the classical schools and saints of Indian philosophy and wisdom traditions the focus is not to begin from the outside variety and unite the units by an emergent phenomenon, even if we take the most realist schools.

Epistemological analysis in Indian thought is subservient to experiential paradigms. Indian schools of thought, in general, have one common thread – that is, to relate to a larger, deeper and holistic concept/entity called 'self.' Whether it is for affirmation or denial, Indian thought engages in rich analytic thinking to form a philosophy about 'self.' Both analysis (structured and 'leading-to-next' kind of hierarchical thinking) and experience are used as epistemological tools in an integral manner to form distinct but inter-related ontologies. Metaphors and imageries are used as epistemological tools for creating transcendence in thinking and thereby experiencing. The aim is not to arrive at structured and classified/listed knowledge of an*other* object/phenomenon but understanding in relation to an abiding entity whether it be the self/no-self/matter.

Another interesting feature of Indian philosophical thinking is the importance given to the way of living or lifestyle subscribed to by the schools, no matter how realistic or idealistic their metaphysical position is. The understanding of a particular school of thought will not be fulfilled by 'understanding' its epistemology or even worldview, but by following a lifestyle which is prescribed. Experience is the core of understanding. This would primarily require the student's mind to follow certain rules and discipline of forming integral and inter-related connections rather than individual and isolated relationships. This is a major difference when we compare it with the dialogues in the West on 'consciousness.'

The therapeutic value of analysis and self-oriented integration of understanding are given more importance than its cognitive value, in their philosophical thinking. The reference for the starting premises and concluding thoughts is the 'person,' and his/her experience and the situation he/she is in. The route taken is from the situation of the person (as 'given') to the reorientation and re-organisation of his/her response based on transpersonal experiences. The most part of imagination and striving is for what is possible from what is given.[12] Hence the style of discourse adopted in their presentations is more metaphorical and non-linear than hierarchical and localised.

The classical approach to spiritual experiences is to disengage from 'ordinary' experiences and engage in 'transcendental experiences.' The implication in such an approach is that there is a division between, and a travel from, the 'ordinary' to the 'transcendental' experience. The major thesis which is missed is that spiritual experience is not another kind of experience in another world and relating to another set of objects forsaking and condemning the given 'ordinary' experienced world to a hierarchically lower order. Spiritual experience, according to Advaita, is reorienting and thereby reconstructing any experience from the Self's point of view. The ontological thesis of Sankaracharya upholds I-consciousness as 'something-which-is-already-there.' Spiritual experience is reconstructing any experience from this ontology. 'It is there across, above, below, full, existence, knowledge, bliss, non-dual, infinite, eternal and one' (*Atmabodha*).

The difference between an 'ordinary' experience and a 'spiritual' experience is that in the former case the experience is given meaning from the point of view of self, and in the latter case it is from the point of view of Self. In both experiences there is an identity that relates to and generates meanings. In the first case the identity is caused and defined by the situation. In the latter case the identity defines the situation by responding to it from an integral point of view.

This thesis could be subjected to skepticism and criticized as *ad hoc* rationalization for not being soteriological. It is also one of the reasons why consciousness described by Acarya is often mistaken as *niskriya* (inactive) in its literal sense. The notion of *maya* too has invited many misconceptions about it, the major one implying a passive homogeneity to pure consciousness. The main argument behind such misconceptions can be traced back to a monistic labelling of Advaita.

Current discussions on 'consciousness' mostly focus on either of the two problems: how simple physiological functions co-ordinate and work together as one single system; how and why a subjective orientation ensues. Will the focus on the ontology of Self and human experience give a different picture about consciousness? In the first case the attempt is to build into 'consciousness' and in the second case the attempt is to build from 'Self.' The categories of thinking needed for the two cases are different. One is for the allocation of new knowledge within a system, and the other is for transformation of knowledge a-systemically. Experience is the common concern and mystery for both the discussions, though it is not the beginning point for the first school of discussion. But can we give up the experiential primacy of consciousness totally or give it secondary importance? This seems to be not so easy, and more importantly, less meaningful.

Endnotes

[1] See David Chalmers, 'The Puzzle of Conscious Experience', *Scientific American*, December 1995, pp.62-68.

[2] See Ray S. Jackendoff, *Consciousness and the Computational Mind* (Bradford: MIT Press, 1987).

[3] See David Chalmers, www.nih.gov/news/NIH-Record/06_27_2000/story01.htm, presentation at the symposium entitled Scientific Approaches to Consciousness: Reductionism Debated, 2000.

[4] See Rodney M.J. Cotterill, 'Evolution, Cognition and Consciousness,' *Journal of Consciousness Studies*, 8, No.2 (2001), pg.4.

[5] See Evan Thompson, 'Empathy and Consciousness,' *Journal of Consciousness Studies*, 8, No.5-7 (2001), p.1.

[6] See Francisco Varela, Evan Thompson & E. Rosch, *The Embodied Mind: Cognitive Science and Human Experience* (Cambridge: MIT Press, 1991).

[7] See Paul S. Churchland & T. J. Sejnowski, *The Computational Brain* (Cambridge: MIT Press, 1997).

[8] See Daniel Dennett, *Consciousness Explained* (London: Penguin Books, 1991).

[9] See Richard Dawkins, *The Selfish Gene* (Oxford: Oxford University Press, 1976). See also Blackmore, *The Meme Machine* (Oxford: Oxford University Press, 1999).

[10] Francisco Varela & Jonathan Shear, ed., *The View From Within: First Person Approaches to Consciousness* (Imprint Academic, 1999).

[11] Sangeetha Menon, 'Towards a Sankarite Approach to Consciousness Studes,' *Journal of Indian Council of Philosophical Research*, 18, No.1 (January-March 2001), pp.95-111.

[12] Sangeetha Menon, "Binding Experiences for a First Person Approach: Looking at Indian Ways of Thinking (darsana) and Acting (natya) in the Context of Current Discussions on 'Consciousness,'" in Chakraborti, Manas K Mandal and Rimi B Chatterjee, eds., *On Mind and Consciousness* (Shimla: Indian Institute of Advanced Study, and Kharagpur: Department of Humanities and Social Sciences, Indian Institute of Technology, 2003), pp.90-117.

Engaged Contemplation for a Troubled World

William Grassie

Some years ago, when my daughters were young [today they are college students], they came home from elementary school with a new nursery rhyme. This was not a song that their teachers had taught them, but rather one that was passed along by the children themselves on the playground and lunchroom. The singing of the rhyme involved a series of rubs and pinches to a companion's back, a kind of Shiatzu massage accompanied by the sing-song refrain:

> *People are dying,*
> *Children are crying,*
> *Concentrate!*
> *Concentrate!*

I don't know where the rhyme originated. Perhaps it is a minor epiphenomenon in our elementary school; perhaps it has some broader circulation among English speaking children. Indeed, I have since encountered it among other children in the United States. In any case, at the time I took it to be a kind of revelation from our collective unconscious. I was stunned into silence and despair at the kitchen sink in the midst of the dinner preparations. Would this be the twentieth century's equivalent to the medieval English nursery rhyme about the Black Plague, still sung by children today:

Ring around the roses,
Pocket full of posies
Ashes, ashes,
We all fall down.

After some bewildering moments with the images of Bosnia and Rwanda then, and Iraq and Tsunami now, as precursors of what is yet to come on a grander scale, the dark clouds of despair and powerlessness passed and I went back to my work preparing dinner, playing with my children, preparing the next day's lessons for my university students, paying some bills, and relaxing to watch some mindless television program before dropping-off to sleep. *People are dying, children are crying,* but I have a life to live and obligations to fulfil.

And so these dark premonitions come and go, as they have so many other times in my life. The contradiction of modernity is that even as technology and organization have dramatically improved the breadth and reach of human life, they have also created new and greater insecurities and dangers. The paradox of prosperity is that even as living standards have increased to undreamed of bounties, poverty has also grown in mind-numbing scale. The incongruity of the Global Village is that we can not only communicate at a distance, we can also do harm to each other across great range with the ruthless efficiencies of modern weaponry.

In my brief lifetime, born in 1957, the human population of the world has doubled to over 6 billion. In the same period, the consumption of fossil fuels has quadrupled, fuelling previously unconceivable wealth and prosperity. This exponential growth in population and consumption patterns is unprecedented in human history. Seen in biological terms, however, the economic idol of compounded interest is part of a human development pattern on Earth more akin to cancer within an organism or an invasive weed species within an ecosystem. Species that grow exponentially, take for instance a simple bacteria culture in a Petri dish, exhaust their ecosystem and experience a population collapse.

We still don't know what the future holds for the more complex cultures of *Homo sapiens.* For a third of the world, the collapse of human cultures and populations is not an abstract possibility, but the daily struggle to survive malnourishment, disease, unemployment, cultural dislocation, and the social unrests that accompany such deprivations. Half of the world's 6000 languages are expected to go extinct in the next generation. So for many today, brought to my comfortable home and consciousness through the global media, the collapse has already begun. It may be all they have ever known of a brief and bitter life on this planet.

And it is especially poignant that the *people* who *are dying*, and *children* who *are crying* are often the same. Some 13 million children will die of poverty related causes this year, a death toll in children alone that exceeds the peak death toll of any year of World War II. I know of no moral calculus that allows us to rank such suffering, except to say that the mortal dangers and moral choices that impinge on our era are no less than those that challenged the world over 50 years ago in the midst of a global war. In the words of Holocaust survivor, Samuel Pisar: "Today, the dangers are of a different order — more complicated, more universal, more widespread. Courage in the face of the 'enemy' has become a much subtler ingredient, because we can no longer threaten to eliminate a hostile power without, at the same time, threatening to eliminate ourselves. Moreover, the enemies are manifold; they are everywhere and nowhere; they are difficult to locate, difficult to resist, and difficult to contain."[1]

So, as I live comfortably in the United States, privileged among the privileged of the world, there is a knowing part of me that looks over my shoulder as I travel through the days of the week. The exponential growth in human population and consumption has significantly altered every bioregional ecosystem on the Earth and ominously altered the chemical compositions of the atmosphere and biosphere as a whole. Vast regions of the Earth have been destroyed, species are going extinct, the entire planet is in the midst of a technological domestication, in what can be understood as a new chapter in the evolutionary epic of the planet. Perhaps future paleontologists will look back on this as the end of the Cenozoic era, the incredible fluorescence of biodiversity and complexity that has occurred over 67 million years since the last mass extinction. Perhaps there will be no future paleontologists to look back at all. And those future generations that do look back on us may do so with great disdain for our having indentured them with a polluted and vastly depleted planet on which to live. When economist philosopher, Robert Heilbroner, considered the prospect of a population and environmental collapse in his 1974 book,

An Inquiry into the Human Prospect, he noted that political freedom and democratic government would not fare well at a time of such desperation. Heilbroner writes: "Indeed, might not the people of such a threatened society look upon the 'self-indulgence' of unfettered intellectual expression with much the same mixed feelings that we hold with respect to the ways of a vanished aristocracy — a way of life no doubt agreeable to the few who benefited from it, but of no concern, or even of actual disservice, to the vast majority?"[2]

I see those future generations and the children of the world today looking upon our own self-indulgent academic luxuries and intellectual leisure here at this conference engaged in esoteric scholasticism. All of our claims for relevance in today's troubled world should be seen as a promissory note, an obligation yet to be repaid to the world.

The prospects of a global economic, social, and environmental collapse for *H. sapiens* in this Petri dish which we call Earth is part of the apocalyptic nightmare that haunts my waking hours. It would seem that a calm and rational study of business-as-usual in the world today would indicate that we are heading towards multiple catastrophes. In a statement signed by some 1500 leading scientists from over 70 countries, including 99 of the 196 living Nobel laureates, humanity is warned that we must have urgent and fundamental changes in our way of living "if vast human misery is to be avoided and our global home on this planet is not to be irretrievably mutilated"[3] That we continue to be "calm" and "rational" in the light of such proclamations is perhaps a further indication of the depths of the dysfunctions in which we are immersed.

In spite of such an impressive scientific consensus, there are others, who are no less calm and rational, or impassioned and emotional, who read the tea leaves in the newspapers, journals, and stock-markets and see the dawn of a great new era of prosperity and advance. The unprecedented growth in productive technologies, the development of global communication systems, global economic trade, new advances in medicine and biogeneic engineering, the decline in human birth rates, and the end of the Cold War are some of the indicators that the future may not be as grim as I and colleagues have painted. Still others see the very exigencies of our global environmental predicament as the catalyst of a global religious-cultural transformation, a New Age, that will usher in peace and sustainable prosperities through the enlightenment for all the inhabitants of the world. Still others look nostalgically towards a revival of some fundamental religious tradition as the path to our salvation and a brighter future in these troubled times.

We desperately need these utopic daydreams to inspire and motivate us in the difficult struggles with resistance and frustration. The word "utopia" was coined in 1516 by Sir Thomas More from the Greek, *ou-topas*, literally meaning "no-place" or "no-where." And as the French philosopher Paul Ricoeur points out, the view back on ourselves from the *nowhere* of some hoped for future, or some golden age past, also provides a valuable critique of the traditional justifications for what is business-as-usual today. There is a creative power in this dream of a no-where, because by motivating and inspiring, it has the capacity to redirect history's unfolding for individuals and nations alike. As a place from which to critique the cultures of business-as-usual, utopias also provide critical analytic perspectives on the ideologies for dominant and domineering social and cultural hierarchies. Utopias and other-forms of wishful thinking, however, can also be dangerously dysfunctional and escapist. Ricoeur writes: "[W]e are always caught in this oscillation between ideology [e.g., a cultural tradition] and utopia. . . we must try to cure the illness of utopia by what is wholesome in ideology — by its element of identity, which is once more a fundamental function of life — and try to cure the rigidity, the petrification of ideologies by the utopian element."[4]

So my argument today is really a kind of dystopia - a feared future that is abundantly realized in the present - but this is only part of the story. It is not really about whose predictions of the future are more apt, the dystopias of doom-sayers or the utopias of dream-weavers. I see enormous positive potential in both technology and religious-cultural transformation as vehicles for creating a healthier and safer planet, though in this discussion I have emphasized the present and future cataclysmic. The questions are more complex: which technologies used-how, whose cultural traditions changed-how, how does one "direct" technological development or social transformation to desired ends, who benefits, who decides, and what are the unintended and unforeseen consequences of different world-views and world-doings. To predicting the future, there will be no end; both our fars and hopes can be self-fulfilling prophecies and self-confounding deceivers.

What I really want to reflect on with you is whether the rhyme my children brought home from their classmates at school might also contain some profound insights into what we must know and do such that the epic of evolution and the unfolding of human life might continue to the mutual benefit of all beings. Perhaps the task of creating a better world is not about predicting the future, but paying attention to the present and honouring the past that has brought us to this present moment. My daughters playfully sang these words as a game without any conscious awareness of their horror:

> *People are dying,*
> *Children are crying,*
> *Concentrate!*
> *Concentrate!*

The proposition contained here, as some kind of message from our collective unconscious in the voice of innocence, may be that if we could just *concentrate, concentrate* on what is really going on right now on this planet, in our communities, in our own lives, then the intractable problems might become solvable. Pay attention to suffering, but don't add to the world's pain by suffering to pay attention. It is unlikely that we can change ourselves or society, unless we awaken to the dysfunctions as a problem in the first place. In the first step of an addict's long journey of recovery, one has to recognize that there is a problem here. Sounds simple enough, so why don't we do it, why don't we pay attention to the *people dying* and *children crying* all around us, right now.

There are two main obstacles to embarking on the children's imperative in the nursery rhyme: denial and powerlessness. We don't concentrate on the world's problems, let alone our own, because we feel powerless and live in denial. I will argue that recovering alcoholics, addicts, and those enmeshed in addictive relationships may have some of the greatest insights into denial, powerlessness, and transformation. Here are some folks who have made urgent and fundamental changes in their way of living. I believe they can teach the rest of us how we as a society might make such changes on a global scale, "if," in the words of the world scientists, "vast human misery is to be avoided and our global home on this planet is not to be irretrievably mutilated."

For a long-time, alcoholics live in denial of their affliction, believing that their drinking behaviour is not really out-of-control and self-destructive. As things start to deteriorate with work and family and friends, alcoholics will often place the blame for their problems on others and feel justified in hitting the bottle anew as the only solace from mounting difficulties. The addict lives in denial, unable to see drinking or substance abuse as a problem in itself. Curiously, spouses, children, friends, relatives, and coworkers may be in just as much denial about this situation as the alcoholic. Indeed, the diseases of alcoholism and addiction infect all those intimately involved with the substance abuser.

In the First Step of the Twelve Step Program developed by Alcoholics Anonymous (AA), the addicts admit that "we were powerless over alcohol - that our lives had become unmanageable." This awareness of powerlessness and unmanageability is so terrifying that many continue in their addictions unto death or near death. Sometimes a careful intervention of family and friends can help provoke this awareness sooner, but it may also be futilely self-destructive for these family members and friends to make a job out of rescuing the alcoholics from their addiction. If the addicts are powerless to control their addiction, then it is for sure that others can't control it either. At some point, different for each alcoholic, they "hit bottom" in crisis and are confronted with the miserable reality of their sickness and the task of reconstructing their lives.

I am arguing by analogy that human society, no less than individual humans, can function like alcoholics and substance abusers. We are addicted to fossil fuels, increasing consumption, media stimulation, compounded interest, growth in GNP, and so on. And it is so terrifying to confront our collective powerlessness over these substance and spirit abuses that we live in denial. Everything about our lives would have to change to kick our addiction, but we won't do that unless we hit bottom, unless some kind of economic and environmental collapse hits us over the head and says *"People are dying, children are crying, concentrate, concentrate!"*

How and at what point we hit a collective bottom and confront the self-destructive and out-of-control reality of our collective consumptive diseases is a mystery to me. Perhaps it happens one person at a time; perhaps it needs to happen in the collective unconscious as some kind of societal Twelve Step Recovery Program. I know it requires both new ways of thinking and acting. Sometimes we can think ourselves into new ways of acting, but we also need to act ourselves into new ways of thinking. As the Alcoholics Anonymous slogan goes: "Don't Think, Don't Drink!" Our polluted thoughts may not be a very good guide in our recovery. We'll need some kind of collective sobriety first, before our "positive thinking" will lead to a "New Age," and not just more of the same escapist denial and selfish-justifying rationalization.

Perhaps some of us can help others to recognize these dangerous dysfunctions in our body politic without becoming obsessed with our own addictive control illusions. The danger in intervention, in working to help society confront its sicknesses and get into recovery, is that we end up playing a role in the addictive system as codependents and enablers. In other words, we end up enmeshed in the dysfunctions through rescue behaviour and our own obsessive desires to control that which is unmanageable. As enablers we ameliorate the symptoms of the dysfunctions, but in so doing prolong the addiction. Eco-justice and peace do-gooders, like me, are in great risk of becoming part of the problem, instead of their hoped for solutions; as if we could ever really stand apart from the dysfunctional systems in whose society we learned to speak, act, and breathe.

Al Anon, the Twelve Step Recovery Program formed by spouses and children of alcoholics, is very clear on this point. Step Four of the Twelve calls for making "a searching and fearless moral inventory of ourselves." In Al Anon especially, the danger is in doing someone else's inventory instead of your own. You are your own problem. Your real problem is not your addicted husband, wife, or parent. Go back and do your First Step again. You are not in control. Your real problem is not George W. Bush or Osama bin Laden. Go back to Step One.

It is a fearful thing not to be in a control, like driving a speeding car without a steering wheel or brakes, not unlike driving on the streets of India. So much of our lives in childhood and adult years is based on the acquisition of new competencies and power, such that we might better manage our lives and be productive members of society. This is good and as it should be. There is, however, this deeper mystery to life of an ultimate powerlessness and finitude. In this sense, we do not and cannot control our existence. This illusion of self-control arises sometime after infancy and leaves sometime before death. This doesn't mean that we do not make significant decisions in our lives or that we can't hold ourselves and others accountable for those decisions. It just means that the big decisions are beyond us. Perhaps this is why both young children and people who are dying have so much to teach us about how to live the big questions in life, like what is the meaning and purpose of it all in face of the absurdity of inevitable death.

Addiction, I believe, can be seen as a very natural outgrowth of a normal development in human life towards greater competencies and powers. Addictions develop as a quest for greater control over feeling-good and being-happy, though addictive diseases ultimately lead to intense pain and misery. In this sense, alcoholics and addicts can be thought of as "failed mystics," because they are searching for the highest goodness and pleasure that life has to offer, albeit in the wrong way. They follow the false "spirits" of liquor, instead of the Spirit of generosity that imbibes in the very existence of the Cosmos and our own Being. To fail as an alcoholic and embark on recovery is really an invitation to become a religious mystic. So for society to fail in its addictive quest for prosperity, security, or the always-better-life can be thought of as an invitation to confront life's deeper mysteries and become religious mystics.

Step Two in the Twelve-Step Recovery Program of AA talks of coming "to believe in a Power greater than ourselves" that "could restore us to sanity." Step Three talks of making "a decision to turn our will and our lives over to the care of God as we understand God." This is a very open-ended religious philosophy, though enormously powerful in transforming desperately sick people. One can be Christian or Buddhist, Jewish or Muslim, Secular Humanist or Fundamentalist. Like Buddha's near starvation on the road to Enlightenment, or Jesus's forsaken despair while dying on the Cross, or the Hebrews groaning cries to God in their captivity, this transformational moment in an addict's life begins with a confrontation with agonizing powerlessness over an affliction.

The paradox of powerlessness is that it leads to restoring sanity in life. The power that we have is to "turn our will and our lives over." We do not have power over the addiction itself, but this higher Power does. God, as we understand God, has the power to turn us into recovering addicts. Our global civilization's desires for control, pleasure, and greater consumption will continue, but we might be living on the mend, not acting obsessively upon these destructive desires.

Comparing our global economic, social, and environmental problems to an addiction is a helpful, but limited analogy. For while an addict can live and live better without booze and drugs, we must eat, work, reproduce, survive and find community in the social and biological systems that surround and sustain us. We can't simply "stop drinking" fossil fuels, for instance. So our afflictions are actually more like an eating-disorder. Over-eating, anorexia nervosa, and bulimia are perhaps closer analogies to our collective dilemma. But the Twelve-Step Recovery Programme has been a helpful resource for those afflicted by such disorders. Dozens of self-help groups for any number of compulsive behaviour illnesses have modeled themselves on AA and Al-Anon. Seen as a separate religious movement, millions of local AA groups and their prolific off-spring around the world would have to be counted as one of the great world religions today, alongside of Christianity, Islam, Judaism, Hinduism, Buddhism, and so on. The Twelve-Step Program, however, is not a separate religious movement, but is spread through religious practices around the world. In the anonymity of their meetings, Jew, Christian, Hindu, and Atheist can all find powerful unity by sharing their personal stories of failure and recovery.

Making urgent and fundamental changes is never easy. People make mistakes even after they have confronted denial and powerlessness. Recovery is a continuous practice. To aid in this practice, a number of slogans have been passed on in the Twelve Step Program:

Let Go and Let God
Easy Does It
Live and Let Live
First Things First
One Day at a Time
Keep It Simple
Think
Listen and Learn
How Important Is It?

Keep an Open Mind

But for the Grace of God

These slogans have become part of my spiritual discipline, not only in confronting the legacies of addiction in my family and myself, but also as I confront the larger addictive systems which are leading to a global economic, social, and environmental collapse. As I head off to the store in my car, I hear myself saying, "How Important Is It?" and "Keep It Simple" and "First Things First." Sometimes I even have the presence of mind to realize that I don't really need to go shopping today at all, so I have more time and energy to "Think" and to "Listen and Learn." When I am overwhelmed and anxious with the business-as-usual of my own life or of the world, I hear myself saying "Let Go and Let God" and "One Day at a Time" and "Easy Does It." When I judge and criticize others or when I look to others with envy or embarrassment, I repeat the slogans "Keep an Open Mind" or "But for the Grace of God."

Above all, descending on an airplane at 4000 feet and seeing the haze of pollution that covers and chokes our cities, I repeat the AA slogan, "Live and Let Live." Most of our lives, we exist in that haze of smoke from our engines and furnaces, unable to even see it for what it is, because we live, breathe, and see most of our lives on this horizontal plane within the pollution. The airplane ride into the vertical provides an occasion both to add to that smog, but also to see it more clearly for what it is. So now as I drive around in my car, in my mind's eye I can "see" the effects of our fossil fuel addiction in the memories of flying in and out of airports from Los Angeles, California to Mumbai, India. Our collective behaviour in a multitude of ways is making it increasingly difficult to "Live and Let Live." Climates are changing, ecosystems are damaged, species are going extinct, traditional cultures are vanishing, and the staggering wealth that some few have achieved seems unable to truly satisfy.

Often I am distressed by my relative powerlessness to make significant changes in this world. After all I am just one person with only one vote and voice, with limited financial resources and perhaps too much education. I am coming to understand, however, that I don't have to change the world, that I can't change the world, that our powerlessness is exactly what "it" is all about. Indeed, the very act of concentrating on the enormous problems and confronting our relative powerlessness is what sets the magic working.

That is not all, of course, there are a lot of consequences that follow from the paradox of powerlessness and calling forth our Higher Power. My behaviour must change and my thinking must evolve. "Reduce, Reuse, and Recycle," "Think Globally, Act Locally," "Live Simply, That Others May Simply Live, " and "Everything is Connected" are additional slogans from the environmental movement that can be added to our recovery tool box in seeking global health and sanity.

On one level, the AA slogan "Live and Let Live" brought into the context of our societal dysfunctions is an acceptance of the way-things-are: stop complaining, find contentment in the simple fact of living, admit you're powerless, so don't sweat this big stuff about far away lands and peoples. There is some important truth here. On another level, the slogan can also become a prayer for the way things could be in a world that is healing, in which we can "live and let live," instead of destroying ourselves and others. "Live and let live" is my utopia, a vision of an Earth restored and life and spirit developed to the mutual enhancement of all beings. Like the escape into the vertical of the airplane, my dream, this slogan, is both part of the problem and an opportunity to solve it.

At the heart of the acquisitive discontent of the prosperous and bodily-affliction of the poor is a spiritual vacuum in our global civilization. I have interpreted the children's rhyme as to say that the way to create a safer and healthier world is through a profound awareness of present conditions and not a predictive managerial control of the future's unfolding. *Concentrate, concentrate*, on what is really going on right now. Be a witness to both the suffering and the joy of others and ourselves. The reason that we do not pay attention to the world in all its manifestations is that we are paralyzed by fear of our existential powerlessness and blinded by the numbing powers of denial.

To learn more about our resistance to abandoning self-destructive behaviour and the dynamics of fundamental change, I examined the process of recovery from alcoholism and addiction as an analogy to our ecological and socio-economic dysfunctions. In the Twelve-Step Program, we can see the paradox of powerlessness and the centrality of a Divine power in the process of creating urgent and fundamental change in an individual or a social system.

So I turn now to some concluding thoughts on the importance of the world religious traditions to integrating the past, living fully in the present moment, and thereby giving rise to a better future. Religions are both part of the problem and a critical part of the solution to our self-destructive predicament in the late twentieth century at the end of the Cenozoic era. Like the airplane, religions can add to our spiritual "air-pollution," but also provide opportunities to see clearly what this world really looks like from a transposition from the horizontal into the vertical realm of the Divine. This is what Christians call the difference between *chronos*, linear time, and *kaiyros*, the eternal time of the Divine in the moments of communion.

Religions are still a big part of our collective dysfunctions, sources for intolerance, barbarism, escapism, and triumphalistic self-rationalizations. It is not always easy with religion to, in the words of another Twelve Step slogan, "take what you like and leave the rest." In spite of these failings, however, it would be pure foolishness to think that we can live well without religion. Religions are the repository of thousands of years of human attempts to deal with the existential dilemma of life, death, and community. Religious traditions are the accumulated wisdom and failures of different cultures and the passing of many generations. There is something here more than fantasy and wishful thinking. Some Higher Power is manifested, for instance, in the lives of individuals who have literally been saved from life-threatening addictions.

And if an addict is a failed mystic, and if society can be like an addict, then we are somehow failing collectively in our search for group mysticism. We need to reclaim and renew the role of mythic inspiration and ritualized disciplines in order to sustain purposeful and transformative living.

There are many paths that can lead to a spiritual fulfillment of the empty-longings of our collective Self. In trying to live more fully in the present moment, adopting a Buddhist-like discipline of Mindfulness, let us also be extremely pragmatic. Even as the Buddha taught the *Dharma* with *Upaya* towards the efficacious Enlightenment of all sentient Beings, so too can we try to separate the wheat from the chaff. Do what works.

Experiment, practice, see the results of your spiritual and moral labours as they manifest themselves in your life and the lives of others. Jesus taught that by their fruits, they shall be known. George Fox, the founder of the Quaker movement to which I belong, wrote in 1656 that when one is faithful, energetic, and courageous for the Truth, "then you will come to walk cheerfully over the world answering that of God in everyone."

Concentrate, concentrate is also an invitation to pay attention to what is good and beautiful in life without getting lost in pleasure-seeking. Tears and laughter come easily to children. Our inabilities to witness to the suffering in the world no doubt diminish our capacities to enjoy the goodness of the world. So the imperative in the children's rhyme is also to turn all of living into play. The invitation is to know the flowers, breathe deeply, explore frivolities, laugh enthusiastically, and play with a child's abandon. Alan Watts, the great Western interpreter of Eastern religions, writes: "The ways of liberation make it very clear that life is not going anywhere, because it is already *there*. In other words, it is playing, and those who do not play with it, have simply missed the point." There is a Japanese Buddhist saying that points without direction to the paradoxical truth of the children's imperative: "Before Enlightenment, chop wood, carry water; after Enlightenment, chop wood, carry water."

The solution to our problems may lie in a new appreciation of the mundane and common place of our daily living. Though the privileged of the world no longer need to chop wood and carry water as a daily necessity, yet we too can turn our daily life into a continuous liturgy that invokes the Holy. Concentrate on what is before you, not what is in the future. Jesus taught: "So do not be anxious about tomorrow; tomorrow will look after itself. Each day has troubles enough of its own."(Matthew 6:34).

Not only can we look to traditional religious teachings, but even modern science offers a powerful mytho-poetic story of creation. This modern scientific cosmology can re-inspire reverence and gratitude in the face of the enormous topographies of space-time and the many improbable miracles that have turned recycled stardust into this human being that looks back with awe upon itself and the stars from which it came.

Mathematician and philosopher, Alfred North Whitehead, in the ripples of Relativity Theory and Quantum Mechanics, wrote that "past actualities, future possibilities, the present holds within itself the complete sum of existence, backwards and forwards, that whole amplitude of time, which is eternity." Whitehead suggests that there is something about living in the present, "one day at a time" to use the AA slogan, that holds the key to preserving the past, transforming the future, and experiencing the eternal. It is in some renewed ability to pay attention to what is really going-on, to *concentrate, concentrate*, that we will find ways forward out of our global predicaments. In this eternal moment, the past intersects with the present to unfold into future possibilities. We must resist the temptation to be paralyzed by uncertainty, insecurity, and insignificance. The story of the Cosmos is one of erring with the elegantly improbable. Hope is always justified, if not always realized. So throw yourself into the curve of the Universe. A couplet from Goethe offers a profound insight into human nature, human doings, and our cosmogenesis: "Whatever you can do, or dream you can, begin it. Boldness has genius, power and magic in it."

Our bold dreams and our committed doings in this present moment will create some kind of future that, for good or ill, is too complex for anyone to predict. While we can only interpret but not predict the unfolding of natural evolution and human history, we can do something about the troubles enough of this day. If we are appropriately mindful of this day, we may be blessed with the insights of mystics throughout the world's religions. The Buddha-nature is reflected in all things, like the diamonds in Indra's net, each reflecting the perfections of all others. Jesus preached the Good News in an impoverished and oppressed corner of the Roman Empire that the reign of Heaven is in our midst, right now, even, especially, among the poor, the sick, the outcast, and the young. Allah, we are repeatedly told in the Koran, is merciful and compassionate. We need not fear the future. What we need to do is recover and recreate powerful group mysticisms to replace the bankrupt false-gods of power and prosperity.

The Trappist monk, Thomas Merton, a powerful advocate of peace and justice in our world through the practice of engaged-contemplation and an early pioneer in Christian-Buddhist dialogue, described his encounter with the Buddhist tradition in Southeast Asia just before his untimely death. "The thing about all this is that there is no puzzle, no problem and really no *mystery*. All problems are resolved and everything is clear, simply because what matters is clear. The rock, all matter, all life is charged with *dharmakaya*. . . everything is emptiness and everything is compassion. I don't know when in my life I have ever had such a sense of beauty and spiritual validity running together in one aesthetic illumination."[5] In my life I have had small epiphanies of the Reign of Heaven in our midst, of the *Dharmakaya* in all matter, and of the marvellous scientific intricacies of our cosmosgenesis. These moments give me great hope and a peace of mind in the face of my powerlessness and challenge me to act responsibly in spite of finitude. I have experienced some illuminations of the Holy Spirit and indwellings of the Buddha-nature, which have enriched my life beyond measure and filled me with joy. Seek and you shall find.

These religious traditions leave me with a series of paradoxes: a broken world that doesn't need to be fixed and a realization of ultimate perfection that calls forth compassionate acts of healing. A Bodhisattva gives with no apprehension of self, nor of a recipient, nor of a gift. With total dedication to supreme enlightenment, a Bodhisattva does not apprehend any enlightenment. Jesus speaks in similar paradox, "By gaining his life a man will lose it; by losing his life for my sake, he will gain it" (Matthew 10:39). It seems to me that similar to the paradox of powerlessness, there must be something in all these inconsistencies that we cannot and should not force into resolution. There must be some great wisdom embraced in the wholeness of these dichotomies, rather than splitting them off in two. We need not choose between freedom and discipline, grace and self-help, free will and determinism, justice and mercy, planning and laissez-faire, custom and innovation, continuity and change, realism and idealism, faith and good works, nature and nurture, individuality and codependent-origination, particularism and universalism, science and religion. With grace and our own spiritual initiative, we can contain the tensions and ambivalences as creative guides from the Divine.

The fundamental emotive and intellectual dissonance that I experience in my life in the late twentieth century at the end of the Cenozoic era is the tension between despair and hope, between powerlessness and responsibility. The depths and margins of that very tension, along with our laughter and our tears, will be our guides in our truth-seeking and good-doing in the coming millennium. Jesus taught us that we might enter into the reign of Heaven, if we can become like children. My children have given it to me and I pass it on to you as a prayer and perhaps also an antidote for these troubled times.

People are dying,
Children are crying.
Concentrate!
Concentrate!

Endnotes

[1] Samuel Pisar, *Of Blood and Hope*, (Little, Brown 1980), p.307.

[2] Heilbroner, *An Inquiry into the Human Prospect*, (Norton 1974), p.26.

[3] Union of Concerned Scientists, 1992.

[4] Ricoeur, p.312.

[5] Thomas Merton, *The Asian Journal of Thomas Merton*, New Direction Publ, 1975.

Contributors

Amin, Yusuf is a Professor in Pharmacology at the Department of Illmul Advia, A.K. Tibbiya College, Aligarh Muslim Univeristy.

Bracken, Joseph is a Professor of Theology (retired), Xavier University, Cincinnati, Ohio, USA.

Duffy, Kathleen is Professor of Physics at the Department of Chemistry and Physics, Chestnut Hill College, Philadelphia, USA.

Grassie, William is the Founder and Executive Director of Metanexus Institute, New York, USA.

Henri, Sarojini was former Professor of Systematic Theology at Gurukul Theological College, Chennai.

Keepin, Will is the President and Executive Director of Satyana Institute, Seattle, USA.

Kozhamthadam, Job is the Founder and Executive Director of Indian Institute of Science and Religion (IISR) Delhi.

Kulkarni, N.V. is an engineer turned research-scholar in the field of science-religion dialogue in Pune.

Menon, Sangeetha is a senior Faculty member at the NIAS (National Institute of Advanced Studies), Bangalore.

Minz, Nirmal is a Lutheran Bishop and scholar who founded the Gosner College, Ranchi, India.

Pandikattu, Kuruvilla is a Professor of Philosophy and Director of JDV Centre for Science and Religion at Jnana-Deepa Vidyapeeth, Pune.

Pereira, Lancy is a Microbiologist and former Principal of St. Xavier's College, Mumbai.

Singh, T.D. was the Founding President of Vedanta and Science Educational Research Foundation and the International Director of Bhaktivedanta Institute.

Virk, Hardev Singh was former Professor of Physics and Guru Nanak Dev University, Amritsar.

Index

A

Aborigines of Australia 223
Absolute Monism 119
Absolute Reality 1
Acintya 135, 141
Acintya-guna-svarupam 135
Adenine 54
Advasis 225, 226, 228, 230
Advaita 155, 254, 255
Agape 40, 151
AGGS 232, 237, 238, 240
Agnostic 35
Ahamkara 153
AIDS 37
Ainu people of Japan 223
Alcoholism 257, 262
Algorithm 133, 142
Allah, Shah Wali 211,212
Allamprabu 110
Amino acids 54, 130
Anawim of Yahweh 156
Anaximander 120
Angela of Foligno 108
Annalen der Physik 205

Annus mirabilis 205
Anubhuti 235

Apeiron 120
Arber, Werner 140
Archer, W.G. 223
Aristotle 8, 80, 90
Arjuna 67, 113, 143
Arnold, Matthew 198
Arrow of Time 94
Arwah 214
Atman 72, 103, 117, 236
Atoms 87, 114, 126, 129, 130, 135, 140, 163, 233
ATP (adenosine triphosphate) 130
Augustine of Hippo 132
Aurobindo 40, 190
Autopoiesis 170
Axon 51, 52, 61
Ayurveda 39

B

Baigas 226
Batak people of Sumatra 223
Battis, Peter Conil 100
Bell's Theorem 67
Bergson 10, 179, 202
Berkeley 10, 64
Bern Office 205
Bernstein, Jeremy 11

Berry, Thomas 75

Beynaam, Lawrence 11

Bhagavad Gita 67, 72

Bhakti 44

Bible 10, 86, 226

Big Bang 31, 33

Biocomputers 47

Biodiversity 140, 253

Biogenetic engineering 254

Biogeography 139

Black ants (*Loha Chinti*) 226

Black holes 32, 34, 88, 132

Black Plague 251

Bodhisattva 266

Boehme 110

Bohm, David 43, 64

Bohr, Niels 13, 31

Bombelli 127

Bontec 223

Bosnia 252

Bousso 132

Brahman 72, 98, 117-119, 154, 161, 236

Brahmanas 247

Brane 89

Brief History of Time 33, 35

Browne, E.G. 136

Bruteau, Beatrice 190

Buber, Martin 152

Buddhism 40, 72, 173, 236, 260

C

Capra, Fritjof 11, 46

Cardano, Girolamo 127

Carnap, Rudolf 89

Category error 12

Catherine of Siena 108

Cenozoic era 253, 263, 266

Central Order 10

Chalmers, David 242

Chance 50, 140

Chance 8, 32, 56, 57, 85

Chaos 7, 143, 176

Chardin, Teilhard de 176, 196

China 24, 160, 202

Christ Omega 204

Christian personalism 192

Christian *advaita* 155

Christian Ashram 155

Christian Ethics 156

Christian-Buddhist dialogue 265

Clockwork metaphor 92

Cloud of Unknowing 105

Complementarity principle 8, 234

Comte, Auguste 7

Consciousness 3, 5, 9, 19, 20, 22, 29, 63, 68, 70, 73-77, 81, 101, 106, 107, 111, 113, 114, 117, 119, 121, 131, 166, 188, 192, 203, 217, 233, 234, 236, 239, 242-245, 247-249

Convergence 188, 191

Copernicus 8, 23

Cosmic Christ 181, 182, 188, 204

Cosmic evolution 170, 174

Cosmic religious feeling 207, 208

Cosmo-theandric vision of reality 155

Cosmogenesis 265

Cosmology 33, 34, 48, 94

Creation 17, 70, 72, 73, 92, 97, 133, 136, 164, 167, 172, 181, 183, 186, 188, 191, 216, 225, 230, 231, 238, 264

Creative Evolution 179

Cytoplasm 52, 53, 59

Cytosine 54

Cytoskeletons 87

D

Dark Night 24, 86, 113
Darwin, Charles 164
De brogile, Louis 10, 234
De-divinization of the world 196
Deikman 102
Delacroix 117
Democritus 14, 163
De Molinos, Miguel 116
Dendrites 51, 52
Descartes, Rene 90, 164
Devaloka 227
Devandan, Paul David 222
Deveswarupa 227
Davies, Paul 142
Dharma 263
Dharmakaya 266
Divine Matrix 173
Divine Milieu 183, 189, 202, 204
DNA 46, 52-54, 56, 59, 140, 142
Dupre, Louis 103
Dyson, Freeman 51
Dystopia 255

E

Easwaran, Eknath 77
Eckhart, Meister 42, 73
East-West Dialogue 17, 22, 43, 38, 144
Eco-centric epistemology 227
Ecological balance 225
Ecosystem 252, 253
Eddington, Arthur 94
Einstein, Albert 4, 68
Eldridge, Niles 165
Eliade, Mircea 230
Elwin, Verrier 226
Embryology 29, 139, 147
Emerson, Ralpoh Waldo 42
Empedocles 80

Enchanted Darkness 29
Enlightenment 8, 72, 150, 179, 185, 191, 196, 197, 199, 255, 259, 263, 266
Entelechy 167, 169
Epicurus 14
Eternal Spirit 10
Evolution 139, 164, 179
evolution 7, 42, 56, 68, 74, 94, 125, 139-141, 144, 165, 166, 169-171, 174, 177, 180-184, 187, 201-203, 232, 243, 265
Exoterism 213
Explicate order 65, 67-71, 73

F

Faster-than-light phenomena 126
Ferguson, Kitty 85
Feuerbach, Ludwig 197
Feyerabend, Paul 87
Fine-tuned 128, 141
Flew, Antony 48, 57
Force-fields 93
Fossil fuels 252, 257, 260
Fossil record 147, 177
Four forces 129
Fox, George 264
Freud, Sigmund 198
Friedrich 197

G

Galileo 23, 33, 80, 132, 163
Gassmann product 87
Gauss 99, 134
General Relativity 30, 91-95
Genetic engineering 47
Genetic information 59
Genetic revolution 14
Genome 59
Ghazali, Al 23, 213, 219

Global Village 252
Gnosis 212, 216
Gödel's Incompleteness Theorem 135
Goethe 265
Gonds 226
Gospel of Thomas 72
Gould, Stephen 165
Grand design 164
Grassie, William 251
Grof, Stanislav 72
Gotra 225
Gravitational constant 128
Gravitons 129
Great Chain of Being 15, 43, 46
Greek atomists 14
Gregersen, Niels Henrik 169
Griffiths, Bede 43, 154
Gerald 47, 49
Guanine 54
Guenon 214
Gunas 96, 97
Guru Nanak 238, 239, 240
GUT theory 8

H

Hadith, Ahl Al- 211
Hawking, Jane 35
Hawking, Stephen 8, 32, 86
Hayyan, Jabir bin 218
Heilbrone, Robert 253
Heisenberg, Werner 4, 10
Harmony of the universe 207
Henry 144
Heraclitus 65
Hidden Face of God 47, 49
Hidden face of God 50, 58
Higg's field 96
Hinduism 72, 155, 173, 190, 211, 213, 222, 260

Hinton, James 119
Hocking 5
Hoffmann, Banesh 205
Holographic structure 65, 69, 74
Homeopathy 39
Horgan, John 120
humanist pantheisms 190
Hume, David 7
Huxley, Aldous 65

I

Ignatius of Loyola 5, 158, 183
Illumination 113
Imaginary numbers 127, 128
Immunogenetics 47
Implicate Order 65, 67, 70, 71, 73, 75
Incarnation 152, 158, 177, 180, 182, 204
Indeterminism 11
Indra's Net 65, 265
Inertia 96, 187
Information 49, 50, 52, 56, 171
Inge, W.R. 1
Innate principles 164
Inner Net of the Heart 63, 71, 74, 75, 78
Integral model 63
Interconnectedness 12, 184, 203
Intuition 9, 20, 40, 88
Intuitive knowledge 102, 227
Inversion condition 134
Islam 72, 211, 212, 213, 214, 215
Islam and Science 214
Islamic Medicine 215, 216
I-Thou relationship 152

J

Jacob, Francois 135
James, William 2, 111

Jnaneswara 109, 110
Jeans, James 10
Jesuits 161, 178
Jivanmukta 43
Jnana yoga 64
John of the Cross 103, 107, 108
Jones, Richard 11
Jones, Rufus 2
Joshi, Murli Manohar 11
Julian of Norwich 72

K

Kabir 44, 105, 110, 120
Karma 39
Keats, John 198, 200
Kekule, Friedrich 15
Kenotic cycle 182
Kepler, Johannes 8, 23
King Janaka 104
King Ursula 187
Kingsley, Peter 80
Kohlberg, Lawrence 42
Koran 265
Kosko, Bark 133
Krause 106
Krishna 67, 138
Krishnamurti 43, 64
Kuhn, Thomas 80, 86, 200
King, Martin Luther 74, 76

L

Lagrange's Theorem 87
Lakatos, Imre 87
Lama, Dalai 43, 64
Law, William 103
Leibniz 88
Leucippus 163

Loevinger, Jane 42
Logic of discovery 165
Logical Positivism 7
Loop quantum gravity 89
Lucasian Chair 8

M

M-theory 31
Magico-religious power 230
Mahabbah 213
Makhafah 213
Malays of Malaysia 223
Mandela, Nelson 21
Mandelbrot set 69, 70
Mandukya Upanishad 235
Manglacharan 238
Maoris of New Zealand 223
Marx, Karl 7, 197
Maslow, Abraham 42
Materialism 75, 234
Mathematical mysticism 10
Matrix theory 89
Maunavrata 153
Maxwell, Clerk 88, 90
Maya 81, 152, 158, 236, 249
McCarthy 64
Mechanical Philosophy of Nature 6, 7
Mechanistic conception of the world 236
Meerabai / Mirabai 44, 110
Meiotic 132
Memes 243
Mendelian genetics 140
Merton, Thomas 265
Microcosm 65, 69, 103
Mindanao people of Philippines 223
Missiologists 222
Mitochondria organelles 131
Molecular biology 20, 29, 46

Monads 110

More, Thomas 255

Morphogenetic 165, 166, 169, 171, 174

Mother Teresa 74, 76, 151

MRI 37

Mukerjee, Ajit 72, 274

Munda, Ram Dayal 223

Mundas 226, 231

Mystery 38, 39, 94, 127, 128, 131, 132,
        135, 138, 141, 189, 196, 198, 199,
        201, 204, 207, 209, 257, 258, 265

Mystical Body of Christ 182

Mystical Milieu 185, 188

Mysticism 1-9, 11-17, 19, 26, 28, 32, 42-
        45, 47, 49, 51, 62, 76, 78, 79, 85, 99,
        100, 103, 104, 114, 126, 132, 135,
        141, 144, 151, 154, 156, 157, 160

Mysticism and modern science 5, 211

Mysticism and reality 4

Mysticism and religion 4

Mysticism and renunciation 4

Mysticism of Service 149

Mysticism of the Margins 156

Mysticism of the marketplace 157

Myth and Reality 230

N

Naam 232, 238, 239, 240

Nanotechnology 47

Natural Selection 50, 56, 57, 125, 139,
        140, 147, 164, 166

Neo-Darwinism 140

Neural information processing 244

Neural networks 55

Neurobiology 29, 47

New age spirituality 157

New Science of Life 166, 174

Newton, Isaac 90

Newtonian Mechanics 6

Nicholas of Cusa 23, 48

Nimbargi Sampradaya 105, 110

Nirguna 238, 239

Nirvana 153

Nishkama-karma 153

Niskriya 249

Noetic quality 237

Non-linear iterative process 82

Non-local 126

Nucleotides 54, 140

O

Obscurantism 5, 6

Observer-observed distinction 11

Omega Point 121, 188, 202, 204

Oppenheimer, Robert 64, 132

Oraons 223, 226, 231

Organismic view of reality 231

Origin of Species 139, 141

Overbye, Dennis 145

P

Panikkar, Raimundo 149, 154

Parallels between the worldviews of
        physicists and 11

Paramatman 154

Parmenides 80, 81

Pascal, Blaise 49

Passivity 187

Patanjali 106

Pauli W. 9

PCR (polymerase chain reaction) 133

Penrose, Roger 32, 86

Perennial Philosophy 15

Perennial philosophy 12, 43

Personal Knowledge 200

Pfleiderer, Otto 126

Phenomenon of Man 202

Phillips, William 142

Physical constants 128

Picasso 24, 55
Pisar, Samuel 253
Planck, Max 30, 57, 144
Planck's constant 128
Plank length 89
Plato 8-10, 44, 80, 81, 87, 138, 163
Pleromization 182
Plotinus 8, 44, 109, 137, 138
Poincare, Henry 144
Polanyi, Michael 165, 167, 169, 200
Polypeptide chains 54
Popper, Karl 86
Postmodernism 150
Practical Mysticism 126
Prakriti 96
Pre-Socratic thinkers 163
Principle of divergence 139
Principle of unification 91
Probability wave 93
Progressus ad infinitum 100
Ptolemy, Claudio 132
Punctuated equilibrium 165
Purusha 97
Puys 178
Pyruvate 131
Pythagoras 8

Q

Qanoon, Al 214
Quaker movement 264
Quantum Mechanics 30, 31, 93, 95, 127,
        233, 264
Quantum nonlocality 67
Quantum Questions 25
Quwa 214

R

Rabia 44
Rahner, Karl 157

Ramana Maharishi 42
Ranade 105, 111, 119
Ravindra, Ravi 75
Recombination 140, 147
Redemption 182
Reductionism 8
Re-enchantment 197, 208
Relativity Theory 64, 264
Religious fanaticism 155
Ribosomal RNA 53
Ricoeur, Paul 255
Rogers, Murray 32, 80, 86, 127, 136, 222
Rolle, Richard 107
Roy, S.C. 226
Rumi, Jalaluddin 21, 76
Rushd, Ibn 218
Russell, Bertrand 7
Ruysbroeck 110
Rwanda 252

S

Al-Safa, Ikhwan 218, 219
Sai Baba 154
Saint Jnanadeva 102
Saint Martin 100, 111
samadhi 228
Samkhya theory 96
samsara 153
Sankaracharya 249
Santhals 223
sarguna 239
Dastras 226
Sat-cit-ananda 154
Satt 238, 239
Scaramelli 106
Schaefer 33
Schiller, Friedrich 197
Schroeder, Gerald 47, 49
Schroedinger, Erwin 67

Schuon 214

Science of evolution 177

Scientific method 64, 85, 199, 236

Scientism 215, 219

Self-actualization 42, 172

Self-realisation 152, 154

Self-transcendence 42

Sense of wonder 196, 198, 206

Sharpe 136

Shebastari 77

Sheldrake, Rupert 43, 165, 166, 174

Shuhudiyyah 213

Siberian shaman 220

Sina, Ibn 214, 217

Singbonga 231

Singularity theorem 32, 33

Smith, Huston 43, 44

Socrates 80

Spacetime 87, 89, 91, 236

Spinoza 207

Spiriton 142, 143, 144

Spirituality of the margins 156

Standard Model 31

String Theory 31, 33, 47, 89, 97

Strong-interaction 10, 12, 14

Structure of Scientific Revolutions 86

Sufi 4, 21, 24, 38, 96, 211

Su Kyi, Aung Sang 74

Summa Theologica 120

Super conductors 87

Super consciousness 42

Superstring theory 88, 94, 95

Supreme Being 143, 227

Suresh, Kumar 223

Suso, Henry 110, 114, 118

Symbiosis 19, 25, 27, 37

Systems' interactions 243

T

Tagore, Rabindranath 44

Tacit Dimension 165

Taitariya Upanishad 110

Tao of Physics 5, 11, 236

Tao te Ching 173

Taoism 173, 236

Tasawwuf 211

Tauler 107, 118, 119

Teresa of Avila 42

Theory of Everything 33, 35, 44

Three Mystical Currents 189

Thymine 54

Tomography 37

Townes, Charles H. 133, 200

Transcendental experiences 248

Transfer RNA 53

Transpersonal 13, 23, 41, 42, 72, 80, 248

Trappist 265

Tribes of Myanmar 224

Trine, Ralph Waldo 137

Trinity 110, 118, 174

Tukaram 114, 115

Turner, Michael 31

Turning Point 5

Twain, Mark 75

U

Ulm 205

Ultimate fundamental particle 8

Ultimate Reality 45, 84, 105, 165, 173, 238

Ummah 211

Unani Medicine 216

Uncertainty principle 8, 93

Underhill, Evelyn 100, 106, 126, 142

Unified theory 95

Universal consciousness 71, 74

Universe in a Nutshell 33
Upanishads 11, 23, 24, 113, 116, 226,
    236
Upaya 263

V

Vafa, Cumrun 132
Varieties of Religious Experience 2
Vedanta 125, 140, 142, 143, 236
Vedic Aryans 97
Virtual reality 88
Vishwa Hindu Parishad 224
Voyage of the Beagle 139
Vyavaharika 152

W

Wald, George 128
Walsh, Roger 80
Watkins, John 86
Watson and Crick 142
Watts, Alan 264
Wave function 33, 128, 233
Wave-particle duality 7
Weber, Max 197
Weber, Renee 43
Weigel 103

Weinberg, Steven 120
Weissman, David 167
What Is Life 142
Wheeler, John 36, 49
Whitehead, Alfred North 150, 169, 171,
    264
Whiteheadian creativity 173
Wholeness 4, 25, 65, 187, 218, 278
Wilber, Ken 11, 13, 41, 76, 157, 160
Williams, Pearce 87
Wisdom traditions 243, 247
Wordsworth, William 198, 201
Wormhole theory 88
Wujudiyyah 213

Y

Yajnavalkya 104
Yugas 238

Z

Zen 72
Zeno 81
Zikr 213
Zukav, Gary 11
Zygon 169

www.ingramcontent.com/pod-product-compliance
Lightning Source LLC
Chambersburg PA
CBHW051143030726
47504CB00004B/1006